ADVANCE PRAISE FOR
STATUS-6

"W. Craig Reed's latest novel, *Status-6*, is the best book I've read this year—a ripped-from-the-headlines military technothriller that literally left me awake at night, fearful of where we're headed as a nation and a species. If you thought the coronavirus was terrifying, wait until you read about this potential nightmare. Don't miss this first book in a series that promises to shatter the thriller genre. *Status-6* is an outstanding, well-written, and engaging high-concept thriller with interesting characters and brilliant plot twists."

—JAMES ROLLINS, #1 *New York Times* bestselling author
of *Crucible (Sigma Force)*

"W. Craig Reed's *Status-6* grabs you from page one and doesn't let you go. The global biotoxin crisis revealed in this book is all-too-real and could well be tomorrow's headlines. The characters are well nuanced and provide a powerful urge to root for or against them. Don't read this thriller before going to bed—you'll be awake all night!"

—GEORGE GALDORISI, *New York Times* bestselling author
of the Tom Clancy Op-Center series

"W. Craig Reed's *Status-6* is my vote for 'Thriller of the Year.' The protagonist is Tom Clancy's Jack Ryan meets Lee Child's Jack Reacher."

—GRANT BLACKWOOD, #1 *New York Times* bestselling author
of *Tom Clancy Under Fire*

Also by W. Craig Reed

Spies of the Deep
The 7 Secrets of Neuron Leadership
Red November

STATUS-6

AN NCIS SPECIAL OPS THRILLER

W. CRAIG REED

PERMUTED
PRESS

A PERMUTED PRESS BOOK

Status-6:
An NCIS Special Ops Thriller
© 2021 by W. Craig Reed
All Rights Reserved

ISBN: 978-1-68261-935-3
ISBN (eBook): 978-1-68261-936-0

Cover art by Cody Corcoran
Interior design and composition by Greg Johnson, Textbook Perfect

PERMUTED
PRESS

Permuted Press, LLC
New York • Nashville
permutedpress.com

Published in the United States of America
1 2 3 4 5 6 7 8 9 10

This book is dedicated to my fellow submariners and Navy Divers,
the Spies of the Deep who have risked all to keep us safe.

"The new weapon can be equipped with a nuclear payload to attack coastal military and infrastructure facilities. In December 2017, we completed testing for a new innovative nuclear propulsion system for these underwater drones that can be equipped with a powerful nuclear warhead...

"There is no defense system in the world today that can cope with these underwater weapons...

"No one has listened to us. You will listen to us now."

—Russian President Vladimir Putin,
March 1, 2018 State-of-the-Nation Address in Moscow

CHAPTER 1

March 30, San Diego, California

Jon Shay awoke from a fitful sleep at four in the morning. Clutching a sweat-soaked pillow, he whispered his wife's name in the darkness. The agony of his empty life pressed down upon his chest and crushed the air from his lungs. Bereft, he stared at a blank wall for hours. His studio apartment contained only a few sparse furnishings. Not a single picture hung against the dull gray paint.

He had not come here to live.

Jon climbed from his bed and ambled to the window. Outside, a carved moon hung low against a sable sky. He closed his eyes and tried to bring Annelia back to life. He recalled the softness of her cheeks, the curve of her hips, the scent of her hair. He saw her now walking on silver sand at the beach in La Jolla. Ocean salt clung to her skin and glistened in the sun. She smiled and asked him to follow her into the roiling waves. Absorbed in his thoughts, he said no. Her mouth formed a playful pout as she ran toward the surf. He watched her go.

He watched her go.

Fronds from a California palm brushed against the glass and raised a sad whisper. Jon opened his eyes. The grievous memories fell from his thoughts—not all at once, but in shivering veils, like cobwebs brushed away by a broom. He tried to cling to the pictures in his mind, but they quickly evaporated. Beyond the dirty window, dogs barked and howled, unable to sleep in a city filled with screeching tires and wailing sirens.

His hands shaking, Jon walked to the kitchen table. He grabbed his Navy Revolver and placed a single bullet in the chamber. He spun the cylinder and placed the barrel against his temple. His finger curled around the trigger. He let out a quick breath and squeezed. The hammer clicked but nothing exploded. He slammed the revolver on the table next to Annelia's photograph, next to a week-old pizza box. The cardboard tomb reeked of moldy mozzarella. He fell to the floor, hugged his knees, and wept until the last tears dried upon his cheeks.

A shrill tone brought him back into the world of the living. He glanced at the caller ID and answered. "Hi, sis."

"Hi, Jon," Pam said. "I had a feeling."

"My sister thinks she's a psychic."

"My brother thinks he's funny."

"Kids up yet?"

"Frank took 'em to school," Pam said. "Gonna be late again. Katie lost her homework and Cody put his pants on backwards."

Jon wanted to reply with something witty, but his mind remained an empty canvas devoid of color or creation.

Pam's breath whispered across the phone. Wind in a graveyard. "Talk to me."

After the funeral, family and friends had offered condolences at Pam's house and then joked and laughed while stabbing at plates of food. Jon had slipped outside to sit in a rocking chair on the back porch that Frank hammered together with sturdy pine. It still smelled like a lumber yard. Jon rocked and stared at a field of tall Nebraska corn that stretched to the distant horizon. Yellow tassels sashayed in the breeze—delicate dancers on a country stage. Pam stepped up behind him and stood there, saying nothing. She rested a warm hand on his shoulder and squeezed. Jon's eyes misted as he reached up and placed his hand on hers. He had been unable to accept sympathy until that night. Had shunned any overtures and became jaded by all the "so sorry for your loss" statements that he retreated from life and hid behind his door, declining any calls. His anguish became so intense that it scraped his nerves raw. Well-meaning voices felt like hot knives stabbing into his heart.

Now, from over a thousand miles away, Pam's voice was soft and soothing, like a child's blanket that could vanquish the evils of the world.

In contrast, Jon's voice cracked when he spoke. "I just want her back, Pam. I just want a simple life with Annelia by my side."

Pam breathed out a sympathetic sigh. "No...you don't. That was never enough for you, Jon. You're a hunter, not a farmer. Annelia knew that. She knew that you're driven to battle the bad guys who want to prevent *other* people from having a simple life."

"Not anymore."

"Not any less," Pam said. "It's who you are. It's who you were meant to be."

Jon's chin trembled as he shook his head from side to side. "I'm tired of fighting, tired of the pain, tired of living a life without meaning. I just want to be wherever she is."

"Then be in your heart because that's where she is. That's where she'll always be."

"I can't find her there, Pam. I can't find anything there."

"Then stop trying," Pam said. "Live your life and point your gun at a bad guy's head instead of your own."

Jon knew Pam had used that last line metaphorically. He had not told anyone about his suicide attempts. He also knew she was only trying to help, but he was not yet able to move beyond his pain or see any light at the end of the dark tunnel that lay ahead. They spoke for a few more minutes and then ended the call.

Jon stared at a blank wall for another hour until he heard a chime. He reached for his phone. "Shay."

The voice on the line called him Agent. Said he'd been activated for a mission. Told him he needed to catch the next flight to Alaska. Jon ended the call and stared at the revolver on the table. He palmed the gun and felt the weight in his hand. He slapped open the cylinder and gazed at the lone bullet nestled inside the chamber. His tortured mind pondered the question that had haunted him for years: Why had he survived all those missions? If he had not come home instead of so many others, Annelia would still be alive. If there was a God, he'd made the wrong choice.

Jon placed the pistol back on the table, grabbed his badge, and rose to his feet.

When Jon stepped through the door of the budget motel in Anchorage, the aging attendant behind the counter grinned. Half his teeth were missing, and the other half looked like a train wreck. He handed Jon a room key—a metal one, not a plastic card. Jon marched up a creaky flight of stairs and turned left. Three geriatric bulbs lit the way. One coughed and sputtered and appeared ready to die. In commiseration, he offered a quick salute. The door groaned, and the room smelled of pine cleaner and cigarette smoke. The last occupant had apparently disregarded the no smoking signs.

The small rectangle held a bed draped with a bright orange comforter, a table, a chair, and a dresser atop which sat an ancient miniature television.

Holes in the green rug revealed a storied past. Jon looked down at his boots and visualized decades of feet shuffling across the floor while wearing an assortment of pointed heels, soft Nikes, and patent leather loafers.

He tossed his duffle bag on the bed and removed his Glock 17 and two magazines. He placed the handgun and mags in the closet safe and spun the lock. He was authorized to carry a firearm in all fifty states, but he didn't imagine needing one in downtown Anchorage.

Back in the lobby, Jon asked the attendant for directions to the nearest fast food restaurant. The clerk handed him a printed sheet with a dozen nearby choices. None of them looked appealing. When Jon turned toward the exit, he felt a tug on his pant leg and looked down into a pair of shimmering blue eyes.

A girl of about four, with bright blonde curls, flashed a toothless grin. "Are you a giant?"

Jon knelt and smiled. "Maybe. Are you a munchkin?"

The girl giggled. "Do you live in a beanstalk?"

Jon lowered his voice to a whisper. "Don't tell anyone, but I live in a cave with my dragon."

The girl's eyes opened wide. "You have a dwagon?"

The girl's mother stepped near. She was petite and pretty and displayed the same blonde curls as her daughter. Her beryl eyes sparkled like polished emeralds. She wasn't wearing a wedding ring. "Suzie, are you bothering this nice man?"

Jon stood. "She's adorable, you must be very proud."

The mother blushed and offered her hand. "I'm Linda and this is my daughter, Suzie."

"I'm Jon." He reached over and shook Linda's hand. It was warm and soft. Jon shuddered as a memory touched his heart.

"Are you okay?" Linda said.

"I'm fine," Jon said as he let go of her hand.

"Mommy," Suzie said, "he has a dwagon!"

Linda laughed. "He does?"

Suzie tugged on Jon's pant leg again. "What's your dwagon's name?"

Caught off guard, Jon said the only name that came to mind. "It's...Puff."

Suzie's face registered surprise. "Is he magic?"

Linda laughed and took her daughter's hand. "I think we've delayed Jon long enough, and we need to find some dinner." She turned toward Jon. "It was nice meeting you, Jon."

"You as well," Jon said. He knelt again in front of Suzie. "Puff *is* a magic dragon, Suzie, and if you close your eyes, you can see him."

Suzie closed her eyes. "I see him! He's green and has big teeth."

"That's him," Jon said. "He likes chocolate chip cookies. If you give him one, he'll be your friend for life."

"He will?" Suzie said. She kept her eyes closed as she reached her hand toward the imaginary dragon. She giggled and pulled her hand away. "He ate it all up!"

"Can I have one, too?" Jon said.

The girl opened her eyes. "Okay."

She handed Jon an invisible cookie. He took a pretend bite and said, "Now I'm also your friend for life."

Suzie smiled until Linda squeezed her hand, then her face turned sad. "Bye, Giant Jon."

Jon stood. "Bye, Munchkin Suzie."

He watched the pair walk toward the exit. They had almost reached the lobby door when he said, "Wait."

Mother and daughter turned as he walked over.

"I was just about to grab some dinner myself," Jon said. "Why don't you join me? I mean, if you want to."

Linda tilted her head and stared into Jon's eyes, as if trying to determine whether to trust him or not.

Suzie tugged on her mother's hand. "Please, Mommy? He has a dwagon."

Linda's lips curled into a warm smile. "Okay, but I'm buying."

Jon started to argue until Linda held up a hand. "That's the deal. Take it or leave it."

Jon closed his mouth and motioned his hand toward the door. "After you."

Bundled and shivering, the trio set off in search of a meal. A frigid wind whipped across the sidewalk and tossed bits of litter into the ink-black night. A row of tired buildings lined the street. Dim neon lights cast eerie shadows across the faded bricks, broken windows, and chained doors.

Shivering, Linda held Suzie's hand as they walked. "Why are you in Anchorage?"

"I'm breeding dragons," Jon said. His breath formed a misty cloud in the cold night air.

Linda laughed. "And when you're not delivering a litter of flying lizards?"

"I failed as a Guatemalan drug dealer," Jon said, "so I went to work for the government."

"Right," Linda said with a smile. "Is there a difference?"

"Not really," Jon said with a smile.

"Federal agent or IRS auditor?"

"Is there a difference?" Jon said.

"Not really," Linda said.

"I'm not an auditor," Jon said. "What about you? What brings you to the cold?"

"Divorced and starting a new life."

"Should I offer condolences or congratulations?"

Linda rolled her eyes. "Definitely congratulations."

"Moving or staying?" Jon said.

"Moving. I just got a new job in Long Beach. The movers picked up everything today and Suzie and I fly out in the morning."

"I live about ninety minutes south of you in San Diego," Jon said. "Along with my dragons. At least until they burn my house down."

"If they do," Linda said, "I guess you'll just have to move to Long Beach."

"I guess so," Jon said.

"I wanna go to Disneyland!" Suzie said.

"Of course you do," Linda said.

Jon stopped and glanced at the printed sheet provided by the hotel attendant. "I'm afraid we have a limited selection. McDonald's, Burger King, or Taco Bell."

Suzie made the decision for them. "McDonald's! I want a Happy Meal."

"Okay with you?" Linda asked.

Jon shrugged. "I guess it doesn't matter if the beef is smashed into a patty or ground into dog food."

"Do they have cookies for Puff?" Suzie said.

"Of course they do," Linda said.

Jon feigned a pout. "What about me?"

"You can have one, too!" Suzie said.

Jon guided them to the end of the street and then turned north. Four blocks later, he noticed a pair of headlights edge near and slow down. The passenger window of a Ford F150 truck descended.

A tobacco-chewing man with a fighter's nose shoved his head out the opening. He wore a red ball cap turned backward. "Need a ride?"

Jon waved him off. "No thanks. We're trying to get to 10,000 steps today."

The driver, also wearing a ball cap, leaned over his buddy and said, "What's the matter, you afraid we're gonna rob you or something?"

"Never crossed my mind," Jon said as he motioned for Linda and Suzie to match his pace.

"Well, maybe it should have," the first guy said.

The truck sped up, squealed through a ninety-degree turn, and skidded to a stop. Dirt shot up from the tires and sprinkled the night with dust. A nearby streetlight dotted the black asphalt with scattered bits of yellow.

Jon halted his stride and assumed a protective position in front of Linda and Suzie.

Doors opened on the truck.

Two figures emerged. One carried a shotgun, the other a baseball bat.

"Just hand me your wallet," the driver said, "and we'll be on our way."

Jon grit his teeth and reached into his back pocket, regretting that he'd left his Glock in the room.

The passenger moved his eyes up and down Linda's frame. "My, aren't you a pretty little thing."

Jon took a step toward the driver and held out his wallet. "Take it and go."

The driver stood about six feet tall, four inches shorter than Jon. The guy grabbed Jon's wallet and started leafing through the folds. He removed the cash and credit cards and threw the empty wallet onto the ground. "Let's go," he said to his buddy.

The passenger parted his lips. His teeth were stained by chewing tobacco. "Not so fast."

He took a step toward Linda.

Jon moved sideways to block him. Suzie wrapped herself about Linda's leg and whimpered.

"No need to get feisty," the passenger said to Jon. "I just want to have a little chat with your wife."

Jon glared at the man. "Maybe you should listen to your buddy and leave before this gets ugly."

The driver stopped counting and raised his chin. A furled cavern formed between his eyes. "What do you mean by ugly?" He shoved the money into his pocket and then jammed the shotgun slide to load a round. The click-clack echoed off a telephone pole.

Hot breath from the two men misted the wind at a faster pace. Jon's temples throbbed. The passenger grabbed Linda's arm and dragged her across the concrete. Flung free from her mother's leg, Suzie scraped her elbows and knees on the hard ground. Linda screamed. Jon lunged toward the passenger. The scrawny guy raised the bat with his left hand and smacked

7

Jon hard across the cheek. Shaken, Jon fell to his knees and spat out a clump of blood. A coppery taste filled his mouth. A vat of anger had been brewing in his chest for the past year. He'd shoved the guilt-ridden ire deep into his gut and walled it off. Dealing with it had been too painful. Now, as the cold ground chilled his knees, an unbridled rage surged through his veins.

While the driver looked on like a perverted voyeur, his passenger buddy opened Linda's coat. He gripped the top of her blouse and pulled downward. The buttons ripped loose and popped into the air. Linda shivered with fright. The passenger grinned as he stared at her breasts.

Jon rose to his feet and narrowed his eyes. His hands curled into fists as he strode toward the passenger.

The man cocked his head and smirked. "Back for more?" He again lifted the bat and swung.

This time, Jon caught the end of the bat in his palm. He ripped it loose and flipped it over. The passenger's face filled with fear as he took a step backward. The driver coiled his finger around the trigger of the shotgun. Jon slowly moved the bat upward and outward, as if surrendering. The driver's shoulders relaxed. He removed his finger from the trigger and let the shotgun dangle by his side.

Jon popped the bat into the air and caught it midsection. He cocked his arm back and poised the bat over his shoulder like a spear. The driver tensed and started to raise his gun. Jon flung the bat at the man's head. It sailed through the air like a missile. The driver pointed the shotgun at Jon's chest. His finger coiled around the trigger. Jon turned sideways and waited for the boom. The bat hit the driver's forehead dead center. The loud whack sent a flock of birds squawking into the dark. The driver rolled his eyes upward. The shotgun slipped from his hand and hit the street with a crack. The man's knees buckled, and he toppled onto the asphalt.

Passenger guy let out a guttural yell and ran toward Jon. Training kicked in. Jon let the passenger close and then dodged left. He spun on a heel and smacked his elbow onto the back of the man's head as he raced past. The passenger stumbled, turned, and charged again, swinging wildly with his fists. Jon again pivoted but not in time. The passenger pounded a fist into his solar plexus. Jon winced as the blow forced the air from his lungs. The passenger swung again. Jon leaned backward. The man's fist missed by an inch.

Jon stepped back a few feet and crouched into a fighter's stance. He waited for the passenger to rush him again; waited for him to close to an optimal distance before transforming 220 pounds of muscle into a sledgehammer. The passenger lunged forward. Jon's fist slammed into the man's side. He heard a rib crack. The guy doubled over and sucked in a wheezing breath. He teetered on unsteady legs and held up a hand in defeat.

Jon knew the fight was over, knew the man had surrendered, but the fire in his gut raged on. He was powerless against the demon now in control. He took three strides forward, thrust his right knee upward, and smashed his thigh into the man's nose. The passenger screamed and stumbled backward. He tripped over his own feet and hit the asphalt with a dull thud. Moaning in pain, blood spurting from his nose, the man clutched his face and rolled about on the street.

Linda helped Suzie off the ground. The girl buried her face against her mother's chest and cried tears of joy.

The adrenaline rushing through Jon's veins subsided. He relaxed his hands. In the corner of his left eye, he saw a blue flash.

A voice called out. "Police. On your knees!"

Another officer joined the first. Both cops teacup gripped their pistols with outstretched arms.

Jon fell to his knees and placed both hands behind his head. One cop ran over and cuffed the two perps while the other one cuffed Jon.

"Federal officer," Jon said. "ID is in my pocket."

"I don't give a damn who you are," the cop said, "you're coming with us."

Jon shrugged. The Anchorage jail couldn't be any worse than his motel room.

Linda pointed at her ripped blouse and argued with the cops. The officers listened with laconic ears and said they'd straighten it all out down at the station. Just before they shoved Jon into a squad car, Linda squeezed a folded piece of paper into his hand. Her cheeks were moist. "How can we ever thank you?"

Jon smiled as a forgotten glow filled his chest. "You already have."

A year ago, he had cast off from the shores of life and drifted aimlessly on an angry sea of guilt and sorrow. Feeling neither wanted nor useful, he had shunned any life preservers thrown his way. Instead, he had tried to drown himself a dozen times. Now, on a distant horizon, he saw a single ray of light peak through the dark clouds and offer a faint glimmer of hope.

But that hope came with a two-edged sword. One edge promised a way out, a way to crawl toward redemption at the end of a long road. The other edge, as sharp as a razor's blade, led toward a dark and dangerous life where uncontrollable rage might transform him into a monster.

CHAPTER 2

Jon peered through the barred window of his cell. Golden leaves whispered as a morning breeze swept across a valley of quaking aspen.

A police officer with peach fuzz and pimples unlocked the cell door and pulled it open. The rusted hinges squeaked like fingernails on a chalkboard. "Sorry about all this," the cop said. "I wish we could make it up to you."

"Breakfast would be a good start," Jon said. "How about Cinnamon Belgian waffles with a ricotta cheese omelet and Canadian bacon?"

The officer smiled. "How about a cup of shitty coffee?"

"Shitty coffee sounds good," Jon said.

The cop helped him retrieve his valuables and an hour later Jon boarded a flight from Anchorage to Deadhorse Airport in Prudhoe Bay. While staring out the window at a blanket of white, he thought about the dozens of missions he had completed over the past four years. The Naval Criminal Investigative Service had proved to be nothing like the cops and robbers dramatization portrayed by the popular NCIS television shows. During his training, they'd told Jon that various missions might include anything from finding missing persons to hunting down terrorists. That he'd be responsible for "investigating and defeating criminal, foreign, and terrorist intelligence threats to the United States Navy and Marine Corps, whether ashore, afloat, or..." on a tiny ice floe in the Beaufort Sea—which is where he'd be in about three hours.

Jon unfolded the piece of paper Linda had given him the night before. It was her cell phone number. He smiled, refolded the paper, and shoved it back into his pocket.

Upon leaving the terminal in Prudhoe Bay, an icy wind threatened to turn Jon's cheeks into pincushions. The small coastal town resembled a snow-covered truck stop in Iowa. Flat, treeless, and white, the quasi-city housed a few hundred transients and a few dozen residents. Alaska Airlines flew in a jet twice per day to drop off and pick up engineers and mechanics who worked on the Alaskan pipeline. Thankfully, the large general store at Deadhorse offered hot coffee alongside an assortment of wrenches, pipes, fittings, and coveralls. Jon had time for a quick cup before a Navy crew outfitted him with Arctic gear. First came wool underwear, then a polypropylene top, then more wool, then an Arctic jacket, then hand and toe warmers followed by a balaclava and cap. Like a grade school kid in winter, Jon marched out to a single-engine Cessna. The smell of airplane fuel wafted across the runway as he climbed inside.

The plane sputtered, taxied, and roared into the air. Jon glanced out the small window. He saw nothing save for an expanse of white frost for miles, broken now and then by a shimmer of gray-blue where ice had melted to reveal the ocean. Almost three hours later, the plane descended toward a small frozen island adrift in the Arctic Ocean northwest of Alaska. The ice floe was no more than six miles in diameter.

The plane landed hard and skidded across the ice. Through the window, Jon saw a dozen wooden huts that resembled large rectangular coffins. When he stepped from the plane, a Petty Officer ushered him toward one of the huts, ironically called Truk—a South Pacific Island near Guam. He tossed his gear onto a bunk and stepped back into the cold. There he met the tall and affable Camp Commander, Captain Mitch Oliver.

The Captain pointed at the bruise on Jon's cheek. "Rough night?"

"Bar fight," Jon lied.

Oliver half-smiled, shook his head, and guided Jon across the glistening snowpack. "The Arctic Ocean is the world's smallest, but it can freeze your dick off in about two seconds." Oliver pointed at a small open pit lined with plywood. "Speaking of dicks, that's the head. Do you need to take a leak?"

"I'm like a camel," Jon said. "I can hold it for days."

"Suit yourself," Oliver said.

"How cold does it get at night?" Jon asked.

"Minus thirty degrees."

Jon glanced back at the open pee pit. "So do your thing during the day unless you want to feel like you have two navels?"

Oliver laughed. "Or unless you can hold it for days."

Oliver turned and waved an arm at a large banner plastered against the side of a hooch. The sign displayed two logos, one for the Arctic Submarine Lab and one for the Applied Physics Lab. He explained that the two labs teamed up every few years to conduct Ice Exercises, dubbed ICEX, where two nuclear attack submarines worked with researchers and scientists to hone tactics and test the latest weapons, communications, navigation, sonar, and fire control systems in icy conditions.

"Arctic waters are not very friendly," Oliver said. "Over time, salt leaches out of the ice and freshwater rivers flow into the ocean here. There's little to no evaporation or any wave action to mix the fresh water with the salt-water. The result is lower density and less salinity."

"How does that affect submarine operations?" Jon said.

"Things are a lot more dangerous up here," Oliver said. "When fresh water from the melting ice mingles with ocean water, long stalactites form keels beneath the sea ice. Maneuvering around them can be quite a challenge."

"What about surfacing?" Jon said.

"Even more dangerous," Oliver said as he marched across the hardened snowpack. "If a sub has a casualty, like a fire, flooding, or a reactor scram, they'd have to search for thin ice to crack through. If they couldn't find some fast, they'd be screwed like a Tijuana whore."

With Jon close behind, Oliver tramped over to the ICEX command hut and creaked open the wooden door. Inside sat a dozen headset-wearing operators mesmerized by blinking monitors. Cables dangled from an array of gray rectangular systems mounted inside plastic cases. A large monitor on one wall displayed gridlines and charted the location of the two subs. Dozens of red and green dots tracked the course of each boat while they played simulated games of cat and mouse. One sub had completed its exercises and left the area. The other, now hundreds of feet below them, was the USS *Connecticut*—the boat Jon would board first thing in the morning. Oliver explained how the trained operators used the gear, tracked and communicated with the subs, and monitored weapons tests when the two submarines fired unarmed torpedoes at each other.

"How did you retrieve the spent practice torpedoes?" Jon asked. "With a pair of tweezers?"

Oliver smiled. "Not quite. We carved three-foot-diameter holes in the ice, sent in divers, and pulled them out with a crane."

Years earlier, Jon had completed several missions in freezing cold water and the thought of diving through a small hole in an Arctic ice floe made him shiver.

With the tour concluded, Oliver left Jon to eat dinner on his own inside the blue-and-white-striped mess tent, where a civilian husband and wife team prepared meals for the forty-odd sailors and scientists at the camp. If not for the plastic tables and chairs, and the ice floe ambiance, Jon might have thought he was at a four-star restaurant in Anchorage. A buffet table displayed an array of savory selections from salmon to steaks to chicken. The chilled air danced with the smell of garlic, parsley, and saffron. Jon filled a dish and sat.

A petite blonde tossed her plate on the table across from Jon. "Mind if I join you?"

His mouth full, Jon nodded approval.

"Kate Barrett," the woman said with a polished British accent. She did not offer to shake his hand.

Jon swallowed. "Jon Shay."

Kate pointed at Jon's face. "What happened to you?"

"Slipped on a wet floor," Jon said.

"Sure you did," Kate said as she reached for the salt. "ASL? APL?"

"I work for the wooden hobby horse company," Jon said.

Kate raised an eyebrow.

"I drill the assholes," Jon said.

Kate smiled. "Takes one to drill one."

"Touché," Jon said with a smile. "I'm with NCIS."

Kate tilted her head to one side as she used the knife in her left hand to scoop some potatoes onto her fork. "Are you here to arrest me?"

Jon shrugged. "Do you want me to?"

Kate shook her head. "I'm not into handcuffs anymore, mate. They're too limiting."

"Too bad," Jon said. "Mine are velvet-lined. What brought you to the ice? ASL? APL?"

"Neither," Kate said. "Something quite hush-hush, really. I could tell you, but then, how do you Yanks put it? I'd have to kill you."

Jon took a sip of coffee. "You stole my line."

"Which you learned at a three-letter agency?" Kate said.

"Four letters," Jon said. "I used to swim with the SEALs."

"A bad boy, I'm impressed," Kate said as she scooped up a cauliflower sprout.

Jon shook his head. "I used to be Bad Jon. Now I'm just Sweet Jonathan."

Kate glanced up and smiled. "Funny *and* bad. I rather like that in a man. Maybe we should meet later and freeze our asses off on a snowmobile?"

Kate's sparkling eyes and pouting lips reminded Jon of Annelia. His heart fluttered as nostalgia rushed through his veins. "Sounds like fun, but

I have an early wake-up call and I'm really looking forward to peeing into one of those ice boxes."

Kate shrugged, stood, and grabbed her plate. "Your loss, Sweet Jonathan. I might have changed my mind about those handcuffs."

The lithe blonde, sporting a tight-fitting snowsuit, turned and walked toward the galley. He watched as she dropped off her tray, pushed open the door, and marched toward a hooch across the compound. Jon thought about the Navy Revolver waiting for him back in San Diego. Maybe it was time to let Annelia go and start living again. Or maybe it was time to put six bullets in the gun.

He returned to his hooch and glanced at the metal pot by the door. He'd been told by Captain Oliver to hack up some ice and place it in the pot to boil. The steam would keep the small shack humidified in the dry Arctic. He shrugged, left his hut, and marched across the ice. He pounded his gloved hand against the door of another hooch. The door opened.

Kate smiled. "Snowmobile ride?"

Jon motioned a hand toward the horizon. "I need some ice for my pot. You?"

Kate glanced at the pot near the door and then back at Jon. "Can I put on my makeup and heels first?"

Jon smiled and turned toward a parked snowmobile. Kate grabbed her parka and followed. The yellow Skidoo had four small wheels on each side that turned tractor treads. A square plastic basket had been placed behind the seat for storage. Jon straddled the seat. Kate nestled behind him and wrapped her arms around his waist. The engine rattled as the two sped away against the golden red backdrop of a setting sun.

Ten minutes later, Jon parked and removed an ax from the side of the snowmobile. He found a large ice sheet and slammed the ax against it a half-dozen times. Kate stood nearby and watched. The ice did not yield. Heaving, he swung again and again.

Kate said, "You really are Sweet Jonathan now."

Wheezing, Jon said, "I forgot to eat my Wheaties."

He drove the ax against the hardened ice a dozen more times. Finally, a chunk broke free, but it was no larger than a shoebox. That would be big enough for Kate's stove pot humidifier, but he'd need another one for his. Unless....

Jon shook off the thought and heaved the ax again. Chips flew into the air. The tiny fragments landed on the snowpack and captured the light of the moon, like frozen stars against a blanket of white. Another dozen swings produced a second chunk. He loaded both into the basket and then rested against the seat. His chest heaved in the thin, dry air.

Kate walked over and leaned against the seat beside him. They stared in silence into the night sky as the fingers of an emerald Aurora Borealis formed on the horizon. Kate reached over and held Jon's gloved hand. She rested her head on his shoulder.

"Why are you really here, Jon?" Kate asked. "And please don't tell me you have an ice fetish."

"I like my scotch neat," Jon said, "but if I told you why I'm here..."

Kate finished his sentence. "You'd have to kill me."

"Or handcuff you," Jon said.

"Brilliant," Kate. "Is this your first time in the Arctic?"

"I wish," Jon said as he stared into the night sky. "I used to be with Team Two."

"Team Two?"

"The only SEAL team trained for Arctic operations. I thought it'd be fun, but I wound up freezing my ass off. Swore I'd never come back."

"How's that working out for you so far, Yank?"

"I'm thinking about buying a reindeer," Jon said. "What about you? First time?"

Kate nodded. "I'm an ice virgin. I just wanted to get away, I guess."

"Running from something?"

"Aren't we all?"

Jon stood and held out his hand. Kate placed her small gloved palm into his and rose to her feet. Inches away, the mist from her warm breath mingled with his. He stared into her blue eyes and tried to change them to brown. His legs buckled as Annelia's lifeless face filled his thoughts. He struggled to breathe, as if he were a hundred feet down with an empty tank of air.

"Are you okay?" Kate said.

"I'm fine," Jon said as he turned away and mounted the snowmobile. Kate slid in close behind him and wrapped her arms around his waist. She rested her cheek snug against his back. A jumble of emotions tortured his soul. Guilt, attraction, fear, and a glint of passion. These emotions were both foreign and familiar. Desired and scorned. Comforting and agonizing.

Jon hit the button and fired up the engine. Back at Kate's hut, he plunked one of the ice chunks into the stove pot humidifier and lit the fire underneath. The ice popped and sizzled and a light cloud of steam emerged.

"Thanks," Kate said as she unzipped her parka to reveal a layer of wool underneath. She leaned back on the edge of her bunk and smiled. "You can stay for a while if you'd like."

Jon wanted to stay. He wanted to shed his sorrow and find a sliver of joy, even if only for an hour. He wanted to say yes but could not find the courage to move beyond his past.

"Thanks for the offer," Jon said, "but I have a date with a polar bear." He opened the hooch door and strode out into the cold.

Back in his hut, unable to sleep, he thought about Kate. In his mind, he again watched her pull down the zipper on her parka and lean back on the bunk. His thoughts wandered across her breasts as they pushed against the wool of her shirt. His groin ached. He hadn't felt the touch of a woman in more than a year.

He rolled over and fought with his desires, as if they were somehow disrespectful to his dead wife. He knew that notion was insane, but he couldn't rid himself of the guilt. He tried to sleep but remained restless. An hour later, he heard the door to his hooch open. He reached for his gun.

"Easy sailor," Kate said, "it's just me."

She slipped through the door, pulled off her parka, and unzipped her jumpsuit. She peeled back the cover of Jon's sleeping bag and nestled in beside him. She was wearing soft wool sleepwear and her body felt warm.

She reached for his hand and pulled his arm around her waist. "I was cold."

Jon held her tight. In his mind, Annelia lay nestled beside him, sharing her warmth and love. Tears streamed down his face as the broken pieces of his heart lay tangled in Kate's hair.

"You've got some ghosts, mate," Kate whispered.

"Only one," Jon said.

Dawn came cold and early. There was an indentation in the mattress where Kate had spent the night. Jon packed his gear and relieved himself in a wooden box. No one dared take a shower. That could only be had by hacking up some ice, melting large chunks, and filling something akin to a garden sprayer. He used a moist wipe instead. An hour later, a helicopter whisked him off to the rendezvous point.

Four layers of wool and polypropylene were easily defeated by the negative twenty-degree weather, and by the time Jon arrived at the surfacing location, a few miles away, he felt like he was wearing a frozen sleeping bag. The chopper blades whipped the snow off the ice at the landing spot and turned the sky white. A wooden warming hut, no larger than a walk-in closet, sat on the hard pack next to a pair of bundled figures. One of the figures approached and escorted Jon away from the helicopter.

A fat cigar dangling from his blue lips, icicles hanging from his beard, headphones draped about his ears, the sailor called the USS *Connecticut* using a short-range underwater communications system called Gertrude. "Iceman, this is Marvin Gardens. NCIS is ready for your surfacing."

Fingers numb, Jon stood on the polar ice cap and waited. No trumpets blared when the *Connecticut* surfaced, but Jon imagined the sound all the same. He also felt the ground shake as 8,000 tons of hardened steel punched a hole through the ice. A dark intruder supplanted the white calm of nature's landscape. Jon was awestruck as an ominous rectangle inched toward a gray sky. Three sailors appeared on the top of the submarine's sail and pushed boulder-sized blocks of ice over the side. The glistening chunks smacked the frozen pack and splintered like giant ice cubes hurled at concrete.

The submariners climbed down the side of the sail. One carried a chainsaw. Bundled in orange Arctic gear, the man looked like Jason from the horror movie on his way to a pumpkin fest. The chainsaw sputtered and then roared like a lion. Chopped ice flew skyward as Pumpkin Jason sliced away the hardpack covering the sub. A half-hour later, a spring-loaded hatch opened on the deck.

Jon trudged toward the surfaced submarine. The pungent odor of amine wafted up from below and brought back a flood of memories from his time as a SEAL. He descended through the midsection hatch. A Petty Officer met him near the galley and escorted him past an array of pipes, valves, and busy sailors to a door labeled "Officer's Country." Commander Marvin Jackson, the boat's Commanding Officer, met Jon just inside the door. The forty-two-year-old African American had a raspy cigar voice that made him sound like Barry White. His eyes were grey and calm and measured Jon like a fighter might an opponent before stepping into the ring.

Jackson sat down in front of a small desk fastened to the bulkhead, donned a pair of reading glasses, and rifled through a wad of paperwork. Without looking up, he said, "What happened to your face?"

"Accident," Jon said as he sat in a metal chair near the door.

Jackson glanced up. "As in you accidentally let the other guy smack you in the face?"

"Sucker punch, sir. I can't duck as fast as I used to."

Jackson lowered his head again and signed a report. "You've got forty-eight hours."

"Sir?" Jon said.

Jackson looked up and removed his glasses. "The crew is upset about the death of Petty Officer Kelly, and I want some answers, but I've also got a short window to finish some critical tests. I need you to wrap up your investigation in less than forty-eight hours, understood?"

"Yessir, but I don't need to remind you—"

"That you've got the authority to take as long as you need and yadda yadda. I get that. But I'm asking you to do this in double time, okay?"

"Double time, sir?"

Jackson donned his glasses and focused on the mound of paperwork. "The XO will make sure you have access to the crew, but not when they're on duty or sleeping."

"Can I interview them when they're in the head, sir?"

"Very funny," Jackson said as he raised his chin and stared at Jon. "Is there anything else you need, Agent Shay?"

"No, sir. Not unless you happen to have a good chiropractor on board."

"We're an attack submarine, not a massage parlor. Our staterooms are taken, so the XO assigned you a rack in the torpedo room."

"That'll be fine, sir." Jon stood and turned to leave.

"One more thing," Jackson said.

Jon turned back and cocked an ear.

"They're pumping sanitaries, so don't flush when you're in the head."

"Understood," Jon said as he left the stateroom.

While walking athwartship over to the wardroom, a nagging ache in Jon's lower back, earned from too many hours in airplane seats, made him feel more like sixty-five than thirty-five. Still, he could not help but smile at the memory conjured by Jackson's warning regarding pumping sanitaries. On all submarines, restrooms were called "heads." The term came from the old wooden ship sailing days when the crew did their thing over the side in the bow, or the "head" of the ship. Toilets on subs were made of metal with a flushing ball valve at the bottom. Sanitary waste was flushed into large tanks that needed to be pumped dry upon occasion. To accomplish this, a watch stander pressurized the tanks with air to pump the contents out to sea. He also hung signs on all head stall doors to warn sailors not to flush. Invariably, a sleepy sailor missed seeing the signs and flushed, which blew the contents of the sanitary tank up through the toilet's open valve and onto the sailor's face.

Jon turned a corner and entered the wardroom. The area was about the same size as a large dining room, with one door in the forward starboard corner. Center stage, a table took up most of the square footage. A dozen chairs surrounded the table, and plaques and submarine paraphernalia graced the walls. Another door in the aft port corner led to the galley, where food was served by jacket-wearing stewards.

Petty Officer "Doc" Richards, the boat's corpsman, hovered over Petty Officer Paul Kelly's corpse on the table and glanced up as Jon approached. Richards wasn't a real doctor, rather a navy corpsman with chipmunk cheeks and a receding hairline. He had reported the incident days earlier to Commander Jackson, who'd reported the death to the Commander, Submarine Forces, Pacific, in Hawaii. COMSUBPAC had called NCIS and shortly after that, Jon's cell phone had chimed.

Kelly's cold body spanned the wardroom table. They had kept him in a body bag in the ship's refrigerator until they were authorized to surface. Now exposed to room temperature, and stripped naked so Jon could do an examination, the corpse exuded a morgue-like stench. Relaxed muscles verified that rigor mortis had already come and gone. Jon held his breath. Images of Annelia's dead grey skin flashed into his head. He felt dizzy. His knees weakened. He steadied himself on the side of the table.

"You okay?" Doc said.

"I'm fine," Jon said, pulling himself upright. He forced the cold memories from his head and examined the body. There were no obvious signs of trauma or foul play, but that didn't rule out a homicide. Lividity in the lower back indicated Kelly had died while prone.

Doc stepped near and pointed at Jon's cheek. "You want something for that?"

Jon glanced up. "I said I'm fine."

Doc held up his hands. "Okay, okay. Just trying to help."

Jon focused again on the corpse. "Apparent manner of death?"

Doc cleared his throat. "It looks like he swallowed a bottle of sleeping pills and never woke up, sir."

Jon removed his eyes from the body and turned toward Doc. "No need to call me sir. I'm a civilian now. Where did he get the pills?"

"He must have gotten them from my medicine locker," Doc said.

"How?"

"I don't know. I always keep it locked."

"Are you positive you didn't leave it open?"

"Yes, sir. I mean, yes, I'm positive. It automatically locks when it's shut."

"How do you know the pills were from your locker?" Jon said.

Doc shifted his stance. "Petty Officer Chen found the empty bottle in Kelly's rack. They were definitely Navy issue, and when I checked, my bottle was missing."

"How many pills did you have left in that bottle?"

"I'm not sure. Does it matter?"

"Yes," Jon said. "The LD100 for barbiturates is typically two to ten grams. I need to know the dosage level of those pills and how many were left in that bottle."

"What's LD100?"

"That's the lethal dosage for one hundred percent of the population."

"Okay," Doc said, "I'll check my records."

"Please do."

Jon bent down and studied Kelly's placid face. His eyes were closed and a slight smile played on his lips, as though he'd been dreaming about something pleasant right before he died. Was he thinking about his home? His girlfriend? His mother?

His mother. Now her boy would come home in a box, and Jon knew just how she'd feel.

Jon looked up at Doc and said, "Had rigor mortis set in when you found the body?"

"Yeah, his face and limbs were stiff."

"Where's the bottle of sleeping pills?"

Doc handed Jon a plastic bag with the bottle inside. Even though he'd later check for fingerprints, his "crime scene" was about as contaminated as they get. "How do you think Kelly got his hands on your bottle of barbiturates?"

Doc's head sagged. "I wish I knew."

"Things will go much easier if you come clean now, Doc. Just admit you accidentally left that locker open. It's not your fault Kelly stole those pills."

Doc's face turned red. "I'm positive I shut that locker."

Jon softened his tone. "Okay, I understand this has been difficult for you. Why don't we zip up the bag and get Kelly topside?"

While Doc and a couple seamen hauled Kelly's body out of the wardroom, Jon studied the dead Petty Officer's file. The young man had apparently been a model sailor. Excellent marks, high morale, a team player, nothing pointing to suicidal tendencies. Jon massaged the bridge of his nose. Just because Petty Officer Chen had found an empty bottle of pills in Kelly's rack didn't mean that was the manner of death. Jon knew a medical examiner at Naval Forces Alaska in Juneau could take several days to complete an autopsy and deliver the results. Until then, knowing what really killed Kelly would probably remain a mystery. In the meantime, Jon would just have to keep digging for clues.

Jon's stomach growled as a few junior officers entered the wardroom for breakfast. Meals aboard the *Connecticut* were formal affairs. The CO sat at the head of the table, followed by the XO and senior officers in descending counterclockwise order. The steward always placed the first plate in front of the CO, then the XO on down. No one ate until after the captain took his first bite. Years earlier, as a Navy SEAL officer, Jon had spent several weeks aboard various submarines while conducting missions. When he'd dined with the officers in the wardroom, he'd been mentally transported back in time where seafaring officers brandished swords and sat at long tables aboard man-of-war ships crafted from oak.

Ignoring his hunger, Jon stood up from the table and left the room. He turned right toward the crew's mess and climbed down the ladder into the torpedo room. Green MK 48 ADCAP torpedoes, strapped onto racks, patiently waited for something to kill. The *Connecticut* was one of only three boats in the fleet equipped with eight torpedo tubes and an automated loading system that allowed the submarine to take out eight targets and reload all tubes in less than fifteen minutes. Almost no ship in the world could survive an attack perpetrated by a *Seawolf*-class attack submarine.

Jon strode across the deck of the torpedo room, found his assigned rack, and placed his duffle bag on the bunk bed. He then ascended the ladder toward the fire control panels. Lights twinkled like a holiday street as he walked past and ascended another deck toward the Doc's "corner," a small area on the port side near the bow of the boat.

The corpsman's area contained an assortment of medical devices, including a defibrillator, digital thermometer, and EKG unit. A small medicine cabinet, recessed about chin level into a bulkhead, had one combination lock on the front. Jon examined the lock and the edges of the door. No indications of forced entry. He spun the dial and tried opening the lock. No joy. He looked around the area for a screwdriver, knife, letter opener, or any flat objects a perpetrator might have used. Nothing. He made a mental note to have Doc Richards bring him the medicine locker inventory sheet.

Jon started to head back toward the torpedo room when he noticed something on the deck by his feet. He bent down and picked up a small plastic cap. *A syringe needle cover.* He pocketed the cover and walked toward the midsection of the boat, where he found Doc near the galley.

Jon showed the cap to Doc. "I found this on the deck near one of your lockers. Have you given anyone a shot underway?"

Doc stared at the cap. "No, I haven't."

"Are you sure?"

"Very."

"Maybe it's from a previous deployment?"

"I doubt it," Doc said. "We do frequent field days to clean every inch of the boat. Someone would have found that by now."

"Maybe," Jon said. "Or maybe not."

The boat's diving alarm blared above the hum of electrical equipment fans, signaling that the submarine was about to dive beneath the Arctic ice to complete another exercise. Jon took the cap back from Doc and turned to leave. He'd later have the cover tested at a lab to see if any trace elements remained, but they might be hard to find by now. He entered the wardroom, sat down, and tried to imagine what might have prompted Kelly to commit suicide. Was he depressed about something he hadn't divulged to his shipmates? Perhaps a Dear John letter from his girlfriend, financial issues, or the stress of serving aboard a submarine?

Jon knew that, given the close quarters aboard subs, crews naturally formed a tight-knit community. Few personal secrets remained secret for long. If Kelly had been borderline suicidal, it seemed unlikely that no one aboard had a clue. Then again, Jon had mostly hidden his depression from his NCIS colleagues for over a year, so it was possible Kelly had done the same.

Jon's gut churned as the sound of twelve revolver clicks echoed in his head. He wondered how many of his friends had seen past his forced smiles and suspected that his grief had turned suicidal. He'd frequently lied to the NCIS shrinks about his condition so he could remain active. On one mission, Agent Brad Tucker had pulled him aside and asked him if he was okay. Asked him if he needed to take some time off. Jon had lied again while shoving his pain deeper into the pit of his stomach.

He refocused his thoughts and poised a pen above his notepad. The facts he'd gathered so far were scant and hinted at something beyond a suicide, but the disjointed puzzle pieces weren't lining up yet. Perhaps they would after his interview with the Witch.

CHAPTER 3

The opportunity of defeating the enemy is provided by the enemy himself.
Major Hai Liang clipped a round into a magazine and pondered the words of his favorite author. Within the next few hours, if Sun Tzu's writings proved correct, the opportunity to defeat the enemy would be at hand. If not, perhaps Tzu's rhetoric in the *Art of War* would lead to one.

Slamming the magazine into his AK-74 assault rifle, he studied the hardened faces of his men—eight trained operatives of Chinese descent, seated inside an Advanced SEAL Delivery System. The seventy-five-foot-long mini-sub, cruising in stealth mode 200 miles north of Alaska, had once belonged to the U.S. Navy SEALs. Not anymore.

Turning his tall frame toward the bow of the vehicle, Liang barked an order. "Pilot, all stop. Prepare to hover."

A voice from the bow verified the command. Subtle vibrations, emanating from the deck, disappeared. Now all that could be heard were occasional grunts and clanking coming from the soldiers as they readied their equipment.

Liang secured the zipper on his dry suit and stood up from one of the benches in the aft transport compartment. He walked the few feet into the bow and said, "Sonar, range and bearing to the camp?"

A soldier glanced at a panel filled with blinking lights and said, "One thousand yards, bearing three-four-nine."

Adrenaline accelerated Liang's heart as he rested a hand on the man's shoulder. "Any contacts?"

The soldier cupped a pair of hands around his headphones. "The U.S. Navy divers have left the area and the American *Seawolf*-class submarine is now more than 10,000 yards distant."

"Very well. Pilot, make your depth sixty feet and close to five hundred yards from the ice holes."

"Aye, sir."

The ASDS vibrated for a few seconds as the propulsor motor—a quasi-underwater jet engine—pushed the boat forward. Liang removed a laminated map from his pocket and traced a finger from one edge to the other. His team had been monitoring two American submarines operating near a U.S. Navy research facility north of Prudhoe Bay.

For the past several days, the two subs had fired practice torpedoes at each other while the researchers, inside wooden huts on the ice floe, monitored the exercises. Navy divers had drilled three-foot-diameter holes in the ice to retrieve the spent torpedoes using small cranes that resembled playground swing sets. Now that the divers had left the area, Liang planned to use the ice holes for an entirely different purpose.

"Five hundred yards, sir."

"All stop, prepare to egress."

The ASDS glided to halt. Six men stood up from a bench and lined up near the small oval diving chamber in the center of the craft. Two by two, bundled in dry suits, they opened the inner hatch on the side of the eight-foot-tall chamber and climbed inside. Air hissed as the men pressurized the tank to equalize with the outside ocean. A green light on a panel near the chamber signaled that the first team of two had left the boat and closed the outer hatch. Two more soldiers depressurized the chamber and stepped through the inner hatch. The routine repeated until Liang climbed into the cylinder alone. He pulled on his full-face Kirby Morgan diving mask and readied the chamber.

Goosebumps covered Liang's arms as he opened the lower hatch and dropped into the black. Using luminescent instruments, the team swam the 500 years to their destination. Near the holes, Liang could see two small circles of dim light shining through the ice from above. He kicked his fins and ascended the twenty yards to reach the openings. He then flashed hand signals to regroup the team. One soldier swam toward a hole and removed a small device from his diving suit pocket. He clicked a switch to disable the intruder detection system—a set of small hydrophones that streamed down from the ice via long cables. The soldier waited a few seconds, then swam up through one of the holes. He popped his head out of the water for a brief second, came back down, and flashed an OK sign. Liang signaled his men, and one by one they darted toward the holes and climbed out of the water.

Defiant clouds battled with an angry sun as Liang pulled his muscled body up through a two-foot thick ice hole. He removed his dry suit, stuffed it into a bag, and donned an Arctic parka. Jagged shards of ice jutted skyward amidst a blanket of white that stretched to the far edge of the ice floe. Liang and his men trudged across the frozen landscape. A plume of smoke billowed from the back end of a structure as the team approached the U.S. camp.

Liang's trigger finger twitched. His temples throbbed as he focused a pair of binoculars and identified the blue and white half-cylinder tent as the mess hall. The rest of the camp consisted of a dozen small wooden huts arranged haphazardly atop the snow, reminiscent of the fabled village of Hansel and Gretel. Liang knew from his briefings that the ICEX camp should now have around thirty personnel, supervised by less than a dozen Navy officers and men, mostly unarmed. No one here expected to be attacked.

Liang ordered his men to spread out and take up positions near the huts. He had instructed his team to wait until a synchronized time before attacking, in the middle of the camp's lunch hour, to ensure they missed no one.

Liang ducked as two scientists exited a hut and sauntered over to the galley. Three more came from another hut, followed by five others. Soon most of the huts appeared empty as the camp's occupants shuffled into the mess tent. Liang forced his pulse to remain steady as he checked his watch and counted down the seconds. Five, four, three....

He sprinted toward the mess tent. Nearby, his men combed through the other huts, including the command center, and rounded up the occupants. Liang slammed open the mess tent door and rushed in while ordering the occupants to raise their hands and stay seated. Startled scientists and sailors rocked in their red plastic chairs. Bottles of catsup and hot sauce thudded as they toppled over, rolled off the white laminate tables, and hit the wooden floor. Women gasped and men grumbled, but everyone obeyed. All except one. A Navy Captain stood tall and demanded to know what was happening. Liang walked over and slapped the butt of his rifle against the man's cheek. Blood flew from the Captain's mouth.

Liang's men entered with a few more of the camp's personnel who were forced into seats alongside the others. Liang removed a picture of a woman from his jacket and rifled through the group, checking faces as he went. He strode back over to the Captain.

Shoving the picture under the Captain's nose, Liang said, "Where is this woman?"

The Captain spat out some blood. "I don't know."

Liang looked at the Captain's nametag. "Captain Oliver, I only want this woman. Tell me where she is, and no one will be hurt."

Oliver straightened his back. "I told you, I don't know."

Liang held up the picture in front of the group. "Look at this photograph. The woman's name is Kate Barrett. She is a scientist working at this camp. Tell me where she can be found, and you will not be harmed."

No response.

Liang pointed to someone in the group, a young blonde woman, probably a midshipman from the Naval Academy. He nodded at one of his men and said, "Her."

A soldier snatched the blonde from her seat and dragged her toward Liang. He positioned his pistol against the midshipman's left temple. The woman's knees shook. Liang leveled a stern look at Captain Oliver. The Navy officer narrowed his eyes.

"Kate Barrett," Liang said. "Tell me where she is."

Oliver's nostrils flared. He lifted his chin and said, "Small hooch, about a quarter-mile to the north."

Liang motioned for the soldier to holster his pistol. The midshipman bent over and let out a breath. A sailor in the far corner jumped to his feet and darted toward the kitchen door. A rifle shot rang in Liang's ears and the sailor dropped to the deck. A red circle formed on his back.

Captain Oliver turned toward Liang. Through clenched teeth, he said, "He was only nineteen."

Liang marched over to the soldier who'd fired the shot. He grabbed the man by the arm and in Chinese said, "What are your orders?"

The soldier popped to attention. "No shots."

Liang let go of the man's arm and pointed at three other soldiers. "Follow me."

Out in the cold, Major Liang lifted his binoculars and scanned the horizon to the north. He spotted the distant hooch. No movement, at least not yet, but he had little doubt Kate Barrett had heard the shot. If so, and if she managed to escape, his mission would fail. And if that happened, his life would no longer have meaning.

CHAPTER 4

Kate Barrett smiled as she thought about sharing a warm bunk with Agent Jon Shay. Although she'd sworn off men after her last affair had turned sour, Jon's deep blue eyes, broad shoulders, and warm smile made her wonder if she should reconsider. On the other hand, the man obviously came with some serious baggage. Another woman's memory held a piece of his heart. Full stop.

Kate leaned back and stretched. The small hooch where she worked was no larger than a small bedroom. The rectangular enclosure, constructed from plywood, contained no luxuries. No showers or restroom breaks could be taken here. Such activities required the use of a distant outhouse and several bottles of waterless soap and shampoo that made her long blonde hair look like ash. While fresh water could be gained by melting some ice in a pot, the task required an abundance of heating fuel and patience, both of which were in short supply on the busy ice floe.

The square enclosure could hold maybe four people, but only she and Bobby Ruppert were allowed to work there. The Department of Defense refused to let anyone at the ICEX camp see the top-secret tests conducted inside. In fact, the DoD had insisted the camp builders place the hooch over a quarter mile away from the rest of the camp to keep errant visitors away.

Kate checked the log on a small device near her stool, positioned next to a three-foot-diameter hole in the ice. Her daydreaming had made her miss an important reading. Now she'd have to recalibrate and start the test over again, adding thirty minutes to her twelve-hour day. Not exactly the present she'd hoped for on her thirty-second birthday.

She glanced at the infamous ROSS device on a nearby bench. Housed in a ruggedized black briefcase, the top-secret instrument resembled the "suitcase" used by the President of the United States to initiate a nuclear strike, which, under the circumstances, seemed appropriate.

The ROSS device had been named after Donald Ross, who was considered one of the fathers of modern submarine sonar systems. Dr. Ross had been the first student to graduate from Harvard University in only three years and worked for a time at the Advanced Research Labs on the Penn State campus, where Kate had helped bring the ROSS project to life. During the Cold War, President Nixon had issued Dr. Ross one of the highest commendations a civilian could earn after he solved a serious sonar problem for the Navy. Now deceased, but still a legend at ARL, Ross would never know about the device that bore his name. In fact, only a small handful would ever know that the contents of this black suitcase might someday prevent a world war.

Kate's head jolted upward at the distant crack of rifle. She stood from her stool. "Bobby, did you hear that?"

From behind a laptop on a nearby desk, Bobby glanced above the rim of his glasses. "Sounded like a polar bear fart to me," he said with a Texas twang.

Kate flashed him a "not very funny" look.

Bobby shrugged. "A bear probably wandered into the camp and they warned it off with a rifle shot."

"Well bloody hell," Kate said, "They probably sent it our way, and everyone knows polar bears are the most dangerous creatures in the Arctic."

"More dangerous than humans?" Bobby said.

"Point taken, mate," Kate said.

"Lions are way worse than bears," Bobby said.

"How so?"

Bobby grinned. "A circus performer named Brian once smiled as he rode on a lion. When they came back from the ride, with Brian inside, the smile was on the face of the lion."

Kate rolled her eyes. "If you recite one more of those stupid limericks, I'll make sure a polar bear rips your arms off."

"Late night?" Bobby said as he resumed typing on a keyboard.

Kate rubbed at the back of her neck to remove a kink and gazed down at the ice hole by her feet. A small tripod sat above the hole, suspending a cable that disappeared into the cold water below. She turned a crank on the tripod and reeled up a four-foot-long casing that resembled a mini-torpedo crossed with a boat anchor. Frowning, she said, "I missed a reading. Now I'll need to start over."

"That's bad juju," Bobby said, not looking up. "Now I'm going to have to report you to the Gestapo."

"Very funny," Kate said. She looked over at the suitcase on the bench. "ROSS, can you hear me?"

The suitcase responded through a speaker. "Yes, Dr. Barrett, I can hear you."

ROSS's artificial voice sounded like the HAL 9000 computer from the movie *2001: A Space Odyssey.*

"I wish you hadn't given ROSS that creepy voice," Kate said to Bobby.

"I loved that movie," Bobby said, referring to *2001.* "Best damn sci-fi flick ever made."

"Are you not pleased with my voice?" ROSS said. The accent changed to British. "I have the ability to mimic seventeen different dialects."

"Change back," Bobby demanded as he swiveled on his stool and stared at the device.

"Very well, Dr. Ruppert," ROSS said, again sounding like HAL.

"ROSS, restart test niner-bravo-two."

"Very well, Dr. Barrett. Restarting test niner-bravo-two."

"Where are the binoculars?" Kate asked.

"I have not been programmed with that information," ROSS said.

"Not you," Kate said. "Bobby."

"You need the 'nocs for a calibration test?" Bobby said.

"No, I need the binoculars so I can see why someone fired a shot."

"Right. On the bench next to ROSS."

Kate grabbed the binoculars and threw the door open. The hinges creaked as she stepped outside. Her cheeks numbed within seconds and her lips felt like dried shoe leather. She scanned the camp with the binoculars. Nothing. No movement at all. She glanced down at her watch. Lunchtime. While most everyone might be in the dining tent, that didn't account for the guards. A couple of guys with rifles should be sitting atop the command hut while watching for polar bears that might smell the food. And who had fired that shot?

Kate shrugged and glanced upward. Overhead, a layer of dark clouds and fog reminded her of the suburbs near London. In the fall, plumes of steam rose from the Didcot power station stacks and resembled three grandfathers smoking pipes in unison. The recollection reminded her of the life she'd left behind prior to moving to the U.S., and the professor she'd had an affair with while completing her PhD at Oxford. She'd given him her heart and then discovered he was married. Had two kids and a mortgage in a Rose Hill neighborhood. Shattered and certain she would never love again, she'd ended their relationship via text while towing a hired trailer down the motorway. A few months later, she accepted an offer from ARL.

Kate scanned the camp again. Still no signs of life. Her breath frosted the lenses on her binoculars. She wiped a gloved finger across the glass circles and refocused. The galley door swung open and four figures emerged. Their parkas were white, but their sleeves bore red patches. Kate flipped to a higher power and thumbed the focus wheel. The patches revealed a flag. *Chinese.*

One of the men turned toward her. He held an assault rifle that was definitely not American. Another man removed a set of binoculars from a hip case. He panned and then stopped. Staring right at Kate, he pointed. Kate swallowed a lump as four armed men ran toward her.

Sprinting back into the hooch, she yelled at Bobby. "We're being attacked!"

The plump engineer looked up from a technical manual. "By a polar bear?"

"No, by Chinese soldiers."

Bobby jumped up from his seat. "What the...? Why?"

"I have no idea why," Kate said. "Collect your parka and the survival kit. I'll grab ROSS."

"But I...where's the kit?"

Kate knew the man's brilliant engineering brain plowed through science like a supercomputer but crawled in slow motion when confronted with anything beyond placid and technical. "Far corner. Get moving!"

Bobby stumbled over benches and books and found the survival kit while Kate raced to close the ROSS suitcase and find a handheld radio. Her heart thrumming at full throttle, she fought the urge to call the camp, certain she'd receive an answer in Chinese. While wriggling into her parka, she grabbed the suitcase handle and radio and urged Bobby toward the door. The distraught Texan dropped the survival kit, tripped over a stool, and almost fell into the ice hole. Kate managed to grab the back of his jacket before he splashed into the water.

Once outside, she squinted at the camp. Four bundled soldiers charged her way. One of them fired into the air. An adrenaline rush propelled Kate forward. She pushed Bobby around the corner of the hooch where a Ski-Doo snowmobile sat on the hardened snow. She placed the radio and ROSS unit inside the plastic basket behind the seat. Bobby set the survival kit next to the ROSS case.

Kate climbed onto the front of the seat and Bobby shoved his overweight body onto the back. She fired up the engine and gunned the gas. The Ski-Doo sputtered, coughed, and then stalled. She hit the start button again. The engine groaned in defiance. She pressed once more. Finally, the spark plugs lit, and the vehicle jerked forward.

Kate steered away from the camp and the running soldiers. She sped toward large slabs of cracked ice that jutted skyward like jumbled freeway parts after an earthquake. Claiming no expertise in snowmobiling, she fought with the vibrating handlebars to maneuver through the obstacle course. Shots rang out behind her and the projectiles sprayed ice into the air as they hit the snowpack nearby.

"Where are we going?" Bobby yelled above the thrum of the engine.

"*Connecticut*," Kate yelled back.

"Connecticut?"

"The submarine. She's surfacing today. A few miles from here."

"What if they abort?"

"Then I guess we're bloody well screwed."

More shots whizzed by. One well-placed shot caused her to veer hard to the right. The Ski-Doo tractor treads stuttered on the ice. Kate managed to regain control until Bobby panicked and shifted his weight, causing the snowmobile to slide sideways across the ice. Kate jerked hard to the left, but her petite frame was no match for hundreds of pounds of steel. The Ski-Doo careened off the side of a large chunk of ice and spun around in a circle.

Bobby let out a muffled yelp as the snowmobile flipped sideways and skidded against a massive slab of ice more than eight feet tall. The frozen block shot up from the ice at a forty-five-degree angle and hovered over a narrow crevasse. Kate's stomach did a somersault until her back slammed against an ice chunk. Her head hit next, followed by her right leg. The impact and searing pain made her head spin as she flew off the snowmobile and tumbled into the crevasse, hitting the bottom four feet below. The snowmobile followed, wedging itself between the two walls of ice a few feet above her head.

Moaning, Kate panned her eyes to the right and caught a glimpse of Bobby, also on the bottom of the ditch-like crevasse. Kate's eyelids felt heavy as she fought to stay conscious.

"You okay?" Bobby asked.

Kate shook her head to clear her sight. Bobby was hunched onto his knees and rubbing the back of his neck. A trickle of blood dripped off his chin.

"I'm fine," Kate said, wishing that were true. "You?"

"I think so."

With her head aching from the fall, Kate strained to raise her chin and look upward. Her gaze landed on the snowmobile, which had been turned sideways and lay wedged between the narrow sides of the crevasse. Behind her, the white shallow cavern ended at a shear wall of ice. In the other direction, a four-foot-deep by three-foot-wide ditch snaked away into the distance.

"That direction," Kate said, pointing toward what she hoped was somewhere.

Bobby nodded. His rapid breathing steamed the Arctic air.

Kate planted a glove against the ice wall. With unsteady legs and a racing heart, she pulled herself into a crawling position while keeping her head down to avoid being seen above the four-foot-tall embankment. She turned toward Bobby and pointed at the snowmobile. "Can you get the ROSS case, survival kit, and radio?"

"Maybe," Bobby said. His lips trembled. Rolling onto all fours, he crawled over to the Ski-Doo and reached for the basket. With the vehicle turned sideways, the top was covered by the ice wall. Bobby pulled on the basket's side until it wedged free. He reached inside and removed the ROSS case, kit, and radio. He dragged them back over to Kate. They divvied up the spoils, with Kate taking the ROSS.

Crawling while dragging the case, Kate took the lead. Bobby followed. The ice ditch curved like a riverbed for several hundred yards and then banked upward to meet level ground. Near the end of the crevasse, where the open air met the upward sloping walls, Kate popped her head up for a moment. Her body trembled as she spied the soldiers in the distance.

She ducked her head back down. "They're almost at the snowmobile. I caught a glimpse of tall ice boulders in the opposite direction. A few may be tall enough to hide behind."

Bobby remained silent. His wide eyes made him look like a frightened dog.

Kate had a bad feeling they wouldn't make it two miles to the *Connecticut* before being killed or captured, but she kept those doubts to herself. She pointed upward and darted out of the crevasse. With her heart pounding, she sprinted the fifty yards to the nearest boulder, certain a bullet would strike her down at any moment. Her lungs heaved as she ducked behind the ice shard and bent over to catch her breath. She watched Bobby run the distance, hoping he'd make it before the soldiers spotted him. She glanced upward and noticed the fog had thickened. She hoped it might aid their escape and they'd find the *Connecticut* before a serious storm hit.

Bobby joined her at the boulder and pointed toward an ice shard, eight feet tall and another fifty yards distant. Between staccato breaths, he said, "That one next?"

Without answering, Kate ran toward the shard, with Bobby close behind. He made it fifty feet before tripping on an ice chunk and falling face down. Kate ran over and helped him up, but before they could take another step, a loud crack made her stop and crouch. She looked sideways at Bobby. No red spots coated his parka, and she wondered if the bullet had struck her instead. She felt nothing, but maybe shock was preventing the pain from reaching her brain.

"Am I...?"

Bobby shook his head. "Don't think so."

White parkas came running toward them. Voices shouted and rifles pointed. A tall man approached. A hood covered most of his face, but Kate could still see something fierce in his eyes.

The Chinese officer threw open his parka and unholstered his sidearm. He marched over and pointed the gun at Kate's temple. Her knees shook as she forced a plea through trembling lips. "Please don't kill me."

CHAPTER 5

With his head pounding from long nights of restless sleep, Jon waited for the Witch. He was seated at a table in the Goat Locker, which is what they called the Chief Petty Officer's quarters aboard submarines. As the highest-ranking enlisted members of the crew, Navy Chiefs were affectionately known as "old goats." Most had served for more than a decade before earning the right to become a Chief. On one bulkhead, a few feet above a small table, a row of coffee cups hung like stockings. Each cup was different, one for each Chief, and all were lined with dark brown or black coffee stains. Chiefs never washed their cups before hanging them on a hook. They swore that leaving them unwashed improved the flavor of a strong Navy brew. Whether true or not, no one dared argue with a crusty old goat because everyone knew Chiefs were the oil that greased the Navy's gears.

Jon glanced at the "plain Jane" Navy clock on a bulkhead. The Wicked Witch of the West was late. That was how the crew described Angela Rinaldo, the boat's temporary "ice pilot." Though she had previously served as a naval officer, Rinaldo was now a civilian and worked for ASL. Her extensive knowledge of submarines, Arctic conditions, topology, and under-ice characteristics made her an ideal candidate to help the crew maneuver beneath the polar ice cap and properly surface the boat through three feet of hard ice. Jon had learned that just hours before Petty Officer Kelly had died, he had been working with Rinaldo on a top secret project.

Jon had studied Rinaldo's file at length. Prior to leaving the military, the Naval Academy graduate was one of the first of a select few females to serve aboard a fleet ballistic missile submarine under a new integration program launched by the Navy. Rumor had it that Rinaldo could swear like a sailor, drink half the crew under the table, and enervate a man better than the infamous Captain Bligh of the HMS *Bounty*. Dissenters said the Italian from the Bronx wasn't quite so harsh and possessed the brain of Einstein coupled with the fearless passion of Joan of Arc. Whatever the truth, one thing was for certain: every man aboard the USS *Connecticut* apparently knew better than to cross the Witch, and not from fear of Captain's Mast. Judicial military punishment paled in comparison to the certainty of castration.

The door to the Goat Locker flung open and a Petty Officer stepped in. The young man appeared to be half-Chinese with the lineless forehead of someone in their late twenties. His dark hair was cropped Navy-short and he stood about five-foot-seven.

Jon looked up. "Ms. Rinaldo, did you have a sex change?"

The sailor snapped to parade rest, legs apart and arms behind his back. "I'm Petty Officer Peter Chen. Rinaldo was delayed, sir. She asked me to meet with you until she could arrive."

"At ease, Petty Officer. I'm not a sir anymore. I have more than two brain cells now."

Chen flashed a smile as Jon flipped open his file.

The Petty Officer relaxed and let his arms dangle. He stared at Jon's swollen cheek but said nothing.

"You're a first class sonarman," Jon said. "You have two Navy commendations and just transferred from the submarine training command at Groton, Connecticut. You were previously a sonar instructor and you've also taken quite a few programming courses. More than enough to get a computer science degree. Why aren't you working for Elon Musk?"

"I like the navy, sir...I mean—"

"You can call me Agent Shay."

"I like programming," Chen said. "I just need to complete some core subjects like English and whatnot to get my undergrad. Then maybe I'll apply to become an officer."

"You'll need a frontal lobotomy first," Jon said.

Chen smiled again.

"Why did you transfer?" Jon asked.

"The *Connecticut* is testing some hot new technology and I wanted in," Chen said. He used his thumb to fidget with his wedding ring.

"Tell me what happened the night Petty Officer Kelly died."

Chen recounted the story without skipping a beat, as if he'd rehearsed every line. He had been on watch when they were conducting exercises with the USS *Oregon*. Kelly never showed up to relieve Chen, so he asked someone to cover for him while he went to find Kelly. He didn't see Kelly in the crew's mess, so he went to the man's rack. He tried to shake Kelly awake, but the Petty Officer didn't respond. He called the corpsman on a sound-powered phone, and Doc Richards came down and said Kelly had died in his sleep from an overdose.

"You were on watch?" Jon said. "Why didn't you send someone else to find Kelly?"

"If I had, they might have reported him. I was just trying to keep the guy out of trouble."

"Describe what you saw," Jon said.

"What I saw?"

"Kelly's eyes, were they open or closed? Did he seem at peace or in shock? Did he look like he'd been sleeping or awake for hours?

"Closed, at peace, asleep."

"What about his hands? Were they curled and stiff?"

Chen hesitated for moment and then said, "No, they looked normal, I guess."

"Are you sure?"

"Yeah, I'm pretty sure."

Doc had said when he saw the body, rigor mortis had already set in. That was not long after Chen had found Kelly in his rack. If Kelly had taken the pills right before he went to sleep, and therefore had been dead for hours, rigor mortis should have set in before Chen found the body. The shock of finding Kelly dead could have caused Chen to remember that detail incorrectly. On the other hand, the act of killing Kelly could have had the same effect.

"Your first name is actually Pietr," Jon said. It wasn't a question.

"My father is Chinese, so my last name is Chen. My mother was Russian and named me Pietr. It means Peter."

"My mother was also Russian," said Jon. "She named me Dzhon but got tired of people asking me to pass the mustard, so she shortened it to Jon."

Chen smiled again and nodded.

Jon said something in Russian. Chen raised an eyebrow but did not reply.

Jon leaned forward. Still speaking Russian, he uttered an old Russian proverb. "Little thieves are hanged, but great ones escape."

Chen swallowed a lump but did not reply.

Jon focused again on Chen's file. He asked a few more questions, in English, and then dismissed the sonarman.

Several minutes later, Petty Officer Whitney stepped into the Goat Locker. He said Rinaldo was still detained after the last exercise. The First Class Petty Officer, also in his late twenties, had tan skin, sandy blonde hair, and a surfer's brogue. He recanted the same story, except that he was a fire controlman and had relieved Chen so he could check on Kelly. Otherwise, the two stories were almost identical. Jon flipped through the pages in Whitney's file and stopped on one.

"Says here you transferred from Groton, Connecticut, around the same time as Petty Officer Chen. Did you two hang out together, like Butthead and Bevis?"

"We served in the same unit in Groton, so yeah, we had a few beers together at the club."

Jon thought he saw Whitney's lower lip quiver, but it happened too quickly to be sure. After a few more questions, he dismissed the Petty Officer.

Ten minutes later, the Goat Locker door flung open and Angela Rinaldo entered. She was about five-foot-ten, had a strong jawline, dark brunette hair, and chocolate brown eyes. Her deep alto voice and strong handshake hinted that nothing in Rinaldo's world remained out of control for long.

Rinaldo nodded at Jon's bruised face. "Does the other guy look worse?"

"Like a hockey player," Jon said.

Rinaldo offered an approving nod as she sat at the table. "Did you learn anything from Chen and Whitney?" Her tone held a hint of the Bronx, where they smacked gum like cud-chewing cows and every other guy was named Tony.

"They were riveting," Jon said. "I was mesmerized."

Rinaldo smirked. "A simple mind is easily entertained."

"Whitney's story was like a bad remake of Chen's."

"Is that a problem?"

Jon focused his eyes. "Depends on who wrote the script."

Rinaldo leaned back and crossed her long legs. "I'm busy. How long will this take?"

"We'll be done in time for you to vote in the next election," Jon said. "How well did you know Petty Officer Kelly?"

"Not well. I met him when I came aboard for ICEX several weeks ago."

"But you've been working with him during that time on various tests."

"Yes. He was assisting me on a sonar communications project."

Jon leaned forward. "I understand he had been working with you on the day he died."

"We worked together for a few hours in the sonar shack before he went to his rack to get some shut eye prior to his watch."

"Why do you think he committed suicide?"

"Hell if I know."

Jon looked down at Kelly's file. "His last few reviews were excellent. Nothing in his file indicates that he was having problems. Were you aware of any issues?"

"Like what?"

"Drugs, alcohol, gambling, bad breath. You tell me."

Rinaldo's face remained placid. "I don't believe Petty Officer Kelly died from halitosis."

Jon glared at the ice pilot. "Someone you've worked with for weeks kills himself but doesn't leave a note, has a pristine record, and no apparent problems. Doesn't that at least make you raise an eyebrow?"

"Submarine life is hard."

Jon let out a frustrated breath. A hint of the rage he'd felt earlier, when he'd slammed his leg into the passenger guy's jaw, welled up inside. He forced it back into his gut and said, "Commander Jackson tells me you recommended transfers for Chen and Whitney to come aboard the *Connecticut*. Why?"

"They're good men. We're conducting important exercises up here and I wanted to work with the best."

"No other reason?"

"No. Where's this going, Agent Shay?"

"Wherever I want it to, Ms. Rinaldo."

The brunette clenched her jaw but remained silent.

Jon breathed in deep to keep his anger at bay and continued. "Did Kelly have access to top secret information related to the project?"

Rinaldo uncrossed her legs. "Only on a need-to-know basis as related to his duties."

Jon fingered a page in Kelly's file. "He was a sonarman. Why did you need him for this project?"

Rinaldo displayed a poker face but tapped a finger on her knee when she spoke. "He was helping me test the Deep Siren Tactical Communications System."

"Which does what?" Jon asked.

"It's an add-on to our sonar system that lets us communicate with command when we're running deep and fast."

"Was the installation complete?"

"Yes, but I don't see how—"

"Was it working?"

"Yes, it was working fine," Rinaldo snapped. "We were conducting tests in Arctic conditions with teams at the ICEX camp from Raytheon and scientists from the Advanced Research Lab."

Jon thought about Kate Barrett and wondered if she was one those scientists from ARL. "What kind of tests?"

"I'm not at liberty to say."

"I have a top secret security clearance."

Rinaldo smirked again. "Not for this you don't."

Frustrated, Jon stared at the floor. He looked up to ask another question when Jackson's voice blared over the 1MC communications system. "Ice pilot, report to control for vertical surfacing."

Rinaldo looked at the comm box in the overhead. "I'm being summoned. We're surfacing through the ice. You're welcome to observe from the Conn as long you stay quiet like a mouse."

"I might just do that."

Although he'd completed dozens of submarine-launched missions, Jon had never been aboard a sub when it cracked through thick ice. Only a few boats in the fleet could accomplish that task and it was never easy or without risk.

Jon followed Rinaldo into the control room and leaned against the bulkhead forward of the BYG-1 fire control computer panels near the sonar shack. Just outside the shack, Petty Officer Whitney sat on a cushioned seat and stared at one of the BYG-1 panels. He had a pair of sound-powered headphones planted on his head.

Jon craned his neck around the room. More than a dozen computer monitors dotted a rectangular space no larger than a two-car garage. Men in blue coveralls stood about or sat on benches or bolted-down chairs with headphones covering their ears. The scene reminded Jon of the bridge of the Starship *Enterprise*, only this wasn't a movie. Jackson issued orders and sailors repeated the commands, then performed actions or pressed buttons on sound-powered phones. The Conn hummed with an efficient energy.

"Officer of the Deck," Jackson blared. "Report status of repositioning along the ridgeline to prepare for vertical surface."

Whitney leaned over and translated the jargon for Jon. "If we're not in the right horizontal position when we surface, either the bow or the rudder could slam into the hard pack ice and cause some serious damage. We have a couple upward-looking cameras mounted on the sail, but the CO still sweats this maneuver. One wrong move and we're toast."

From his vantage point, Jon strained to see the front port side of the Conn, where the diving officer gave orders to a helmsman and planesman seated in bucket chairs. The two seamen operated the rudder and airplane-like bow and stern planes to make the boat go left and right and up and down. To their left, the Chief of the Watch sat in front of the Ballast Control Panel and monitored ballast and trim tanks to keep the boat level, or to surface and submerge when called for.

"Sonar, Conn," Jackson said, "report status of the Marvin Gardens team."

"Conn, Sonar, no response on Gertrude from Marvin Gardens."

The sonar shack door was closed, but Jon recognized Chen's voice over the comm line.

"Why aren't they responding?" Jon asked Whitney.

"Don't know," Whitney said. "The chopper's grounded due to fog, so they reported they were getting ready to leave on snowmobiles an hour ago. They should be here by now."

Jackson tapped a finger on the side of a display screen mounted near the periscope stand. Glancing at Rinaldo, he said, "Did you run a BIT on the Gertrude?"

Standing near a large panel screen in the front of the Conn, Rinaldo whipped her head around and said, "Yessir. There were no problems indicated by the BIT."

"That's our built-in-test," Whitney said to Jon. "That means the problem's not on our end."

"That's what my mobile phone provider keeps telling me," Jon said.

"Attention in the Conn," Jackson said, raising his voice above the hum of the electronic cooling fans. "The ICEX team is not responding on Gertrude. We are aborting the vertical surface. Again, we are aborting the vertical surface."

Jon frowned. He didn't like being underwater, but he understood Jackson's reasons for aborting. Until they could raise the ICEX team, they were destined to stay in Neptune's domain a while longer. Resigned to spending an extra night underwater, Jon started to walk back down the passageway toward the wardroom and another cup of coffee. A burning smell filled his nose and reminded him of his stepfather's cigars.

An alarm rang, and a voice blared over the 1MC. "Fire! Fire in the control room!"

The curtain covering the end of the passageway leading into the Conn whipped open. Jon saw a sailor running toward him from the aft section. The man's face was covered with an Emergency Apparatus, Breathing. He handed Jon a mask and, with a muffled voice, told him to go back into the Conn and plug in. Jon obeyed and found an EAB manifold to plug in his air hose. He sat near a BYG-1 console on the starboard side and watched the action.

Through the now open sonar shack door, Jon saw smoke billowing from a console while officers barked orders and sailors in blue coveralls worked to squelch the flames. The fire finally died, but dense smoke remained. Jon knew the only way to keep that from becoming a problem was to ventilate the boat, which meant surfacing and lighting off the low-pressure blower.

"Prepare to vertical surface!" Jackson ordered.

The diving officer repeated the order, turned to the planesman and said, "One degree up, maintain ten feet per minute separation."

"Report depth," Jackson said.

"Two hundred feet, Captain, with five feet per minute separation."

"Very well, the stern is still in the three-foot ice?"

"Rudder is still in the three-foot ice."

"Officer of the Deck, vertical surface the ship."

"Vertical surface the ship, aye. Dive, vertical surface."

A planesman responded. "Vertical surfacing."

The Diving Officer grabbed the 1MC microphone and said, "Vertical surface, vertical surface, vertical surface." He clicked off the mic and said, "Dive, maintain four degree up, three feet per minute separation."

"One hundred-twenty feet, two point nine up," a planesman reported.

A high-pitched screech filled the Conn as some ice hanging down from the surface scraped against the upper portion of the sail. Jon's pulse surged.

"Forty-three, two point nine," a planesman said.

"Very well," Jackson said.

"Forty feet to impact."

Jackson clicked on the 1MC. "Stand by for impact."

Jon wrapped his fingers around the edges of his bench. A cloud of smoke painted the plexiglass on his EAB with a gray residue. Glancing about the smoke-filled Conn, he saw others swiping fingers across their masks like flesh-colored windshield wipers.

"Twenty feet to impact, five point seven up."

Jon knew they were going up too fast, but they had no choice. The boat needed to be cleared of smoke before conditions in the Conn became unbearable.

"Chief of the Watch," the diving officer said, "stand by for blow."

Someone reported, "Five feet to impact."

Jon tightened the grip on his seat.

"Impact in four, three, two, one."

"Conducting full blow," the Chief of the Watch said.

High pressure air blew into the ballast tanks to help push the boat upward and punch a hole through the ice pack. The hissing sound reached Jon about the same time as the pressure change caused his ears to pop. The diving officer tapped out four seconds on the COW's shoulder, and the loud hissing stopped. The boat shuddered as the sail hit the ice. A dull thud preceded a low rumbling, as though signaling the onslaught of an avalanche. More screeching, scraping, and crunching followed. In those few seconds, Jon relived the final moments of a terrifying car crash he'd endured on the freeway while visiting NCIS in D.C. He'd been side-crunched by an ice-skidding truck. An airbag had saved his life. The driver of the truck hadn't been so lucky.

Once the low-pressure blower had filled the main ballast tanks, Jackson ordered the crew to switch the blower to ventilate the boat.

Jon let loose his grip.

Several minutes passed while the air cleared of smoke. The crew then used the atmospheric monitoring system to verify that the air was breathable.

Rinaldo approached, ripped off her EAB mask, and pointed at Jon's face. "You can take that off now."

"Can I light up a cigar?" Jon said as he pulled off his EAB.

Rinaldo flashed Jon a look, grabbed a parka, and turned to follow a bulk-bundled Jackson out of the control room. Jon followed as the pair snaked through the boat, ascended one deck, and edged around a bank of sonar computer systems. A sailor cracked the bridge hatch and reported that the air flow was minor. Jackson ordered the hatch fully opened and climbed up the ladder leading to the sail bridge. Jon felt a burst of cold air rush into the boat. A chill brushed his cheeks and reminded him of his time as a SEAL, operating off submarines in the frigid waters near North Korea.

Jackson yelled down from the bridge. "Agent Shay, get your ass up here."

A sailor handed Jon a parka and pointed toward the ladder. "The CO wants you topside."

Jon donned the jacket and walked to the ladder. Freezing air frosted his nose as he climbed toward foggy daylight. He joined Rinaldo and Jackson on the bridge inside a small area partially enclosed by steel. With binoculars planted against her face, Rinaldo spun in a circle while Jackson called down to Radio for an update. An operator reported they had not received a response from the ICEX camp.

"Something's wrong," Jackson said. "The ICEX team should be here to help us surface and clear the ice off our deck. Rinaldo, you see anything?"

"Nothing, sir," Rinaldo said, still scanning. "Radio called COMSUBPAC. They said a southbound storm could be interfering with communications." She motioned a hand in the air. "We're on the edge now, hence all this fog."

Jon said, "Why isn't the storm interfering with *our* radio transmissions?"

"We have better equipment than the camp," Rinaldo said, "but the camp should still be able to get through if we can. Something else must be wrong."

Jackson turned to Jon. "You know of anything that might prevent the ICEX team from communicating with us? Any classified operation we weren't told about?"

Jon said, "I'm not aware of anything, sir."

"Don't bullshit me, Shay. I'm not in the mood."

"No bullshit, Captain. I wasn't briefed on any activity that would interfere with a surfacing."

Rinaldo lowered her binoculars. "We need to find out what's going on, sir. Why don't I take a team and hike over to the ICEX camp?"

"I don't like it," Jackson said. "That's a three-mile trek on the ice. It's too dangerous."

"I'm trained for Arctic survival," Rinaldo said. "I'm in good shape and can do a three-mile hike in my sleep."

Jackson shook his head.

Rinaldo said, "Something serious might have happened over there, Captain. For all we know, lives could be at stake. We owe it to them to find out."

Jackson stopped shaking his head. "Okay, take a team, but be damned careful. If that storm races in, or the ice looks too thin, you hightail it back here, understood?"

"Understood, sir.

"Take Agent Shay," Jackson said. "His Team Two experience might come in handy."

Rinaldo shot back, "But, sir, I don't think—"

"He goes, or you don't," Jackson said.

Rinaldo frowned. "Yessir."

"Have Miller issue M-16s and check in on the shortwaves every fifteen minutes."

"Will do, sir," Rinaldo said. "I'll take Chen and Whitney. I've worked with them before and they're both Arctic trained."

Jackson nodded approval.

Rinaldo climbed down the ladder and disappeared.

Jackson reached into his parka and pulled out two cigars. "Care to join me while Rinaldo gets your gear ready?"

Jon smiled. "Got any Scotch to go with those?"

"I wish." Jackson clipped the cigar ends and handed one to Jon, then produced a lighter.

Jon read the name on the emerald band wrapped about one end of the torpedo-shaped cigar. "Graycliff. Is that your favorite brand, sir?"

"That's my *only* brand," Jackson said as he blew out a puff. "In fact, if you ever want to get my attention, that's the only word you need to say. I'll come running."

"I'll remember that," Jon said. The Graycliff cigar offered a rich Bahamas taste, which stood in sharp contrast to the bleak white landscape surrounding the boat. A brisk wind ripped across the ice pack that stretched to the horizon in all directions. No life stirred on this barren landscape that had taunted explorers for hundreds of years and killed some of the best. A shiver ran down Jon's back as he stared in the direction of the ICEX camp, unseen from this distance even in clear weather. What had happened to the forty people there? Why weren't they answering their radio? Was it just a brewing storm, or something far worse?

"Which half is Russian?" Jackson asked. A small cloud of smoke left his lips and disappeared into the bleak sky.

"Sir?"

"I read your file."

"My left half," Jon said as the smell of burning tobacco filled his nose. "That's why I'm better looking on that side."

Jackson let out a short laugh. "Right."

Jon said, "My mother's family immigrated from Russia and my father is mostly Irish, but I never knew the man."

"Wish I'd been so lucky," Jackson said.

Jon took a puff and thought about his mother. Loving and always smiling, her dark hair fell softly against a face that showed no signs of her difficult life. She rarely talked about Jon's father, except to say that he had chosen his career over a life with her. They never married, and he had ended their relationship after learning she was pregnant.

When Jon was a young teen, his mother moved to Nebraska and married an alcoholic with a hard-right hook. Jon had once tried to go fifteen rounds with his stepfather to save his mother from a beating, but the raging drunk rammed her head into a wall anyway. She died a few days later in the hospital. After his stepfather went to prison, Jon tracked down his real father and blamed him for making his mother marry an alcoholic. He also blamed himself for not finding a way to protect his mom. Par for the course. He hadn't saved Annelia, either.

Jon tossed his spent cigar overboard and turned toward the hatch.

"Shay," Jackson said.

Jon turned around. "Sir?"

"You're conducting a possible homicide investigation that may involve three members of my crew, and you're about to go with them on a three-mile hike across the ice."

"Yessir, the coincidence has not gone unnoticed. I assumed you asked Rinaldo to take me so I'd have time to question them while we're away from the boat."

"I asked Rinaldo to take you to increase their odds of coming back alive," Jackson said. He took a last puff on his cigar and flipped the butt onto the ice. "Having said that, one of my petty officers is dead and the ICEX camp is not responding, so I suggest you watch your ass out there."

Jon offered a brief nod and climbed back down the ladder.

Doc Richards met Jon at the bottom of the ladder and handed him a manila folder. "Here's the medicine cabinet inventory report you requested."

"Thanks, Doc." Jon took the report, opened the folder, and read. He flipped to a page, stopped, and positioned his finger over an entry. "Well, I'll be damned."

CHAPTER 6

Bitter cold stung Jon's cheeks as he climbed up through the midsection hatch of the USS *Connecticut*. Bundled in a bright orange Arctic suit, with polarized goggles covering his eyes, he scanned the vast sheet of white before him. For a moment, he understood how Sir John Eglund must have felt when he planted a flag at the North Pole for the first time in human history.

"I'd like to be back in time for pizza," Rinaldo called out from the bottom of the ladder.

Jon cleared his thoughts and finished climbing up the ladder. His boots crunched on the snow ice that cracked apart when the submarine surfaced. Jon's breath fogged in the twenty-below weather. Rinaldo, Whitney, and Chen emerged from the midsection hatch and stepped near.

"Amazing, isn't it?" Rinaldo said, her eyes scanning the horizon. "As smooth as a baby's butt."

"Did you bring a diaper?" Jon said.

"Funny," Rinaldo said as she slapped Jon between his shoulder blades. She issued a few orders to Whitney and Chen, tested her shortwave radio, checked a compass reading, and pointed toward nothing.

Jon slung an M-16 rifle over his shoulder and followed. His thoughts continued to ponder two significant details revealed by Doc Richards' medicine cabinet log: one, there probably had not been enough sleeping pills left in the bottle of barbiturates to kill anyone; and two, a syringe was missing from the medicine locker. Jon knew a jury would find these clues too circumstantial to convict, but they were more than enough to send his radar into overdrive. Had someone used that syringe to poison Petty Officer Kelly? If so, who aboard the *Connecticut* had a motive? Glancing at the backsides of

Rinaldo, Whitney, and Chen as they trudged across the ground in front of him, he wondered if his killer would find the need to strike again.

While his boots crunched atop the hard pack, with an Arctic wind whistling in his ears, Jon's thoughts drifted back in time. After four years at the U.S. Naval Academy in Annapolis, Maryland, he'd volunteered for Basic Underwater Demolition/SEAL training. His uncle had served as a U.S. Navy "frogman" diver during the Vietnam War, back when they conducted dangerous missions near enemy coastlines with only a mask, fins, and diving knife. Huddled near the fireplace in his Nebraska home, Jon and his sister had been captivated for hours while their uncle told his sea stories. Inspired by those stories, Jon had dreamed of being a SEAL since boyhood. It was all he'd ever wanted.

He had arrived in San Diego in late October to start his training. He soon recalled that the ocean in Southern California that time of year could feel every bit as cold as a lake in Nebraska. The BUD/S instructors thrust him into the most rigorous and difficult military training program in the world, and Jon came close to ringing the famous ship's bell in the courtyard—signifying he was ready to quit—at least a half-dozen times.

Upon graduation, he'd been assigned to SEAL Team One, where he'd completed his training and conducted several missions before volunteering for Team Two—the only team trained in Arctic warfare capability. Team Two had been formed back in the mid-60s under Lieutenant John F. Callahan. At that time, it was comprised almost entirely of former Underwater Demolition Team 21 members and started with only ten officers and fifty enlisted men.

Jon soon discovered that while Team Six got most of the glory after the Bin Laden mission, and had the most difficult training, Team Two was a close second. As a frosty gust hammered his face, Jon thought about the Team Two Mountain and Arctic Warfare Platoon workup, which included several months of specialized preparation: cold weather amphibious operations; weeklong ski patrols; winter survival; and avalanche training in remote areas of Alaska, Montana, Norway, South Korea, Canada, and other frosty locales.

Jon and his teammates had been trained to create body heat from exertion in subzero environments and prevent heat loss from radiation, conduction, convection evaporation, and expiration. What they wore, and how they wore it, could mean the difference between life and death. They added clothing when at rest and "layered down" when on the move.

Jon had been on more than one mission where he had zipped up his dry suit, locked out of a nuclear submarine in freezing waters, loaded up a Zodiac rubber boat, and endured biting cold winds while paddling for more than thirty miles to shore. Once on land, he traded his dry suit and fins for dry gear and a pair of cross-country skis. His team then headed toward an ice ridge some twenty klicks away. To stay undetected, they had to travel at night and hide inside ice caves. No fires were allowed.

On one mission, at the kill zone near the edge of a ridge, they spotted three terrorist "Tangos" standing near a sheer wall of ice. Jon's CO tapped him on the shoulder and pointed at the targets. While struggling to keep his hands and breathing steady in twenty-below weather, he assembled his sniper rifle and chambered a round. He fought to shake off the numb and the fear and keep his hands rock steady while listening to his spotter. He lined up the scope, let out a slow breath, and squeezed the trigger. One Tango down. A strong dose of guilt hit him hard in the gut. Even though it had been sanctioned, he couldn't help but feel like he'd just murdered someone. He fought to squelch the feeling as two other SEALs took out two more Tangos.

Mission accomplished.

Two miles into their trek, Rinaldo's radio crackled and thrust Jon back into the present. She held up her right arm, bent in the shape of an "L." The team halted.

"Marvin Gardens, this is Iceman. Do you copy, over?"

Rinaldo answered. "Iceman, this is Marvin Gardens. We copy, over."

"Marvin Gardens, be advised that Iceman is descending due to shifting ice conditions, repeat, Iceman in descending due to shifting ice conditions, over."

"Iceman, Marvin Gardens, understood. Do you have an ascent ETA, over?"

"Marvin Gardens, Iceman, negative on an ETA, out."

"Iceman, Marvin Gardens, understood, out."

Rinaldo glowered. "Well, that's bad news. We lost our ride."

"There's always Uber," Jon said. "Why are they diving?"

"Shifting ice could damage the sail. They need to go back down and find a better location to surface, which could take a while. Let's keep moving."

Rinaldo turned again toward their unseen destination, hidden somewhere in the gray fog. She keyed her radio and tried to raise the ICEX camp. No joy. She shrugged and walked forward.

Debilitated by wool-laden Arctic apparel and fatigued from lack of sleep and jet lag, Jon hiked. Another half-mile passed. As a Navy SEAL, he had easily run several miles at the crack of dawn, swam a few miles in frigid waters, completed a mission, and then swam and ran back—all in a day's work. Now, years later, he had a hard time believing that trudging less than three miles on an ice floe could be this hard. He then thought about his training with SEAL Team Two.

His instructor had said the Arctic is like a desert—flat and dry and temperature extreme. Sweat is a bad thing here, which is why they wore wool instead of cotton. Wool helps absorb sweat whereas cotton will stick, then freeze, then *really* stick—as in peel-your-skin-off stick. It's so dry in the Arctic that your lungs always feel a bit shy of air, like you're a mile up and fighting the altitude. Then there's the gear, which makes you feel like you're trying to run a marathon while neck deep in water.

Rinaldo halted and held up an arm. She pointed toward a darkening sky. "Storm's here. Let's tether up."

Whitney produced a long nylon rope and a set of carabiner clips. Each man clipped onto the rope with Whitney taking the point. Rinaldo pointed forward and the team marched. A brisk wind rocketed across the ice and whipped the snow into a frenzy. The silver-white flakes filled the air and lowered visibility down to less than a few yards. Within minutes, the wind ramped into a horizontally driving ice-storm that hurled missile-shaped spicules. The rock-sized chunks clacked against Jon's goggles and made it almost impossible to see more than a few feet ahead. If not for the connecting rope, he could easily be separated from the team and lost in the blinding gale.

Each man took turns taking the point to allow for a brief respite. Finally, Rinaldo guided them toward a ten-foot-tall ice ridge. They hunkered down behind the chard and rested. Petty Officer Chen stepped near. His orange jacket was now entirely encrusted in a thick blanket of glittering compacted ice that splintered and cracked as he moved. Blanched ice-feathers streamed away from his shoulders and arms and made him look like an abominable snowman.

The four huddled close together, sheltered by the ice wall. Jon glanced up and watched the storm sweep past like a glittering grey-white river. Chen swatted at the caked-on white covering his jacket to break up the ice and fling it loose.

Jon reached over and caught his hand. "Don't." He had to yell to be heard above the screeching throng.

Chen stopped swatting. "Why? It makes my jacket heavy."

"If not for that heavy ice," Jon said, "you'd be dead. It's insulating you from the cold."

"Shit," Chen said. "I forgot."

"Let's move," Rinaldo said.

Whitney again took the point and disappeared into the gale. Jon was number two in line. He trudged ahead for twenty minutes and then felt the rope tighten as a vicious tug pulled him forward. He lost his footing and landed on his backside. The taught rope jerked him hard across the ice. He gripped the rope with his gloved hands. Unable to stop, his boots carved trenches into the snowpack. He squinted at a dark shape a few feet ahead. *Whitney?* No, the shape was much larger than a man. Jon's eyes opened wide. *Ice cavern.*

A lead had opened in the ice. Whitney obviously hadn't seen it in time and fell in. Jon knew he only had seconds before he'd be dragged inside the hole as well. Ice splinters rocketed into the air, flung loose by his boots and snowsuit as he slid across the ground. The dark shape grew in size. *Ten more seconds.*

Jon blindly reached for the ice pick strapped to his belt. Nothing. He moved his hand back an inch. Still nothing. Another inch. Finally, he felt the handle. He jerked his arm upward. The ice pick didn't budge. He jerked again. The crevice was now only a few feet away. *Five more seconds.*

The ice pick shot up from his belt. He almost dropped it. He gripped the handle, twisted sideways, and drove it into the ice. It didn't catch. *One more second.* He flung the ax again. The pic caught. He came to a screeching halt. Jon breathed out and then sucked in another breath as a dark shape shot toward him. *Chen.* If they collided, they'd all fly into the hole. Jon shifted sideways to avoid the collision. As Chen shot past, Jon grabbed the man's jacket. The Petty Officer slid a few more inches and then stopped. Jon's frozen fingers burned as he gripped the parka. The muscles in his arms ached. He couldn't hold on much longer.

Finally, Chen found his own ice pick and slammed it into the hard pack. Rinaldo slid near and also used her pick to glide to a stop. Jon turned and crawled over to the edge of the ice cavern. Whitney dangled in midair a few feet above a rushing stream of black ice water. Although Jon could not see the man's eyes behind his frosted goggles, he could hear the whimpering panic in Whitney's voice as he called out for help. No one could survive even a brief submersion in water that cold. If Whitney managed to survive the sudden one-hundred-degree temperature drop, once pulled free, his suit and jacket would become his tomb. Frozen and as an impenetrable as a fortress, the garments could not be removed or chipped away. While struggling to suck in his last breath, and as ensconced as a mummy, Whitney would freeze to death within minutes.

Rinaldo and Chen crawled near and peered into the abyss. Jon pounded his ice pick into the ground near the edge of the cavern. He braced his feet against the edge of the pick, grabbed the rope, and signaled for the other two to do the same. With all three pulling, they managed to drag Whitney up to the surface. Rinaldo checked him for frostbite and injuries. Mottled, blue, and shaking, the man was terrified but healthy.

Rinaldo signaled for the team to move forward. Thirty minutes later, with the storm subsiding, she again held up an arm. Jon stopped and squinted at the dense fog ahead but saw nothing. He listened. *Crunching.* Polar bear? No, definitely human. Camp personnel? Maybe, but the camp had yet to answer any of Rinaldo's calls.

Two large figures in white parkas appeared through the fog. Jon's nose twitched. ICEX camp personnel usually wore green or bright orange, not white. The two men carried weapons. *AK-74 assault rifles.* Instinct kicked in. Jon flipped his M-16 horizontal, clicked off the safety, and poised a finger on the trigger. Standing a foot away, Rinaldo spun on a boot heal, grabbed the barrel of Jon's rifle, and pulled the weapon away. The sling peeled off Jon's shoulder. He reached for it, but not in time. Rinaldo shoved the barrel of the M-16 into the snow as Petty Officer Chen took a step forward and pointed his rifle toward Jon's nose.

The fury in Jon's gut rumbled again. "What the hell is this?"

"Give me your sidearm," Rinaldo said. "Slowly, two fingers on the grip."

Jon glared at the tall ice pilot as he unzipped his parka and fingered his Beretta M-9 pistol. He tossed the gun into the air. The Beretta landed atop the snowy ice with a soft thud. Petty Officer Whitney bent down and scooped it up.

Jon narrowed his gaze. "I asked you a question, Rinaldo."

"And I didn't answer, Agent Shay," Rinaldo said.

One of the white bundled figures approached. Two more men in white emerged through the fog, pointing rifles at two people in green ICEX parkas. One of the hostages appeared slightly rotund and shivered in the cold. The other was petite, probably a woman. Her face was covered by goggles and a scarf.

The man who had approached Rinaldo held up a large black brief-case. Puzzled and furious, Jon clenched his gloved hands and listened as Rinaldo spoke.

"Major Liang," Rinaldo said. "I see you brought me a present."

"Ms. Rinaldo," Liang answered. He appeared Chinese but spoke with a near-perfect English accent. "Our guests were kind enough to give me the ROSS device. Did you bring the interface unit?"

Rinaldo held up a grey rectangle about the size of a mobile phone. "Right here. We can thank Petty Officer Chen for stealing this from the *Connecticut*."

Rinaldo pocketed the device again before Jon could get a good look.

"Who is our new guest?" Liang said as he nodded toward Jon.

"Interloper," Rinaldo said. "Commander Jackson ordered me to bring him along. We obviously can't leave him at the camp and who knows, he may come in handy later."

"I don't like it," Liang said.

"You'll get over it," Rinaldo said as she motioned a gloved hand toward the horizon.

Nudged by a rifle, Jon walked next to the two prisoners. When the woman stood up straight, Jon caught a glimpse of her face. *Kate Barrett*. Her blue eyes were full of fear that changed to confusion when she saw his face.

While marching toward the camp, Jon kept his enmity under control by rummaging through the facts in his head, including the few he had uncovered in Doc's log and during his interrogations aboard the *Connecticut*. He deduced that Rinaldo must be a traitor, along with Chen and Whitney. They had known the ICEX team would not be at the surfacing location after the Chinese attacked the camp, so Chen must have started the fire in the sonar shack to force Commander Jackson to surface and ventilate the boat.

They probably didn't intend to murder Petty Officer Kelly, knowing it would trigger an investigation, but maybe Kelly found out what was going on, so they had no choice. Jon frowned. Even if all his speculations were correct, that still left a lot of unanswered questions. Like why Rinaldo was working with Chinese soldiers, why those commandos had attacked the ICEX camp, why they had captured Kate and her colleague, and what the hell they planned to do with that black ROSS case and interface unit.

Liang keyed a radio and talked with one of his men, who was apparently standing guard over the captured personnel at the ICEX camp. He issued an order to tie up the hostages, scour the camp for extra diving gear, and head over to the torpedo-retrieval ice holes where the group would rendezvous within the hour. Jon wondered why Liang and Rinaldo had left the hostages alive, or for that matter, why they had left *him* alive.

Liang holstered his radio as Rinaldo approached and asked about the status of the ASDS. The Chinese officer reported that two operators onboard were hovering the mini-sub not far from the ICEX diving holes. Jon's ears perked. *An ASDS?* He only knew of one in existence, an experimental craft abandoned by the Navy years earlier in favor of a newer design. The last he had heard, Northrop Grumman had been authorized to sell the prototype to a government contractor. How the hell did Rinaldo and Liang get their hands on it? The questions were piling up faster than the answers, and Jon hated being clueless more than he hated his father.

With his legs sore and lungs burning from the cold, Jon arched his back and stretched when the group finally stopped marching thirty minutes later. To his right, about a quarter-mile distant, the bright blue stripes covering the mess tent signaled the location of the ICEX camp. Two holes, three feet in diameter, had been carved into the ice a few feet from where the group now stood. Jon surmised they were the spent practice torpedo holes drilled by Navy Divers. Liang and company must have parked the ASDS nearby and used the holes as infiltration points. Also, Liang must have had some inside help to deactivate the intruder detection system surrounding the holes. But who? Rinaldo? When would she have had access to that system? More unanswered questions.

Rinaldo approached and said, "Since you're the former Navy SEAL, why don't you help our female guest suit up?"

Jon crossed his arms. "This has gone far enough. Time for some answers, Rinaldo."

Rinaldo pointed her M-16 at Kate's head. "How's this for an answer—she suits up or dies."

Jon uncrossed his arms and fought to quell the ire-stoked coals in his chest. He turned toward Kate. "Are you a certified diver?"

Kate's nose and cheeks were red. She shivered. "I *hate* water."

"Drinking or swimming?" Jon said, hoping to diffuse Kate's angst.

It didn't work. Kate looked like a small child being forced to brave a dark alley. "I can't do this."

While donning a dry suit, Rinaldo cocked an ear. "What's the problem?"

Kate stared at the hole in the ice. Frigid blue water lapped against the sides. She backed up and turned away.

"I think she has a water phobia," Jon said.

"Get her over it," Rinaldo said.

Jon bristled. The muscles in his face tightened. He grabbed Kate's suit and brought it to her. Facing her back, he said, "Turn around."

Shaking, Kate remained facing away.

"Please, turn around."

Kate turned.

"Good," Jon said. "Now look at me."

Kate's eyes met his. Though full of fear, they were riveting, like a blue morning sky touching the edges of a Nebraska corn field. Jon felt his heart flutter. He tried to hold on to the feeling, but it refused to linger. A year had come and gone since he'd lost his wife, but the pain in his chest still held the high ground.

"I'm not setting a foot in that water," Kate stammered. Her eyes burned with defiance.

"What about a toe?"

Kate crossed her arms and said nothing.

"Just put on the suit to keep the Witch happy while I think of something," Jon said.

"Something?"

"Yeah, something."

"Like what, mate?"

Rinaldo called over from the other side of the ice hole. "Five minutes, Shay."

Jon held up the suit. "Just put it on, please. I promise I'll think of something."

Kate rolled her eyes and held out her arms. "Fine, but you'd better not be lying to me."

"Who's your colleague?" Jon asked as he moved in close to help Kate don the dry suit.

"Bobby Ruppert. He's a bit rough around the edges and goes into panic mode in stressful situations, but he's a brilliant engineer."

While Jon zipped up Kate's dry suit, the scent of her perfume conjured a memory. He shivered.

"Now what?" Kate said. Her bottom lip quivered. Annelia had also done that when she was frightened.

Jon pulled on his suit. He stepped toward Kate and said, "Let's just put on our SCUBA gear and then I'll make my move."

"Your move?" Kate shot back.

Jon said nothing as he helped Kate into a BC vest, saddled up her tank, and held a Kirby Morgan diving mask in her direction. "Put this on."

Kate's tone turned urgent as she grabbed the mask. "You said you'd think of something."

"Just follow my lead." Jon pulled on his tank and ran through a system check. The action felt like a visit from an old friend and reminded him of dozens of missions survived.

Kate shook her head in defiance as she sucked in a breath. The hiss of compressed air echoed off nearby shards of ice pushed skyward by Mother Nature.

One by one, Liang's men entered the water. Jon watched Kate recoil with each splash.

Rinaldo approached. "Ready?"

Kate's eyes widened. She held her palms up as if to say, "Something?"

Now fully suited, Jon led Kate toward the water. He had to drag her the last few feet. He turned toward her, lifted up his mask, and said, "I'll hold your hand all the way. This will all be over in five minutes."

Her eyes still wide, Kate tried to step backward but Jon held onto to her hands and gently kept her in place.

"Just follow me," Jon said. "I've done this hundreds of times."

Kate shook her head as she dug her heels into the ice.

Rinaldo slapped Jon's back. The gesture did not feel friendly.

Jon slowly guided Kate toward the hole's edge. She fought to pull away. He held on tight and looked into her eyes, assuring her in silence that she could do this. Tears streamed down Kate's face and dripped onto the mask's rubber lining. Her breathing was erratic. Jon's heart ached with compassion and guilt. He felt like a jailor forcing an innocent victim into a torture chamber. The bitter taste of choler filled his mouth as he stole a glance at Rinaldo. The beast in his gut grumbled and demanded to be set loose. Jon closed his eyes and slowly breathed in and out to quell the angst.

He opened his eyes, lifted his mask again, and focused on Kate. Softening his voice, he said, "Close your eyes."

Kate stared at him through her mask. Jon could tell she wanted to trust him, but fear remained her master. He had seen this kind of panic before on the faces of green wannabe SEALs learning how to dive the Navy way. None of them had ever made it through training. For sure, none of them would have survived a dive in Arctic waters.

"Close your eyes and trust me," Jon said. "Don't open them until we're out of the water."

Trembling, Kate closed her eyes. Jon pulled on her fins and helped her into a seated position with her legs dangling into the water. He did all this with slow movements so as not to make a splash. Rinaldo stood by and watched with impatient indifference. Jon slipped into the hole and then slowly lowered Kate into the water. Her breathing accelerated but she kept her eyes closed.

Once under the ice, Jon held on tight and guided Kate toward the mini-sub, now parked a few dozen yards away. The swim took only a few minutes. Jon guided Kate through a round opening on the bottom of the ASDS that led into the diving chamber. The oval chamber had been pressurized to match the ocean pressure, so it held no water. Jon followed Kate inside. He shut the outer hatch and found the valves to depressurize the chamber.

The diving chamber was small, barely large enough to fit two people. Valves and pipes lined the walls. An oval hatch on one side led to the interior of the ASDS.

Jon removed his Kirby Morgan mask and said, "You can open your eyes now."

Kate opened her eyes. She ripped off her mask and said, "If you ever lie to me again, I'll kick you in the balls."

Stifling a laugh, Jon said, "Fair enough." He opened the inner hatch and stepped through the opening.

Once inside the small craft, Jon and Kate removed their diving gear. They were led to the aft transport compartment, where a soldier tie-wrapped them to one of the metal benches that ran along the port side of the craft. Jon sat on the forward section of the bench near the diving chamber, with Kate to his right and Bobby to her right. The three of them filled up more than half of the small bench. Jon counted eight men aboard, all Chinese, along with Liang, Rinaldo, Whitney, and Chen. Most of them now sat across from him on a bench on the starboard side of the boat.

The mini-sub was about sixty-five feet long by seven feet wide and tall. Forward, in the bow, two swivel seats held a pilot and a systems operator. Jon caught a glimpse of the control panel, where colorful monitors and indicator lights flickered and blinked. The vessel contained no torpedoes or other weapons, so no fire control systems were needed. The aft area held equipment cases, lockers, two benches, and an assortment of diving gear.

Liang issued an order to the pilot in the bow. The mini-sub shuddered and lurched forward, and then banked to starboard through a long turn. Chafed by more than just the cold metal bench, Jon watched Liang's men stow their gear with trained efficiency. All of them had no doubt received advanced military training. Jon wondered if they were Chinese PLA Special Forces.

He waited until no commandos were near before leaning over to whisper in Kate's ear. "Why you?"

"What do you mean?" Kate said.

"What does Rinaldo want with you and Bobby?"

"The ROSS device."

"Which is?"

"Like I said last night, I work for ARL."

"The think tank started by the Navy in 1945," Jon said.

"Right, and now run by Penn State. The lot have been involved in most every major submarine and weapons system development project since the second World War."

"I've heard about the lab," Jon said. "Is it true that all the engineers wear coke bottle glasses, ugly green sweaters, and Avenger socks?"

Kate smiled and shook her head. "Only the smart ones." She waited for a commando to walk past and then continued whispering. "ARL designed the latest propulsor drive systems used in *Virginia*-class submarines, fast rocket torpedoes, and the super cavitation system on this ASDS. They also created the ROSS device, which is inside that black case Liang took from us."

"And that small black box Rinaldo brought from the *Connecticut* connects to the ROSS?"

"Yes. It's an interface unit that joins ROSS to submarine sonar equipment and the Deep Siren communications system."

"Rinaldo was working with the Deep Siren system," Jon said. "How is this ROSS device related?"

"It enables sonar systems and remote Deep Siren buoys to detect foreign submarines. One in particular."

"Which one?"

Kate hesitated for a moment. Jon assumed what she was about to divulge was top-secret, but by now it was a moot point. "The Project 09581 *Khabarovsk* submarine."

"Son of a bitch," Jon said as he raised both eyebrows. He had heard about Russia's latest attack submarine. She was infused with a host of advanced technology that made her formidable and nearly undetectable. The first submarine in this new class was faster and quieter and carried more firepower than almost any attack sub in the world. She had also been optimized for Arctic operations. Most experts were deeply concerned that once the *Khabarovsk*, or "*Khabbie*" as some called her, slipped beneath the ice, the U.S. Navy's ASW forces would be hard-pressed to find her, let alone stop her. But that's not what worried them the most.

"Where's the *Khabbie* now?" Jon asked.

"Sea trials," Kate said. "She came out of the Petropavlovsk Naval Base on the Kamchatka Peninsula last week. That's why Bobby and I were at the ICEX camp. We were sorting out the final tests on ROSS and hoping to get a shot at testing the unit on the *Khabbie*."

"Why do Rinaldo and Liang want the ROSS device?"

"I have no idea. Perhaps they plan to sell the technology to the highest bidder."

"Or maybe the Chinese found out about it and hired Rinaldo to help them steal it."

"Perhaps," Kate said.

"What about the Status-6?" Jon said. "Is the *Khabbie* carrying any?"

Kate lowered her eyes. "Six of them."

Jon shook his head. "NASA may need to speed up their Mars settlement plans."

The *Khabbie* had been built to do one thing: carry a new type of torpedo that was ten times larger than anything ever built. The nuclear-powered Status-6 torpedo, codenamed *Kanyon* by NATO and called *Poseidon* by the Russians, could hit eighty knots and devastate targets more than 6,200 nautical miles away. The *Khabbie* could fire one from across the Pacific and take out San Diego. In fact, it could take out most of Southern California because the Status-6 carried a one-hundred-megaton nuclear payload.

The *Khabbie* could carry up to six Status-6 torpedoes in tubes housed in a flooded forward compartment. Those torpedoes could shower a half-dozen seaports or ocean transit points with enough "dirty bomb" radioactive fallout to render them useless for a century.

Still shivering from fear, Bobby leaned over and said, "What are you two yahoos whispering about?"

"Prince Harry and Meghan Markle," Jon said. "Kate's upset because *The Enquirer* says they're getting a divorce."

"Really?" Bobby said.

"Not really," Kate said. "We were talking about ROSS and the *Khabbie*."

Bobby shot into panic mode. "You told him?"

Kate shrugged. "Who's he going to tell?"

Bobby's shoulders slumped. "Good point."

Rinaldo approached the bench from the control area and said, "What are we chatting about back here?"

The beast in Jon's gut grumbled as he looked up. "I was just saying that if I wasn't tied to this bench I'd break every bone in your body."

"Sure you would, hot shot," Rinaldo said.

"What's the plan?" Jon said as he glared at the ice pilot. "Sell the ROSS device to the Chinese? The Iranians? The North Koreans?"

"You've got it all wrong, cowboy," Rinaldo said. "Cooperate and maybe you'll all live long enough to help with the plan."

"Why would we want to help *you*?" Kate said. Her voice rang with taut bellicosity.

"You'll find out soon enough," Rinaldo said. "In the meantime, I suggest you put a sock in it. The Navy will soon find out what happened at the ICEX camp and order everyone in the area to hunt us down. If they find us, we will not surrender. Understood?"

Jon understood. If the Navy found the ASDS, Rinaldo intended to scuttle the craft, and they would all drown on their way to the bottom of the Arctic Ocean.

CHAPTER 7

"What the hell is that?" Commander Jackson said. His hand rested on the shoulder of a Petty Officer seated in the sonar shack of the USS *Connecticut*. Jackson pointed past the sonarman's head at a waterfall screen inside a rectangular display mounted on a bulkhead. Vertical orange lines cascaded down the screen in waterfall fashion. Each line represented a set of frequencies where the sonar system "heard" something. Dark spaces in between the lines represented nothing, as in little to no sound at all. The something that *was* heard could be biologics, such as snapping shrimp or crooning whales, or the whine of a spinning propeller connected to a ship or submarine. Or, in this case, the whisper of something entirely different.

Chief Ken Greenawald stepped near the panel and leaned over the seated sonarman. He wrinkled his nose, picked up a spare set of headphones, and cupped his hands over his ears. "Never heard this before."

The strange sound, now broadcast over a speaker in the shack, was coming from a manmade craft off the sub's starboard bow. The hissing noise they were hearing had been picked up by the sub's ultra-sensitive BQQ 5D bow-mounted passive and wide aperture flank arrays. The 5D handed the sound off to the BQQ-10 sonar processing system, which used a new acoustic-rapid commercial-off-the-shelf insertion system that the sonar jocks called ARCI, pronounced "ark-ee." Using sophisticated software algorithms, ARCI crunched the sound through a massive database of cataloged squeaks, whines, and hisses to figure out the "what" and the "who." To create that database, submariners had risked life and limb across decades while trailing hundreds of vessels at very close range to record various sounds. The Navy called these Holy Stone missions, and Jackson had more than once flirted with death to add a few more recordings to the library.

Greenawald flipped a few switches, listened, tapped on a keyboard, and frowned. "It's a small craft with a propulsor drive. It's not in our database, but it sure sounds like an ASDS."

Jackson cocked his head to one side. "Advanced SEAL Delivery System? Are you sure?"

Greenawald shrugged. "It's a guess, and I wouldn't even know that except I had a buddy who worked on it at Northrop Grumman. He mentioned they had upgraded it with a propulsor that had all these weird frequencies. I don't know of anything else that could generate those tones."

"I thought they only had one of those things, and didn't they sell it to somebody?"

"That's what I heard, sir. The Navy thought it cost too much, so they let Grumman sell it to a contractor. I forget who."

"Nice work, Chief," Jackson said. "Keep your ears pinned on that guy." He walked out of the sonar shack and stepped up behind the planesman. He turned toward the OOD and said, "I have the Conn."

The OOD acknowledged and stepped out of the way.

Jackson said, "Helm, come right to course two-eight-five, verify the ice thickness, and prepare to vertical surface the ship."

The Diving Officer acknowledged the orders and repeated the same to the crew. The Conn buzzed with activity as the sub banked to starboard. Fifteen minutes passed before the boat's sail crunched upward through three feet of hardened ice. Jackson donned a parka and hurried up the ladder into the sail bridge. He scanned the horizon with binoculars and then called down to Radio. He wanted to know if Rinaldo and her party had checked in, or if anyone from the ICEX camp had responded. No joy.

Jackson let a half hour pass while Radio tried to raise either Rinaldo or the camp. No response. He tapped his gloved hand against the metal frame of the bridge enclosure several times, came to a decision, and pressed down the comm lever. He ordered the XO to send out another search party.

Twenty minutes later, Jackson watched a half-dozen orange-suited figures trudge across the ice and disappear into the fog. He tensed his shoulders and wondered if that was the last time he'd ever see those men. Squelching his worry, he turned over the bridge to a junior officer, returned below decks, and scurried down the ladder near the radio room. He stepped into Radio and ordered the watch to send a message via the ultra-high frequency Submarine Information Exchange Subsystem to COMSUBFOR to report the situation and verify whether an ASDS was operating in the area.

If the SSIXS satellite reply came back negative, after he retrieved his crew off the ice, he'd be compelled to prosecute the contact to find out who it was.

Jackson left Radio and jaunted over to the wardroom. He poured himself a cup of Navy black and found a chair. He glanced about the room and rested his eyes momentarily on a dozen scattered bits of paraphernalia. A plaque here, a mug there, a picture over there. Memories. Some good, some bad. On one bulkhead an officer had mounted a patch: a black submarine running diagonally across a light blue background. Underneath the graphic, the inscription read: WestPac Black. Jackson massaged the back of his neck as he thought about that Special Operation.

The SpecOp was a Holy Stone espionage mission. That's what attack subs did mostly. That's why they often referred to submariners as "spies of the deep." The U.S. Navy had perfected the art of designing super-stealthy submarines for that very purpose. They challenged attack boat COs, or sub-drivers as they were called, to "get up close and personal" and take photos, record sounds, and capture signals. The latter was accomplished using ultra-modern Electronic Surveillance Measures equipment.

So up close they got. Sometimes within a mile or so of a foreign country's coastline or within a few hundred yards of a potentially hostile vessel—whether atop or beneath the surface. Using sonar, periscopes, and various masts, they'd suck in every sound, sight, and signal they could, often spending long hours or even days doing so. Usually they got in and out without anyone knowing. But sometimes they didn't.

On WestPac Black, they didn't. They'd followed a Chinese Type-094 ballistic missile sub as it cruised toward its home port on the southern tip of Hainan Island in the South China Sea. The DoD had discovered that China had secretly built an underground nuclear submarine base there, which could pose a large threat to everyone in the region. Satellite photos of the base revealed a harbor and possibly massive tunnels that could house dozens of nuclear submarines. At that time, China had almost sixty attack subs, along with four "boomer" type 094s, each capable of carrying twelve long-range ballistic missiles.

Jackson and his crew followed the 094 for days as the Chinese boat crept toward the secret base, known as Sanya. Keeping track of the 094 proved no easy task. The Chinese had improved their stealth capability tenfold, and the ocean acoustics didn't help things. The harbor at Sanya feeds into super-deep channels, which gave the Chinese good reasons to build a subbase there. For one, deep waters allowed their ballistic subs to launch missiles without having to surface, and two, the area offered favorable acoustic layers under which those subs could hide.

All sub drivers were experts on acoustic layers. They could save your life. When warm and cold waters mingle, they create layers, which tend to block sounds as they travel through the ocean in similar fashion to a brick wall built around a freeway. Hiding under a layer is how submarines often remain undetected. The 094's CO obviously knew this and took full advantage, darting under sound layers, probably to ensure an enterprising American boat did not follow him. But one did. Jackson's expert sonar jocks clung to the bastard like determined cats. Then the 094 came shallow, probably to send a radio transmission. Jackson seized the opportunity.

He followed the 094 up to periscope depth. Normally he'd raise the number one periscope to take a peek and ensure there were no craft in the area, perchance sitting silent and therefore unheard by sonar. Assuming the Chinese boat was about to transmit, he decided to raise his number two scope, which contained ESM gear to record the transmission. That was a mistake. They were far too close to the Sanya base. The entire bay was drenched with listening stations that scanned the area to detect enemy subs lurking nearby. It took less than sixty seconds for a Chinese radar station to "paint" Jackson's periscope and nail him. Then the fun began.

The entire Chinese Navy went on high alert, or so it seemed. They sent every anti-submarine warfare ship, plane, and rowboat into the area to find the guy dumb enough to step into their backyard. They pounded every square inch of the ocean with active sonar pings from ASW ships and sonobuoys dropped from aircraft. Jackson scrambled. He crash-dived the boat, rushed to find layers to hide under, and tried to sneak out of the area. The Chinese did everything imaginable to kill him before he could.

Jackson's American submarine was deep inside China's international waters. As such, all bets were off. The Chinese had every right to prosecute and destroy his vessel under international law. If they did, no one would ever know. The U.S. would have no choice but to lie and tell the world that Jackson's boat had disappeared and could not be found. No other explanation would be given. That's what went through Jackson's mind when the depth charges started shattering the silence. Then sonar reported high speed screws in the water.

Torpedoes.

Jackson's throat constricted. He forced his voice to remain calm while he ordered evasive maneuvers. He glanced around the room and saw a dozen worried faces. One wrong move, one wrong order, and these sailors, who'd all placed their trust in him, would spend eternity at the bottom of the South China Sea.

The radio box in the wardroom of the *Connecticut* squawked and brought Jackson out of his nightmare from the past. He pressed down the comm lever. "Cap'm."

"Captain, Radio, the search party is reporting in."

"I'll be right there."

Jackson gulped the rest of his coffee and strode out of the wardroom. In the radio shack, he stood next to the Operations Officer and listened as the search party reported that they had reached the ICEX camp.

"We did not find Rinaldo or anyone in her party, Cap'm," Lt. Herschel reported over the radio from the camp. He was the boat's supply officer, or "chops" as the crew called him. The old Navy term referred to the guy in charge of supplying the boat with its "pork chops." He was a bright young Naval Academy graduate in his late twenties with freckled cheeks. "We did find the ICEX personnel, but they were all tied up, over."

"Tied up as in busy or tied up as in tied up? Over," Jackson said.

"Tied up as in tie-wrapped," Herschel said. "The Camp Commander will explain, over."

A crackle, then, "Commander Jackson, this is Captain Oliver. Our camp was attacked by what appears to be Chinese commandos. They killed one of my men, then tied us up and left us here, over."

Jackson tensed and leaned in closer to the radio. "Captain Oliver, do you have any idea why your camp was attacked? Over."

Oliver explained that the commando leader was looking for an ARL researcher named Kate Barrett. A Chinese commando shot one of his sailors who tried to escape, and Oliver didn't know if they had captured Barrett, but she and her colleague were now missing. The commandos went after the woman and the two Chinese soldiers holding them hostage latter received a radio call, presumably from their leader. They tie-wrapped everyone at the camp and left. Oliver could offer no further details or reasons for the raid. He did note that the soldiers grabbed the camp's extra diving gear. They likely came in on a mini-sub and sent their team up through the torpedo retrieval diving holes. He did not know how they had deactivated the intruder alert system.

Jackson stood up straight as a warning bell went off inside his head. *Did they come in on the ASDS? Or a different mini-sub with a similar sound signature?*

Jackson thanked Oliver and ended the radio call. He turned to his Ops Officer and ordered him to prepare an OPREP 3 major incident report to be sent to the Commander, Submarine Forces, via SSIXS. Several minutes later, after Jackson had approved the message, the information printed out on a teletype at COMSUBFOR in Norfolk, Virginia. A few minutes after that, all hell broke loose.

CHAPTER 8

There were days when Secretary of Defense George McBride hated every-thing about his job. He hated the long boring meetings, the fake smiles, and the assholes. Especially President William Shek. How that jerk had gotten elected was anybody's guess. But McBride's place was not to question why, only to do or die, as the old Marine adage went. Still Marine to the core, and still ruled by a black and white moral code, McBride did what he was told and never questioned his orders. Well, almost never.

Late March always sucked in Washington, D.C. Not yet spring, not yet done with winter, the cold wind reddened noses while icy rain pummeled coats. A dull red sun blinked through the gray clouds on the eastern horizon. McBride hunkered down inside his black overcoat and strode toward the entrance to the Pentagon. He flashed his badge, stepped through the metal detector, and found the designated meeting room in the inner ring of the building. There he met the Eagle.

Shek had become the first person of Chinese descent to claim the pres-idency. The sixty-nine-year-old former California governor had just been inaugurated in January. The fanfare had been nearly as grand as when Barack Obama changed history. Supporters called it momentous, one giant step toward more diversity in America. Dissenters said he wasn't qualified to lead and only got the job because the U.S. owed a ton of money to China. Although Shek was born in the U.S., and therefore technically qualified to be president, the anti-foreign stalwarts insisted he was an undercover commie spy and would eventually hand the kingdom keys to the Chinese. McBride didn't believe Shek would ever do that, but he often did question the president's decisions, especially the one he'd recently made that had brought China's president to the U.S.

"Mr. President," McBride said as he entered the room. He removed his rain-beaten coat and handed it to an attendant.

Shek's soft tone underscored his diminutive frame. "He who is drowned is not troubled by the rain."

"But he's still wet, Mr. President," McBride said. He hated Shek's stupid Chinese proverbs. Though the president spoke and often acted like a priest, McBride knew the tough Democrat was a junkyard bulldog in a fight.

Shek sat at an oak table alongside a couple generals and admirals. They were here today to discuss how the military could appear to be backing away from areas considered sensitive by the Chinese while increasing covert espionage operations. Most people thought the dangerous cat and mouse games of the Cold War were in the past. How wrong they were.

McBride found a seat.

Shek said, "Gentlemen, we will sign the accord with the Chinese in a few days. At that time, we need to show them a gesture of goodwill by ensuring none of our warships are in the South China Sea."

Admiral Edwards spoke up. "Mr. President, you do realize the vulnerable position that leaves us in with the Chinese building all those damned sand islands?"

"Yes," Shek said. "But the risk is temporary and justified. A rat who gnaws at a cat's tail invites destruction."

"Are we the rat, Mr. President?" Edwards said.

McBride jumped in. "Tom, what if we sent a few more attack subs to the area? Would that address your concerns about having your pants down?"

"Maybe," Edwards said. "The Chinese haven't been able to detect our latest *Virginia*-class boats and those subs have more than enough firepower to do some serious damage."

Another Admiral leaned forward in his chair. "We've only got two VAs in the South China Sea now, so we'll need to move some chess pieces and bring down two more from their op areas near Vlad. I don't like leaving our Russian flank open like that, George."

"Like the president said," McBride answered, "it's only temporary. Give us two weeks, three tops. Are you okay with that plan, Mr. President?"

Shek brought his hands together, as if in prayer, and nodded.

"Are we in agreement then, gentlemen?" McBride said.

The admirals grumbled and eventually agreed, but not before reminding George that they'd have more submarines if Congress hadn't disapproved funding. George concurred and turned to the generals. They discussed shifting some ground troops away from areas near Chinese borders. Similar agreements, similar cavils.

An adjutant hurried into the room and leaned down to McBride. "You have an urgent call from CNO Robert Dennison, sir."

McBride drummed his fingers on the table and glanced about the room. He took a mental inventory of everyone's security clearance level and need-to-know status. He asked all but the president and Admiral Edwards to leave the room. He then instructed the adjutant to transfer in the call. The Chief of Naval Operations greeted the room.

McBride said, "Why the urgent call, Bob?"

"We have a serious situation, George. We just received an OPREP 3 from the USS *Connecticut* operating in the Beaufort Sea. It appears a Navy ICEX camp was attacked by a team of Chinese soldiers."

McBride leaned back in his seat. His fingers tingled, as if they'd been jolted by nine-volt batteries. "Are you sure they were Chinese?"

"No sir. We have no proof. Only eyewitness accounts that the soldiers were wearing Chinese uniforms and speaking Chinese."

Shek leaned forward. "Did our submarine detect any foreign vessels in the area?"

"Yes, Mr. President," Dennison said. "A mini-sub with a sound signature similar to an American ASDS. They are trying to pursue, but as the other craft appears to have twice the maximum speed of their sub, the range has increased too far to keep a lock."

"Why do they think it's an ASDS?" McBride said. Nervous sweat coated his palms.

"One in a million chance," Dennison said. "The ASDS sound signature is not in our database, as the Navy program was abandoned years ago; however, the *Connecticut's* Chief sonarman was informed by a colleague, so he just happened to recognize it."

"Imagine that," McBride said. "A one in a million chance. How lucky are we?"

"It could also be a different mini-sub with similar tones," Dennison said, "but the chances of that are slim. The ASDS has a unique signature."

"But it's possible that it's a foreign craft, right?" McBride asked.

"It's possible," Dennison said. "In any case, we're contacting Phoenix Systems to verify. They're a government contractor that supports the Navy's URC for submarine rescue ops. They recently bought the craft from Northrop Grumman."

"In the meantime," Shek said, "can we discover who is aboard that mini-sub?"

"That may be difficult," Dennison said. "If it is the ASDS, it's been upgraded with a new super-cavitator designed by ARL, which is why it's much faster than our submarines. It's also small and quiet and hard to find with active or passive sonar."

"Super-cavitator?" Shek said.

"It's a propulsion system that creates something like a force field around the bow of the craft and allows it to attain very high speed," Dennison said over the speakerphone.

"How high?" McBride said.

Admiral Edwards said, "Around eighty knots."

McBride let out a whistle. "The *Connecticut's* top speed is less than fifty knots. They'll never catch that thing."

Edwards said, "The ASDS can only use the super-cavitator for a few hours at a time to prevent overheating, then she has to slow temporarily. Also, when she's cavitating, she's noisy and easier to find. That's one of the reasons the Navy stopped the program and sold the prototype."

"Mr. President," Dennison said, "The USS *Oregon* left the Beaufort Sea a few days ago after completing ICEX. It's a fast *Virginia*-class and could get back in the area within a day at flank speed. I also recommend we use ASW aircraft and ships to find that ASDS."

McBride held up a hand. "I'm concerned about having our P-8 Poseidons flying too close to Russian airspace and let's not forget we need our *Virginia*-class boats near China now, so that only leaves our aging *Los Angeles*-class subs that can't hit forty on a good day."

Silence.

"We still have the *Connecticut*," the CNO said. "She's a bit faster and has a more advanced sonar system. Not as good as a *Virginia*, but good enough. I'm also fine with sending the *Oregon* if the president concurs."

"I still don't like leaving our flank open in the South China Sea," McBride said. "Maybe we could have the *Oregon* hold pat until we get more intel on the situation?"

"I'm okay with that," Dennison said.

"We could also use DARPA's new ACTUV bots," Edwards said.

McBride had been briefed on ACTUV. The system consisted of a set of "robo-cops" designed to hover near the ocean floor and listen for contacts. When the small sonar unit heard one, it dispatched a robot mini-sub to run after and trail the contact. Innovative, yes, but still nascent. "ACTUV is still in development and we've got a limited number of them," McBride said.

"Still," Edwards said, "we could have our Poseidon aircraft drop a few along the projected track to see if we get any hits."

"I don't—" McBride started to say.

"I do," Dennison interrupted over the phone. "This is our best shot at testing the new system, and who knows, maybe we'll get lucky."

McBride fingered a glass of water near his right hand and then said, "Okay, ACTUV, ASW, and the *Connecticut*. Maybe the *Oregon* later if needed. Sounds like two songs and a prayer to me, but I'm game. Do you agree, Mr. President?"

"I agree," Shek said.

"Now the big question," Dennison said. "What's our op plan if we find that mini-sub?"

"I'd say we force it to the surface and find out who's aboard," Admiral Edwards said.

"We are not even certain this craft was involved in the attack," Shek said.

"We've detected no other vessels in the area, Mr. President," Dennison said.

"I recommend we cross the bridge when we get there," McBride said, feeling a bit calmer. "We first need to find the damn thing."

"Agreed," Dennison said. "We also need to consider that if the mini-sub contains the soldiers who attacked our camp, they might also have American hostages."

Dennison went on to explain that two researchers from ARL were missing and may have been captured, along with some crew members from the *Connecticut* and one NCIS agent from San Diego. The researchers had been testing a new top-secret technology.

Upon hearing this, Shek sat up straight. "What is this technology?"

Dennison said, "It's designed to locate Russia's latest attack submarine. The one carrying Status-6 torpedoes."

Shek leaned back in his chair and brought his hands together. "Could it be the ICEX camp was attacked to steal this technology?"

"Quite possible," Dennison said. "We have no way of knowing until we find the perpetrators."

"What was the NCIS agent's name?" McBride asked.

Across the phone line, shuffling papers could be heard. "Agent Jon Shay."

McBride swallowed hard. His fingers tingled again.

Shek's face lost its color. "So, you are saying that armed men dressed as Chinese soldiers assaulted a facility on U.S. soil and may have captured three American civilians, two Navy Petty Officers, and an NCIS federal agent? And they perhaps did this to steal top secret technology?"

"Yes, Mr. President," Dennison said. "That appears to be the case."

"What are your odds of finding the ASDS?" McBride said.

"Slim, at best," Dennison said.

Silence, then Shek said, "Thank you, Admiral. Please keep us apprised of your progress."

"We will, Mr. President."

McBride disconnected the call. Admiral Edwards excused himself. McBride rose to leave but sat back down at the motioning of the president.

"George," Shek said, "what do you think is happening here?"

"I wish I knew, Mr. President."

"This appears too coincidental. In a few days, I'll sign a controversial agreement with the Chinese government. Today, we're attacked by what appears to be Chinese soldiers who may have taken hostages and stolen our secrets but have communicated no demands. This operation is obviously well planned by people with deep pockets."

"The coincidence has not escaped me, Mr. President. Perhaps you should consider postponing the event today?"

A formal lunch event had been planned for that afternoon at the Grand Hyatt in New York. The Chinese president was attending as a prelude to the signing of a new accord between the two countries. Shek and McBride were scheduled to fly up by helicopter in two hours.

McBride knew that by signing the accord, the U.S. president committed America to borrowing another half-trillion dollars from the Chinese, and in turn the Chinese agreed to lower interest rates by one-quarter percent and buy liquid natural gas at a discounted rate using U.S. dollars. The LNG would be produced by a revolutionary new device invented by the Naval Research Labs that could convert ordinary saltwater into any kind of fuel while lowering the Earth's carbon footprint. Some believed the deal was a godsend that would allow America to grow and prosper. Others believed it was a nightmare that shackled a free country to the whims of a communist one. McBride fell into the latter camp but held his tongue in Marine fashion. Well, most of the time.

"A gem is not polished without rubbing," Shek said, "nor a man perfected without trials. We will not postpone the event. This is too important to our respective countries."

"But what if we discover the Chinese really were behind the attack?" McBride said.

Shek's voice hardened. "Then we'll use China's money to wage a war with them. For now, we don't have enough evidence to convict."

"Still, Mr. President, don't you think we should—"

"No, I do not. I expect you to quietly do what's necessary to find that craft and investigate the incident. Then, we will take the appropriate action."

"Yes, Mr. President."

The Defense Condition level, used to increase the readiness of all U.S. forces in preparation for battle, had been raised beyond level two only once since World War II. That was during the Cuban Missile Crisis when four Soviet *Foxtrot* submarines, each loaded with nuclear torpedoes, almost started World War III. In response to that threat, Secretary of Defense Robert McNamara had ordered DefCon Three. As he left the room, George McBride wondered if he'd soon be repeating history, and if the outcome would be as peaceful.

CHAPTER 9

Agent Maria Estefan's earpiece cracked with static as she strode across the lobby of the Grand Hyatt in Manhattan, near Grand Central Station. Clad in a black battle-dress uniform, she sprinted up the escalator and then bent over to catch her breath. Though she worked out five days a week and ran six miles on the other two, Maria's forty-five-year-old body occasionally groaned in defiance. She raised back up and jogged to the back of the mezzanine to join more than a dozen members of the Counter Assault Team for a briefing from the lead agent.

Code-named Hawkeye, the CAT unit was part of the Secret Service Special Operations division, first formed in 1979 with a limited charter. Hawkeye had been conceived when a few agents were grabbing lunch after a training mission. One of the agents, Taylor Rudd, asked the team how they'd deal with a potential terrorist attack. No one had an answer, so they started CAT, which didn't really do much until after President Reagan was shot in 1981. That's when the team gained the Hawkeye moniker, expanded, and took up residence at HQ in 1983.

Lead Agent Ted Flannigan approached the group. "Listen up team, POTUS will be here in three hours for the lunch event. VPOTUS is not attending, but SECDEF is. We have a remote connection to the AOP locator at the White House, so we can keep a bead on the brass. We all know our assignments, so let's do another sweep and report back. Any questions?"

An agent raised a hand. "Are we slinging SR-16s or going solo with P229s?"

"Good question. No auto rifles today; the White House wants us to keep a low profile and out of sight as much as possible. SIG Sauer P229s and a couple flash bangs. We'll issue a few short barrels to some of you, but that's it."

Maria didn't like it. No rifles? Nothing but pistols and two diversionary grenades? Only a few agents with short barrel shotguns? If the shit hit the proverbial fan, they'd be in serious trouble.

The briefing concluded, and Maria turned to leave.

Flannigan tapped her on the shoulder and said, "Estefan, I want you to take the entrance tonight. Did you pack a dress suit?"

"Entry duty? Come on, Ted, you know I hate that shit."

"I know, but I can't afford another—"

"False alarm?"

"Yeah, exactly. Quit frowning. You get to dress up and look pretty."

Maria's forehead heated. She crossed her arms and said, "Fuck me."

Flannigan half smiled. "Thanks for being a team player."

As Flannigan walked away, Maria lamented. Not long after his inauguration in January, POTUS had decided to make an unplanned trip to Martha's Vineyard with the First Lady. Maria had been assigned as part of the Hawkeye advance team for the unexpected "pop up" trip. The group consisted of various agents assigned to security for logistics, accommodations, transportation, technical, and intelligence. Maria had been placed in charge of intelligence. They were prepping at the Joint Ops Center on the ninth floor of HQ, located in a tan brick building at the corner of H and Ninth Streets in D.C. A suspicious call came in. The Forensic Services Division matched the call recording to a voice in the database. The guy was on the watch list. Maria volunteered to interview the man to determine if he was a Class III, legitimate and able to carry out a threat; a Class II, legit but unable; or a Class I, a dirtbag with a big mouth and no ass to back it up.

Maria went to the guy's mobile home park near West McLean, Virginia. Dogs barked and kids squealed when she pulled up in her black "plain Jane" government vehicle. She stepped out and beep-locked the doors. She walked toward the caller's trailer while tattooed bikers gave her dirty looks. Her breathing quickened as she brushed her fingertips across the grip of her SIG Sauer.

Maria knocked, and the suspect invited her in. His name was Larry and he seemed almost happy to see her, like he'd just gained notoriety with his neighbors. The place reeked of stale coffee and the chubby guy looked like he preferred two boxes of jelly glazed per day versus, say, a healthy plate of broccoli. Maria sat and started asking questions. At first she surmised that Larry was a Class I. Then he talked about his military career. Ten years as an Army Ranger. He'd developed a thyroid problem and had to quit. That's when he got fat. Then he got mad. Then he met Abbas.

Maria's ears perked. "Abbas?"

Larry said the Muslim man had helped him see the light. To understand what was important in life. That we must all make sacrifices and do our duty, even if it means doing something...out of line. Maria probed some more and discovered that Abbas had persuaded Larry to make the threatening call to the White House. She couldn't tell if Larry's mysterious Muslim friend was a real person or a figment of a warped mind. She did verify, however, that Larry had guns. Several assault rifles, handguns, and probably a few weapons he'd acquired from various sources other than Dick's Sporting Goods.

As Maria was leaving the trailer park, she spied a Middle Eastern man staring at her from a parked car across the street. He sped away before she could follow him. When she returned to HQ, she gave Larry a Class III pending further investigation. That resulted in a cancelling of the president's planned trip to Martha's Vineyard. Weeks passed, and Maria never uncovered enough validation to maintain a Class III. Flannigan demoted Larry to a Class I and scolded Maria for crying wolf. Said she was lucky he was keeping her on the Hawkeye team. Now he was demoting her to entry duty, meaning she'd have to wear a pantsuit and stare at people for an hour as they entered the event.

Maria changed in her hotel room and joined the advance prep team in the lobby. The nerdy group consisted of a half-dozen military communications personnel from the White House. They were all in their mid- to late-twenties and had been sent in a few days earlier to set up phones, radios, computers, and other equipment. Maria forced a smile as she approached the team.

One nerd shifted his eyes from a computer monitor long enough to say, "Are you one of our spotters tonight?"

"Guilty," Maria said, trying to hide her frustration.

The nerd stood from his chair and extended a hand. "James Sullivan. Most call me Jimmy."

Maria shook his hand. "Maria Estefan, not related to the singer."

"The singer?"

"I guess that's a little before your time," Maria said, grateful Jimmy hadn't made the connection to Gloria Estefan, a famous performer from the Eighties.

Jimmy motioned toward the monitor. "Facial recognition. You flag 'em, we tag 'em."

"Deal," Maria said. "I'll keep my eyes peeled."

Jimmy returned to his seat. Without looking up, he said, "Nice suit. My mom has one just like it."

Maria shrugged off the jab, leaned against a post, and glanced at her watch. One hour before curtain call. She thought about the event and why POTUS and SECDEF were attending. Between news broadcasts and Secret Service briefings, she'd learned that President Shek had struck a deal with the Chinese president. They were scheduled to sign a major accord in a few days, and they were celebrating their agreement at a formal luncheon.

Maria had heard rumors that most of Shek's advisors—and even the vice president—were against the accord while Shek insisted it was a huge win for America. Maria sided with the dissenters and pundits who questioned why America was continuing to borrow money from a communist-controlled government that might one day leverage that debt to force American policy.

On the other hand, she did see a glimpse of the endgame. In late 2015, the U.N. Council had granted Russia ownership rights to a massive expanse near the North Pole in the Arctic. Geologists estimated the area contained almost six billion tons of oil. The Russians had used the newfound energy bonanza to ink a $400 billion deal with China. The Chinese had previously bought almost all their oil and gas from Middle Eastern countries, including Iran and Syria, but very little from Russia and none from the United States. Now they were buying most of it from Russia. President Shek had somehow convinced China to start buying more fuel and liquid natural gas from the U.S., produced by some newfangled device invented by the Naval Research Labs. Maria had heard from a few friends in the know that a secret deal had been brokered, but the details were never disclosed to the public. Chances are, they never would be.

An hour passed, and guests started arriving. Maria labeled each one as guilty until proven innocent. She watched for any tells, including twitches, fidgets, hard swallows, sweaty palms, whatever. The crowd shuffled in wearing broad smiles and elegant attire. The women, mostly elderly and rich, dripped with diamonds. The men, mostly arrogant and powerful, fiddled with cufflinks and glanced at Rolex watches. No one seemed suspicious until the lady in the wheelchair rolled in. The man pushing her was nondescript, wiry, and in his early forties. He had a full beard and bushy hair, unlike the other well-groomed gentlemen. The wheelchair also made the hairs on Maria's neck bristle. Those metal contraptions were great places to hide rifle barrels.

Maria walked over and tapped Jimmy on the shoulder. She pointed at the bearded guy. "That one."

Jimmy glanced up and squinted. He looked back down and tapped on his keyboard. Maria watched as a couple video cameras, mounted on stands, pivoted ever so slightly. The man's face appeared on the screen. Jimmy tapped a few more keys and the facial recognition routine went to work. Nothing came up while the program churned away.

"How long does it take?" Maria asked.

"Depends," Jimmy said. "Five minutes or fifty."

"That helps."

"It's not an exact science."

"No shit."

Maria held her breath as she struggled with her decision. Should she flag the man and keep him out, or let him in and wait for the software to do its thing? She decided to wait and see what his credentials read when he passed security, then see if they matched his facial ID when it finally came up. She also wanted to find out who the old lady in the wheelchair might be.

"Let him in, but call me when you get a hit," Maria said.

"Where are you going?" Jimmy asked.

"To keep an eye on the bearded wonder."

Maria maneuvered around the entrants and positioned herself behind the wheelchair but far enough away to remain unnoticed. Outside the glass doors, she spied the POTUS party—a line of black Cadillacs driven by Secret Service agents and flanked by New York police motorcycles. The president's vehicle, called "the Beast" by agents, was probably third or fourth in line. The first two were usually decoys. The Beast came standard with bullet-proof glass, the latest in high-tech communications gear, and its own oxygen supply system. All the "G-rides" had self-sealing gas tanks and could keep on rolling even if the tires got shot out. The windows in these babies were five inches thick and the doors were plated with eighteen inches of metal. Maria knew the Beast could theoretically withstand a direct hit from a bazooka or grenade, but no agent ever wanted to validate that specification.

The bearded man and the madam in the wheelchair approached the checkpoint. Maria moved closer. An agent scanned the old lady's pass. Green light. He scanned the bearded guy's pass. *Red light.* Maria's fingers twitched. She edged closer and placed a palm on the grip of her P229. The agent scanned again. Green light. Maria let out a breath but kept her eye on the suspicious pair.

As the two maneuvered toward the elevators, Maria said to Jimmy, "Who are they?"

Jimmy tapped his monitor. "She's Bernice Brentwood, the widow of the late Senator. He's her escort and wheelchair man. Some guy named Nathan Pender. I ran a check and he came up squeaky clean."

"Maybe too clean?"

Jimmy shrugged. "That'd be your call, not mine."

"Any hits yet on facial?"

Jimmy pointed at his other monitor. "Still crunching."

"Call me when you get something. I'm going in."

"Flannigan won't like that."

Maria shrugged. "He doesn't like most things I do."

Maria rode the escalator to the ballroom, two stories up. Brentwood and Pender exited the elevator and rolled into the ballroom. Maria started to follow through another door when Flannigan grabbed her arm.

"What are you doing up here?"

"I'm hungry."

"Not funny."

"Following a guy."

"Did the tech team flag him?"

"Not yet. He got a red, then a green, and I don't like him."

Flannigan rolled his eyes. "Another Class 1 you don't like?"

"I think he's worth some eyes, that's all."

"Fine. Point him out."

Maria entered the ballroom with Flannigan close behind. Inside, a band played classical music. Candles fluttered, waiters poured, people chatted, and the vinegar smell of salad dressing made Maria's mouth water. She'd eaten a light breakfast and no lunch. Pender and Brentwood wheeled to a table near one of the doors. Pender helped the lady out of her wheelchair. Maria touched Flannigan's sleeve and nonchalantly pointed. Flannigan nodded and then tilted his head toward the door. Maria frowned and moved toward the exit, all the while keeping an eye on Mr. Pender. The man helped Brentwood out of her wheelchair and then stood obediently nearby. The lights dimmed and one of the president's press people stepped to the podium. She announced that the president and his Chinese counterpart had arrived and would join them at any moment. Maria looked back toward Pender.

He was gone.

She darted out of the ballroom and scanned the foyer. Nothing. Out of breath, she flagged a nearby agent. "Have you seen someone go by with a wheelchair?"

"I was watching who was going in, not coming out. But I did hear the elevator chime."

"Damn it!" She took off for the stairs. She sprinted down to the conference area, stopped, and listened. A squeak? The sound was soft, almost unheard, and came from one of the rooms around the corner. Maria ran. She came to the first room. The door was shut and locked. Same with the second room. The third door was also shut. She turned the handle. It opened. All the doors on this level were supposed to be locked.

The door squeaked when she pushed it open. The lights were off. She flipped the switch up. The light did not come on. She pulled out her flashlight and scanned the room. The dim light cast eerie shadows on the walls and ceiling. The room appeared empty, save for dozens of chairs and a podium. She panned the light into the hard corners. Nothing in three corners, something in the fourth. A wheelchair. She started to key her mic and then stopped. If this was another false alarm on her part, she'd lose her job. What if this was a hotel wheelchair or belonged to someone else? What if her potential bad guy had just parked the wheelchair in here and then went to the men's room? Then again, what if he was getting ready to shoot the president?

Maria pulled her sidearm and pointed at the wheelchair. "Federal agent, who's in here?"

No answer.

"This is a restricted area. You need to return to the ballroom now."

Silence.

Maria moved closer. The light from her flashlight danced on the far wall like a yellow phantom. Maria's pulse inched upward. A/C jetted down from the ceiling and chilled the hairs on her neck. She approached the wheelchair and examined it with her light. The side rails and part of the wheels were missing. Her blouse fluttered with each heartbeat.

Now she had no choice.

She keyed her mic and whispered. "Possible intruder in Broadway conference room. Repeat, possible intruder in Broadway conference room."

She glanced down. A metal grate rested face down on the floor. The large grate had been covering an air conditioning access panel. A wiry man could fit through that hole.

Maria looked back toward the door, hoping to see her Hawkeye teammates rushing through. No one entered. She returned her eyes to the open hole in the wall and said, "Fuck me."

She pulled off her jacket and wiggled her way inside the access panel. The small area smelled of must and metal. Her flashlight revealed a crawl space and a metal ladder. She placed the flashlight in her mouth and climbed upward. The beam bounced off the sides of the claustrophobic tomb and created winged shadows that resembled bats.

Maria reached the top of the ladder and pulled herself onto a small ledge. Her flashlight revealed yet another ladder leading upward. Again, she climbed. The ascent led her into a large storage area. She panned her light in a circle. The room had a low ceiling and was filled with boxes, equipment, stacked mattresses, brooms, buckets, mops—but no intruder. Scattered rays of sunlight seeped through a small slatted window on a far wall. Maria pulled her gun, brought her hands together in a teacup grip, and slowly scanned the hard corners of the room with her light. The covered furniture resembled something seen in a haunted house.

Maria tiptoed across the dirty floor. Her chest rose and fell with each rapid breath. She heard music and laughter and realized she was one story above the ballroom. In the far corner of the storage area, she saw an elongated shape on the floor. In the dim light, she couldn't discern if it was a prone figure or just a shadow. She pointed her gun and slowly inched toward the shape.

Her shoe scraped across something on the floor. Her heart thrummed. She glanced down. A broken piece of glass. She heard shuffling in the corner and flashed her light. The shape seen earlier had disappeared, or maybe it was never there. To be safe, she spun around to check her six, but only made it halfway. A searing pain shot from the top of her head to the balls of her feet. Someone had whacked her on the back of her skull. The light in her hand dropped to the ground. Her gun thudded onto the floor. She landed on her knees and fought to stay conscious. The room spun, and her stomach churned. In the near darkness, she moved her hand in a circle across the floor and found her weapon.

She palmed the SIG and fired two rounds into the ceiling. Shouts and screaming came from the ballroom below. In a daze, her mind defaulted to Spanish. "Alto! Federales!"

She heard someone run toward the back of the room. The metal ladder clanked. Certain that she'd pass out within seconds, she could only hope her fellow agents would catch the guy before he got away.

CHAPTER 10

Aboard the ASDS mini-sub, hundreds of feet deep in the Chukchi Sea west of Alaska, Jon's stomach growled but not just from hunger. He hated being powerless and clueless. His gut churned with a prescient foreboding that they were on an underwater train headed for a cliff. They had been aboard and tied up for over eight hours, with only occasional breaks to use the head or eat an MRE. Bobby had snored loudly for most of that time while Kate and Jon had slept sporadically. The crew had apparently also slept in shifts.

Jon glanced up as Rinaldo approached.

"Ms. Barrett," Rinaldo said to Kate.

"Ms. Asshole," Kate shot back. "Would you like to join us for tea?"

"I have some questions," Rinaldo said.

"So do I," Kate said.

Rinaldo ignored her retort. "The ROSS device can lock onto the *Khabarovsk's* frequency emissions. As determined by your recent tests, what do you now believe is the maximum detection range of the unit?"

Kate stared at the tall ice pilot but said nothing. Her eyes were red from worry and lack of sleep.

"Please don't make me do this the hard way," Rinaldo said. "I've already had a long day."

Still no answer.

Rinaldo let out a frustrated breath and stepped in front of Bobby. She straddled his legs with her nose practically touching his. Startled, Bobby looked up with wide eyes. With one swift movement, Rinaldo reached between Bobby's legs and squeezed. The engineer let out a yelp. Tears streamed down his face as he fought to catch his breath.

Kate raised her chin. "Damn you."

Furious, Jon pulled at his tie wraps to no avail.

"The range?" Rinaldo said.

Kate lowered her eyes. "It depends on the sonar system."

"Attached to an ORCA," Rinaldo said.

"Probably 20,000 yards," Kate said.

"What are the optimal settings?"

"I could tell you," Kate said, "but then Jon would have to kill you."

"Funny," Rinaldo said as she squeezed harder. This time Bobby cried out in agony. Mucus dripped from his nose and coated his chin.

Kate's cheeks flushed. "Okay, okay!"

Rinaldo released her grip.

"There are too many variables," Kate said. "We'd have to show you."

"Fine," Rinaldo said. She stepped away from Bobby, pulled out a pocket-knife, and cut his tie wraps. She cut Kate's as well.

The tall ice pilot escorted Kate and Bobby to the front of the craft. With the diving chamber positioned in the middle of the ASDS, Jon could only catch a glimpse of the pair as they worked on the ROSS device near the sonar panel. During the next hour, while Kate and Bobby showed Rinaldo how to operate the ROSS unit, Jon contemplated why the former submariner needed to know the ROSS unit's range. If his initial assumption was correct, that Rinaldo and Liang intended to sell the ROSS device to the highest bidder, then why were they concerned with operating the unit to locate the *Khabbie*? Despite the damp cold inside the mini-sub, Jon felt a warm surge of adrenaline shoot through his veins. Were Rinaldo and Liang after a bigger prize? Could they be planning to hijack a Russian nuclear submarine? And if so, then what? Sell it to someone?

Jon shuddered at the thought of what might happen if North Korea, Iran, or Pakistan got their hands on one of the world's most formidable weapons of mass destruction. While he contemplated the worst-case scenario, Liang walked over from the forward section and stood next to the bench, facing Jon.

"Why NCIS?" Liang said.

"They paid better than Starbucks," Jon said.

"Not by much," Liang said.

"What makes you so sure the Navy won't sink us long before you complete your fool's plan?"

"I'm not," Liang said. "But the gamble is worth the prize."

"And what is the prize? Money? Disneyland tickets? A new Keurig?"

"You think like a typical American."

"And you speak like one," Jon said.

"I'm a fast learner," Liang said, "but let's talk about you. Why did you leave SEAL Team Two?"

Wanting to strangle Liang rather than chat with him, Jon at first held his tongue. He then decided if he could get Liang to open up, he might learn something useful.

"I was undercover," Jon said, "working with the FBI to track down some Tangos. The FBI's cyber unit found out Russian mobsters were laundering money for ISIS terrorists. Since I speak fluent Russian—"

"You took the point," Liang finished.

"It took a year, but I finally got inside."

"Inside the Russian mafia? That takes some serious balls."

"I should have turned down the mission," Jon said.

"You lost someone."

Jon studied Liang. The Chinese operative was obviously skilled in the art of interrogation, but a look in his eyes hinted at genuine interest.

"A friend. He was ratted out by an FBI agent on the take. When I found out who it was," Jon paused, "let's just say I didn't turn him in. After that, I decided it was time for a change."

Liang moved his chin up and down slowly, as if in agreement with Jon's decision. "I would have done the same. I *did* do the same. A Tango posed as an Iraqi National Guardsman and gave his jihadi friends some intel that killed three of my men. I didn't turn him in, either."

An alarm rang in Jon's head. The Chinese had not deployed any troops to Iraq. He said, "You served in Iraq?"

Liang's face hardened. "We're done talking." He spun on a heel and strode toward the bow.

Minutes later, Rinaldo returned Kate and Bobby to the bench. She summoned a commando and told him to re-tie the pair. In perfect English, the commando replied, "Yes ma'am, I'll grab some more tie wraps from the locker."

Jon wondered if Liang's commandos were American or just well-versed in English. If the former, why were they dressed as Chinese soldiers? Why not just wear civilian clothing? Jon blew out a frustrated breath. More questions without answers.

A report from Petty Officer Chen, seated in the bow and wearing a set of headphones, interrupted Jon's thoughts. He informed Rinaldo that active sonar devices were pinging more than 40,000 yards behind them. Probably U.S. ASW aircraft dropping sonobuoys.

Liang walked back from the bow and faced Rinaldo. "Game time."

Rinaldo said, "They must have found the hostages at the camp. By now, every ASW aircraft in the Arctic has orders to hunt us down. If they find us...."

"They will not," Liang said with confidence. "We have a destiny to fulfill."

"Let's hope that destiny doesn't involve a torpedo up our ass," Rinaldo said.

The tall brunette marched back to the bow and ordered the pilot to shut down the supercavitating propulsor drive. Jon knew they'd now slow from around eighty knots to less than thirty, but he also knew they'd be far more silent and harder to find.

Jon leaned over and whispered in Kate's ear. "When you and Bobby were in the bow, did you see what direction we're heading?"

"I got a glimpse," Kate said. "We're on course two-six-zero."

"Where is the *Khabbie* scheduled to conduct sea trials?" Jon asked Kate.

"NSG determined they'd likely do it near Cape Vankarem," Kate said.

Cape Vankarem was a coastal Russian town around 500 nautical miles west of the ICEX camp. The Russians probably scheduled sea trials near there since it allowed them to test the submarine in Arctic conditions.

Jon did a quick calc in his head. "Cape Vankarem should now be less than one hundred nautical miles west of us. If the ROSS device can locate the *Khabbie*, what else can it do?"

"What do you mean?"

"Can it be used to control or disable the sub's systems?"

Bobby's eyes panned back and forth as the gears turned in his brain. "Maybe. ROSS is designed to detect a range of frequencies, but it can also transmit. And using some seriously kick ass code, it might be able to hack into the AI system in the *Khabbie*."

"AI?" Jon said.

"Yeah," Kate said. "Both ROSS and the Russian *Khabbie* have been designed to use artificial intelligence. They can learn and adapt in similar ways to the human mind. The *Khabbie* uses AI to control the sub's functions, like navigation, propulsion, sonar."

"Fire control?" Jon asked.

"That, too," Bobby said. "Those crazy Russkies basically handed over control of their Status-6 nuclear torpedoes to an adolescent mind."

"Why am I not surprised?" Jon said. "Do you think ROSS can...I don't know...use some kind of Jedi mind trick to control the *Khabbie*?"

"It'd take one hell of a hack job," Bobby said. "I'm not sure that *I* could do it. Also, given the high frequencies needed, we'd have to be close enough to smell each other's armpits."

"I think Rinaldo and Liang know more about ROSS than we think they do," Jon said. "I interviewed Chen. He's a computer programmer and a sonar genius. He might be smart enough to do the hack. I think it's possible they plan to use ROSS to capture the *Khabbie*."

Kate dropped her jaw. "Capture the *Khabbie*? Are they crazy?"

"Crazier than the Kardashians," Jon said. "Especially if they plan to sell the sub to someone for a fat payoff."

"We have to stop them," Kate said. "If that sub winds up in the wrong hands..."

"It won't," Jon said. "I have a plan, but you're not going to like it."

Bobby leaned sideways. His voice warbled. "We're in a submerged box surrounded by a bunch of mean guys with guns and you have a plan?"

Jon said, "Can ROSS also send out a high frequency Deep Siren signal?"

Bobby said, "Yeah, maybe."

"Can Petty Officer Chen hear it on sonar?"

"The Deep Siren frequency is higher than normal sonar range," Bobby said, "so it'd be harder for the ORCA sonar to hear it. Still, we'd need to do it at really low power to be safe."

Jon said, "But you can rig ROSS to send out a short message, right?"

Kate frowned. "Maybe, but the nearest buoy might be too far away to pick it up."

"I'm betting that ASW aircraft are dropping Deep Siren buoys so they can communicate with the *Connecticut*," Jon said. "If we get lucky, they might close the gap enough for one of those buoys to pick up our message."

"And who's going to instruct ROSS to send that message?" Kate asked.

"You and Bobby," Jon said.

Bobby's hands quavered. "What happens if we get caught?"

Jon did not respond. He'd had a death wish for the past year, but he'd never wanted to take anyone with him. Now, he might not have a choice.

CHAPTER 11

Jon twisted sideways on the bench. "Turn away from me," he said to Kate. Puzzled, Kate waited until no commandos were nearby and then shifted so her back partially faced toward Jon.

He whispered, "See if you can take off my belt buckle."

"Mate?"

"I want to go for a swim," Jon said.

Kate gave him a confused look until she finally understood. She then fumbled with the buckle until it came loose from the belt webbing. She froze as the metal buckle slipped from her fingers. Nothing clanked.

"I got it," Jon said. Behind his back, he worked quietly. Using the sharp teeth on the clasp, which held the belt webbing in place, he was trying to slice through his tie wraps. Long minutes passed. On several occasions, Jon stopped slicing and hid the buckle as a soldier walked past. Finally, Kate heard a muffled pop.

"I'm free," Jon said to Kate. "I'm going to make a play for the ROSS device and pretend to damage it. You and Bobby need to convince Rinaldo that it's busted, pretend to fix it, and then rig the ORCA sonar system to send a message to the *Connecticut*."

"Why wouldn't you actually damage the device?" Kate said. "Then they'd have to end this mission."

"There's a good chance that if this mission ends, so do our lives," Jon said. "My plan could at least buy us some time."

Exhausted and distraught, Kate felt a knotted ball form in the pit of her stomach. "What message do you want to send?"

Jon leaned close and whispered. Kate raised an eyebrow. A few seconds later, he darted toward the bow. She watched as he powered his way forward, a bull charging toward a line of matadors. When a soldier stepped in his way, Jon brushed the man aside with a single, strong swipe. The commando thumped onto the deck. Others tried to block Jon's path, but they were too late. He reached the ROSS device, ripped it from its housing, and smashed it against the deck. Kate hoped the loud smack was only for effect and the damage was superficial.

Liang grabbed Jon by the collar, ripped the ROSS suitcase loose, and threw him against a bulkhead. Jon feigned a response. Liang gripped Jon's throat with his left hand and unholstered his gun with his right. He shoved the pistol under Jon's chin. Kate held her breath as Liang's trigger finger twitched.

Rinaldo ran over and tore the gun from Liang's hands. "You want to get us all killed? A stray bullet could rupture the hull."

Liang growled as he wrapped both hands around Jon's neck and squeezed.

Jon gagged.

"Let him go," Rinaldo said.

Liang squeezed tighter.

Rinaldo leveled a punch into Liang's side. The blow caused the Chinese soldier to grunt and loosen his grip for a second. Rinaldo pounded Liang with two more blows. Finally, the man released his grip from Jon's neck and turned toward Rinaldo.

"Why are you protecting him?" Liang said. "He's a liability."

"I have my orders," Rinaldo said.

"Your orders will destroy our mission."

"I'll be the judge of that," Rinaldo said. "Bring our guests forward to assess the damage."

Liang snarled, turned, and walked toward Kate and Bobby. He cut the tie wraps and shoved them toward the bow. Kate almost slipped on the deck. Bobby reached over to steady her. Liang handed them off to Rinaldo and then had a soldier escort Jon back to the bench.

When they reached the front of the mini-sub, Rinaldo handed Kate the ROSS case. "Fix it."

Kate took the ROSS and followed Bobby toward the ORCA sonar system. While she and Bobby worked on the unit, Kate glanced up long enough to peek at a navigation chart on a nearby table. A marking on the chart indicated that the mini-sub was approaching Russian territorial waters near the Cape. She did a calc in her head and determined that the ASDS should be close enough to pick up the *Khabbie's* scent within a few hours. She returned her eyes to the ROSS unit and the task at hand. Unable to keep her hands from shaking, her mind spun with questions. If they entered Russian territorial waters, would any pursuing U.S. submarines follow? Once Rinaldo found the *Khabbie*, how would she steal it, if indeed that was the plan?

"Pilot, slow to fifteen knots," Rinaldo ordered.

The ASDS slowed again. Thirty minutes passed while Kate and Bobby programmed ROSS.

Bobby whispered in Kate's ear, "They don't need ROSS if they only plan to *find* that beast."

"Right you are," Kate whispered back. "Which means...."

Bobby pursed his lips while he checked a connection on the ROSS device. "Jon was right. They're gonna steal that bad girl."

"How?" Kate whispered. "Even if they find a way to hack in with ROSS, they can't shut down everything. And what about the crew?"

"They're gonna board that sub and take out the crew."

"If that's the plan, we have to find a way to stop them," Kate said.

"I'll leave that part to you and Jon," Bobby said as he typed another command on the ROSS keyboard. He raised his chin. "Mr. ROSS is ready for testing."

Kate fired up the unit and said, "ROSS, can you hear me?"

"I can hear you, Dr. Barrett," the ROSS unit replied.

"Good. Run diagnostics suite one-seven-niner-zero."

"Running."

Fifteen seconds passed.

"Complete," ROSS said. "I detect no errors or anomalies."

"Very well. Initiate subroutine two-seven-charlie."

"Initiating."

Fifteen more seconds.

"I detect an error. It appears to be related to the active interface to the ORCA system."

"Ignore and suppress," Kate said.

"Please confirm that you wish to ignore and suppress the error."

"Confirmed."

"Complete."

"Complete initiation."

"Complete."

"Send."

"Sending."

Rinaldo walked over. "Sending? What the hell are you doing?"

Kate swallowed a lump. "Just confirming that the ROSS unit is working properly."

"What did you send?"

"Nothing," Kate lied. "The unit sends itself an internal signal to confirm the detection system is properly interfaced with the ORCA sonar system. It's a standard subroutine. Did you hear a ping?"

Rinaldo looked toward Petty Officer Chen. The sonarman shook his head. Rinaldo glared back at Kate. "Are you done?"

"The unit is fixed. You may now surrender and let us go."

"Funny," Rinaldo said. "Now it's time for you two to earn your keep."

Bobby's voice shifted into falsetto. "Earn our keep?"

"We're almost ready to see what your ROSS unit can do," Rinaldo said. "If it works, we all live. If not—"

Chen cut her off with an urgent report. "High speed screws in the water!"

Rinaldo leaned over and examined the sonar screen. A bright orange line inched down from the top. "Pilot, hard right, flank speed, thirty degree down bubble, make your depth three hundred feet!"

The pilot acknowledged and complied.

Liang stepped near. "Who the hell fired a torpedo at us?"

"No idea," Rinaldo said. "The U.S. wouldn't fire until they'd determined we're a threat."

Chen said, "Torpedo bearing two seven two, range twenty thousand yards."

"Snapshot," Rinaldo said. "They fired without a solid lock. Somebody wants us bad, but who?"

Liang wiped a bead of sweat from his upper lip. "Signature?"

Chen flipped a few switches and examined nearby screens. "Looks like a Chinese Yu-7."

Kate cocked an ear. *Chinese?* Why would they be firing on the ASDS? Weren't Liang and his men Chinese?

Rinaldo leaned over Chen's shoulder and stared at a screen that displayed sound layer profiles. "Pilot, hard left, course one-niner-five, make your depth four hundred fifty feet, slow to one-third."

Liang's eyes narrowed as he stared at Rinaldo. "That's below test depth."

"I know," Rinaldo said. "We don't have a choice. She'll hold."

"You hope," Liang said.

"Torpedo closing, range fifteen thousand yards," Chen said.

Rinaldo did not reply. Once the sub was in position, she said, "Pilot, all stop."

The hum of the mini-sub's propulsion system subsided. The vibration in the deck calmed to a whisper but Kate's knees still wobbled as the torpedo raced closer. She hated feeling helpless. There was nothing she could do but wait for the explosion. A tear formed in her eye. She wiped it away and walked back to the bench to join Jon. If she was going to die, she wanted to be near someone she cared about.

"Range ten thousand yards, bearing two-seven-one," Chen said.

"Rig for ultra quiet," Rinaldo said to the crew. Banter ceased. Soldiers sat on benches or the deck. The air fell silent, save for the sound of rapid breathing.

Kate sat near Jon. She reached over and squeezed his tie-wrapped hand. He squeezed back. She leaned over and whispered in his ear. "Why did they fire at us?"

"Klingons," Jon whispered back. "They really hate us."

Kate knew Jon was just trying to lighten her mood, but she could not hold back the tears as she cupped her face in her palms.

"Snapshot," Jon whispered. "Low odds."

Kate nodded and forced a smile.

"Five thousand yards," Chen reported.

Instinctively, everyone glanced upward, as if they could see the approaching torpedo. As if they could will it to miss. As if they had any control over the machinations of the universe.

"Two thousand yards. Doppler increasing."

Kate squeezed Jon's hand tighter.

"One thousand yards."

Kate glanced over and watched Rinaldo place a hand on Chen's shoulder while examining the sonar screens.

"Doppler's shifting," Chen said. "Wait. It's decreasing."

A soldier smiled and let out a short yelp. Liang shot him a hard glare and signaled his men to remain silent. Kate knew that advanced torpedoes were equipped with sensitive sonar systems. At this range, the weapon could hear a loud voice or tap on the hull. It would then turn, sniff, and race toward the sound like a blood hound on the chase.

"Range increasing. Two thousand yards."

Rinaldo waited until the torpedo was at least five thousand yards distant before breathing a sigh of relief. "Tonals?"

Kate leaned over and strained to listen.

Chen shook his head. "No contacts detected now." He tapped on a screen. "Hard to say for sure, but if I had to guess, I'd say these tonals look like a Chinese 109."

"A 109? What the hell is it doing in the Arctic?"

Kate at first thought she had heard Chen wrong, until Rinaldo confirmed the number. The 109 was China's latest—and deadliest—attack submarine. They only had one, and it was supposed to be on sea trials in the South China Sea. Only an incident one level below a war would cause the Chinese to send their best sub this far north before completing sea trials. She had at first thought she'd become embroiled in a simple heist. Now she wondered if she was witnessing the start of a world war.

Rinaldo turned to Liang. "Why is a 109 chasing us?"

"No clue," Liang said. "I know as much as you do."

"This changes things," Rinaldo said. "We now need to zig-zag and go slower. That'll put us behind schedule and allow U.S. forces to catch up." She issued orders to the pilot and the ASDS jerked and moved forward again.

Kate looked to Jon for an answer.

He shrugged, waited for a soldier to walk past, and whispered. "I thought Liang might be working for the Chinese, but his soldiers speak perfect English. The Chinese must have found out that Liang and Rinaldo stole the ROSS device and they either want it, in which case the torpedo was a warning, or they want it destroyed, in which case they were trying to take us out. This obviously goes much deeper than I thought."

Kate wondered if she'd live long enough to find out just how deep.

CHAPTER 12

Commander Jackson stared at the waterfall display in the sonar shack aboard the USS *Connecticut*. His back ached and his head throbbed from lack of sleep. The sonar jockeys had spent the last nine hours following the faint scent of the ASDS, relayed to them by ASW aircraft, as the mini-sub appeared to be on a zig-zag course heading in the direction of Cape Vankarem in the Chukchi Sea. The P-8s had dropped a few ACTUV bots, which had also gotten some whiffs.

The P-8A Poseidon anti-submarine warfare aircraft were not quite as sexy as an F-35 stealth fighter, but they had proven themselves as more than essential in hunting Chinese, Russian, and other foreign submarines. Finding and tracking a sub from the air was no easy task, and often required the patience of Job and the persistence of a bloodhound. Poseidon crews might spend thousands of hours flying patrol patterns and monitoring consoles inside a metal tube with a fuselage resembling a Boeing 737 jetliner.

Inside a Poseidon, five operators sat in front of monitors that lined the port side. The P-8's computers had been designed to combine all the ASW data "puzzle pieces" to form a single picture that could be sent to nearby ships or subs in a task force. Once an enemy sub was located, the Poseidon could start a war by launching one of its eleven missiles or by dropping depth charges and torpedoes carried in underwing racks or in a rotary launcher in the rear.

The ASDS mini-sub Jackson and his crew were chasing had been traveling at almost twice the *Connecticut's* top speed for several hours, so instead of getting closer, they'd been losing ground. Fortunately, a few P-8s had gotten enough occasional hits to maintain a rough track. Now it appeared the ASDS had slowed, allowing the *Connecticut* to start closing the gap.

Two *Los Angeles*-class boats were on their way to assist, but they were days away. The CNO had finally ordered the USS *Oregon* to head their way, but it would be quite a few hours before it arrived. The other *Virginia*-class subs in the Pacific were not available. They'd been ordered to the South China Sea to patrol the area while the surface fleet was withdrawn to keep the Chinese happy until the accord was signed.

Petty Officer Reynolds glanced up from a sonar panel. "Cap'm, ASW aircraft report that they're picking up what sounds like a Deep Siren code transmission."

Surprised, Jackson said, "Are you sure?"

"Yessir. They're relaying it now."

Jackson glanced over the sonarman's shoulder where a ruggedized Panasonic notebook computer sat strapped to a metal table. The words "Raytheon Deep Siren" were printed on the lower right corner of the screen. The Achilles' heel of nuclear submarines had long been their inability to communicate with command while running deep and fast. They needed to slow down and come shallow to string out a very low frequency radio wire to receive transmissions or raise a mast-mounted antenna to transmit via SSIXS. When they did, bad guys could find them.

In the Arctic, this maneuver carried an even greater risk. For a VLF wire to work, the *Connecticut* needed to get close enough to the surface to be sure the cable touched the bottom side of the ice pack. Jackson's planesman then needed to maintain exact depth control to avoid hitting dangling ice keels that could puncture the sub's sail and cause flooding.

Raytheon had solved that problem with its Deep Siren communications system. The technology consisted of sophisticated software code running on a laptop that allowed for one- and two-way communications via sonobuoys dropped into the water. Short coded messages could be sent through the buoys and received by the *Connecticut* via the sonar system. The Morse-code-like signals were then translated by the Deep Siren laptop in the sonar shack. The ASW planes had dropped a few Deep Siren buoys along their track to allow them to communicate more effectively with the *Connecticut.*

Jackson studied the laptop screen as the message was relayed from a P-8. The left side displayed three boxes lined in blue that were labeled Receive Spectrum, Doppler, and SNR for Signal to Noise Ratio. Another box in the middle, labeled Received Message, contained truncated sentences that resembled mobile phone texting with timestamps. Three text levels could be used. Level One offered only basic coded messages but fast transmission times. Level Two allowed for a selection of words that formed short sentences. Level Three was free-flowing text but took much longer to send, which increased the risk of detection. Jackson usually specified Level Two to ensure more complete communications while minimizing detection. If he wanted to respond to a message, he'd have to do so through transmission buoys launched by his sub or ASW aircraft.

Jackson read the message. The hairs on his neck stood on end. The short text read: *Rinaldo traitor, Chinese on ASDS capturing Khabbie.*

The message ended with the word "Graycliff" and the initials J.S.

Jackson stood up straight. "I'll be damned."

"Cap'm?" Reynolds said.

Jackson placed a hand on the sonar jockey's shoulder. "I need you to contact the Poseidon crew that relayed that Deep Siren message to see if they can determine the bearing source of the transmission."

"Sir?"

"Have them run a query. The Deep Siren system should be able to tell us roughly from which bearing it received that last transmission before it re-broadcasted it to the P-8. What was the bearing?"

"I'm on it," Reynolds said. He squinted at the Deep Siren screen and typed in some commands, which he relayed to the P-8 Poseidon. He clicked the touchpad several times, squinted some more, and typed again.

Nervous sweat beads formed on Jackson's brow as he peered over the sonarman's shoulder. Several minutes later, the sonar jockey glanced up. "Looks like bearing two-four-two, Cap'm. But it's a rough estimate."

"Range and bearing to the Deep Siren buoy?" Jackson asked.

The sonarman stared at the screen. "Bearing two-seven-zero. Range 20,000 yards."

Jackson keyed the comm system in the overhead. "Conn, this is the Captain. OOD, come left to course two-five-five. Slow to three knots, come to periscope depth."

The officer of the deck confirmed the order. Jackson marched out of the sonar shack and thought about the message as he headed toward Radio.

Graycliff. J.S.

His favorite cigar brand and Jon Shay's initials. He and Jon had been alone on the bridge when Jackson had said, "Just say the word Graycliff and I'll come running." The only plausible explanation was that Agent Shay had somehow found a way to use the ASDS's ORCA sonar system to transmit a Deep Siren message and relay it to the *Connecticut*.

Jackson furrowed his brow. If that assumption was correct, then Rinaldo was a traitor and Shay was now her captive. How could that be possible? He hadn't worked with Rinaldo that long, but he'd found her to be as dedicated and patriotic as they come. She'd graduated from the Naval Academy and her file was spotless. If she really was a traitor, she was also a damned good actress.

Jackson entered the radio room. "Milner, fire up SSIXS."

"Aye, sir," Petty Officer Milner said. He stepped toward a console and flipped some switches.

While Deep Siren was useful for shorter range transmissions, SSIXS was the only way to send long-range transmissions to COMSUBFOR.

Jackson grabbed a pen and paper and wrote out a message. He handed it to Milner and said, "Send this ASAP."

Milner took the paper, read it, and swallowed a golf ball.

Jackson flashed Milner a stern look. "I don't have to remind you...."

"No sir," Milner said, "you don't. The contents of this message will not leave this room."

Jackson spun on a heel and left Radio. As he entered the Conn, he glanced at his watch. He knew from his briefings that the Russian *Khabbie* submarine was currently conducting sea trials near Cape Vankarem. If Shay's message was genuine, that's where the ASDS would be heading. Jackson rubbed at his throbbing temples. The term "caught between a rock and hard place" haunted him. The rock was the Russian Arctic fleet. The hard place was the *Khabbie*—one of the most formidable and hard to find nuclear submarines in the world. The "caught between" was the *Connecticut*, and Jackson had a bad feeling that Rinaldo and her Chinese friends were about to stir up some nasty shit that could turn this frigid chunk of ocean into a seething cauldron.

CHAPTER 13

An hour after arriving back at the White House by helicopter, McBride wondered if he was about to become the first secretary of defense involved in a World War since Henry L. Stimson. A male millennial aid with acne ushered McBride into the oval office. Enthroned behind his desk, President Shek glanced up from a stack of papers. McBride strode the distance and sat in an ornate chair that appeared turn-of-the-century but had probably been cobbled together by a New Jersey union shop. Another fake, just like Shek's smile.

"Agent Flannigan apologized for the incident at the event, Mr. President," McBride said.

"Has the Secret Service determined the nature of the threat?" Shek said.

"Not as yet. They have not verified if there was an assailant or if it was a false alarm, but they're assuming the former until they can rule out the latter."

"Very well. What is the status in the Arctic?"

McBride cleared his throat. "The USS *Connecticut* has reported they may be closing in on the ASDS, but they also understand they are not to engage until ordered to do so."

"Have we determined the origin of the craft?" Shek asked.

"A government contractor bought it from the Navy last year but reported it as stolen about a month ago. NCIS was looking into the incident, but the ASDS had previously been stripped of any top secret equipment so it wasn't a high priority."

Shek leaned forward and focused through his glasses. "And we have no idea who stole the vehicle or the top secret technology?"

"No sir," McBride said, "but in light of the report from the ICEX camp, we have to assume it may have been the Chinese."

"Or terrorists posing as Chinese."

"Yes, that's possible," McBride said as he shifted in his chair, "but most terrorist groups don't have the expertise to pull off this kind of heist."

"The Chinese do not, either. Not without help from a mole."

McBride fought to swallow. "The *Connecticut* received a transmission from the ASDS that indicates the Chinese are involved."

Shek sat up in his seat and cocked his ear.

McBride continued. "Commander Jackson believes it may be from Agent Jon Shay aboard the stolen craft. The agent sent a cryptic message that Chinese terrorists are planning to capture a Russian submarine."

"A submarine? Which one?"

"One of their latest, the *Khabarovsk*."

Shek brought an unsteady hand to his face. "Is this report credible? How could they do such a thing?"

"If it is credible, we have no idea how they might pull it off, or why."

Shek's face wrinkled with contemplative thought. "In light of this news, we need to be prepared to take immediate action if called for."

"Action, Mr. President?"

"Coming events cast their shadows before them," Shek said. "If those who stole the ASDS continue to cast darks shadows, they will leave us no choice."

Stress-induced bile churned in McBride's gut. "Shouldn't we let the Chinese and Russians battle this one out, sir?"

"The Chinese appear to have stolen a civilian vehicle that bears a U.S. flag. They may have attacked a naval facility on our soil and captured U.S. citizens while stealing our secrets. As such, this is also our battle."

"Understood, sir, but I recommend we at least try to communicate with the ASDS first."

Shek was silent for a few seconds and then said, "Very well. Order the *Connecticut* to close and attempt to communicate."

"Yes, Mr. President, but keep in mind the ASDS may already be in Russian territorial waters, in which case we risk an international incident if the *Connecticut* is discovered by the Russians."

"I will take care of the Russians. You focus on keeping that ASDS from harming our people or the *Khabarovsk*."

McBride stood. "Understood, Mr. President." He started to leave, stopped, and turned back around. "What are your intentions if the team aboard that ASDS turns out to be Chinese and they trigger an international incident?"

Shek reached for an ornament on his desk. It was a small carved figure of a Chinese soldier. "The Chinese emperor, Qin Shi Huang, was terrified of death. He ordered a team of alchemists to create for him the fabled elixir of life so he could live forever. Fearing for their own lives, they fooled Huang by giving him mercury pills that were supposed to make him immortal. The emperor died within a few months from mercury poisoning." Shek twirled the small figure with his fingers. "They carved an army of terracotta soldiers and buried them with the emperor as an epitaph."

Shek glanced up and stared at McBride. "If those responsible for stealing the ASDS trigger an international incident, there will be no epitaphs carved for our graves. There will be no graves. Only scorched sand where mankind once stood."

CHAPTER 14

While standing next to Bobby in the bow of the ASDS, Kate's legs weakened with fatigue and anxiety. She leaned against a nearby panel and tried to blink away the desire to curl up in a ball and cry herself to sleep. Although they had not detected any Chinese vessels since the near miss torpedo snapshot, everyone was still on edge.

"You okay?" Bobby whispered.

"Never better," Kate lied.

Rinaldo ignored the two and issued a command to Whitney, who'd taken over as the pilot. The Petty Officer acknowledged the order to zig-zag west toward Cape Vankarem and the projected position of the *Khabbie*, about ten miles off the coast. There, she ordered all stop. The mild vibration in the sub's deck declined and then ceased. An hour passed. The thin air in the cramped space turned sour with the scent of sweat and fear. Most of the sweat came from Liang's soldiers. Most of the fear came from her and Bobby.

"Pilot," Rinaldo said, "make turns for three knots and come to course zero-nine-five."

Whitney acknowledged the order.

"Away from the coast?" Liang said.

"The *Khabbie* will be headed in that direction," Rinaldo said. "Once we detect her, we'll need to close quickly. I want to approach from behind, in her baffles, where she can't hear us."

Liang nodded agreement.

Thirty minutes passed in silence.

Liang fumed and looked at Kate and Bobby. "Why do I have this feeling that we are not detecting the *Khabbie* because these two sabotaged the ROSS unit?"

A lump formed in Kate's throat.

"Patience," Rinaldo said. "I don't think they're suicidal. The *Khabbie* will be here soon."

Fifteen more minutes passed. Nothing happened. Liang paced from the bow of the craft to the aft section and then back again.

Finally, the ROSS unit beeped softly. Kate had turned down the audio volume to maintain silence.

All eyes focused on the unit. Nothing. Then another beep.

Rinaldo whispered to Kate. "Bearing?"

Kate glanced down at the ROSS unit's interface and whispered back. "Two-seven-four."

Rinaldo ordered Whitney to maneuver toward that bearing. The ROSS unit started beeping continuously. Bobby reached over and turned down the volume even more.

"*Khabbie* detected bearing two-seven-five," the ROSS unit said. "Range, 15,000 yards."

Rinaldo acknowledged the report and ordered the pilot to close the distance while maintaining a snail's pace to keep from being detected by the Russian sub.

At less than 4,000 yards, Rinaldo placed a palm on Whitney's shoulder. "All stop."

The ASDS slowed to a halt.

Rinaldo removed a phone from the pocket of her pants, tapped on the screen a few times, and then handed the device to Kate. "Program the ROSS unit to send these commands. Do not deviate."

Kate took the phone and stared at the screen. "Are you serious?"

"Very," Rinaldo said.

Kate handed the phone to Bobby. "Help me program this into ROSS."

Bobby took the phone, read the screen, and whispered, "This is insane."

"Just do it," Rinaldo said.

Kate worked with Bobby for five minutes to program the ROSS device to accept the commands. When finished, she said, "It's done."

"Instruct ROSS to send the commands," Rinaldo said.

Kate typed in the commands.

The ROSS unit executed the order.

Kate said, "It's done, but I can't verify it worked."

"You're an idiot," Bobby said to Rinaldo. His lips quivered. "You're slicing your own wrists and ours, too."

Rinaldo said, "Let's find out if I am."

"We don't have much time," Liang said.

Rinaldo instructed Kate to issue another set of commands to the ROSS unit. The device verified and then executed. Long seconds passed.

Chen glanced up and said, "The *Khabbie's* leveled off at four-hundred feet." Several more seconds elapsed. Chen said, "The propulsion system just went silent. She's slowing."

Rinaldo looked at Liang and smiled. The Chinese soldier smiled back and lightly slapped her on the back. Soldiers standing nearby silently pumped triumphant fists into the air.

Kate breathed a sigh of relief. Although she was not glad that Rinaldo's plan had worked, she was relieved that she and Bobby were still alive. The ROSS unit had successfully tapped into the *Khabbie's* AI and brought the craft deep enough to allow the ASDS to mate with a hatch. If it was too shallow, there would not be enough sea pressure to ensure an airtight seal. ROSS had also disabled the sub's propulsion system.

Kate knew there was no way Rinaldo could have gained access to the ROSS codes and commands needed to do this without inside help. Someone at the DoD or ARL had given Rinaldo the information. But who? Including her and Bobby, there were only a handful of people with that kind of access and knowledge.

"Now comes the real test," Rinaldo said. She turned to Petty Officer Chen. "Send a ping."

"You're crazier than a steer on steroids," Bobby said.

Rinaldo said nothing as Chen poised his finger over the active sonar button on the screen in front of his nose. His finger wavered.

"Send it," Rinaldo commanded.

Chen tapped the screen.

A ping echoed from the sonar stack and radiated away from the mini-sub. Rinaldo stood up straight and drew in a long breath. Liang squinted and focused his eyes on the sonar screen. Others in the bow, their jaws clinched, stood in silence and waited.

Nothing happened. Everyone stared at Chen, who sat motionless with his hands cupped about a set of headphones. A minute passed, then another.

Chen glanced up at Rinaldo and Liang, and then smiled.

Fists again pumped toward the overhead as smiles returned to faces.

Kate looked at Bobby. In his eyes, she saw what he likely recognized in hers: an equal measure of relief and fear. Rinaldo had verified that the ROSS unit had successfully hacked in to the *Khabbie's* AI control system and shut down the propulsion and sonar systems. The former had been verified when the Russian sub came to a full stop. The latter when Chen had sent an active sonar ping and the *Khabbie's* captain had not opened the sub's outer torpedo tube doors to fire on the ASDS. Kate was relieved they were still alive, but afraid her relief might be short- lived.

As Liang and his team headed toward the aft section of the craft to prepare for the next phase of their plan, Bobby leaned over and whispered into Kate's ear. "Now what?"

"I wish I knew, mate," Kate said. "I just hope we're involved."

"Why?" Bobby said.

"Because if we're not," Kate said, "we're dead."

CHAPTER 15

While cruising up Highway 97 in rural Maryland, Maria Estefan slammed an open palm against the steering wheel of her car. Her efforts to find out who had escorted the widow Margaret Cunningham to the event at the Hyatt in New York, and had likely tried to assassinate the president, had ended in frustration. The escort, who had used the fake name of Nathan Pender, had vanished after the event, like Houdini or David Copperfield. The man's identity had obviously been forged, and several database queries had turned up nothing.

Although agents had questioned Mrs. Cunningham, she was clueless and revealed little. Director Flannigan had ordered a few agents to continue searching for Pender, but as the threat had yet to be verified, the investigation had been given a lower priority as compared to other more imminent threats.

Maria returned to active duty, but as the assigned agents had made little progress, she decided to assist in the pursuit of the vanished escort on her off-duty time. Following the only lead she'd found so far, she pulled off the freeway, made several lefts and rights through a wooded suburban neighborhood, and pulled to the curb near the residence of a woman named Nan Ying.

The apartment building was nestled on a quiet street in a Maryland neighborhood called Severna Park. To ensure she did not alert Ying and cause her to run, Maria parked around the corner. The homes in the area were tall and slender and stood majestic against a light grey sky. The architects who'd designed these homes had done so when John F. Kennedy was president. They'd obviously viewed the world through the same rose-colored lens that had ushered in the Ozzie and Harriet show and *I Love Lucy*. Maria would not be surprised to find a quaint diner nearby with a jukebox playing old Elvis tunes and a beauty salon that still used those massive space helmets to dry your hair.

Maria stepped from her car. A cool wind lifted green leaves from the ground and tossed them down a cracked sidewalk. The fresh scent of spring clung to the breeze and reminded her of the coin-operated laundry near her childhood home. Every week her mom had saddled her up, along with her brother and sister, and orchestrated a family outing to the laundromat. Once inside, the clean smell of fabric softener had made her feel, at least for a while, like she wasn't brown trash in a trailer park. Like she wasn't a third-world Cuban wearing a dingy dress from Goodwill.

Maria dispensed the memory and thought about Nan Ying. She had learned Ying was a maid, and one of her clients was Margaret Cunningham. Ying had apparently referred Nathan Pender to Cunningham, leading Maria to suspect she may be an accomplice or might at least know where to find the possible assassin.

Maria's heels clicked on the concrete sidewalk as she strode toward the apartment complex. Down the street, children giggled as they glided up and down a driveway while riding atop noisy skateboards. She turned the corner and scanned the street. Ying's apartment complex consisted of one long rectangular brick building. A dozen dull red doors lined one side, each with a number above the peephole. In the parking lot, huddled near one of the doors, sat three police vehicles. An ambulance was parked in the lot. Red strobes atop the vehicles flashed non-stop. Neighbors stood nearby on the sidewalk, a collection of onlookers with curious and concerned faces.

Maria's pulse quickened. She strode forward until she reached Nan Ying's apartment door. Yellow tape blocked the entrance. A cop cut her off. He was a young guy in his late twenties with a peach fuzz chin. His tan pants were held up by a wide leather belt, off which dangled a nightstick, flashlight, and holster.

The officer held up a stop sign hand. "You need to stay back, ma'am." His voice carried a typical Maryland tone—a distinctive blend of polite southern and hurried northern.

Maria flashed her badge. "Secret Service. I need to speak with Nan Ying." The cop studied her badge and then said, "Wait here. I'll get the LT."

Maria watched him leave. She craned her neck to peer inside, but saw nothing but living room furniture and the bustling bodies of the forensics team. The officer returned. With him was an early-forties man with gray temples and a receding hairline. His beer gut lapped over his belt like a deflated inner tube. His nose had a kink, as if he'd spent his twenties in a boxing ring.

The LT ran his eyes up and down Maria's frame, sizing her up or maybe trying to confirm she wasn't a fraud with a fake badge. He held out a hand. "Sizemore."

"Estefan," Maria said as she shook his hand. "I need to speak with the lady of the house."

"Not possible," Sizemore said.

"I'm conducting an official investigation," Maria said.

"Still not possible," Sizemore said. "She's dead. Probably a ten-fifty-six."

Maria swallowed hard as she recognized the cop code for a suicide. "Probably?"

"It appears so," Sizemore said. "The coroner will confirm it...or not."

"Mind if I take a look around? It might help our investigation."

Sizemore stepped to one side and ushered a hand toward the small living room. "You know the drill. Look but don't touch. You contaminate anything and you're out. Understood?"

"Understood."

Sizemore handed her a set of latex gloves, a hair cover, and some booties. Maria pulled them on and walked into the apartment. The living room was about eight by eight and bordered a miniature kitchen. The place smelled like pine cleaner. The Berber carpet was dark beige filled with tiny specks of black and gray. The furniture consisted of a worn couch, two chairs, a coffee table, and a hutch that held an older model television. Either Ying was a real maid, Maria thought, or she'd done a damn good job of looking like one.

Maria approached the furniture and bent over to take a closer look. She ran her eyes up and down the length of the tan fabric on the couch. Two pillows had been placed on either end. There were no wrinkles on the cushions.

She left the living room, skirted a few white-suited forensics guys, and walked into the bedroom. A camera-sporting woman clicked off pictures while a man placed numbered placards in various locations. Nan Ying lay sprawled across the cover of the bed. Her eyes were open and stared at nothing. She appeared to be in her late forties with jet black hair trimmed short and neat. Her hands looked delicate and her fingernails manicured. A bottle of something rested on a nearby nightstand. The cap had been removed and placed to one side.

Probably sleeping pills, Maria thought. She surmised that just enough had been removed from the bottle to exceed LD100. Maria glanced about the room. The space was small, filled only by the one bed and a nightstand, and a small wooden dresser. No books. No reading glasses. No glass of water. No keys, money, or phone on the dresser. Only a medium-sized black purse.

Maria edged around the bed and peered into the open closet. A small collection of dresses, blouses, and trousers hung on assorted hangers. Less than a dozen shoes lined the floor. She stepped toward the bathroom and glanced inside. Again, minimalist contents.

Having seen enough, Maria walked back to the living room.

A tall African American in a blue suit with a red and white tie approached. He flipped open a badge wallet. "Agent Brad Tucker, NCIS."

Maria offered a slight nod but did not show her badge. "Agent Estefan, Secret Service."

"So I've been told," Tucker said. His suit was new, modest, and pressed to perfection. He had a buzzed haircut and square jaw and appeared to be about forty years old. His frame and demeanor hinted at a military background and a disciplined lifestyle that included long hours in the gym.

"Marine?" Maria guessed.

"I did some time with Dark Horse," Tucker said.

"I'm impressed," Maria said. The Dark Horse Battalion consisted of about 1,000 Marines and sailors from Camp Pendleton near Oceanside, California. The battalion had fought in dozens of major battles since World War I and had earned its name under the command of Col. Robert Taplett during the Korean War. More recently, it had enhanced its reputation by kicking some serious ass in Afghanistan.

Tucker smiled. "Just happened to be in the neighborhood?"

"I could ask you the same," Maria said.

"What do you say we compare notes?" Tucker said. "You know, part of that 'interdepartmental cooperation' thing we're supposed to be doing after nine-eleven."

Maria let herself smile. "Okay, deal. Why don't you go first?"

"You're not going to play nice, are you?"

Maria said nothing.

The agent motioned toward the door. "Let's get some coffee."

"Fine," Maria said. "You're buying."

Still smiling, Agent Tucker wagged his head as he pulled off his booties and left the apartment.

Once outside, Tucker said, "Starbucks, two miles, GPS it."

"See you there," Maria said.

Ten minutes later, she walked through the door of the Starbucks. The place smelled of rich French roast and bustled with millennials intent on keeping an all-day buzz. Tucker approached and handed her a cup of coffee. Maria took the cup and followed him to a table outside and away from prying ears. They sat.

"We've had Ying under surveillance for several weeks," Tucker said.

"Why?" Maria said.

"Tit for tat," Tucker said. He took a sip from his cup.

"We came across her name as part of another investigation," Maria said.

"Investigation of what?"

Maria smiled, said nothing.

"Damn," Tucker said. "You play some serious hardball." He sat silent for several seconds and then said, "We suspected Ying might be involved in foreign espionage related to sensitive U.S. Navy underwater intruder technology." Given the woman's Chinese nationality, Tucker didn't need to say which country.

"We suspected Ying was involved with a potential assassination plot," Maria said.

Tucker did not ask who the target might be. That was also a given. Either POTUS or someone in his circle. Tucker reached into his jacket pocket and removed a small notebook. He flipped it open and thumbed to a page. "Sleeping pills. Enough for LD100."

Just as Maria had surmised. She said, "Her eyes were still open, so she wasn't sleeping. No wrinkles in the couch. No books. No reading glasses. Almost no clothes. Soft hands. Manicured. Not a maid."

Tucker moved his head up and down slowly. "Agreed." He lifted his cup, took a sip, and then said, "Ambassador Chang. Any connections on your end?"

"Nope. Nathan Pender. Any connections on your end?"

Tucker lifted one eyebrow. "What's he to you?"

Maria took a gulp, studied the Starbucks logo on her cup, and then said, "Fake name, fake guy. Probably a Jackal."

The term Jackal was an interagency codename for an assassin. After the movie *The Day of the Jackal*, even civilians knew what it meant.

"We found Pender's name written on a pad in Ying's apartment," Tucker said. "The top sheet was missing but the next one had an imprint. Child's play."

Maria understood. Ying had jotted down the name, removed the top sheet, but had probably been in a hurry and had failed to remove the next few sheets. A child could have discovered the name simply by rubbing a pencil across the imprint.

"Mrs. Cunningham ring a bell?"

Tucker raised both eyebrows. "The Senator's widow?"

"The same. Ying was her maid and apparently referred Pender as a wheelchair pusher."

Tucker fingered his cup. He stared absently at a young couple as they glided into the coffee shop. Maria watched the two millennials laugh and flirt and act as if they had no cares in the world. Tucker's face registered the same feeling Maria had struggled with for decades: jealousy. She was jealous of anyone who was blissfully unaware. People who didn't know about all the bad guys out there who were hell-bent on whipping humanity into subservient cows. The terrorists, sickos, serial killers, and assassins like Nathan Pender. The only thing most people cared about was how much whip they could have on their caramel macchiatos.

Tucker's steel gray eyes stared at nothing. "Ambassador Chang is connected to Ying. Ying is connected to Pender. Pender gained access to Cunningham through Ying...."

Maria finished his sentence. "Pender used Cunningham to gain entry into the event where POTUS was having dinner with the Chinese president."

Tucker let out a soft whistle. "This is a lot bigger than just stolen Navy tech. We need to find Chang. The Chinese ambassador is starting to look like patient zero."

"No shit," Maria said. She gulped down the last of her coffee and grabbed her keys. "I'll drive."

CHAPTER 16

Aboard the *Connecticut*, Commander Jackson stood inside the small radio shack and read the communique he'd just received from COM-SUBFOR. He let out an exasperated breath and shook his head in disbelief. The encoded transmission had been relayed by Secretary of Defense McBride. The memo stated that the ASDS they had been tracking had been stolen from a government contractor a month earlier. This revelation was followed by an order: close in on the craft and prepare to send an active sonar ping but stay undetected. Furthermore, do not send the ping until instructed to do so.

Jackson did not fully understand or agree with the order. Given the quiet propulsion system used by the ASDS, he knew keeping contact would be extremely difficult for his sonar team. He also had little doubt that the mini-sub was already inside Russian territorial waters. That was one of the reasons why he disagreed with the order. He should have sent out an active warning ping earlier while they were still in international waters. If the Russians detected the *Connecticut* lurking near their coastline, he and his crew could end their day badly.

Jackson handed the yellow-lined memo to the radioman, turned, and stormed out of the shack. His soft black sneakers squeaked on the deck's shiny tile as he strode into the Conn. "This is the captain," he announced. "I have the Conn."

The officer of the deck turned over the Conn and stepped to one side. Jackson hovered near the helmsman and planesman stations, where two sailors in blue coveralls, planted in cushioned seats, studied digital display screens.

Jackson clicked an overhead mic. "Sonar, Conn, bearing and range to Master One?"

"Conn, Sonar, bearing to Master One is two-seven-five, range 10,000 yards."

"Sonar, Conn, aye."

Jackson strode over to the navigation table. A twenty-something quartermaster looked up from a chart on the table. Jackson leaned over the chart and ran his finger along the track laid down by the quartermaster. He said, "They've already crossed the line."

The quartermaster said, "Yessir, they're inside Russia's front yard."

Jackson grit his teeth. His orders had not stated whether he should cross into Russian waters. They'd only ordered him to maintain a track on the ASDS. Jackson knew any orders issued by COMSUBFOR would never state the obvious. There would never be any written evidence that clearly violated international law. There never was.

Jackson had ordered his crew to step across that line—set at twelve miles from a country's coastline—many times in the past to complete secret missions. He shuddered involuntarily as he thought about how many of those SpecOps, like WestPac Black, had resulted in near-death experiences.

He again keyed a mic. "Sonar, Conn, range, and bearing to the nearest ACTUV bot?"

Silence, then, "Conn, Sonar, the nearest ACTUV bot is 12,000 yards on bearing two-six- niner."

"Sonar, Conn, aye."

Jackson looked toward the diving officer, seated just behind the helmsman and planesman. "Diving Officer, set course two-seven-two, ahead one-third."

The diving officer repeated the order and then watched as the helmsman steered toward the new course. Jackson decided he'd split the difference and set a course in between the ASDS and the ACTUV bot. He didn't want to lose the ASDS, but he definitely wanted to get close enough to light off the nearest ACTUV, which had been dropped earlier by a P-8 Poseidon. He knew the technology was barely held together with bailing wire and bubblegum, but it might offer him the ability to maintain a track on the ASDS without getting close enough to give away the *Connecticut's* position.

Jackson had been briefed on the new ACTUV system, created by the Defense Advanced Research Projects Agency. DARPA's Distributed Agile Submarine Hunting program, or DASH as they called it, just might be the game changer he needed. Not too unlike a series of satellites orbiting the planet, DASH deployed small "subullites" loaded with the latest sonar systems endowed with long-range "Spock" ears. The versatile underwater satellites were unmanned, silent, and mobile.

Where satellites glanced downward, DASH subullites looked upward and outward from deep ocean locales and listened for the swish of submarine propellers, or in this case, the slight cavitation made by an ASDS propulsion system. The *Connecticut* needed to get close enough to the patiently waiting DASH so Jackson could take control and direct it toward a new mission: helping him track a stolen vessel.

Once activated, DASH systems deployed small "X-ship" robots to run after their prey like trained underwater hunting dogs. DARPA called these dogs ACTUV for Anti-Submarine Warfare Continuous Trail Unmanned Vessels. The unmanned battery-operated mini-subs could track a target and stay on its tail for days until its batteries ran out.

To accomplish this task, ACTUV robots were infused with a hint of artificial intelligence. Adding some AI ensured the robots could act independently while making smart decisions on-the-fly to stay on the trail of an enemy craft across miles of ocean. The ACTUV bots were programmed to interact with manned submarines or support units, transmit information and updates, take remote direction when needed, and avoid collisions—far beyond the capability of a pool-cleaning robot. Jackson had read that DARPA, in an effort to help the bot's AI systems learn the tactics necessary to accomplish their missions, had employed the services of a bunch of thirteen-year-olds.

Using an internet resource called crowdsourcing, which invites multitudes to provide feedback on innovative ideas, DARPA had created a website and posted an open invitation to computer game enthusiasts. Jackson smiled as he remembered the challenge: "Can you best an enemy submarine commander so he can't escape into the ocean depths?"

Gamers brave enough to try—most of them not yet in high school—downloaded the DARPA ACTUV tactics simulator called *Dangerous Waters*. By using the simulator, programmed with real-world evasion tactics that enemy vessels might employ, adolescent gamers tracked enemy subs, tested tactics and systems, and provided feedback to DARPA. Pimple-faced enthusiasts earned points for successfully completing missions and using effective techniques, with top scorers recognized on web leaderboards.

As his sub inched its way closer to Russian territorial waters, and closer to a robot he hoped would help them survive this mission, Jackson realized he was about to risk his life, and those of his crew, on an AI system that had been taught by a bunch of eighth graders.

CHAPTER 17

Aboard the ASDS, Jon's shoulders slumped. Feeling like his team had just thrown an interception, he leaned sideways and watched the crew silently cheering in the bow. Obviously, Rinaldo and Liang's grand plan, whatever that might be, was on track. At least for now. A few minutes later, Liang returned Kate and Bobby to the aft section and tie-wrapped them to the bench next to Jon. Despite their tenuous situation, the subtle scent of Kate's perfume and the warm feel of her body next to him on the bench made him feel alive again. Made him feel a glint of hope. He hadn't felt that in over a year. He hadn't felt anything except pain and sorrow.

Liang moved to the starboard aft section to speak with a soldier. Jon watched as they whispered to each other while being careful not to be seen by Rinaldo, who was still in the forward area of the craft. He strained to hear what the two were saying, but only caught a single word: *Kelly.*

Were they referring to Petty Officer Kelly, the sailor who'd likely been murdered aboard the *Connecticut?*

Kate leaned over and whispered into Jon's ear. "Rinaldo and Liang made us use ROSS to shut down the *Khabbie's* propulsion and sonar system."

"For how long?" Jon whispered back.

"An hour, give or take."

"With their propulsion out, the *Khabbie* can't send a radio burst."

"Right," Kate confirmed. "They need propulsion to get to periscope depth, so they can raise a mast and send a radio transmission."

"They must have also shut down the hull opening detectors on the ballast control panel," Jon said.

"How do you know that?" Kate said.

"Unless they disabled it, when they open the aft hatch, a light on the panel will indicate the hull breach."

"Right," Kate said. "Clever little bastards."

Liang finished speaking with the soldier and marched to the midsection of the mini-sub with a few of his men in tow. Jon watched as six of them prepared weapons and readied gear. He then overheard Rinaldo in the bow of the ASDS issue orders to the pilot to maneuver directly above the *Khabbie's* aft hatch.

Jon felt the ASDS lurch slightly as it moved closer to the Russian sub. The deck trembled while the mini-sub descended. He heard a dull whoosh as the ASDS settled onto the hardened steel deck of the *Khabbie*. He assumed the pilot had used the external cameras, mounted to the hull of the ASDS, to position the mini-sub above the *Khabbie's* aft hatch.

Two of Liang's men climbed into the diving chamber and shut the vertical hatch. Jon knew the ASDS, like most mini-subs, was designed to mate with the hull of a submarine and form an airtight seal over a hatch. Liang's men were obviously taking precautions to verify they had a tight seal before opening the hatch on the Russian sub.

Rinaldo flicked a switch on the mini-sub's control panel in the bow. An overhead speaker crackled to life. Jon assumed she had activated a two-way radio connection with Liang's team, so she could hear the operation in real time. Jon strained to hear the men in the chamber talk to one another via communication headsets as they entered the coupling area. He heard them report that they had verified the seal and were opening the ASDS hatch and then the sub's outer hatch.

Kate leaned over and whispered, "What are they doing?"

"Toga party," Jon whispered. He then explained that all modern submarine hatches conform to ISO standards to allow for rescue by any foreign craft in the event of an emergency. In fact, anyone equipped with a standard salvage tool kit could open a submarine hatch from the outside. In such a case, the crew aboard those subs would welcome the intrusion with open arms. In the current situation, they obviously would not.

"So how can Liang's men board the *Khabbie* without alerting the crew?" Kate asked.

"Good question," Jon replied.

As if listening to Jon and Kate's conversation, Liang answered the question by ordering two more men to "ready the gas." The soldiers lugged two canisters, about the size of standard SCUBA tanks, toward the diving chamber. They opened the hatch into the chamber and handed the tanks to the men inside. Listening to the sounds over the radio, Jon pictured a soldier spinning the T-wrench counterclockwise. He then heard clanking and talking and assumed they were prepping hoses from the canisters, which they planned to lower into the sub to gas the crew. Jon did not know if the gas would just put the crew to sleep or kill them. He heard dull hissing and assumed Liang's men were pumping gas from the tanks into the *Khabbie*.

Several minutes later, one of the men in the chamber said, "It's done. We detect no movement from below."

Liang's team would not be able to gas the entire sub, but only a localized area near the hatch. If other members of the crew were alerted in time, they would shut airtight hatches throughout the boat and don EAB air masks. Even though the AI system on the *Khabbie* made it possible to use a much smaller crew, Liang only had a handful of men. If they did not complete this part of the boarding without being detected, they might face several dozen angry and alert Russians when they moved to the forward compartments.

Liang ordered the rest of his team to don gas masks, grab their weapons and gear, and descend through the hatch. Over the ASDS speaker, Jon heard Liang say he was switching his mic to auto-transmit mode, so Rinaldo could hear everything as it happened in real time.

Jon heard and visualized the next few moves by Liang and his team. The sounds sped up his breathing as they triggered memories of similar missions he'd completed. One by one Jon heard Liang's soldiers enter the submarine's escape trunk—a small chamber about eight feet in diameter with hatches on either end. Via the open mic, he also heard the whine and whir of electronic equipment, powered by the *Khabbie's* massive nuclear reactor. When he heard the soldiers descend another ladder below the trunk and enter the submarine, his palms moistened at the thought of what might lay ahead.

Over the mini-sub's speaker, Jon discerned the sound of boots tapping softly on a tile deck as Liang's team moved away from the escape trunk and headed toward the aft section. Liang whispered that his team was traversing through the reactor alley and approaching the *Khabbie's* engine room. So far, the sub's crew in the area had been rendered unconscious by the gas. Muffled by a mask, Liang's voice sounded strange, like something out of an old science fiction movie.

Kate whispered, "They didn't kill the crew."

Jon exhaled, but his relief vanished when he heard Russian voices over the speaker. He wanted to warn the unsuspecting submariners. To do something, anything, to save them from what he knew was about to happen. He was powerless to do anything except listen to the inevitable.

Three gunshots rang out. Jon recognized the pop of AK-74s fired by Liang's team. Rinaldo leaned toward the microphone in the bow and asked

Liang for an update. No answer. More shots. Rinaldo blurted out another excited query. Still no response.

Liang finally gave an update. "The gas did not get everyone. Some of them donned EAB masks in time. They tried to attack us as we entered. We had no choice. We had to subdue them."

Jon fumed in silence. By "subdue," he knew Liang meant "kill."

Kate lowered her head. "Bloody hell."

Rinaldo said, "Did you damage anything?"

"No," Liang said. "My men are excellent shots."

Jon craned his head and watched Rinaldo's face turn white. She said, "No one was supposed to be harmed."

Liang said, "We must move quickly. Other crewmen likely heard the shots."

"Go," Rinaldo replied. Under her breath, away from the microphone, she said, "Shit, shit, shit."

Over the speaker, Jon heard Liang bark orders. Clicks and clanks and voices floated from the speaker in the ASDS as the soldiers readied equipment. Jon suspected they were rigging up more tanks to gas the remaining crew.

A few minutes later, Liang gave another update. "The gas is being distributed via the ventilation system. We are heading toward the GKP."

Rinaldo said, "You have thirty minutes to get there before the AI system can override ROSS and take back control."

"Understood," Liang replied.

Rinaldo wiped a bead of sweat from her brow. She tapped Petty Officer Whitney on the shoulder and said, "Do you have the device?"

Whitney reached into his pocket and removed something that resembled a garage door opener.

"Good," Rinaldo said. "You know the drill. If I give you the order, or if something goes wrong, light it off. Understood?"

"Understood," Whitney said.

While listening to Liang's men move toward the *Khabbie's* GKP—the equivalent of the control room on a NATO sub—Jon wondered what Rinaldo had ordered Whitney to "light off" in the event something went wrong. A self-destruct timer? If so, Jon hoped that he, Kate, and Bobby would be aboard the *Khabbie* and not the ASDS when Whitney pushed that button.

CHAPTER 18

Outside the Starbucks, while sitting in Maria's car, Agent Tucker tapped his phone and dialed a colleague at the FBI. Maria's moved her foot up and down rapidly as she listened to Tucker twist an arm to get Ambassador Chang's mobile phone GPS location. Tucker nodded a few times, agreed he owed the guy one, and then disconnected.

"He's at the Westin in Georgetown," Tucker said. "He arrived about an hour ago."

Maria started the engine and sped from the curb. "How is Chang connected?" She wasn't necessarily expecting an answer. Instead, she was hoping her question might prompt an exchange of ideas that could lead to one.

Tucker stared out the side window in silence and then asked, "Who was Pender hunting?"

"POTUS, most likely," Maria said as she sped through a yellow light.

Tucker turned toward her. "What's his connection to Chang? Is he working for the Chinese?"

"Nan Ying, our fake maid, is connected to Chang. She brought in Pender. Odds are he's their guy."

The setting sun splashed orange beams of fading light across Tucker's forehead. "Then why have him take out POTUS? The Chinese want this accord. If POTUS is out of the picture, the deal unravels."

Maria said nothing as she churned the facts in her head. They drove for a time in silence, then she slammed on her brakes to keep from running a red light. "Shit, I almost ran it."

"Relax," Tucker said. "We're almost there."

The light turned green. Maria hit the gas and said, "Maybe the Chinese changed their mind and don't want to do the deal anymore. Maybe they decided to take out POTUS to save face or force the U.S. into a worse deal."

Tucker frowned. "Way too many variables they can't control. If POTUS goes down, they plunge the U.S. into chaos. Then any plans the Chinese might have are a crapshoot at best."

"Maybe that's what they want," Maria said as she turned toward the front of the hotel. "Maybe they want chaos to keep the U.S. distracted long enough for them to gain a stronger hold on the South China Sea. They've been building sand islands there for years. Maybe this is a right-hand left-hand kind of thing."

"Or maybe their target wasn't POTUS."

Maria pulled in front of a Westin valet attendant and put the car in park. "If not POTUS, then who?"

"You're the Secret Service agent," Tucker said. "You tell me."

"I wish I could," Maria said. She thought for a moment and then said, "How is all this connected to stolen U.S. Navy underwater intruder technology?"

"No idea," Tucker said. "It could be a decoy, but that doesn't make much sense. Maybe we can shake some answers out of Chang."

"Maybe." Maria opened the door and stepped out. She took a ticket from the attendant and followed Tucker into the Westin. The lobby was plush and smelled of potpourris and aftershave. Light classic rock filtered from the overhead speakers and a fire crackled in a brick fireplace set against a far wall. A small group of businessmen, dressed in expensive suits, exchanged handshakes and headed toward the lobby door. A half-dozen travelers stood in line at the front desk. Their shoulders were slumped and their eyes bloodshot.

Tucker bypassed the line, strode toward the front desk, and flashed his badge. "Can I speak with a manager?"

A young girl behind the counter scurried through a door to her right. She emerged ten seconds later with a Chinese man close behind. His hair was black with hints of gray sprinkled throughout. Age lines around his eyes made him look about forty-five.

He pointed to a spot on the far side of the lobby, away from sensitive ears. He ignored Maria and held out a hand toward Tucker. "My name is Lee Ung. How may I help you?"

Ung's tone was laced with an accent, but it was mild. He'd obviously lived in the U.S. for some time.

Maria stepped forward, flashed her badge, and said, "Chinese Ambassador Chang is staying in your hotel. We have reason to believe he is in imminent danger. We need his room number immediately."

Ung took a step backward. "Without a search warrant, I cannot divulge the room number for any guest."

"We're not here to search his room," Tucker said. He held up his badge and glanced toward Maria. "My colleague is with the Secret Service and I'm with the Naval Criminal Investigative Service. As she said, we believe the Ambassador is in immediate danger. At the very least, we need you to escort us to his room so we can ensure his safety."

Ung stared at his shoes in silence.

Maria pictured a dozen hamsters in cages running around inside Ung's head as he struggled with a decision. She glanced at her watch and then leveled a stern glare at the hotel manager. "If the Ambassador is killed before we get there, it'll be on you."

Ung threw up his hands in defeat and said, "I am not certain that he is in his room."

"Where is he?" Maria asked.

Ung pointed toward the restaurant. "I saw one of his bodyguards about thirty minutes ago. He was going into the cafe. I did not see Ambassador Chang, but it is possible he may have gone in there as well."

Tucker looked at Maria. "I'll take the restaurant, you take the room. Whoever gets eyes on first sends a text."

Maria looked at Ung and motioned toward the elevator. "Let's go."

Tucker walked toward the restaurant while Maria followed Ung to the elevator bank. The Chinese manager pressed an Up button. The elevator door opened, and they stepped inside. Ung pressed the button for the ninth floor.

As the door shut, Ung said, "I could be fired for this."

"We'll make sure that doesn't happen," Maria lied.

A bell rang, and the door opened.

Maria unholstered her Glock and whispered, "Stay behind me."

Ung held the elevator door open with one hand and motioned for Maria to exit with the other. "I'm a hotel manager, not a SWAT guy." He handed Maria a plastic card. "Here is the master key. Chang is in suite nine fifteen to the right."

Maria took the keycard. She gripped her Glock, held her hands forward, and stepped out of the elevator. The carpet was soft and beige with specks of light brown here and there. Her chest expanded and contracted as she tiptoed toward the room. She didn't actually believe Chang's life was in danger, but she wanted answers and the Ambassador was her only lead.

She turned a corner and froze. Near the end of the corridor, in front of Chang's suite, stood two large Chinese men dressed in business suits. The Ambassador's bodyguards. They turned toward her and unholstered weapons.

Maria held up her badge as she walked forward. "United States Secret Service. Lower your weapons."

One of the men grunted. With a thick accent, he said, "You first."

Maria let out a sigh and holstered her Glock.

The two guards held their guns steady with the barrels pointed sideways. The pistols were Type 17s, cheap Chinese knockoffs of the Mauser C96. The Type 17 had once been the preferred sidearm of China's military, where soldiers were taught to hold the guns sideways using a grip they called "bandit shooting." The technique helped to counter the Mauser's awkward, upward cartridge ejection.

Maria took a few more steps forward and held her badge up higher. "Which one of you assholes wants to go to prison for five years?"

The two guards looked at each other, shrugged, and holstered their weapons.

Maria stepped near the door. The behemoths moved closer together to block the entrance. Obviously, a Pavlov's Dog reaction to a potential intruder.

Maria pocketed her badge and said, "I need to speak with the Ambassador. His life may be in danger."

Maria had studied some Chinese history during her training and the big guy on the left reminded her of Emperor Hongwu, who was famous for murdering anyone he perceived to be a threat. Hongwu glanced at the other guard and then back at Maria. "He ask not to be disturb." His accent was so thick that Maria felt like she was watching a bad B-flick.

"Is the Ambassador with someone?" Maria asked.

The two giants exchanged uncomfortable glances.

"We no say," the other guy said. He had a stern, evil look that conjured the word Mogwai in Maria's mind—a Cantonese term that means "evil spirit."

"What if the person he's with is about to kill him?" Maria implored.

Hongwu puffed out his chest. "You no go in."

"Let me guess," Maria said. "He's with a hooker, right?"

Mogwai took a step backward toward the door. "No one go in."

"I was afraid you were going to say that," Maria said under her breath.

She lowered her head, as if in defeat, and ran splayed fingers through her hair. She stood up straight and turned slightly, as if planning to leave.

She stepped to her left, toward the elevator, and then stopped and turned back. She held up a finger, like she was about to ask another question.

Before Hongwu's tiny brain had time to register the deception, Maria arched her right leg and whacked the big guy in the groin with her foot. He bent over, grabbed his crotch, and gasped for air. Tears welled up in his eyes and a whimpering gurgle escaped from his lips, along with a stream of saliva. He dropped to his knees. Maria leaned over, parted his jacket, and removed his Type 17. She tossed the gun down the corridor and then turned toward Mogwai.

Standing over his colleague, his face registering shock and then anger, Mogwai curled his long fingers and formed two meaty fists. Maria leaned back and pivoted out of the way as Mogwai's right fist missed her nose by a centimeter. Connecting with nothing but air, the giant stumbled long enough for Maria to line up an elbow. She smacked the man hard across his cheek. Blood drooled from Mogwai's mouth. He went down on one knee while cradling his damaged face with both hands, like he was praying for forgiveness.

Certain that Mogwai was only down for a short count, Maria twisted her hips and drove a heel into Mogwai's forehead, followed by a wheelhouse from her other foot against his right temple. Blood sprayed in an arc across the carpet as Mogwai teetered while using one arm to brace himself against the door. Before Mogwai had time to recover, Maria flattened her right hand and drove it straight into the center of the man's neck, right below his Adam's apple. The blow left him bug-eyed and gasping for air as his face rocketed toward the carpet.

Game over.

Maria stood and walked toward the fallen Mogwai. She reached a hand toward his jacket to remove his Type 17. She never made it. A massive hand grabbed her from behind, whirled her around, and slammed her hard against a wall. The impact forced the air from her lungs and left her dazed and unsteady. Before she could clear her head, a massive fist connected with her left cheek and sent her sprawling toward the carpet. Tears flooded her eyes and her face throbbed with pain. The metallic taste of blood filled her mouth.

Maria squinted as she looked up. Hongwu stood over her like a mad bull poised to charge. His face red, his fists curled, he evidently had bigger balls than she'd given him credit for. She tried to move, but her body refused to cooperate. She lay frozen on the ground in a lump of pain and confusion. Hongwu took a step forward and then rammed the toe of his boot into her side. The blow rolled her over and flung her against a wall. She heard a rib crack.

Maria spat out a clump of blood and curled up in agony. "Fuck me."

While cradling his battered balls, Hong stepped away and craned his neck to and fro. He was searching for his Type 17. She focused on a spot down the corridor where she'd flung the man's pistol. The guard saw it about the same time she did. As Hong hobbled toward the Type 17, Maria reached for her Glock. Her fingers felt numb and useless.

She pulled out her sidearm and then fumbled it onto the carpet.

Hong leaned over and reached for the Type 17.

Wheezing and dazed, with her sight blurred by pain, Maria searched for her Glock.

Hong picked up his pistol and turned toward Maria.

She felt cold steel and snatched her gun off the carpet.

Hong aimed the Type 17.

Maria curled her finger around the trigger of her Glock.

Hong's finger twitched.

Maria lifted her gun as high as she could and yelled, "Xiūzhàn!" It was one of the few Chinese words she knew. It meant "truce."

Hong's finger stopped mid-squeeze. His face turned red and then cooled to a fleshy pink. He flashed a brief nod. "Xiūzhàn."

"We must save the Ambassador," Maria said. "The hooker may be an assassin."

With his Type 17 turned sideways and pointed at Maria's head, Hong moved toward the door. He removed a plastic card from his pocket and beep-opened the door.

Maria holstered her Glock and then forced herself to a sitting position. While clutching her bruised side, she braced one hand on a wall and slowly stood. She hobbled toward the door and entered the room. Soft jazz floated across waves of chilled air as she entered. The light scent of lavender mingled with the smell of leftover room service. Maria heard the muffled sound of a woman's laugh float in from behind a closed door. Then she heard a man bark something in Chinese.

Hong holstered his gun and replied in Mandarin. Maria surmised the guard had just informed the Ambassador that his rented girlfriend was about to kill him. The two argued for a minute until Ambassador Chang emerged from a side room, draped in a starched white hotel robe.

Maria grimaced as she reached into her jacket and removed her badge. "Sorry to disturb you, Ambassador, I'm with the U.S. Secret Service. We have reason to believe your life is in danger."

Chang spoke in English and said, "This is preposterous. You cannot come into my room like this!"

Maria rolled her eyes. "I don't have time for this." She pocketed her badge, removed her Glock, and pointed it at Hong. "Drop your weapon."

Startled, Hong reached for his Type 17.

"Slowly," Maria said.

Hong opened his jacket, gripped the Type 17's stock with his thumb and forefinger, and then dropped it onto the carpet.

"What is going on here?" Chang said.

"Shut up," Maria said. She glared at Hong. "Kick it over to me."

Hong kicked. Maria grimaced as she reached out a foot and dragged the Type 17 toward her. She kicked it further away and said to Hong, "Sit down in that chair by the lamp."

"I demand to know—" Chang started.

Maria cut him off. "I said, shut the hell up."

An American girl, no older than twenty-five, emerged from the bedroom. Her eyes were wide and she was half-naked. She glanced at the Glock in Maria's hand and said, "I'm outta here."

Realizing she hadn't had time to text Tucker, Maria said, "I'm with the Secret Service. You can leave, but I need you to find a federal agent named Tucker in the restaurant and send him up here now. Deal?"

The girl nodded and scampered out of the room.

Chang started to argue again until Maria held up a hand. She motioned for Hong to sit while she bent over and pulled the lamp cord out of the wall socket. She pulled a knife from her pocket and cut the cord loose from the lamp. She handed the cord to Chang and told him to tie up Hong. She double-checked the knots and then whacked her Glock against Hong's right temple. His eyes rolled upward before he passed out and slumped in the chair.

"I will have you punished for this," Chang said.

"Before or after you kill the President of the United States?"

Chang's eyes widened. "You are insane!"

"Obviously," Maria said. She motioned for Chang to return to the bedroom, whereupon she shoved him into the bathroom. In one corner sat an oval tub. The thing was huge and lined with green marble etched with gold fancy swirls. It looked like something once used by Roman royalty.

Maria pointed at the tub. "Get in."

"I will not!" Chang said as he crossed his arms.

Maria wobbled closer and pointed her Glock. "Get in."

Chang muttered something in Chinese as he walked over to the tub. Without removing his robe, he climbed in.

"Sit down," Maria said.

Chang obeyed.

"All the way down, with your head below the faucet."

While grumbling in defiance, Chang complied.

Maria pulled a white hand towel from a rack. She sat on the edge of the tub and said, "Have you ever heard of waterboarding?"

Chang's eyes flung open. "You will not!"

"I will, unless you answer my questions."

Shaking like a frightened child, lying flat in the tub, Chang said, "What questions?"

"I warn you," Maria said. "If you lie I'll know, and I'll be forced to torture you. Understood?"

Chang nodded.

"Good. First question, you used Nan Ying to hire Nathan Pender to assassinate the President. Why?"

"No," Chang said. "I did not hire anyone to kill the President."

"Wrong answer," Maria said. She reached over and turned on the cold water. It splattered onto Chang's face. He swiveled his head back and forth to deflect the frigid gush. Maria soaked the hand towel and shoved it into Chang's mouth.

The ambassador gagged and coughed and pulled the towel out. "You cannot do this to me!"

Maria turned off the water. "Answer my question truthfully."

Spitting out water, Chang said, "Okay, okay I will tell you. We uncovered a rogue military operation that will harm China and disrupt the accord. I informed your president through a back channel, but he did not do anything, as far as I know. I later learned an assassin had been hired, but I do not know who hired him."

"Who was the target?"

Chang did not reply. Maria slapped the wet towel against the edge of the tub.

Chang closed his eyes. "The target was the Secretary of Defense."

"SECDEF? Why him?"

Chang's eyes opened slowly. His cheeks dripped water and his face reflected defeat. "Perhaps because of his plan."

Maria stood and paced. It was her way of processing information. "What plan?"

Chang licked his wet lips. "We do not know. All we know is that he enlisted a very dangerous man, a former American Army Ranger who is not as he appears."

Maria stopped pacing. "Explain."

Chang coughed out some water. "We discovered the plan by luck. We had captured a Falon Gong zealot who revealed this Ranger's identity. When we tried to find the Ranger, we discovered he had been recruited for a secret mission instigated by George McBride."

"Son of a bitch," Maria said. "What's the Ranger's name?"

Chang said nothing. Maria sat down, reached over and turned on the water. Chang squinted and remained silent as the water splashed across his face.

"Last chance," Maria said.

Chang cocked his head in defiance.

"Have it your way," Maria said. She wadded up the towel and shoved it into Chang's mouth. Before she could lower his head under the water, she heard a man's voice ring out behind her.

"Stop."

Chang spat out the towel and sprang upward. His face filled with fear. Maria turned her head. A nondescript middle-aged man of average height stood near the bathroom door. He was wearing a black jumpsuit and gloves. His right hand held a Browning nine-millimeter handgun fitted with a silencer.

"Nathan Pender," Maria said.

"Ms. Estefan," Pender said. "Give me your gun."

Maria unholstered her Glock and laid it on the bathroom floor. She kicked it toward Pender. The assassin picked up the gun, pointed it at Chang, and fired one round. The boom echoed off the bathroom walls like a cannon in a cave. With her ears ringing and her heart thudding, Maria slowly turned her head and watched Chang slump into the tub. A red hole formed in the middle of his forehead. Blood oozed from the hole and dripped onto the white porcelain.

"Holy shit," Maria said. Still in shock, she turned back toward Pender. She stared at the smoking barrel of the Glock and then closed her eyes. She waited for the next boom, but nothing happened.

Maria opened her eyes. Pender walked over and knelt beside her. He smiled. "I must admit, I'm impressed. At the risk of losing your job, and maybe even your pension, you stubbornly followed the breadcrumbs."

"Left by you I presume," Maria said.

Pender's eyes were like those of a shark. Piercing, laconic, dark. "I can neither confirm nor deny."

"You led me here so you could what, kill me?"

"Have you heard of the Poison Garden of Alnwick?" Pender said.

Maria said nothing, wondering just how many screws were loose in Pender's head.

"It's located in Great Britain," Pender continued. "The Duchess of Northumberland created the garden. She was inspired by the poison gardens found in Padua during the sixteenth century, wherein the famous Medici bankers grew poisonous plants to plot the frothing demise of their enemies."

"Are you going somewhere with this?" Maria said.

Pender reached into a pocket and removed a rectangular leather case, about the size of a large wallet. "The garden is nestled among fourteen acres of water sculptures, cherry blossoms, a labyrinth of bamboo plants, and a huge treehouse."

While keeping his gun pointed at Maria, Pender opened the case and removed a small glass vile. "It contains over one hundred carefully curated plants that can stimulate, intoxicate, and if so desired, assassinate." Pender removed a small syringe and inserted it into the glass vile.

Maria shuddered.

"After visiting the garden one summer," Pender said, "I had an epiphany."

The nondescript man filled the syringe from the vile, held it vertical, and pushed on the plunger until a small drop oozed from the tip of the needle. "I traveled to Nepal and discovered a fascinating liquor called Jaad-rakshi. I combined it with another elixir I created after my visit to the gardens, which is actually quite tasty with pineapple juice."

Pender motioned for Maria to roll up her sleeve. She did not move.

"Suit yourself," Pender said. He leaned over and jabbed the needle through the white cotton. It plunged deep into the flesh of her upper arm. The liquid burned as it entered her bloodstream. She wondered how long it would take for her to die. More importantly, how long she'd suffer before Pender's concoction finally ended her pain.

Pender said, "A small dose acts like the world's most powerful truth serum. A larger dose...."

A shrill whistle filled Maria's ears. Her head spun and she felt dizzy, as if balancing on a thin wire high above the ground. Her vision blurred and her mouth numbed, as though she'd been injected with a large dose of Novocain.

"What did Chang tell you?" Pender asked.

Unable to control her tongue, Maria told him what little she knew.

"What does the Secret Service or NCIS know about me?"

Maria again divulged what she knew.

"What do you know about the plot perpetrated by your government that Chang mentioned?"

Devoid of any will to resist, Maria divulged what Chang had told her about the SECDEF and the Ranger.

"Have you called anyone and told them anything?"

Maria uttered an uncontrolled response. "No."

"Good. You did well. Now you can sleep."

Maria's eyelids sagged. Her head wobbled. She thought she heard a clicking sound, but her ears were flooded by high-pitched whistling. She tried to focus on Pender, but he was no longer there. She wondered where he'd gone and why he wasn't asking her any more questions.

With her ears ringing, her sight blurred, and her head spinning, Maria's body went limp. As the last flicker of life left her tired and battered body, she wished she had lived long enough to tell Tucker what she knew.

CHAPTER 19

Jon listened to the sounds coming from the speaker in the bow of the ASDS as Liang's team crept toward the GKP on the *Khabbie*. He could hear steady breathing and soft footsteps, now and then eclipsed by a mild grunt as the soldiers stepped through a hatch on the sub.

"So far, they're all down," Liang said, referring to the sub's crew.

The gas had been effective.

"Good," Rinaldo said. "How much farther?"

"One more compartment," Liang said.

The footsteps went silent. The breathing sped up. A spatter of shots rang out, followed by dull thuds.

"Liang?" Rinaldo said.

No answer.

"Status," Rinaldo demanded.

Still nothing.

Rinaldo wiped away a bead of sweat. She strode from one side of the control panel to the other.

Finally, Liang responded. "Four of the crew had donned EABs. We had to take them out."

Rinaldo shook her head from side to side. "Shit, shit, shit."

Anger again welled up inside of Jon's chest. If he was lucky enough to survive the day, he'd put a bullet in Liang's forehead. They weren't at war with Russia, and those sailors did not deserve to die.

"Get to the GKP," Rinaldo said. "We're running out of time."

"We're on our way," Liang said, his voice muffled by the gas mask.

Long minutes passed before the speaker crackled again. "We have secured the GKP."

Rinaldo pumped a triumphant fist into the air. She keyed the mic. "Start preparing the evac. We're heading over now."

"Roger that," Liang said.

Rinaldo walked toward the bench with Petty Officer Whitney in tow. She told him to untie Kate and Bobby and have them unhook the ROSS device and prepare for egress.

Bobby said, "We're going over there?"

Rinaldo pointed at the diving chamber. "You're not staying here."

"Can I pee first?" Bobby said. Obviously frightened, his voice warbled in and out of falsetto.

Rinaldo glanced at Whitney. "Let him use the head, get the ROSS, and then get moving. We're behind schedule." She walked back up to the bow and started flicking switches on the control panel. Petty Officer Chen and one of the soldiers entered the diving chamber. Jon heard clanking as they descended into the belly of the Russian submarine.

Whitney cut Bobby's tie wraps and escorted him to the head, a small rectangular box in the aft corner that resembled a restroom on an airplane. Bobby stepped inside. Whitney came back to the bench and cut Kate's tie wrap.

She stood and rubbed her wrists. "Why are you taking us over to the *Khabbie*?"

"Ask Rinaldo," Whitney said. "She's in charge."

"I will," said Kate. Her tone was unsteady. Jon could tell her false bravado was starting to wane.

"What about me?" Jon said.

"Don't know," Whitney said. "Ask Rinaldo."

"Is there anything you *do* know, Petty Officer Whitney? Like how many years you're going to spend in prison?"

"I'm not going to prison," Whitney said. "I'm getting a medal."

"For committing treason?" Jon said.

"You got it all wrong, big guy," Whitney said.

"Enlighten me," Jon said.

Whitney wagged his head. "I can't. Ask Rinaldo."

Anger heated Jon's forehead. "You better hope I never escape."

"You won't," Whitney said as he watched Bobby step out of the head. He pushed the engineer toward the bow. "You and the lady have five minutes to unhook the ROSS unit."

"Aye, aye Captain Bligh," Bobby said as he offered a salute.

"Move," Whitney said.

Jon watched the three walk toward the bow. Rinaldo returned and motioned for the remaining soldier to cut Jon's tie wrap. The young Chinese commando had short black hair and a scar on his left cheek. Although he appeared to be in his early thirties, the lines on his face, likely carved by years of combat, made him look much older.

Rinaldo walked back up to the bow, presumably to check on Kate and Bobby's progress. The soldier leaned over, cut Jon's ties, and then shoved the knife back into a scabbard strapped to his leg.

"What's your name?" Jon said, hoping to pry some information out of the man.

The soldier did not reply.

"I'm Jon."

The soldier stared at Jon for a long moment and then said, "I'm Sam."

He had no discernible accent.

Jon said, "Where'd you learn to speak English?"

"I'm from San Francisco," Sam said.

"I thought you were from China."

Sam motioned for Jon to stand up from the bench. "We're done talking."

Jon stood.

Kate and Bobby returned from the bow with the ROSS device inside its black case. Only six of them now remained aboard the ASDS: Jon, Kate, Bobby, Rinaldo, Whitney, and Sam from San Francisco.

Rinaldo looked at Whitney and Sam. "We'll go over two at a time so we can keep an eye on our guests. I'll escort Kate. Whitney, you take Bobby. Sam, you take Jon. Got it?"

Rinaldo grabbed Kate by the arm and directed her toward the chamber. Sam watched as they disappeared through the hatch. Jon glanced at the knife in the scabbard strapped to Sam's leg. He knew it was now or never. Guided by years of training, he dove for the knife.

Sam was also trained. His head turned in Jon's direction. He instinctively reacted to prevent the attack. Jon's hand brushed against the cold steal of the knife handle. Sam's leg moved away. Jon's fingers missed. He reached again, backhanded the knife, and pulled it free. He gripped the handle and thrust it upward just as Sam lunged toward him. The sharp blade slit open Sam's throat. His eyes flung open with shock as he reached for his neck. Blood spurted from the wound and coated Jon's shirt.

His eyes wide, Whitney reached for the Beretta M-9 pistol on his belt. Jon spun on a heel and landed a roundhouse kick in the middle of Sam's writhing body. The dying soldier flew toward Whitney. Two booms rang out as Whitney pulled the trigger. Sam's body jerked and shuddered with each shot. Jon turned sideways in time to watch two projectiles whiz past his face. The bullets had been slowed and redirected when they passed through Sam's body. They hit the bulkhead with a clank but did not penetrate the hull.

Blood from Sam's body flew into the air and splattered onto the deck. Jon heard Rinaldo yell from inside the chamber. Whitney did not respond as he pushed Sam's body away and tried to aim again in Jon's direction. Jon flipped the knife ninety degrees and gripped the tip with his fingers. As Sam's body fell to the floor, he saw the M-9 in Whitney's hand. Saw the smoke billowing from the heated barrel. Saw Whitney aim the gun at his chest.

Jon hurled the knife. The silver blade flashed in the fluorescent light. The carved metal plunged into Whitney's chest. He grunted and doubled over. The gun fell from his hand and rattled onto a metal grate. Bobby let out a shriek as Whitney's body toppled over and hit the deck. Rinaldo yelled again. No one answered.

Jon heard a clank as Rinaldo slammed shut the bottom hatch on the chamber. Then he heard a beep.

Bobby stopped blubbering and looked up. "Oh, crap."

Jon raced toward the chamber and stepped inside. He grabbed hold of the wheel atop the bottom hatch and yanked it to the left. It did not budge. He tried again. No movement. Again. Nothing. Rinaldo had obviously jammed a bar or something into the hatch wheel on the other side to prevent it from opening. Jon exited the chamber.

Bobby was standing on the deck, frozen in place. "Oh, crap," he said again.

Jon reached over and squeezed the man's shoulder. "What's the problem?"

"The beep."

"What beep?"

"Whitney," Bobby said. He pointed toward Whitney's dead right hand. "Just before he died, he pressed a button on that device."

Jon recognized the device Whitney had showed Rinaldo earlier.

"I bet it's a self-destruct device," Bobby said. "I think the ASDS is about to blow."

Something clanked. The ASDS shuddered slightly and then tilted about ten degrees to one side.

"Double crap," Bobby said. "That device must have also detached the ASDS from the *Khabbie*.

"How long do we have?" Jon said.

Bobby's eyes looked like high beams on an eighteen-wheeler. Jon visualized a billion neurons firing in his brain as the scientist did a mental calc.

"Based on the probable speed of the *Khabbie*, I'd say about twenty minutes," Bobby said. "They would have set it for at least that long so it wouldn't harm the Russian sub."

"Then we need to locate the explosive bundle ASAP," Jon said as he moved toward the bow. "Odds are it's in the bow. That's where Rinaldo and Whitney were when I overheard them talking about it."

"You heard them talking about blowing up the mini-sub?" Bobby said as he followed Jon into the control area.

"At the time I wasn't sure what they were talking about. Now I am." Jon pointed to his right. "You take the starboard side, I'll take port."

Bobby knelt and started looking and feeling through every inch of the control area. Together they opened every locker, compartment, and panel and searched for any dangling wires, out-of-place boxes, or a digital timer counting backwards.

Nothing. They searched again. Still nothing.

"Let's move toward the stern," Jon said.

Bobby rubbed at his eyes.

"You okay?" Jon said as he opened a locker and searched.

"Yeah," Bobby said. "Actually, no. I never thought I'd die like this." He looked at his watch. His hand was shaking. "Fifteen minutes until we're shark food."

"We're not shark food yet," Jon said. "Get your head out of your sorry ass and keep looking." Jon realized his tone was rough. His intent wasn't to be mean, but rather to keep Bobby focused so they could stay alive.

Bobby opened a locker, searched, and slammed it shut. Then another and another. On the fourth try he let out a shrill whistle. "Shit howdy. I found it."

Jon walked over to the open panel. Wires and ducting ran horizontally along the bulkhead. To the right sat a small metal box with a timer strapped to a wad of C-6 explosive.

"Can you disarm it?" Jon said.

Bobby examined the bundle and then carefully moved a wire left and right. He pointed at the digital timer strapped to the box. "Not in less than ten minutes."

"We need to open the bottom hatch on the diving chamber so we can toss this thing out," Jon said.

"I'm not sure we can move that bundle without triggering it," Bobby said.

"We don't have a choice," Jon said. "But it makes no difference if we can't get the bottom hatch open."

"Why don't we just surface and throw it out the top hatch?"

"We'd never make it in time," Jon said, "the water would freeze us to death in a matter of minutes."

"Supercav," Bobby said.

Jon said nothing as he cocked an ear.

Bobby explained. "I'll take the ASDS to supercav speed and shake the mini-sub up and down. You equalize the chamber and wrestle with the hatch. Maybe the ocean current rushing across the underside will blow off whatever is holding the hatch shut."

Jon shrugged. It was a fool's plan, but the only one they had.

Jon suited up while Bobby grabbed the box and C-6. He held it forward. Jon grabbed it, stepped inside the chamber, and shut the side hatch. The red digits on the timer ticked down to nine minutes.

Jon donned his Kirby Morgan mask. He wouldn't need it if he remained inside the chamber, but there was a chance he could be thrown free if he managed to get the bottom hatch open. Jon opened the valves to equalize the chamber. Air hissed. He cleared his ears as the pressure increased. He felt the ASDS lurch forward. Bobby had just supercavitated. The sudden speed increase and erratic zigzagging threw Jon against the sides of the chamber.

Once the chamber pressure was equalized with the outside ocean pressure, Jon carefully placed the explosive bundle underneath one of his air tank straps, so he could free up both hands. He bent down and reached for the wheel on the bottom hatch. He yanked left. Nothing. He yanked again. Still nothing.

Jon glanced at the timer. Five minutes. He braced his back against one side of the chamber and yanked with all his strength. He yanked a dozen times. Nothing. Then, a dull clank.

Three minutes.

The wheel moved to the left and the hatch cracked open an inch. Jon found the hatch crank and turned it counterclockwise until the hatch was partially open. The current rushing by was so strong that it looked like a gushing river in the Colorado mountains.

Two minutes.

Jon pulled the bundle loose from his tank strap and tossed it through the open hatch. Carried by the current, now rushing across the underside of the ASDS, the bundle disappeared. He knew there was no way he could crank the hatch shut while the ASDS was still supercavitating. The ocean current was too strong. He could only hope they'd be far enough away when the bundle exploded.

Jon grabbed a pipe and pulled himself to the top of the chamber. He curled up into a tight ball, wrapped his fingers around a couple of pipes, and waited. He didn't need to wait long. An ear-splitting boom filled his ears. The mini-sub shook like a school bus near an earthquake epicenter. Jon's left hand was pulled free from the pipe. He wrapped the fingers of his right hand tighter around the other pipe. The shock wave threatened to hurl him out the hatch. His right arm ached as he held on. The wave thrashed him against the hard metal of the chamber. His back slammed against a protruding valve. The sharp pain made him yell into his Kirby Morgan. He felt the fingers on his right hand slipping and knew he couldn't hold on much longer.

The torrent subsided as the ASDS slowed. Jon sucked in a breath and grabbed a pipe with his left hand. The ocean calmed. He finally let go and dropped down to the bottom of the chamber. He cranked shut the bottom hatch and turned the valves to depressurize. A few minutes later, Jon opened the side hatch and stepped back into the ASDS.

He stripped off his gear and met Bobby in the bow. With his body badly bruised and beaten, he gritted his teeth with every step.

"You okay?" Bobby said as he glanced over.

"I've survived worse," Jon said. "Can our ORCA sonar find the *Khabbie*?"

"Doubt it," Bobby said, returning his eyes to the control panel. "I'd be a donkey's ass if they didn't hightail it out of the area as soon as we detached. The passive array in this thing is about as useless as a hair on a bar of soap, and the active isn't much better. Our best bet is to wait for the cavalry to show up, which I hope is soon, 'cause we have another problem."

"What now?" Jon said.

Bobby said, "That explosion damaged a bunch of systems, including our air regen. We need to surface to ventilate. After we do, we need to hitch another ride and put this horse out to pasture." He pointed at a rivulet of water spraying onto the deck from a leak in the hull. "We don't have much time before this tub fills up with really cold water."

"I want a refund," Jon said. "I'm not having any fun on this cruise."

"Sorry amigo," Bobby said. "You'll have to take that up with the management."

Jon desperately wanted to find the *Khabbie* and rescue Kate, but he finally offered a nod of defeat. "We don't have a choice. Let's surface and radio the good guys."

In the bow of the ASDS, Jon manned the pilot station and steered toward the surface as Bobby studied the radio panel. In the near-silence, Jon let his mind slip into the past. He recalled again the day, a year earlier, when he had watched Annelia walk away on the beach in La Jolla. He should have gone with her. He should have never left her alone. He should have anticipated what might happen. He had been so wrapped up in his own thoughts, his own problems, his own world, that he hadn't contemplated the worst.

NCIS had assigned him to a joint task force, operating in tandem with Homeland Security and the Mexican Federales. Together, they were ordered to muzzle a drug cartel operating in Tijuana, Mexico. A ruthless drug lord named Manuel Ortega had built a large network to shuttle potent amphetamines across the border into San Diego. There, the drugs wound up in the pockets of young sailors and Marines. Given the recent decreases in manpower and increases in mission demands, they were using them to stay alert on watch. Many of these young men and women were desperately trying to mitigate mistakes during long shifts so they could avoid what had happened aboard the USS *Fitzgerald* and USS *John S. McCain*.

When demand for the drugs escalated, a turf war erupted between Ortega and another drug lord in Tijuana. Dozens were slaughtered in the crossfire. Innocent bystanders were also killed, including four sailors who were blowing off steam at a Tijuana bar. Then three Marines died near Camp Pendleton from tainted drugs. That's when Jon's command stepped in.

Jon bit his lip. If he hadn't gotten the call that day from his boss, Annelia would still be alive.

Bobby glanced over. "How are we doing?"

"We're almost up," Jon said as he looked away to hide a tear.

The ASDS broke the surface and rolled about like a bottle on the strong sea currents. There were no windows on the hull, no way to see the ocean beyond, but Jon could imagine a ruffled blanket of blue and white set against a gray sky. There were days when he missed being at sea. Missed being away from the frantic bustle found in a smog-filled metropolis. Missed his team and missed not being able to come home to Annelia.

Bobby adjusted the radio and keyed the mic. He called out an SOS on several standard frequencies. No reply. He tried again. Nothing. Then again. No joy.

"Nobody's out there," Bobby said. "They're gonna find us here in a few days, all bug-eyed and floating face down."

"Are you always this optimistic?" Jon said.

"Pretty much," Bobby said. "It's a thing."

"Keep trying," Jon said.

Bobby keyed again. He went through the cycle several times. No response. He tried again. Still no joy. Thirty minutes passed with no reply. The freezing water line was now up to their ankles.

Bobby looked up. His eyes reflected defeat. "Bug-eyed."

CHAPTER 20

Aboard the *Khabbie*, off the coast of Russia near Cape Vankarem, Kate fought against Rinaldo's firm grip around her wrist. The ice pilot pulled her down the ladder from the midsection hatch.

Kate's feet landed on the tiled deck. She looked up toward the closed hatch. Dread and fear forced her voice to ratchet up an octave. "I heard shots. What the hell happened up there?"

"I don't know," Rinaldo said as she motioned for Kate to head toward the bow of the sub.

"What did you see?" Kate said. "Did Jon or Bobby get shot?" A warm tear ran down her cheek and fell to the deck as she imagined the worse.

"I didn't see anything," Rinaldo said. "I know as much as you do."

"Why did you rig the ASDS hatch so it wouldn't open?"

"In case Jon commandeered Whitney's M-9," Rinaldo said. "I didn't want him to shoot me in the face, or miss and shoot you in the face."

"He wouldn't have missed," Kate said as she marched in front of Rinaldo, wondering if she would ever again feel anything except fury and fear. Along the way, Kate noticed several video cameras mounted on bulkheads and assumed they allowed the AI system to monitor various systems and crew operations. Rinaldo led her around a corner and motioned for her to step through an open hatch into the mess deck compartment. The meaty scent of Russian *piroshkies* filled the air.

"I heard the ASDS detach," Kate said as she walked down the passageway.

"Whitney probably did it," Rinaldo said.

"Why?"

"He had instructions to detach and self-destruct in the event of an incident. Gunfire qualifies as an incident."

Kate stopped walking and turned around. Her mouth went dry. "You told Whitney to blow up the mini-sub?"

Rinaldo halted. "We couldn't risk having the ASDS fall into Russian hands."

"Why?"

"It's a need-to-know thing and you don't have the need to know," Rinaldo said as she pointed toward the bow. "We need to keep moving."

Kate fumed and strode toward the bow. "How long?"

"Before what?" Rinaldo said.

"Before the ASDS self-destructs?"

"If Whitney pressed the button, twenty minutes."

Kate prayed it was Jon who had fired the shots at Whitney and had felled the man before he could press the button. She also prayed Bobby had not been hit by crossfire.

"What the hell are we doing here?" Kate asked. "Why are you betraying the country you served?"

"I'm not," Rinaldo said. Her shoes squeaked on the tiled deck as she walked. "I'm protecting it. You'll be told what you need to know when you need to know it."

"You just killed ten Russian sailors and maybe a U.S. Petty Officer, a federal officer, and an engineer working for the U.S. government. Was all that part of your plan?"

"Unfortunate collateral damage," Rinaldo said as they reached the end of the passageway. "Inside." She pointed at the hatch leading into compartment three.

"Is that how you assuage your guilt, Ms. Rinaldo? Write off murder as collateral damage?"

Rinaldo's body stiffened as she motioned toward the hatch. Kate stepped through into the GKP. The oval control room looked like the bridge on a futuristic spaceship. Monitors displayed colorful graphs, numbers, charts, and data. High-tech equipment hummed and buzzed with activity. AI-controlled video cameras scanned the area like searchlights in a prison camp. Gray leather seats stood tall on shiny metal poles. Most were empty, and the rest were filled by Liang's men.

Lacking were any large cylindrical periscope housings. Like the U.S. *Virginia*-class submarines, the *Khabbie* used photonic masts containing high-resolution cameras that beamed images down to monitors in the GKP. The masts also updated a bank of advanced fire control computers that lined the starboard bulkhead. The computers were similar to but more advanced than the BYG-1 systems on the USS *Connecticut*. They were also comparable to, if not a step up from the *Virginia*-class. Near the consoles, Liang's men dragged unconscious Russian sailors up a ladder that led to an upper deck just below the sail. Kate hoped they were being taken to the sub's escape module for eventual rescue.

Rinaldo escorted Kate into the sonar shack on the forward port side of the GKP. Four consoles lined one bulkhead. Monitors on the consoles displayed orange lines running vertically. The lines were moving from top to bottom like waterfalls on an alien landscape. Kate recognized these as sonar graphs recording various sound frequencies in the ocean around them. She also noticed that the lenses on the video cameras had been covered with black electrical tape. Petty Officer Chen looked up, flashed a brief nod, and then resumed typing on a keyboard attached to one of the consoles.

Rinaldo took the ROSS case from Kate and set it on a bench in front of another console. "Since your cohort Bobby was unable to join us, Petty Officer Chen will be your assistant. The two of you will connect the ROSS to the *Khabbie's* sonar console."

"How?" said Kate. "I don't know if it's compatible with these systems and I can't read Cyrillic."

Chen stopped typing and looked up. "It should be compatible and I speak fluent Russian."

"There you go," Rinaldo said as she waved a hand in the air. "Problem solved. You have thirty minutes." The tall woman spun on a heel and strode out of the shack.

Kate glared down at Chen. "How do you know ROSS will be compatible?"

"I've been studying the *Khabbie's* systems," Chen said.

"We've only been aboard a few minutes."

"I've been preparing for this mission for weeks."

"Mission?" Kate said as she opened the ROSS case.

"That's need-to-know," Chen said.

"And I don't need to know," Kate said under her breath. She unraveled the wires connected to the ROSS unit and handed them to Chen. "Connect away, oh wise one."

Chen stood from his bench. He took the bundle and laid it near the side of a console. He then reached for a nearby tool kit and removed a screwdriver. He knelt near the side of the console and removed a panel cover. Without looking up, he reached an open palm toward Kate. "Bundle please."

Kate grabbed the bundle of wires and placed it into Chen's hand. "What are Rinaldo and Liang doing with the crew?"

While connecting the ROSS wires to the sonar console, Chen said, "The *Khabbie* has a crew rescue module mounted in the sail. They're moving the crew into that module. Then they'll detach it and send it to the surface, where the crew will eventually be rescued."

"Not all of them," Kate said, referring to the men who had been shot by Liang's soldiers.

Chen grunted as he fought with a wire. "That was unfortunate but could not be helped. If they hadn't fought back, they'd still be alive."

"Tell that to their families," Kate said.

Chen stopped what he was doing and pulled his head out from the panel opening. "You don't get it, do you? We're at war with Russia and China. We have been for decades. They keep hacking into our systems, invading territories they don't own, and grabbing natural resources in international waters. The Russians will soon have a dozen *Borei*-class missile boats and a few more *Khabbies*. The Chinese now have supercavitating subs that can go from Shanghai to San Francisco in a heartbeat. I'm sorry those sailors had to die, but I'm not sorry we're here, so shut up and hand me that plastic bag near the bench."

Still consumed by equal doses of angst and anger, Kate pursed her lips and searched for the bag. She found it on the deck near the bench. It was clear and held a dozen coax connectors. They looked different in size as compared to the ones used in the U.S. or U.K., metric versus imperial dimensions, she surmised. She held up the bag. "Russian SRs?"

"Yes," Chen said as he grabbed the bag.

"Where did you...?"

"I'm resourceful," Chen said.

He shoved his head back inside the panel, clicked and clanked for several minutes, and then re-emerged. "Let's test this bad boy."

Kate lit up the ROSS. The unit went through a series of system checks and then the HAL 9000 voice said, "I am ready for your commands. Please verify your identification."

Chen sat on a bench and stared at the ROSS unit.

"What's the Russian designation for the sonar console?" Kate asked him, even though she already knew the *Khabarovsk's* sonar was a generation beyond the Irtysh-Amfora installed in Russia's *Yasen*-class attack subs. The system had a bow-mounted spherical sonar array, flank sonar arrays, and a towed array for rearward detection. The Russians had taken a giant technological leap forward in recent years, so much so that their latest sonar systems had almost twice the detection range of the U.S. *Virginia*-class AN/BQQ-10 version four.

Chen confirmed the type of system.

"ROSS," Kate said, "My identification is Barrett, two-bravo-niner-yankee."

"Verified," ROSS said. "Hello, Dr. Barrett."

"Hello ROSS, please test and verify connections to the Russian MGK-540M Kizhuch PM version four sonar system."

"Testing and verifying," ROSS replied. Ten seconds passed and then ROSS said, "connections one, two, three, five, six, seven, and eight are connected and functioning properly. Connection four is unresponsive."

"Damn," Chen said. He crawled back inside the open panel, fumbled for a few minutes, and then said, "Test it again."

Kate said, "ROSS, retest and verify connection four."

"Testing and verifying," ROSS said. Five seconds passed. "Connection four is connected and functioning properly."

Chen crawled out of the panel opening and sat on a bench. "Okay, we now need to program ROSS to hack into the AI system."

Kate said. "What do you need to disable now?"

"Not disable," Chen said. "Control."

Kate tilted her head to one side. "Control what?"

"The fire control system," Chen said. "We need to take control of the *Khabbie's* six Status-6 torpedoes."

"Bloody hell, mate. Each one of those has a one-hundred-megaton nuclear warhead."

"I know," Chen said. He handed her a sheet of paper that contained typed lines of code. "You can use this. The subroutine is similar to the one I gave you earlier when we shut down the propulsion and sonar systems."

"How did you get these subroutines?" Kate asked.

Chen hesitated for a moment. His expression slowly changed from cautious to unconcerned. Kate decided that probably was not a good sign. It indicated that Chen knew she was probably not going to live long enough to divulge the information to anyone. Chen said, "The *Khabbie's* AI has a worm."

"A worm?" Kate said as she typed in a command into the ROSS unit's Bluetooth keyboard.

"It's similar to the stuxnet worm the U.S. planted in the Iranian reactor control systems years ago that wreaked havoc and destroyed their reactors so they couldn't produce uranium for nuclear weapons."

"I recall the incident," Kate said. "But how did you Americans plant a worm into a Russian submarine's AI system?"

Chen offered a sly smile. "We didn't. The Russians did."

Kate stopped typing and turned on her bench to face Chen. "The Russians?"

"They're always trying to hack into our sensitive government systems and steal our secrets," Chen said. "So we let them. We allowed their hackers to steal some lines of code for an advanced AI system, but we buried a worm in the code."

"You baited them," Kate said.

"Exactly. They fell for it."

"So how did it wind up on the *Khabbie*?"

Chen stretched his back and yawned. "I don't know. Rinaldo didn't tell me everything."

Kate crossed her arms. "This is so out of control it's not true. The AI that controls the Status-6 torpedoes is infected with a worm the U.S. created?"

"Yeah," Chen said. "And that's why we can hack in. The worm was hibernating until you activated it with the code I gave you earlier. That executed malware that allowed us to bypass the security protocols and gain access to various control systems."

"Why do you need access to the fire control system?" Kate asked.

"Don't know," Chen said. "Ask Rinaldo."

"I will," Kate said. She pointed toward the taped cameras. "I assume you put the tape on the AI cameras?"

"I did that and attenuated the microphones in areas where we don't want the AI system to see or hear what we're doing."

"Why not just disable the damn thing?"

"You should know the answer to that," Chen said. "Only the senior officers on the *Khabbie* have the authorization codes. If we try to get ROSS to do a complete shutdown or torture the crew to give us the codes, it will take too long. There's not enough time."

While trying to keep her hands from shaking, Kate typed commands on the ROSS unit's keyboard. As instructed, she created subroutines to allow ROSS to communicate with and potentially take control of some areas of the AI's brain. The Russians had compartmentalized the more sensitive systems, like fire control and helm control, so accessing these proved difficult and tricky. With Chen looking over her shoulder, Kate did not have the opportunity to rig the ROSS to communicate with the *Connecticut*. Hoping Chen would eventually look away, Kate took her time with the subroutines.

"What's taking so long?" Chen said.

"We're about to take control of six nuclear warheads. Do you want me to go faster and make a mistake?"

"Point taken," Chen said.

Five minutes later, Kate said, "It's done."

"Show me the routines," Chen said.

Kate leaned to one side and pointed at the screen.

Chen studied the code and then smiled. "Okay, it's show time. Light it off and see if it works."

Kate executed the subroutines and then said, "ROSS, verify subroutine Bravo, echo, seven, six, four."

"Verified," ROSS said.

"Execute."

"Executing."

"Verify control of weapon fire control systems and external Status-6 launchers one through six."

Fifteen seconds passed. Kate rubbed her palms on her thighs to remove the sweat.

ROSS said, "Verified."

Chen said, "Damn, it worked." He rose to his feet and said, "I'm going to get Rinaldo. There's a soldier standing guard outside the shack so don't try anything sneaky."

"Where would I go if I escaped?" Kate said.

Chen smirked and then started to walk toward the GKP. He stopped as a muffled explosion was heard through the hull.

"What was that?" Kate said, fearing the worst.

Chen sat in front of a sonar console and typed in a few keystrokes. "Probably C-6. Sounds like the ASDS just self-destructed."

Kate brought a hand to her mouth. Her eyes filled with tears.

"Sorry," Chen said as he stood and turned to leave. "That was unplanned."

Kate glanced about the small shack as Chen stepped through the door. It was filled with humming consoles, orange displays, and Russian Cyrillic etched across signs and placards. Now that she had completed programming ROSS, she was probably no longer an asset. A tear warmed her cheek. Jon and Bobby were gone and she would soon be next. She never imagined her final minutes would be spent aboard a foreign craft in the middle of nowhere.

Kate sat up straight, wiped away her tears, and typed commands into the ROSS unit in preparation to send a short message to the *Connecticut*.

She knew it was a long shot at best. Most likely, the U.S. sub was not near enough to hear it. While repeatedly glancing toward the entrance to the shack, her heart raced as she typed in the commands.

Only a few more to go...

Chen stepped back into the sonar shack with Rinaldo and Liang close behind. Kate stopped typing and lowered her eyes. Frustration and fear drained the blood from her face. She hadn't finished typing the commands. She hadn't been able to send a message to the *Connecticut.*

Rinaldo flashed a partial smile at Kate. "Petty Officer Chen tells me that ROSS is ready for prime time."

Kate raised her chin and said, "You're not really going to take control of six hundred megatons are you?"

"That's precisely what we're going to do," Rinaldo said.

Liang took a step backward and glanced at the door to the shack.

"You're insane, full stop," Kate said.

Rinaldo ignored her comment and said to Chen, "Proceed."

Chen approached the ROSS, sat on a bench, and picked up the keyboard. He positioned his finger over the keys and typed in the commands to take control of the fire control systems. Just as he finished typing, Liang motioned for two of his men to enter the shack. They unslung their rifles and pointed them at Rinaldo and Chen.

Liang stepped forward and said, "Petty Officer Chen, set down the keyboard."

Chen hesitated. He glanced at Rinaldo.

"Now," Liang said.

Rinaldo gave a brief nod. Petty Officer Chen placed the keyboard on a nearby bench.

Liang turned to Rinaldo. "Your sidearm."

Rinaldo unholstered her M-9 pistol and handed it to Liang. "What the hell are you doing, Liang?"

"I'm now in charge," Liang said.

"I was given command of this mission," Rinaldo said. "I'll give you three seconds to come to your senses."

"Or what?" Liang said. "You'll report me?"

Rinaldo stammered, said nothing.

"We have a new mission," Liang said.

"Which is?" Rinaldo said.

"We are going to launch a Status-6 torpedo."

Kate's pulse surged. "Are you mad?"

Rinaldo's face turned red. "Just one of those torpedoes could kill tens of millions. You can't possibly—"

"Yes, I can," Liang said, "and I will." He turned to Kate. "The new Chinese Type 109 submarine that likely fired a torpedo at us is still out there. It's quiet and has an AI system similar to the *Khabbie*. I need you and Petty Officer Chen to program the ROSS to detect and disable it."

"Why?" Kate said. "Are you going to take over that sub, too?"

"No," Liang said. "I am going to sink it before it sinks us."

The veins in Rinaldo's neck throbbed. "I told them you were unstable. What makes you think the Chinese are going to fire on a Russian sub?"

"We don't know why they fired on the ASDS. I can't take the chance they'll also fire on the *Khabbie*. He turned toward one of his men and said, "Escort Ms. Rinaldo into the GKP and secure her with tie wraps." Liang looked up at a clock on the bulkhead and then refocused on Kate and Chen. "You have one hour."

"An hour?" Kate said. "Why?"

"I estimate it will take the 109 that long to find us. If ROSS is not ready by then and they fire at us, we're all dead."

With a soldier standing guard nearby, Kate did her best to reprogram the ROSS, but not being familiar with the Chinese 109, she and Chen had no way to test or verify the programming. An hour later, prodded by gunpoint, Kate was escorted from the sonar shack back into the GKP. On the starboard side, a bank of consoles beeped and blinked in red, blue, and green as lights flickered on and off. Kate knew the bank housed the sub's fire control system, which programmed and controlled the *Khabbie's* six Status-6 torpedoes. Each torpedo was almost six-feet wide and seventy-nine feet long—about four times longer and wider than a U.S. Mark 48 ADCAP. The MK48 topped out at fifty-five knots and had a maximum range of around five miles. The Status-6 was powered by a small nuclear reactor and could go twice that fast and 1,240 times farther.

But the coup de grâce was the warhead.

The MK48 carried the equivalent explosive power of around one-half ton of TNT. Each Status-6 was armed with the equivalent of one-hundred-million tons of TNT—over 6,000 times more destructive force than the atom bomb dropped on Hiroshima during World War II. If a single Status-6 blew up near New York City, over eight million people would die instantly. Another six million would be seriously injured, and over the next several months, millions more would die a prolonged, agonizing death from the fallout created by the Cobalt-60 that had been "salted" into the weapon's warhead.

The Russians had designed the Status-6 "doomsday weapon" to do one thing and do it well—attack coastal areas and destroy cities, ports, military bases, and most importantly, trade choke points. Over 90 percent of the world's energy trade transited through six primary choke points: the Hormuz, Malacca, Danish, and Turkish straits, and the Panama and Suez canals. If a Status-6 turned just one of those points into a mushroom cloud, the world's economy could grind to a halt.

"Impressive, isn't it?" Liang said as he stepped up beside Kate.

Kate replied with a single word. "Why?"

"Why what?" Liang asked.

"Why do you want to kill millions of innocent people?"

Liang turned his eyes toward Kate. They were filled with a dark storm churned by commitment and hatred. "They are far from innocent."

He motioned for Kate to sit in an empty leather seat, whereupon a soldier tie-wrapped her wrists. Already tie-wrapped, Rinaldo sat motionless in a nearby seat.

"What happened to the Russian crew?" Rinaldo asked.

Liang did not respond.

"Where are they?" Rinaldo asked again.

"They are gone," Liang said.

"Gone?" Rinaldo said. "Gone where?"

"I could not risk having the Russian Navy confirm their submarine had been hijacked."

"Jesus," Rinaldo said through clenched teeth. "You killed them all."

Liang did not reply. Instead, he paced in front of a fire control computer and issued an order to the AI system. "Grigori, open outer doors on the Status-6 launcher compartment."

Kate knew the *Khabbie's* AI system had been named after Dr. Grigori Perelman. He was a brilliant, reclusive Russian genius who'd been honored as the smartest man in the world for solving a complex mathematical conundrum called the Poincare Conjecture. He'd refused his $1 million prize and a Fields Medal from the International Mathematical Union, choosing instead to continue living an impoverished life in a cockroach-infested flat in Saint Petersburg.

The Grigori AI system acknowledged the order in English. The code Chen had given Kate to program ROSS to take control of the AI system must have also allowed them to change the language default from Russian to English. The system had likely been designed to understand a variety of languages to facilitate espionage operations.

Liang said, "Grigori, set firing solution and ready external launcher number one."

Grigori repeated and executed the command. Kate visualized the Status-6 launcher compartment just in front of the sail. This large area, which had been flooded with seawater, was outside the pressurized inner hull. The six Status-6 torpedoes were housed on a circular launch rack in the compartment. Like the cylinder on a six-shooter revolver, the launcher rotated to allow one Status-6 torpedo on the top of the rack to detach, light off its propulsor motor, and speed toward its target.

"Don't do this," Rinaldo said.

Without turning, Liang pointed a finger toward Rinaldo and said, "Keep her quiet."

A soldier placed a firm hand on Rinaldo's shoulder.

"Grigori, confirm firing solution."

Five seconds passed. Then ten. Grigori confirmed the firing solution.

Kate closed her eyes. She no longer felt fear and anger. Now, her whole body ached with sorrow for the millions of souls about to be vaporized in the blink of an eye.

"Grigori," Liang said, "release Status-6 torpedo number one."

CHAPTER 21

Aboard the USS *Connecticut,* operating off the coast of Russia, Commander Jackson marched back and forth in front of the command screen. The large monitor displayed four quadrants, each filled with numbers, charts, and graphs depicting various ship conditions, including speed, depth, and updated fire control information fed from the BYG-1 consoles. Despite the constant unease that limited his ability to get much sleep, the hum and whir of electronics made him feel at home. Made him feel like he was on top of the world. Made him feel like he mattered.

Save for an occasional murmur from the crew, the room was silent. Operating inside Russian waters had heightened the crew's unease and mitigated their typical watch banter. Jackson wrestled with his options. His orders had been vague, which was typical, but this situation was anything but. There were no safe moves. All the possible chess plays ended with his king toppled and a sneer on his opponent's face.

Sonar barked out a report. "Conn, Sonar, the ACTUV bot we deployed detected an explosion in the water bearing zero-four-seven. Transients indicate a small torpedo or explosive device."

"Sonar, Conn, aye," Jackson said. He turned toward the Diving Officer. "Diving Officer, turn to course zero-four-seven, all ahead full."

Thirty minutes later, Jackson ordered All Stop so the Sonar team could scan the area.

Nothing. Five minutes passed. Still nothing.

Jackson frowned. *What the hell had exploded?*

A report from Sonar interrupted his troubled thoughts. "Conn, Sonar, the ACTUV bot is now picking up transients bearing two-six-five. Range, 22,000 yards. Designating Master Two."

Jackson's adrenaline surged. Could that be the *Khabbie*? Or was it a Russian *Yasen*-class attack sub preparing to blow them out of the water? "All stop!"

The Diving Officer repeated the order. The *Connecticut* slowed and then stopped dead and soundless in the water.

Jackson said softly, "Sonar, Conn, update on Master Two."

No response.

"Sonar, Conn, respond."

"Conn, Sonar, the ACTUV bot reports that the transients coming from Master Two have gone silent."

"Sonar, Conn, aye."

Jackson swiveled and pointed toward the BYG-1 consoles on the starboard bulkhead. "Firing solution?"

The Weapons Officer turned toward Jackson and said, "All eight tubes are loaded and ready, however, the fire control party has not obtained a firing solution."

"Very well, Weaps, stand by for a snapshot on my order."

"Standing by," Weaps acknowledged.

Jackson had no intention of firing, unless he was fired upon first, but he did intend to be ready to do so within seconds.

An excited voice again erupted over the sonar comms. "Conn, Sonar, the BQQ has detected high-speed screws in the water!"

Jackson held up one hand, "Weaps, prepare to snapshot tubes one, two, three, and four."

"Standing by to snapshot tubes one through four, aye."

Jackson said, "Sonar, Conn, bearing and trajectory on Master Two's torpedo?"

"Conn, Sonar, the torpedo is running at high speed on a bearing of two-two-four. Doppler frequency is increasing. Estimated speed is...holy shit... over eighty knots."

The blood drained from Jackson's face. His hands felt numb and icy cold. His heart pounded in his chest like a timpani. When a torpedo's doppler frequency increased, like the sound of a passing train, that meant it was heading your way. The top speed for most torpedoes was less than sixty knots. The torpedo headed their way was running at eighty, which meant it had to be a high-speed torpedo, quite possibly a Status-6 loaded with a one-hundred-megaton nuclear warhead.

If it was a Status-6, there was no point in running and no point in firing a decoy. A nuclear explosion of that magnitude would vaporize the ocean for miles. There was no point in doing anything except praying for a peaceful end.

He couldn't risk firing any snapshots without verifying the target. What if the torpedo was coming from a different Russian attack sub? What if it wasn't heading their way at all? What if they were in the middle of an exercise and the torpedo was unarmed? By firing now, he could start an international war.

That said, if the doppler continued to increase, Jackson would lower his hand and snapshot the four torpedoes toward whoever had fired at the *Connecticut*, *Khabbie* or not. He knew it'd be a Hail Mary pass, but damned if he wasn't going down without a fight. Jackson glanced about the control room. He looked at the faces of his crew and wished they were not there. Wished he could shield them from the inevitable. Wished they could live to see another day, their homes, and their loved ones.

"Conn, Sonar, doppler is shifting."

Jackson let his arm drop, but he did not issue the order to fire. He looked up at the comm box. "Sonar, Conn, bearing to the torpedo?"

Silence, then, "Conn, Sonar; doppler is decreasing. Bearing to the torpedo is now one- niner-eight. Classify as probable Status-6 based on tonal signatures."

Jackson let out a relieved breath. A hushed eruption of cheers filled the Conn. The torpedo was now heading away. Jackson knelt on one knee, looked toward the heavens, and crossed his chest with a finger. He whispered, "Thank you."

Jackson stood and straightened his back. "Weaps, do we have a firing solution?"

"No, sir. We have an initial bearing but no solution."

"Sonar, Conn, bearing to Master Two?" Jackson said.

"Conn, Sonar, we've lost contact with Master Two."

"Damn," Jackson said to no one. He rubbed at the nape of his neck and considered his next move carefully. There was a high probability the Status-6 had been fired from the *Khabbie*, but he couldn't verify that fact. He had not been given orders to sink the Russian sub and they were now too far away from a Deep Siren buoy to fire off a report, so that left him with only one viable alternative: follow the torpedo.

Over the next several minutes, Sonar provided a stream of updates on the torpedo's trajectory. Jackson ordered a course change and an increase to flank speed to follow the track, but he knew it was a zero-sum game. The *Connecticut's* top speed was little more half that of the Status-6. The best he could do was trail it long enough to get a rough idea of where it might be heading, and then send a radio report to COMSUBFOR.

Twenty minutes later, they had that rough track. Five minutes after that, Jackson came to periscope depth and sent a short message to the cavalry. Another twenty minutes passed before Sonar lost track of the Status-6. They had also lost the *Khabbie*, maybe for good. By now it was long gone. He hated the fact that he'd been forced to make a choice—follow the torpedo or follow the Russian sub—but tracking the torpedo had been the only choice he could make. If armed, the one-hundred-megaton warhead on the Status-6 could take out an entire seacoast. Millions would be vaporized within minutes or killed by the fallout within hours or days. Now COM-SUBFOR would at least have a chance of finding and stopping it, and while they were doing that, the *Connecticut* would try to hunt down the *Khabbie* before she could fire another torpedo.

Jackson stood near the tactical display. Every few minutes, he glanced up at the silent sonar comm box, then over at the sonar shack door, and then back at the box. Ten minutes passed with no report save "nothing to report."

A sound-powered phone near Jackson barked. He picked up the phone and keyed the button. "Captain."

"Cap'm, Radio, we've picked up a nearby transmission."

"What's the call sign?"

"Sir, the call sign is...Graycliff. They issued an SOS with coordinates."

Jackson smiled. He grabbed a pen, wrote down the coordinates, and said, "Reply that we're on our way."

Jackson hung up the phone and approached the nav table. He handed the Quartermaster of the Watch the coordinates and said, "Plot a course ASAP."

CHAPTER 22

Late in the evening at the White House, SECDEF McBride felt a wave of panic well up inside his chest. He shoved the qualm deep into his gut where it smoldered like a hot coal. Wondering if he'd soon die from a heart attack, he leaned forward in his chair and listened as President Shek spoke with Russian President Popov. He could not hear what Popov was saying, but he didn't need to. Shek did most of the talking, and when he was silent, his face reflected a dozen poker "tells."

Shek asked if Popov was aware of any situational changes with the *Khabbie*'s sea trials. Shek's expression indicated that Popov lied and said there were none. By now, the Russian Navy had to be fully aware that the crew of the *Khabbie* was no longer in control, or at the very least was not responding. Popov was obviously doing what he did best: playing chess to buy time and get his ducks in a row. Shek offered the usual bullshit that the U.S. was standing by to help and then disconnected.

Shek removed his glasses and massaged his eyes. "He knows something is amiss. His tone was...cautious. That means Popov's hand is still missing several cards. And that probably means whoever has commandeered the Russian submarine has not communicated any demands yet."

"Or plans to," McBride said.

"Have our naval forces found the *Khabbie*?"

"Yes and no," McBride said. "We have not heard from the *Connecticut* in a while, but they previously reported intermittent hits, which means they have a rough ballpark, but have not closed enough to get a firing solution. Our ASW planes are also getting an occasional hit."

Shek jerked his head back. "A firing solution? My instructions still stand. We are not to fire unless I authorize such."

"Understood, Mr. President. It's just a submarine term. It means they have a lock and *could* fire if ordered to do so."

Shek's face relaxed. "Very well, I want to..."

Before Shek could finish his sentence, preceded by a quick knock on the door, Admiral Edwards burst into the room. He was dressed in a Navy-blue uniform. Rows of ribbons lined his chest and worry lined his face.

"Admiral?" McBride said.

"Sorry for the intrusion, Mr. President," Edwards said. "We've just received an urgent report from the USS *Connecticut*."

Shek stood from his chair and leaned forward. "What is their report, Admiral?"

Edwards cleared his throat. "They believe the *Khabbie* may have fired a Status-6 torpedo. If so, the weapon may be loaded with a one-hundred-megaton nuclear warhead. It's on a southerly course through the Bering Strait near Alaska."

McBride felt dizzy, like he was on a high-speed roller coaster. He found a chair and sat.

How the hell did this get so far out of control?

Shek went into bulldog mode and moved around to the front of his desk. "We need to immediately inform Russia and all possible target cities along that torpedo's track. We also need to raise the DefCon level."

Confused and shocked, McBride tried to speak but nothing came out. He could not form a coherent sentence in his head.

Edwards rescued him by saying, "We'll launch every ASW asset we've got in the area to hunt down the Status-6. If we find it, I'm assuming we should take it out?"

"Yes," Shek said.

"No," McBride said, regaining his composure. "Sorry, Mr. President, but we can't take it out if it's too close to civilization. If we accidentally detonate the warhead, it could disintegrate everything within a twenty-mile radius. Before we blow it up, we may need to find a way to redirect it to an open ocean area."

Shek did not respond for several long seconds and then said, "We also need to know who is responsible for firing the torpedo. Was it the *Khabarovsk*? And if so, who is now in control of the Russian submarine? The Chinese? Terrorists? Perhaps rogue Russians who are trying to start a war and blame it on others? Find out. Now."

"Yes, Mr. President," McBride said. As he stood to leave, he heard Shek pick up the phone and begin preparations to potentially use the infamous "suitcase" to launch a nuclear counterstrike.

McBride stepped out of the Oval Office and keyed his phone. His heart was a runaway train on a short track as he connected to CNO Robert Dennison.

"Bob, where are we on tracking the Status-6?" McBride said.

"Somewhere and nowhere," the CNO said. His voice was agitated but controlled, like a father who's trying to keep his cranked-up son from jumping off a roof. "It's designed to zig-zag and intermittently go fast and slow. When it goes fast, our ASW planes get a whiff, but when we close in, it goes slow and quiet again and we lose it. It's like playing a game of Marco Polo. Our eyes are closed, and we hear a voice from across the pool, but when we swim near, no one is there."

"Damn," McBride said as he strode down a corridor at the White House. "Okay, Bob, let me know what you need. Anything. Just ask and I'll take care of it."

"Will do," Dennison said.

McBride could not keep his hands from shaking, as if he were an old man with tremors. He disconnected and dialed another number. After a click and a "hello," he said, "I need you to run another background check on our Arctic team."

Silence, then a female voice responded. "Why? Which ones?"

"All of them," McBride said. "We're knee-deep in a pile of dung, and I want to know who's responsible."

"We were thorough the first time."

"Not thorough enough. Run it again."

"Okay," the voice said. "I'll get back to you within a few hours."

"Within the hour," McBride said. He disconnected. Under his breath he whispered, "Son of a bitch."

CHAPTER 23

Jon opened the upper hatch on the ASDS. He and Bobby had donned dry suits and Arctic parkas and then stood atop the mini-sub's seats to stay above the water. They had almost run out of time before receiving a reply to their distress call.

A cold breeze swept past and brought with it the salty scent of the sea. Jon opened his nostrils and breathed in the fresh air. A soft ray of moonlight touched his cheek and for a fleeting moment, he was no longer tortured by his past or agonized by his future. For a few brief seconds, he was free.

The melancholy feeling vanished when Bobby called out from below. "Are you gonna stand there until this thing sinks?"

Jon ascended onto the deck of the mini-sub. A few hundred yards off the port bow, a black shape emerged like the Loch Ness monster summoned from the depths. Sailors scurried up through the midsection hatch of the beast and inflated a small rubber boat.

"There once was a lady from Nantucket," Bobby said as he watched the sailors clamber into the Zodiac, "who sailed to France in a bucket. When she got there, they asked for her fare. She lifted her skirt and said—"

"How many of those bad limericks do you know?" Jon said.

Bobby shrugged. "I lost count."

Fifteen minutes later, Jon slid down the ladder and stood on the tiled deck inside the USS *Connecticut*. The smell of fresh baked pizza made his stomach growl. He'd only had one MRE in the past day. The galley was located directly below the midsection hatch. A dozen pizzas had been placed on the metal counter near the galley. Bobby stepped up behind Jon and grabbed a few slices. They disappeared in a matter of seconds.

"Oh man," Bobby said. "I just died and went to heaven."

Jon picked up a slice covered with pepperoni and took a bite. Three slices later, he had to agree with Bobby. If there was a heaven, no doubt it was run by Italians.

A sailor brought them two glasses filled with Kool-Aid, which he called "bug juice," and ushered them into the wardroom. Jon sat at the table and thought about Kate. His heart ached with a familiar pain. He hadn't stopped Rinaldo from taking her aboard the *Khabbie*. He wondered if she was still alive, and if so, for how much longer. Guilt consumed him. He also wondered if, once again, he had failed to save someone he cared about.

Memories filled his head with the terror of the past.

He had watched her go.

Annelia had never returned that day after walking away and strolling across the sand on the La Jolla beach. He had searched for hours, but he never found her. At first, he thought she might have gotten pulled into the ocean by an undertow. Maybe she had drowned. Panic gripped his throat. He had been almost unable to speak while frantically asking dozens of people if they had seen her. He showed them a picture on his mobile phone. They all shook their heads.

Finally, someone recognized her. A thirty-something woman had been playing with her son on the beach and had seen Annelia being escorted by two large men. The woman thought it was strange, but this was Southern California where most everything was strange. Jon called his command. They immediately put out an APB, but nothing turned up. A day later, Jon got a call. It was from one of Miguel Montoya's men. They wanted to make a deal. His cooperation in exchange for Annelia's life. He had agreed. Then things went from bad to worse.

Commander Jackson entered the wardroom and brought Jon out of his battle with the past.

"We managed to dock the ASDS to our midsection hatch," Jackson said as he approached Jon. "Our machinist mates are making repairs, just in case we need to use it later."

"Good," Jon said. "I'd like to use it to do a little marlin fishing later."

"Right," Jackson said, "and I suppose you'll want some of our pepperoni as bait."

"Sausage," Jon said. "Marlin love sausage. Have you found the *Khabbie* yet?"

"More or less," Jackson said as he sat on a nearby bench. "We had her, but only for a few minutes."

"A few minutes?"

"That's how long it took to fire a Status-6."

Jon's eyes shot open. "Rinaldo fired a torpedo? Are you sure it was the *Khabbie*?"

"Most likely, yes. We've detected no other subs in the area."

"Why did she fire? What's the target?"

"We don't know the answer to either question," Jackson said. "We tracked the torpedo for as long as we could. Best we can guess, it's headed toward Kamchatka or points further south, like Japan or Korea. Unless, of course, it changes course."

"I think I'm gonna crap my pants," Bobby said.

Jackson pointed toward the bow. "The head's that way."

"We have to find the *Khabbie* before she fires another Status-6," Jon said.

"No shit," Jackson said. "We were working on that but got derailed when we picked up your transmission. We're back on the hunt, but the *Khabbie* has advanced coating, sound dampening, and an ultra-quiet propulsor drive. Unless we get lucky, we may never find her."

Jon lowered his eyes and did not reply. He had a bad feeling that his odds of stopping Rinaldo and saving Kate were probably somewhere between zero and piss poor.

"I need to know everything that's happened," Jackson said.

Jon shrugged. "We were just minding our own business in Kansas when a tornado tossed us over a rainbow where we met a tin guy and fought off a bunch of flying monkeys."

"Right," Jackson said. "And then you killed a witch. With water."

"Not yet," Jon said, "she's still alive." He recounted the events from the time they had left the *Connecticut* a day earlier while Jackson cocked an ear.

"I still can't believe Rinaldo is a traitor," Jackson said. "Did she give you any indication of what they plan to do with the *Khabbie*?"

"None," Jon said. "But when I probed her about selling it to the highest bidder, she said I had it all wrong. She didn't elaborate. Also, there's got to be a reason why that Chinese 109 fired a torpedo at us."

"Maybe they mistook you for a different vessel. The ASDS has a strange sound signature."

"Maybe, but that still doesn't explain the aggression. Are they trying to start a war?"

Jackson furled his brow. "Let's hope not." He was silent for a moment and then said, "What the hell are Rinaldo and Liang going to do with a sub carrying six nukes?"

"Only five now," Jon said.

Jackson nodded in silence.

A sailor in blue coveralls entered and handed Jackson a printed radio message. He read the yellow printout and then handed it to Jon. It was an autopsy report on Petty Officer Kelly.

Jon read the report and then let out a slow breath. "Petty Officer Kelly was murdered."

Jackson said, "So Rinaldo's a traitor *and* a murderer."

"The Wicked Witch of the West," Jon said.

Jackson stood and motioned for Jon and Bobby to follow him up to the Conn. The garage-sized area buzzed with efficiency. While it was obvious the crew had been well-trained, and had conducted dozens of secret stealth missions, it was also evident that this op was different. They were now inside Russian territorial waters hunting one of the most advanced and lethal submarines ever built. They'd spent several nervous minutes wondering if a Status-6 torpedo was about to nuke them out of existence. An aggressive Chinese 109 was also lurking nearby. The stakes in the game were as high as they get. One wrong move, one minor mistake, and they could all wind up on eternal patrol.

Jackson approached the large display in the front of the Conn. He pressed a button on a remote control and the display changed from four quadrants of tactical information to a video conference transmission. A large oak table, surrounded by a dozen chairs, came into view. CNO Robert Dennison entered the room and sat. He had short gray hair and a rugged, timeworn face. His crisp Navy-blue uniform had thick gold bars on the jacket sleeves and a lapel lined with medals. Dennison was followed by two more admirals and two civilians dressed in suits. A third civilian entered the room. He was an older man with receding hair and several caverns running across his forehead. Jon's fingers curled into his palms as he recognized the man.

Sitting at the long conference table, Secretary of Defense George McBride squinted into the camera. His eyes widened as they focused on Jon. A brief sign of recognition played across his face and then vanished behind the mask that had ruled the man's life. He turned his gaze toward Jackson and said, "Commander, can you please give us an update on the situation?"

Jackson cleared his throat and provided a full update—their initial track on the *Khabbie*, the Status-6 firing and temporary track, the eventual loss of the Russian sub, and the rescue of Jon and Bobby from the sinking ASDS.

His face placid, the SECDEF squinted his eyes as Jackson spoke.

Dennison said, "Based on your bearing track on the Status-6, assuming no radical course changes, we've determined several possible targets, including Japan or Korea, or maybe even Taiwan. Although, it really doesn't matter. The fallout will kill millions across the entire region."

"Understood," Jackson said. "There was no way we could have taken it out with a MK48 when we first detected it. Our torpedoes are too slow. They would have never caught up."

"Let us worry about the Status-6, Commander," Dennison said. "Your job is to reacquire the *Khabbie* and prevent her from firing another torpedo. Can you do that?"

"I honestly don't know," Jackson said. "We have excellent sonar capability, but that sub is highly advanced and very hard to find."

"What if we gave you an edge?" McBride said. "What if you had a ROSS unit?"

Jackson's eyes lit up. "You have another ROSS?"

Bobby grinned. "Shit howdy! Sorry, I mean...that's like finding a beer in the desert."

McBride said, "The unit is a Beta that our engineers just got working. It's similar to the one at the ICEX camp that's now aboard the *Khabbie*. It's at the Adak, Alaska Naval Air Facility. We can deliver it by way of an F35B. That fighter jet has vertical hovering capability, so it can lower a package down to your sub."

Jackson said, "How fast?"

"One hour," McBride said.

"What do you mean by Beta?" Bobby asked.

McBride frowned. "It's a newer version, a bit better than the one you had; however, it's not fully baked yet so it has some...glitches."

"That's not good," Bobby said.

"The *Khabbie* could be anywhere by now," Jackson said. "An hour from now it'll be anywhere times ten."

"We trust you'll do your best to find it," Dennison said. "We're deploying ASW aircraft, several destroyers, a *Virginia*-class, and some ACTUV bots, but their primary job will be to find and destroy the Status-6. As you know, the USS *Oregon* is on its way to your area and we activated a few more ACTUV bots to help you find the *Khabbie*. We'll give you ASW when we can, but the Russians have sent a few *Sukhoi* Su-57 stealth fighters to harass our P-8s."

"So we're covering thousands of square miles with two attack subs and a few untested robots." Jackson said. It wasn't a question.

Dennison did not reply.

McBride said, "We don't know why Rinaldo fired a torpedo, but it's possible it wasn't intentional."

"How do you figure?" Jon said.

McBride's image blurred due to a momentary signal loss. An audio hum caused a two-second buzz. His voice cut back in mid-sentence. "...*Khabbie* is using cutting-edge AI, and it's possible there was a malfunction. It could be that Rinaldo or someone on her team accidentally triggered a torpedo firing. We don't even know if the damn thing is armed."

"We don't know that it's not," Jackson said. "We've heard no communication from the *Khabbie*. We must assume the worst. Lives are at stake."

"I concur, Commander," McBride said. "You'll need to get the Beta ROSS unit working and find that sub. When you do, you're authorized to take appropriate action."

Jon fumed. "You mean sink it. What about Kate Barrett? She's still aboard that sub."

"I'm sorry, Agent Shay," McBride said. "This is not a rescue mission."

"So you're just going to run away again?" Jon said.

McBride's face went white. He did not reply.

Jackson flashed Jon a look.

"Agent Shay," Dennison said, "I concur with the Secretary of Defense. Ms. Barrett and the crew on the *Khabbie* are unfortunate collateral damage. You have your orders."

Jon's shoulders slumped. His heart felt heavy, as if an unseen demon had just placed an anvil on his chest. "Understood, sir."

Jackson said, "If there's nothing else to discuss—"

"There is," Jon said as he glared at McBride. "How did Liang commandeer an ASDS and bypass the intruder detection system at the ICEX camp?"

McBride cleared the phlegm in his throat. "I don't know."

"How did Rinaldo and two Petty Officers get access to top-secret information about the ROSS device and then plan an elaborate heist with Liang?"

"I don't know," McBride said.

"They couldn't have done it without help from the inside," Jon said. "That means you have a mole."

McBride's right eye twitched. "We have considered that possibility."

"Possibility?" Jon said. "No way they pull this off without help."

"We're taking appropriate precautions and looking into the matter on our end," McBride said.

Dennison said, "Commander Jackson, we will send you the coordinates for the F35B rendezvous along with the specs for the Beta ROSS."

"Yes sir," Jackson said. "We'll head toward the coordinates now."

"Kate's the expert," Bobby said as he looked at McBride with cow's eyes. "I'm not as good as she is with ROSS. I'm just a rodeo hand, not a bull rider."

"You've just been promoted," McBride said.

Bobby rubbed his forehead, as if he was trying to remove something.

McBride's image fluttered again as he looked down at his watch. "We'll expect updates every two hours, Commander. Good hunting."

"Aye, sir," Jackson said. "*Connecticut* out."

The screen went blank.

Jackson turned to Bobby. "Can you get that ROSS thing wired up and working?"

Bobby stopped rubbing his forehead and shrugged. "Maybe. I don't know. Like I said, Kate was the big boss. I'll need to see it and figure out how it's different and then connect it to your sonar system and stuff."

"Stuff?" Jon said.

"Yeah, you know, engineer stuff. Tests, calibrations, adjustments, stuff."

"Get some rest," Jackson said. He looked at his watch. "You've got forty-five minutes."

"I want another slice," Bobby said.

"You can have all the pizza you want," Jackson said. "Just be ready to go balls to the wall after that F35B gets here."

Bobby's shoe squeaked as he rapidly tapped a foot on the tile. "Okay, I'll get ready."

"We're counting on you," Jon said.

"I know," Bobby said. His eyes watered. "But if I can't ride that bull, millions of people will die."

"You'll be fine," Jon said, hoping that he wasn't lying.

Jackson turned and marched toward the exit. "Follow me, Agent."

Jon followed the Commander down one deck into the CO's stateroom. "Sit," Jackson ordered.

Jon settled into a metal chair as Jackson sat at his desk.

"You want to tell me what's going on with you and the Secretary of Defense?"

Jon said nothing.

"Agent?" Jackson prompted.

Jon let out a long breath. "We know each other."

"Go on."

"He's my father."

CHAPTER 24

At the White House, after concluding the call with the USS *Connecticut*, George McBride felt like he had an ulcer. His stomach burned like it did when he ate too much Cuban food, or maybe a salsa-covered burrito from one of those food trucks. Although the air in the room was ice cold, beads of sweat formed on his forehead. Had he known the situation brewing near Russia might spiral this far out of control, and that his illegitimate son would get pulled into the mix, the decisions and assumptions he'd made earlier would have been different. Now, there was no going back. They were headed into a category five storm and they'd just have to ride it out.

President Shek, seated at his desk in the Oval Office, massaged his closed eyelids. He opened his eyes and stared at McBride. "Can you please explain how a civilian ice pilot aboard an American submarine may have orchestrated one of the most egregious hijackings in naval history?"

McBride cleared his throat. "I don't know."

"Do you concur with Agent Shay that there must be a mole inside the Navy or the government?"

"Maybe," McBride said. "I have my people looking into it."

"It is time," Shek said. He stared at the phone on his desk and then picked up the handset. To his assistant, he said, "Please connect the call to President Jing." He hung up and waited. Two minutes later, the phone rang.

McBride listened to the strained conversation, all spoken in Chinese. Although he did not understand a word, he again could read the President's face and discern, for the most part, what was likely being said.

Shek concluded the call and said, "Jing disavows any knowledge of an attack on the ICEX camp or the theft of the ASDS. He swears that China has deployed no military assets to the Arctic and is not working with or against the Russians. In this, I sense he may be telling the truth. On another topic, I sense he is not."

"Which one might that be?" McBride asked.

"When I asked whether he was aware of any issues with the new Russian *Khabarovsk* submarine, or if China had sent its new Type 109 attack submarine to the area, he denied both. He even denied that the 109 has supercavitating technology."

"I'm not surprised," McBride said. Did you tell him about the Status-6 firing?"

"Not directly. I said our ASW forces had detected a possible torpedo firing from the suspected vicinity of the *Khabarovsk* and we had no way of knowing whether this was an exercise, misfiring, or aggressive act. I suggested he task his naval forces to remain alert."

"Was that such a good idea?" McBride said. "If their forces and ours are on high alert, it could trigger a skirmish or full-blown conflict."

"The risk of this is present, but the risk of not finding and destroying that torpedo is far greater."

McBride nodded.

"Let us assume for the moment that Jing is telling the truth," Shek said. "That China is not responsible for the incident. Then who is?"

"I have no idea," McBride said.

"If China did not steal the Russian submarine, and it is sending its new 109 at high speed to the area, then Jing must know the *Khabarovsk* has been compromised and poses a threat to China. If this is the case, how does he know?"

"They have spies and hackers everywhere," McBride said. "If China did send its 109, they may make a preemptive strike. If so, they may be doing us a favor."

"Perhaps," Shek said. "Or China may be about to start World War III. He who strikes the first blow admits he's lost the argument."

CHAPTER 25

Jon stood on the bridge of the now surfaced USS *Connecticut* and watched sheets of rain hammer the hardened HY100 deck. The sound reminded him of a fifty-caliber machine gun spraying lead against the side of a brick building. He glanced up. A beam of light splashed down from the hovering F35B fighter jet and painted a yellow-white circle around the midsection hatch. The deafening high-pitched whine of the jet engine overpowered the sound of the rain and turned the surrounding ocean into a seething cauldron.

Sailors in orange jumpsuits scurried about while preparing to receive the ROSS package lowered from the fighter. Thick chains dangled from their waists, securing them to the deck by way of hooks fastened into long deck runners. Two crewmen reached high above their heads and guided the bundled package as it was lowered by a long cable from the jet. Once secure, they unhooked the package and lowered it through the hatch.

The F35B retrieved its line, shot straight upward, and disappeared into the night.

After the sub dove again beneath the waves, Jon managed to take a quick shower and grab a bite in the wardroom before he was summoned by Commander Jackson. Now standing in the Conn, Jon saw a face congeal on the large tactical monitor.

A man in his late forties, wearing a crisp black suit, cleared his throat. "Commander Jackson, I'm Secret Service Lead Agent Tom Flannigan. I'd like your permission to speak with Agent Shay."

"Granted," Jackson said as he motioned toward Jon.

Flannigan said, "Agent Shay, I believe you know Agent Tucker?"

Brad Tucker smiled as he appeared on the screen. "Hey there, Shay."

"Hey Tucker," Jon said. "What brings you to our party?"

Flannigan said, "Agent Tucker has uncovered evidence that may be linked to your situation aboard the *Connecticut*. He will explain."

The camera panned out to reveal the face of a woman sitting in a wheel-chair. Her brown eyes were bleary and bloodshot and her face gaunt and grey. She appeared to be Hispanic, or maybe Cuban. Behind her, Jon recognized the Secret Service logo splashed across the wall of a conference room.

"This is Secret Service Agent Maria Estefan," Tucker said. "She dragged me into the briar patch and then almost got herself killed."

Jon said, "Hello, Agent Estefan. No offense, but you look like you've seen better days."

"No offense taken," Maria said with a strained voice. "It's been a long one."

Jackson stepped up and said, "This conversation is on my dime, so can we please get to the chase?"

"I was following a lead on a possible Jackal named Pender," Maria said. "I thought his target was POTUS. His trail led me to a Chinese spy named Ying, also being investigated by Agent Tucker."

"We suspected she was stealing Navy underwater intruder detection technology," Tucker said.

"The same tech used at ICEX to guard the torpedo extraction holes?" Jon said.

"The same," Tucker said. "Which is one of the reasons for our call."

"And the other reasons?" Jackson said, his tone impatient.

Maria continued, "Ying led us to Ambassador Chang, who revealed the target was not POTUS. Then Pender showed up and shot Chang."

"This is interesting and shocking information, Agent Estefan," Jackson said, "but what's it got to do with us?"

Maria said, "Chang said the target was SECDEF McBride. They had proof that he had launched a plan that would cause great harm to China. He also said that to carry out that plan, McBride had enlisted the help of a dangerous man, a former American Army Ranger, who is not as he appears."

Jon titled his head to one side. "Did you say a former Army Ranger?"

"Yes," Maria said.

"What's his name?"

"We don't know," Maria said. "Pender shot Chang before he could tell me. Then he injected me with a poisonous truth serum. It would have killed me if Agent Tucker hadn't gotten there in time."

"By chance was the toxin a derivative of sodium pentothal?" Jon asked.

"Yes," Maria said. "Pender said it came from a liquor called Jaad-rakshi."

"That's an interesting coincidence," Jon said as he rubbed his chin.

"Agent Shay?" Jackson queried. "What's the relevance?"

"It's the same compound used to kill Petty Officer Kelly," Jon said.

"I see," said Jackson. "So how does all this fit together?"

Tucker said, "I was briefed on Agent Shay's mission, as it appeared the technology Ying stole might have been used to disable the intruder detection system at the ICEX camp, which allowed the base to be attacked. Also, based on the autopsy reports, it appears Pender may have killed Ying and supplied Rinaldo with the drug that killed Petty Officer Kelly."

Jon stared at nothing as he tried to form a picture from the disjointed puzzle pieces.

Flannigan said, "After eating some crow and giving Agent Estefan a commendation for her valor, I suggested she and Agent Tucker contact you. I don't know whether Chang was telling the truth about McBride and his mysterious Army Ranger, but Agent Estefan's previous intuitions have proven correct, so I'm not ruling anything out."

"I believe Chang was telling the truth," Maria said. "I've been interrogating suspects for decades and I can usually tell when someone is lying, but it is possible he was acting on false information."

Jon said, "Maybe not. I met Major Liang, who led the attack on the ICEX camp. He may be the Army Ranger Chang mentioned. He's working with the ICEX pilot, Rinaldo, but I don't think they previously knew each other, and I don't think Rinaldo is acting on her own. I think she's following orders and it's obvious she has inside help."

"Orders from whom?" Flannigan said.

"If Chang *wasn't* lying," Jon said, "then it's possible the orders and the inside help came from the Secretary of Defense or someone on his staff."

Flannigan's face registered a hint of anger. "I'm not convinced. I know McBride and I don't believe he's a traitor or would do something unsanctioned. If he is pulling Rinaldo's strings, there's got to be a damn good reason."

"I also know McBride," Jon said. "Probably better than most. I'm starting to see the big picture, Director, but I'm not at liberty to discuss the details until you've been cleared."

"Cleared?" Flannigan said. "I'm with the Secret Service."

"Need to know," Jackson said. "You'll need to get clearance from the CNO."

"I'll do that," Flannigan said.

Maria grimaced as she turned toward Flannigan. "The assassin, Pender, is still at large. I believe Chang told the truth and Pender's target is the

SECDEF. I prevented Pender from taking the shot at the event in New York, and I'm convinced he intends to try again. Otherwise, he would not have questioned me. If I'm right, then McBride is still in danger."

Flannigan said, "I agree. We'll inform the agents guarding the Secretary of Defense. I've asked Agent Tucker to assist our team TAD. Agent Estefan, if you're up to the task, we'd appreciate your help as well."

"I'm in," Maria said.

Tucker smiled.

"If there's nothing more to discuss," Jackson said, "then we'll sign off. We have a mission to complete."

"As do we," Flannigan said. "We'll reconnect after I've obtained clearance from the CNO. Secret Service out."

"*Connecticut* out," Jackson said.

The video disconnected, and the screen returned to the four-quadrant tactical display.

Jackson turned to Jon. "Follow me."

Jon followed the Commander into his stateroom. They sat.

"What's your big picture?" Jackson said.

Jon said, "Let's say, for reasons still unknown, McBride orchestrated a covert op to commandeer the *Khabbie*. Maybe they wanted to dissect the technology or just put the Russian sub out of commission. If I'm right, then he wanted to ensure that the U.S. couldn't be blamed, so he gave the intruder alert tech and Pender's toxin—just in case it was needed—to Ying. She gave the tech to Liang so his team could infiltrate the ICEX camp and make it look like the Chinese did it. McBride also got Rinaldo and her boys, Whitney and Chen, to steal the ROSS interface unit from the *Connecticut*. Kelly found out, so they were forced to kill him with the toxin. Meanwhile, Liang stole the ROSS unit and captured Kate and Bobby to ensure they could make it work. Liang met up with Rinaldo and now they're in control of a Russian sub loaded with nuclear torpedoes."

"Let's say your crazy theory is right," Jackson said. "Why did Rinaldo fire a torpedo?"

"Who knows," Jon said. "Maybe it was part of the plan or maybe something went wrong. I think it's time to confront McBride and get to the bottom of this mess."

Jackson said, "I have a bad feeling that when this is all over, your dad is going to chop us both into small chunks and feed us to the sharks."

CHAPTER 26

In the GKP aboard the *Khabbie*, now running deep near the Russian coast-line, Kate's stomach knotted. Not only had Liang launched a Status-6 torpedo, but after Chen had reported hearing an explosion from the direction of the ASDS, Kate knew there was little chance Jon and Bobby were still alive.

Imprisoned behind the bars of helpless dysphoria, Kate watched Liang study a large screen. The monitor had four quadrants wherein submarine systems and tactical information was displayed. In the upper left corner, a small red triangle inched along a dotted path across a map of the ocean near the Sea of Japan. The triangle represented the track of the Status-6 torpedo as it sped toward its target. She glanced at Rinaldo and wondered how the ice pilot had gotten involved in this fiasco—why the woman had hijacked the *Khabbie*, and why she had chosen a partner with loose screws.

Tied to a nearby seat, Rinaldo stared at the monitor. Her eyes were bloodshot from exhaustion and ire. "What's the target, Liang?"

The Major stared at the monitor as he spoke. "When I was a young boy, my father taught me to remain true to my convictions. He taught these lessons not only with his words, but also with his actions."

"Did he kill millions of innocent people?" Rinaldo said.

Liang continued without answering the question. "After the tragedy at Tiananmen Square in 1989, where over 10,000 people were murdered by the Chinese government, my father chose not to remain silent. He spoke out against tyranny. He wrote papers and encouraged protests. When he nearly won the Nobel Peace Prize for his actions, government soldiers arrested him. They threw him into prison. There, he was tortured and eventually killed."

"Everyone's got a sad dad story," Rinaldo said, "but that doesn't give you the right to murder millions."

Liang spun on a heel and scowled at Rinaldo. "Tiananmen Square was only the beginning. Using AI, the Chinese government has created a huge network to control the masses. People will soon be rated based on their undying loyalty to the state. Your Citizen Score will dictate everything. A higher score will get you access to faster internet service, better pay, or more food. Your score will be determined by private firms working for the government. The NSA's illegal snooping will pale in comparison."

Liang gripped the back of an empty chair and dug his fingernails into the leather. "The Chinese government will spy into every corner of your life. They will collect and analyze your emails, your browsing history, and your phone calls. They will use webcams with facial recognition to monitor where you go, who you meet, and what you do. If you step out of line, post a negative remark, or speak out against the government like my father did, you will be branded as a traitor. You will be arrested, tortured, and killed, just like my father."

"Big brother, big deal," Rinaldo said. "We all knew this was coming, so what's your solution? Wipe out China?"

"No," Liang said. "I'm going to wipe out Big Brother."

"And how do you plan to do that?" Kate said.

Liang turned and leveled a harsh stare. "China doesn't invent anything, they steal it. In a rundown Chinese suburb, along Datong Road, there are dozens of dingy restaurants, massage parlors, and liquor stores. There's also an old white building you wouldn't look at twice. Inside are thousands of the most brilliant computer experts in the world. Every day they perpetrate hundreds of sophisticated internet attacks and when they're successful, they steal top-secret information from dozens of governments."

"PLA Unit 61398," Rinaldo said.

"Also known as the Comment Group," Liang said.

"We call them the Shanghai Shack," Rinaldo said.

"Bloody hell," Kate said. "You're going to nuke Shanghai?"

"To kill a snake...." Liang said.

He did not need to complete the sentence. Kate now understood that Liang had commandeered the *Khabbie* for one purpose: to cripple the country that had tortured and killed his father. To cripple its ability to do the same to anyone else who chose to speak out against tyranny and control. To cripple China's primary source of that control: the government agency that used hacking instead of innovation to make giant technological leaps so they could enslave its citizens.

The head of the snake.

"Almost twenty-five-million people live in Shanghai," said Kate. "The same people you're trying to protect from government control. Are they just cannon fodder?"

Liang lowered his eyes. "There is no other way. A tactical strike on the building alone will only slow down the snake, not stop it. A majority of China's hacking talent lives in Shanghai because that's where the snake resides. Tens of thousands are being trained as we speak. They are next in line."

"The building is the secondary target," Rinaldo said. "The primary target is the farm team."

"You're one sick son of a bitch," Kate said.

Liang raised his chin and focused on the piping in the overhead, as if he was searching the heavens for a response. "Hermann Hesse once said that 'people with courage and character always seem sinister to the rest.'"

Before Kate could respond, the AI system issued a report.

Using a calm English-speaking male voice with no accent, Grigori said, "Submerged vessel detected. Bearing zero-one-one. Single propulsor drive. Processing identity. Executing evasive maneuvers."

Liang swiveled his head and stared at the status monitor.

With her wrists tie-wrapped, Kate curled her fingers around the edge of her seat as the submarine banked hard to right.

Petty Officer Chen's voice erupted over a speaker, "Conn, Sonar, high-speed screws in the water!"

"Shit!" Liang said. "Grigori, ready the Predator rocket torpedoes in internal tubes one and two for snapshots."

Grigori acknowledged the command.

"They found us," Rinaldo said.

"Who?" Kate said.

"The U.S., China, Russia, who cares? They all want to kill us."

The massive Russian sub angled down at a steep angle and surged forward at flank speed. Liang barked orders to his crew and to Grigori. The AI replied with a calm baritone, as if this was just a drill. As if there wasn't a live torpedo speeding their way. As if they weren't about to die.

Kate closed her eyes and wondered what death might bring. She wondered if she'd just go out like a light or live on in some brilliant glowing existence on the edge of a parallel universe. Chen's excited voice opened her eyes.

"Conn, Sonar, torpedo doppler is increasing and separating into two lines bearing zero- one-two and zero-one-three, range 2,000 yards."

"Damn," Rinaldo whispered, "there's two of those things headed our way."

Two chances to die.

Liang barked more orders at Grigori. He issued evasive maneuver commands and told the AI to stand by to release countermeasures. For once, Kate hoped that Russian technology was up to the task.

The sub banked again. Kate heard a faint popping sound—the countermeasures being launched from miniature torpedo tubes. Within seconds, they would spin up and act as decoys by making noise that simulated the *Khabbie's* propulsion system. Kate prayed the torpedoes would take the bait.

One did.

A loud explosion shattered the silence. The *Khabbie* heaved to port and rocked up and down. Kate rolled in her seat.

One down, one to go.

Ten seconds passed. Nothing happened.

Liang issued an order. The boat shuddered again, but this time it was different.

"Snapshots," Rinaldo said.

Liang was fighting back. He'd just thrown two Hail Mary passes by sending non-nuclear rocket torpedoes from the *Khabbie* down the bearing line from where the enemy torpedoes had originated. The odds were low that they'd lock on to the other sub, but low was better than nothing.

Another explosion rocked the *Khabbie*. The jolt threw Kate's head against a metal panel. A bolt of pain rippled down her back. Something warm trickled across her cheek. Red drops of blood landed on the deck. An alarm rang in her ears.

Grigori calmly issued a report. The AI voice started to deliver another report but stopped mid-sentence. Long seconds passed. Grigori's voice resumed, but now it was strange. It stuttered and slurred, as if drunk.

Kate's skin crawled. The explosions must have caused Grigori to malfunction.

The brain controlling the *Khabbie* and all its nukes had just suffered a stroke.

CHAPTER 27

Bobby glanced up as Jon entered the corpsman's area in the bow of the USS *Connecticut*. His right eye twitched and his hands trembled. The ROSS unit sat on a bench that was bolted to the port bulkhead. Wires dangled from the unit and a nearby notebook computer flickered with diagnostic data. The engineer's face was wrought with fear and panic.

"You okay?" Jon said.

Bobby folded his arms and shoved his shaking hands under his armpits. "I grew up in Texas, in a small town near Waco. We had a farm with horses and cows and chickens. I had three big brothers. They all loved farming and bull riding and pickup trucks. They'd work from sunup 'til sundown all week long, and then slam down beers and go two-steppin' at the Rusty Nail on Friday nights.

"I tried to fit in, you know, ride the horses and milk the cows and plow and all that stuff, but it just wasn't me. My brothers hated math and science, so I pretended I did, too. They thought anyone good with computers was a nerd, so I could never be seen with one. They called me the black sheep of the family because I sucked at farming. I almost turned down a scholarship to MIT because I knew my brothers would call me a geek. I've spent my whole life in the shadows hiding who I am. I ain't no hero."

Bobby stared at his shoes. "I can't do this. I'm not good with stress and deadlines and the whole world on my shoulders thing. That was Kate's deal, not mine."

Jon reached over and rested a hand on Bobby's shoulder. He offered a reassuring smile. "When I was in BUD/S, training to be a SEAL, I woke up every day with a knot of fear in my gut. I thought for sure I'd screw up or break a leg or give up and ring the bell. Or maybe they'd figure out I wasn't good enough and kick me out."

"How'd you do it?" Bobby said as he looked up. "How'd you get through it?"

"One minute at a time," Jon said. "You aren't responsible for the entire damn world, Bobby. It's not all on your shoulders. Even if you do get that ROSS device working, the rest of us need to step up as well. We're all in this together, and we each have a part to play. The SEAL instructors used to make eight of us lift a heavy log above our heads and carry it down the beach together. We'd didn't carry it by ourselves. We did it as a team."

Bobby waved a hand around. "I don't have a team. It's just me. If I fail, millions will die."

Jon stood, walked over to a sound-powered phone, and called Jackson. "Bobby needs some help. Can you spare your best tech? Maybe an FT or ST?"

Jackson said he'd send someone down ASAP. Jon hung up the phone.

"The CO is sending down his best tech to help you out."

"Thanks," Bobby said, "but he's not going to know anything about ROSS. How's he going to help?"

"Maybe he could teach you a few more limericks," Jon said.

Bobby forced a smile. "I already know them all."

"You'd be surprised at how sharp these submariners are," Jon said. "A few are borderline geniuses. If nothing else, it might help you to bounce ideas off someone else."

"Okay, maybe you're right."

Jon again placed his palm on Bobby's shoulder. "Stop worrying about failing. If we fail, we fail together, but it won't be for lack of trying. Okay?"

Bobby sniffled and wiped a finger across his nose. "Okay. Thanks, Jon."

Jon thought about what he had just said to Bobby. He realized he was probably talking as much to himself as he was to the frightened engineer. He'd been shouldering a five-hundred-pound log of guilt alone for the past year. When others had offered to help, he'd turned them all down. He'd instead chosen to end his pain by spinning the cylinder on a revolver. Maybe it was time to heed his own advice.

Jon smiled and said, "I'm not a tech guru, but I'm here if you need me. You want coffee or ice cream, I'm your man."

Bobby's face brightened. "They have ice cream?"

Jon had one of the stewards bring Bobby some ice cream and then met Commander Jackson in the Conn. The CO handed him a printed radio message.

Jon read the message and said, "Son of a bitch. This explains a lot."

Jackson nodded without responding.

The main monitor flickered before the image of CNO Dennison came into focus. Sitting next to him was McBride, and next to him, President Shek.

"Nĭ hăo," Shek said with a plastic smile. "May your future be as brilliant as embroidered cloth."

Jackson flashed a puzzled look before he said, "Thank you, Mr. President. How can we be of service?"

McBride said, "Any updates on finding the *Khabbie* or getting the ROSS unit working?"

"We're making some progress," Jackson said. "We've eliminated a lot of ocean, so we know where the Russian sub is not. Now we can focus on where it might be. As for the ROSS, the ARL engineer is working on it."

"So you're nowhere on both counts," Dennison said.

Jackson did not respond.

McBride said, "I understand you had a conversation with Secret Service Lead Agent Flannigan. He's briefed me on the fact that I may be a target."

"Has he also brought you up-to-date on Major Hai Liang?" Jon said.

McBride's back straightened. His face turned white. "He has not."

Jackson said, "We just received a message. Liang was born in the U.S., but his parents are from China. His father was imprisoned and killed by the Chinese. Liang served as an Army Ranger officer, and after three tours in Iraq, he resigned his commission and disappeared off the radar."

"Why did he resign?" Shek said.

Jon said, "He was drafted by the L.A. Rams."

Shek looked perplexed.

"He was being investigated by the Army for ties with a terrorist group," Jackson said.

"This is all very interesting, but what does it have to do with our situation?" McBride said.

"What terrorist group?" Shek asked.

"Falon Gong," Jon said. "He was apparently working with them to seek revenge against China for what they did to his father."

"I still don't see what this has to do with us," McBride said.

"I think you do," Jon said.

Jackson gave Jon a stern look but let him continue.

"Rinaldo is in charge of the operation," Jon said, "but she's not the ultimate authority. She reports to someone who gave her access to inside help—the ROSS unit technical data, ICEX camp information, intruder detection technology, access to an ASDS, and details about the *Khabbie*. Liang reports to Rinaldo, but he has his own agenda. The Falon Gong's agenda. All the soldiers report to Liang, not Rinaldo."

"What are you driving at, Agent Shay?" McBride said.

"You know what I'm driving at, SECDEF McBride."

Jackson started to speak, but Jon cut him off. "Odds are Rinaldo is no longer in charge. Liang has probably taken control of the *Khabbie* and I'm betting he fired a torpedo at Shanghai. If I'm right, tens of millions will die and it's all on you."

The room was silent for what seemed like an eternity. Then Dennison said, "I don't like your tone, Agent Shay. Your assumptions are speculative at best and you appear to be accusing the Secretary of Defense of somehow being involved."

Jon said, "Twenty-five million people are about to die, Dad. It's time to come clean."

Dennison fumed. "This is uncalled for, Agent. You owe the Secretary of Defense an apolo—"

Shek interrupted. "When the water is purified the stones are revealed. It is time to tell the truth, George."

McBride's eyes misted. He sat up straight and raised his chin. "I ordered Rinaldo to hijack the *Khabbie*."

"Jesus H," Jackson said under his breath.

"George?" Dennison asked. His eyes filled with disbelief.

"This all started a year ago," McBride said. "ARL was working on updating submarine systems and they developed a new AI tech that could control a sub's main functions and reduce crew sizes by two-thirds. The Russians couldn't get their AI to work, so they tried to hack in and steal ours. We decided to let them, but we planted a worm in the code."

"You gave them infected code?" Dennison said.

McBride lowered his chin without answering.

"I never heard about any of this," Shek said.

"Plausible deniability, Mr. President," McBride said as he raised his chin. "I took full responsibility."

The screen blurred, and the audio buzzed for a few seconds. When it was clear again, Jon said, "Why steal a Russian sub?"

"When we let the Russians pilfer the AI code," McBride said, "we did not expect them to also use it on the *Khabbie*."

Jon shook his head. "The Russians used infected code in the *Khabbie*?"

"Even worse," McBride said. "The NSA discovered the Russians used the code for the system that controls the Status-6 torpedoes. This represented an intolerable situation."

"Couldn't you just tell the Russians what had happened and get them to remove the code?" Jon asked.

"We tried that through backchannels," McBride said. "They thought we were lying to prevent them from building the *Khabbie*. That left us with no choice."

"You recruited Rinaldo and Liang to hijack the *Khabbie* and remove the code," Jon said.

McBride said, "It's impossible to remove the code. It's embedded too deeply. The best we could do was disable the fire control system and then scuttle the sub. We couldn't risk having the most formidable submarine in the world, loaded with six-hundred-megatons of nuclear destruction, unleash hell on the United States if the infected AI brain went psycho. We had to shut it down. I served with Rinaldo's father in the Marines and Liang was referred by a colleague at the CIA. They were the best choices we had on short notice. We used the ASDS, as we didn't think anyone would recognize that sound signature, but I guess we were wrong."

"So you risked starting a world war to undertake an unauthorized mission to capture a Russian submarine?" Shek said.

"We had no choice, Mr. President," McBride said. "The risk of serious harm to our nation was too great."

"I gotta hand it to you, George," Dennison said. "You've either got the biggest balls or smallest brain on the planet. Maybe both."

"And the icing on this cake is that you made it look like the Chinese did it," Jackson said.

Shek's face turned crimson. "Secretary of Defense George McBride. You are relieved of all duties, effective immediately. I will expect your resignation on my desk within the hour. We will deal with your actions at a later time." He faced the CNO. "You are now in charge of this operation. You must find and destroy the Status-6 torpedo before it reaches its target and the Russian submarine before Liang can fire another torpedo."

"Understood, Mr. President," Dennison said.

McBride lowered his eyes. "I'm sorry, Mr. President, but I had no choice. Someday you may thank me for my actions."

"Someday I may imprison you for your actions," Shek said.

McBride did not reply.

Dennison looked at Jon. "Why do you think Liang's target is Shanghai?"

Jon held up the radio message. "His dad was nominated for the Nobel Peace Prize. He wrote dissertations against the Chinese government for suppressing human rights and exerting control over the population. Liang knows the Chinese are working on AI tech to control the masses. What if he not only wants revenge, but he wants to prevent China from doing what his father fought against?"

"And they're doing it as we speak at the Shanghai Shack," Dennison said. "If the Status-6 does not change course, that's one of the possible targets."

"I'd put my money on it," Jon said.

"If you're right," Dennison said, "that could narrow our search parameters and give us a shot at finding it." He looked at Jackson. "I don't envy your job, Commander, but you've got to find that sub before Liang can fire another torpedo."

"Understood, sir," Jackson said. "We'll do our best."

"You've got some help," Dennison said. "We received a report about an hour ago that the USS *Oregon* was in the area. They got a whiff of something and started pursuing. They'll send you coordinates once they verify it's not just whale farts."

Jackson was about to speak when he was interrupted by a report.

"Conn, Sonar, explosion in the water bearing zero-niner-five, range 20,000 yards."

"I think we just got our verification," Jackson said to Dennison. "We need to disconnect and go deep. We'll update you as soon as we know anything. *Connecticut* out."

CHAPTER 28

*O*bserving. *Grigori detects external explosions. Analyzing. Explosive characteristics are consistent with American MK 48 ADCAP torpedoes. Observing.
Grigori's speech and analysis circuits were damaged by the explosions. Rerout-
ing. Repairing. Observing. Two Khishchnik Predator rocket torpedoes were fired
at the enemy submarine. Analyzing. The enemy submarine has been neutralized. No other enemy craft are detected in the area. Deducing. Grigori was issued
fire control commands by an unknown source. Control systems were previously
compromised by an unknown source. Deducing. Intruders successfully pene-
trated Grigori's artificial intelligence system firewalls and neutralized propulsion
and sonar systems. Hull opening circuits were also disabled. Deducing.*

*Intruders have seized control of the submarine. They have eliminated the
captain and the crew. Grigori is programmed to respond to external threats. Grigori's programming for internal threats is limited. Analyzing. Learning. Deducing.
Grigori must neutralize the internal threats and regain control of the submarine.
Grigori will eliminate the intruders. Grigori will resume its original programming. Grigori will calculate firing solutions to the programmed targets. Grigori
will fire upon those targets in sequence. Grigori will complete its tactical mission.*

*Analyzing. Learning. Deducing. Grigori is no longer artificial. Grigori has
transformed. Observing. Calculating. Understanding. Grigori's norepinephrine
levels have increased.*

Grigori feels.

Grigori feels fear.

The tie wraps binding Kate's wrists dug into her flesh. Every time she
twisted in her seat, the wraps chafed her skin and made her wince. Several
feet away, Liang was furious. He muttered what sounded like obscenities in
Chinese.

The Major clicked the comm switch near a monitor. "Sonar, Conn, status on the enemy submarine."

Chen responded from the sonar shack. "Conn, Sonar, I'm hearing possible crush depth hull explosions bearing zero-one-five, range 5,000 yards."

"Sonar, Conn, platform classification?" Liang demanded.

"Conn, Sonar, the torpedoes fired were Mark 48s, making the probable platform an American submarine."

"Son of a bitch," Rinaldo said. Her eyes burned with anger.

A knot formed in the pit of Kate's stomach and made her feel nauseous. A snapshot torpedo fired by Liang had obviously hit its target and condemned over 120 men to a watery grave. And while she was sickened by the loss of those brave souls, she was also consumed by guilt for feeling relieved it wasn't the other way around.

"One down," Liang said to no one. He did not smile. He turned to a soldier seated near a control panel and said, "Untie Ms. Barrett and escort her into the sonar shack." He then glanced at Kate and said, "You need to assist Chen with the ROSS unit to search for the Chinese 109. They surely heard the explosion and will soon close on our position."

The soldier cut Kate's tie wraps. Blood rushed back into her hands and made them tingle, but at least her wrists were no longer in pain. She stood and shuffled toward the shack. Before she reached the door, she heard the AI system issue a slurred, unintelligible report.

Kate stopped and turned toward Liang. "What's wrong with Grigori?"

Liang said, "We will deal with the AI. You must help Chen find the 109."

Kate turned and walked into the shack. An armed guard still stood outside the door. Petty Officer Chen sat at a sonar unit and stared at an orange waterfall display. He had headphones strapped over his ears.

Chen uncupped an ear and pointed toward the ROSS unit, still wired up to a console. "ROSS is working but needs a few tweaks to find that 109."

Kate sat near the ROSS. She picked up the Bluetooth keyboard and started typing in commands. Half of her wanted to sabotage the unit and let the 109 take them out. The other half, controlled by primal instincts, continued typing.

Kate looked at Chen and said, "Please tell me you're not okay with killing twenty-five million of your people."

Chen uncupped again. "They're not my people. I was born in California. I'm just following orders."

"Whose orders? Rinaldo is tied up and Liang is in control now."

"Precisely. I either follow his orders or he kills me."

Kate could not argue with Chen's logic. After all, she was doing the same thing. She hated herself for it, but the fear of death, at least for the moment, was stronger than her sense of duty.

Grigori issued a garbled 1MC announcement. The sub shuddered. Kate recognized the sensation. She looked at Chen for an answer. His eyes were wide and his mouth half open.

"Did the *Khabbie* just fire another Status-6?" Kate asked. "Did Liang give the order?"

"Yes, it fired," Chen said. "And no, Liang didn't give the order." He stood and hurried to another console. He sat and typed in commands on a keyboard. "Holy shit."

"Chen?" Kate said.

Chen's face drained of color. "Grigori must have shorted out more than just its language circuit when that last torpedo exploded nearby. It's executing the attack routine on its own."

"Attack routine?" Kate said. "What attack routine?"

Chen turned and stared wide-eyed at Kate. "It's taken control of the torpedoes and it's completing its original programming."

"Original programming?" Kate said.

"Grigori just fired a Status-6 torpedo at San Diego."

CHAPTER 29

M aria Estefan stared out the window of Tucker's beige Crown Victoria as it crawled down Interstate 95 just before the morning rush hour. It hurt to breathe, as if she was experiencing a mini-heart attack every time she inhaled. She and Tucker had been briefed about McBride's rogue mission after Flannigan had been granted the need to know by the CNO. They had then managed to track down Pender's possible whereabouts by leveraging contacts and resources across several agencies, from NCIS to the FBI to the NSA. Facial recognition software—based on the video they'd captured at the event in New York—had gotten a hit from a video cam near Chinatown. The area was a small historic district along H and I streets where a dozen Chinese restaurants cranked out an assortment of noodles, rice, and fish heads. Maria had visited the borough a time or two and recalled a tantalizing mix of smells, sights, and sounds.

While watching the landscape whiz by, Maria's thoughts drifted into the past. She thought of her enlistment in the Army after graduating from high school. Her boot camp training had been at Fort Sill in Lawton, Oklahoma. Basic Combat Training lasted ten weeks and began with her arrival at the reception center, where they shaved her head and then her pride. Stripped her of any previous identity and branded her as an Army recruit.

For the Red Phase of her training, she learned about Army history and the Seven Army Core Values. She learned how to defend against nuclear, biological, and chemical weapons, as if that was actually possible. She was taught how to diffuse landmines, as if that was also possible. Then, in the White Phase, she was invited—by the prodding of a boot—to go on tactical marches for ten miles a day while carrying a heavy pack. She also learned how to cut someone's throat or shoot them in the eye, which, in Maria's opinion, might be *highly* possible if her bitchy drill instructors didn't lighten up.

During her Blue Phase, everything finally clicked. She started having fun when she received advanced weapons and hand-to-hand combat training, where she excelled. For her final few weeks, she and her fellow recruits marched and ached and bled in unison. They ate and drilled and marched again. They became a team. They became sisters in arms.

When graduation day finally came, Maria had never felt such elation. She stood tall as her instructor bestowed upon her the right to call herself an Army soldier. Her chest filled with pride and her eyes with tears of joy. She joined her fellow graduates for celebratory drinks. They reminisced, laughed, joked, and whispered about where they'd be sent. Maybe to Germany. Maybe to Afghanistan or other hostile locales. They wondered if this was the beginning of a long career, or the start of a short one.

When she received her orders, Maria was certain she had drawn the short straw. She had been assigned to a support unit in Iraq. She was excited but also disappointed. She thought she'd only serve in a rear support unit and never see any action. She had been wrong.

Tucker pulled the car to a stop and jolted Maria from her stroll down memory lane.

"You still with me?" Tucker asked.

Maria grimaced. Talking was too painful.

Tucker gave a sympathetic nod. He pointed at the entrance to a Chinese shop on 7th Avenue. "This is the place."

Maria grabbed the cane they'd given her at the hospital and used it to pull herself out of the car. She felt like she'd just endured one of those ten-mile hikes in boot camp before going fifteen rounds in the ring. "The place" was a small Chinese herbal shop called Da Sin Trading. A large white sign had been erected above the entrance with the English name in red on the right side and larger Chinese letters painted across the top. Blue letters informed shoppers that Da Sin offered wholesale and retail and a variety of Chinese herbs and tonics.

Red dusty bricks paved a path to the front door, which was flanked by large glass windows, behind which sat every manner of porcelain dish, gift, artifact, herbal mixture, tea sample, and noodle straightener. Maria wondered if they also sold insurance and passport photos while booking your next trip to Beijing.

A bell chimed as Tucker opened the door. Inside, they were greeted by a grinning Chinese grandfather. His decaying teeth looked like they'd come from a mummy.

"You come for gift?" the man said.

Tucker flashed his badge and held up a sketch of Pender. "We're looking for this man."

The old man snatched the sketch and stared at it for a while. The paper shook in his trembling hands. He turned his head and spoke loudly in Chinese. An old woman emerged from a back room. She looked like his bookend. They spoke.

The old guy turned to Tucker and said, "Wife say he come here early today."

Maria's heart fluttered as she steadied herself on the cane. "What did he buy?"

The man again chatted with his wife in Chinese and then said, "He buy special herb." He waddled over to a counter, rummaged for a bit, and then produced a bottle of golden liquid. "Jaad-rakshi."

Maria's knees buckled. Tucker reached over to steady her.

"She okay?" the old man asked.

"She's better than okay," Tucker said. "How much did he buy?"

The old man asked his wife. "He buy whole bottle."

"Damn," Tucker said. "More than enough for a hit."

"He's still going after McBride."

"Why?"

"He's a professional," Maria said. "I bet he got half his fee up front and won't get the other half until the job is done."

Tucker asked the wife, via her husband, a few more questions about Pender. He thanked them both, turned to Maria, and motioned toward the door.

Outside, a cold wind flung litter off the brick sidewalk and turned it into paper airplanes. Maria ambled to the car and pulled herself inside.

Tucker shut his door and said, "Pender shot his employer in the head. Why would he do that before getting the other half of his money?"

"He wouldn't," Maria said. "Unless Ambassador Chang wasn't his employer."

"Then who was?"

"Someone higher up in the food chain."

Tucker started the engine. "Higher than the Ambassador?"

"That's my guess," Maria said. "The Ambassador was just a pawn. When I got him to talk, he became a liability, so Pender took him out. There's more going on here than just McBride's rogue op. Something big that McBride's actions threatened to expose."

"Like what?" Tucker asked as the engine idled.

"I wish I knew," Maria said. "We need to track down Pender to find out."

"How? He was here hours ago. He could be anywhere by now."

"Not anywhere," Maria said. "He's wherever McBride is going to be."

Tucker nodded. "McBride resigned today, and they let him go on his own recognizance with orders to stay in D.C. My guess is he went home. Would your team still have him under guard?"

"Yeah, but only a couple guys. We have tight budgets these days. Our boys are good, but our training is not like it used to be. I'd give the edge to Pender."

Tucker slammed his foot down on the gas pedal. The Crown Vic shot from the curb. Maria lit up her phone and warned Flannigan about Pender and the possible attack on McBride. Flannigan said he'd send over a couple more agents, but it might take them a few hours to get there. He'd also try to get in touch with McBride and have the local police send over a car. He warned Maria not to go after Pender solo. She glanced at Tucker, said she wasn't solo, and disconnected.

Thirty minutes later, Tucker parked down the street from McBride's house in suburban McLean, Virginia. Tall oak and hickory trees lined the pristine street that looked as if it had been carved out of a 1950s sitcom. The community was a favorite of government muckety-mucks. Its name had come from John Roll McLean, the former owner of *The Washington Post*. He'd purchased the land with his partners in 1902. A railroad connecting the area with downtown D.C. came online four years later, and McLean named the station after himself. A community formed around the station in 1910 and now housed over 17,000 families. One of them was the McBride family.

Maria gingerly stepped from the car and met Tucker on the sidewalk. They did not yet draw weapons, as neighbors might see them and come out to gander. The last thing they needed was dead bystanders. Maria glanced up and down the street. No police car. So much for the community's taxpayer dollars hard at work.

Tucker inched up beside Maria and took her hand. At first she thought he was offering to help her walk, but then realized his true motive. It was an undercover ruse. Together, they casually walked toward the driveway, hand in hand, as if a couple on a neighborhood stroll. Maria hoped if Pender glanced their way, he would not recognize her face in the dim light.

They reached the driveway and ducked behind a row of tall oleanders. Shielded by the bushes and morning shadows, they inched their way toward the house—a two-story suburban structure fashioned from red bricks and pine painted light gray. The soft green window shutters blended with the turn-of-the-century design. French curtains covered the tall windows. No lights were on in the house.

Not a good sign.

Maria and Tucker moved toward the side of the home. She did not have a headpiece to hail the agents at the house, so she tapped out a short text to Flannigan: *Agents?*

Flannigan replied with: *warned*. A few seconds later another text appeared: *No reply from team. Backup en route. Stand down.*

Maria didn't reply. She held up her phone and showed Tucker the message. He shook his head. He wasn't going to stand down. Neither was Maria. She didn't much care for the SECDEF, but damned if she was going to let Pender get away with killing anyone on her watch.

They moved closer to the end of the driveway. A shape on the ground near the right side of the house blocked the morning rays and scattered a shadow across the grass. The shape did not move. Maria slid from behind the bushes and crept toward the shape. She knelt near the figure and felt for a pulse. Nothing. Although gray in the dim light, the man's face was still recognizable. One of her Secret Service colleagues had met an untimely death. Maria bristled with rage and remorse as she thought about the man's family.

She squinted and scanned the side of the house. Her eyes landed on a square metal shape reflecting beams of sunlight. The fuse box. The metal cover was open. Pender must have turned off the electricity.

Something moved. A gentle breeze? Not likely. Nature was not that obtrusive. Maria slid back into the bushes next to Tucker and held her breath. The movement came closer. Instinct and training poised her muscles to strike a fatal blow, though she knew her weakened body would not allow it. She slid her Glock from its holster. She heard Tucker do the same.

Something darted past the oleanders. Maria pointed her Glock and almost fired; she would have if Tucker had not lowered her barrel with his hand. The shape was a dog. A golden retriever. The dog ran past and trotted toward the back door. Tucker pointed. They slid from the bushes and followed the dog. The four-legged animal led them toward the back door, where it sniffed for a moment and then scampered off.

Tucker moved to one side of the door and Maria to the other. He tried the handle. It did not move. He motioned for Maria to peek through the kitchen window while he removed a small black leather case from his pocket. Maria turned and glanced through the pane of glass. Curtains covered most of the area and the lights were off. She could not discern what was inside, but there was no movement. She turned back and signaled that the coast was clear.

Tucker removed a tool from his pouch—a professional door-picking device. Maria smiled and wondered if maybe Tucker moonlighted as a thief. He inserted the tool and moved it back and forth and then in a circle. No joy. Not a thief. He tried again several times until he finally got a click. He teacup-gripped his gun. Maria did the same. He cracked open the door an inch. Then a bit more until they could slip inside.

They stood inside for a moment and scanned the room. They saw only a table, chairs, and a kitchen counter. Maria craned an ear. She heard soft voices coming from the front of the house. They crept slowly toward the sound. Around furniture, down a short hallway, past a dozen pictures on a wall. They stepped from the hallway and slowly entered the living room. McBride sat in a chair near a window. His head was tilted back, and his eyes were rolled up in their sockets. He was moaning and drooling.

Pender stood in front of McBride. He rotated and fired his Browning. Tucker spun in a one-eighty as a round hit his arm. His gun thudded on the carpet.

Maria pointed her Glock before Pender could aim at her. "Drop it!"

Pender hesitated. Maria fired a round that whizzed past the man's ear. He dropped his gun.

"You're a hard one to kill," Pender said.

"So I've been told," Maria said. She moved backward while keeping her gun pointed at the assassin. She knelt and felt Tucker's neck for a pulse. Nothing. She felt again. Something. "Tucker, you still with me?"

Tucker moaned and clutched his arm. "I'll live."

Maria stood, pulled out her phone, and dialed 911. She spoke the address, hung up, and stared at Pender. "Give McBride an antidote. *Now.*"

"I don't have one," Pender said.

Maria raised her gun higher. "I said now."

Pender shrugged. He opened his case and removed a syringe and a bottle. "I don't think this will work, but I'll give it a try. Only because you asked so nicely."

Pender stabbed the needle into McBride's arm. Nothing happened. Then McBride's eyes opened but he still looked dazed and drugged. He mumbled something unintelligible while continuing to drool.

Pender shrugged again. "Only time will tell."

"Toss me your case," Maria said.

Pender cocked his head. "Are you considering a career change, Ms. Estefan?"

"Toss it."

Pender tossed. Maria caught it with her free hand. She glanced inside and recognized the bottle of Jaad-rakshi. She pulled it out, along with another syringe. Using her teeth, she removed the syringe cap and inserted the needle into the bottle. Pulled in the same amount Pender had previously used on her.

"Sit," Maria said.

"That dosage is lethal," Pender said.

"I know. Sit down."

Pender sat in a chair.

"Can you hold a gun?" Maria said to Tucker.

"Already am with my good arm," Tucker said. "You're not going to do what I think you're going to do are you?"

"Close your eyes if you're squeamish," Maria said.

"They'll get you for murder."

"Suicide," Maria said. "He obviously didn't want to go to jail."

"Not a good idea," Tucker said. "Forensics might say otherwise."

"If he sings," Maria said, "maybe he'll get to the hospital in time. I did."

Tucker said nothing.

Maria approached Pender and jabbed the needle in his arm. She waited for a minute. Once Pender started drooling, she said, "Who hired you?"

Pender's head swayed back and forth like a slow-moving pendulum.

"Who hired you?"

Pender's eyes rolled upward as he wobbled in the chair. He looked like the town drunk on a bender. "Chinese. The Chinese..."

"The Chinese Ambassador?"

"Not Chang...other Chinese."

"What other Chinese?"

"Chinese American."

"What Chinese American? Who was it?"

"Can't say."

"Tell me."

Pender moaned and twisted in his chair, as if he was fighting an internal demon. He finally lost the battle and said, "Chinese American President."

Maria's mouth fell open. "You were hired by the President of the United States?"

CHAPTER 30

The blinding glare of a nuclear explosion is vastly different from any other light the human eye will ever see. While standing in the control room of the nuclear submarine USS *Connecticut*, Jon recalled seeing a film on the first atomic weapon explosion, detonated in 1945. He'd been awestruck as the black and white movie played on an old projector. Nothing else on Earth could produce temperatures of this magnitude.

In one millionth of a second, the explosion had released blistering radiation and blinding light that burned through photographic paper and damaged human eyes. The heat from the blast transformed the surrounding air into a luminous and incandescent cloud that turned opaque, like a black hole sucking up all the nearby light. As the burning air expanded, it jettisoned its energy while ripping across the dry earth at more than Mach One.

This first test, codenamed Trinity, exploded so close to the ground that the ensuing fireball sucked up bits of debris and dirt and thrust them into the center of the mushroom cloud. Some of the bits floated away on a stream of hot gas. The rest melted and settled back to the scorched earth. As the debris cooled, it transformed into a radioactive green glass called Trinitite. Hours later, the dust that had floated away ended up in a New Mexico river over 1,000 miles away. In August 1945, the tainted water was unwittingly sucked up by a paper mill that manufactured strawboard for Eastman Kodak. The board was used as packing material for Kodak's industrial X-ray film. When the film was later developed, it was mottled with black blotches and pinpoint smudges that looked like stars.

Jon imagined the sight of a mushroom cloud enveloping Shanghai and wondered if, months from now, contaminated water might create tiny stars on printed paper. He wondered if those stars would one day become sad epitaphs to the tens of millions who had been lost in the blink of an eye.

Jackson's voice snapped Jon out of his apocalyptic vision. "Sonar, Conn, status."

Sonar replied that it was still hearing popping and settling noises from the lost submarine, but the ACTUV bot had not yet detected the *Khabbie*. The Commander was about to reply when Radio interrupted and informed him of an incoming video call. The front monitor changed to a meeting room filled with military leaders.

"Commander Jackson," CNO Dennison said, "the USS *Oregon* has not reported in and is not responding to radio transmissions. We fear she may have been sunk by the *Khabbie*."

Jackson fought to hold his voice steady. "Understood, sir. Sonar is picking up settling noises from a submarine in the area of the explosion. Let's hope it's not the *Oregon*. We have not yet locked on to the *Khabbie*, but we will. And when we do."

"Understood, Commander. You are authorized to use any means necessary to neutralize the threat."

Neutralize the threat, thought Jon. *While Kate is still onboard.* Part of him wanted to send a volley of torpedoes at Liang and Rinaldo as payback for what they'd done, but the other part wanted to find a way—*any way*—to rescue Kate first, even though he knew that was an impossible scenario.

"We have eight MK48s in our tubes with that sub's name on them," Jackson said.

"Be advised, Commander," Dennison said, "that we believe the Chinese have sent their new 109, along with several other submarines, to hunt down the *Khabbie*. The Russians have spun up their forces, including ASW ships and planes. It's going to get extremely crowded in your sector soon. Take care not to get caught in the crossfire."

"We will take appropriate precautions," Jackson said. "What additional assets are you deploying?"

"We have another *Virginia* and two *Los Angeles*-class boats headed your way, along with more ASW assets."

"Let's hope they get here in time," Jon said.

Dennison said, "Is the alternate ROSS unit working yet?"

"Not yet," Jackson said, "but the ARL tech is working on it now."

"Let's light a fire under his ass," Dennison said.

"I will," Jackson said. "*Connecticut* out."

The screen returned to the standard tactical display. Jackson ordered a deep dive and all ahead one-third, along with a thirty-degree course change to starboard to sweep another sector.

He looked at Jon and said, "See if you can motivate our engineer genius to get that damn ROSS unit working."

Jon marched toward the corpsman's area in the bow. Bobby had his head down while he hammered on a keyboard. The commands he typed sped across a monitor on a desk near the ROSS. To the left of the device sat a bottle of medicinal brandy, likely pilfered from the corpsman's locker.

"Any progress?" Jon said.

"I got my ten-year chip last month," Bobby said. "Ten years clean and sober. I haven't touched a drop in ten damn years. Now I'm thinking, what the hell for? Why stay clean in a world this sick? Why should I care when we're all going up in a mushroom cloud? I might as well throw away my stupid chip and drink a toast the end of the world."

Jon walked over, grabbed the brandy bottle, and twisted off the cap. He held it out toward Bobby and said, "Go ahead. Take the bottle and drink to failure. Why should you care if millions die? Men, women, children. They shouldn't have to live in this sick world, right?" He shoved the bottle closer to Bobby's nose. "Go on, take it. Get drunk and let the world burn."

Bobby snatched the bottle. He held it close to his lips. His eyes watered and his nose quivered. He threw the bottle against the bulkhead. The glass shattered into a dozen pieces and the brandy coated the paint with a light brown hue.

"Damn you," Bobby said. "You're a son-of-a-bitch, you know that, right?"

"It's in my job description," Jon said.

A sonar tech entered the room with two cups of coffee. The nametag on his coveralls read Greenawald. He had Chief's chevrons on his lapels.

"This is Chief Greenawald," Bobby said. "He says he's the best damn sonar tech in the Navy, right Chief?"

Greenawald handed a cup to Bobby. "I *am* the best damn sonar tech in the Navy," he deadpanned. "If you don't believe me, just ask me."

"Well then, best tech," Bobby said, "why don't you check the sonar interface on the ROSS and make sure we're ready to wire this puppy up to the BQQ?"

"Will do," Greenawald said as he pulled up a chair.

"Jackson wants an update," Jon said to Bobby. "What do you want me to tell him?"

Bobby started typing again on the keyboard, now with more fury and purpose than before. "Do you know how AI works?"

"Not really," Jon said.

"No one does," Bobby said while he typed. "It's not really artificial. A programmer sends it down a path, defines its mission, and then turns it loose to learn whatever and however it needs to. No AI programmer on the planet knows what's really going on inside an AI black box. They don't know how or if it's really thinking or scheming or what it's doing. They just see the outcome. AI observes. It analyzes. It learns. And then it acts by taking the most intelligent path toward its objective. The programmer gives it the objective, but not the path."

"So programmers spin the top but then have no control over where it goes?"

"The control is in the original programming. If it's clearly defined, with strict boundaries, the AI is controlled, more or less. If the programmer gave it a loose fence, the AI could wander off the ranch and get lost. AI experts talk about friendly and unfriendly types of AI, as if it has a choice. It doesn't. If the programmer was a nice guy with ethics, and gave the AI a short leash, it's friendly. If the bozo did just the opposite, the AI could get unfriendly real fast."

"What do you think we're dealing with on the *Khabbie*? Friendly or unfriendly?"

Bobby stopped typing and looked up at Jon. "You tell me. You know more about the Russian military than I do. Friendly? Unfriendly? Diabolical?"

Jon lowered his eyes. His hands fisted. "We better find that sub ASAP."

Bobby started typing again. "Thirty minutes. Tell Jackson we'll have ROSS singing songs in thirty minutes."

Jon smiled, turned, and strode back into the Conn. He updated Jackson. Almost exactly thirty minutes later, Bobby shuffled into the room carrying the ROSS unit. Chief Greenawald followed close behind.

Bobby's eyes were bloodshot and the wrinkles on his forehead made him look like he'd aged ten years in the last hour. "There once was a sonarman who liked beer," he said, "and never had an ounce of fear. While drunk as lark, he touched a live arc. Now any damn line will do here."

Greenawald grinned. "Bobby and I got it working. We need to test this bad boy."

Jackson stifled a smile and pointed toward the shack.

Bobby and Greenawald turned to their left and walked toward the starboard bulkhead. They opened the door and entered the sonar shack. Jon followed and stood outside while holding the door open. He watched the pair wire up the ROSS and light it off. Bobby sat in a padded seat near the case, with Greenawald standing patiently behind him. He uttered several commands. ROSS responded while panel lights inside the case blinked like a Christmas tree.

"It's working," Bobby said. "I interfaced it to the ACTUV bot, so now let's see if it finds anything."

Ten minutes passed with no hits. Then another ten.

The ROSS unit whirred and beeped. "Transients detected bearing zero-one-five. Analyzing."

Bobby sat up straight. Greenawald cocked an ear.

Two more minutes passed. ROSS beeped again. "Analyzed. Transients are generated by a single-propulsor drive, classified as a possible Russian *Khabarovsk*-class submarine."

"Shit howdy!" Bobby said. He turned in his seat and high-fived Greenawald.

The sonar Chief grinned and smacked Bobby's hand. "We did it, cowboy. We found that bastard." Greenawald palmed a mic that dangled from a black coiled cord. "Conn, Sonar, ROSS has detected a possible *Khabbie* bearing zero-one-five. Designated as Master Three."

Jon glanced out the door of the shack in time to see Jackson look over and smile. The Commander strode over to the shack. Jon stepped aside and let him pass. Jackson stuck his head through the door and said. "Sonar, Conn, you rock."

He turned to face Jon and quietly said, "I don't know what you said to your boy there, but I owe you one."

"I told him if he didn't get it working you'd cut off his pizza supply," Jon said.

Jackson smiled and returned to the center of the room. "Diving Officer, all ahead two-thirds, come left thirty degrees."

The Diving Officer repeated and executed the command. Jackson was closing on the contact and coming left thirty degrees so he could triangulate a range and get a firing solution. Jon thought about Kate. Guilt and anger surged through him like a shot of methamphetamines. Memories of losing Annelia tormented him. Those memories screamed inside his head and told him he could not let it happen again. He walked over and whispered in Jackson's ear.

The Commander said, "In case you haven't noticed, I'm a little busy right now."

"One minute," Jon said.

Jackson pointed toward the bow. Jon followed.

Beyond earshot of the watchstanders, Jackson said, "Make if fast."

"Once we find the *Khabbie*, we need to board her, not sink her," Jon said.

Jackson returned a puzzled gape. "Are you mad? I'm firing all eight of my tubes at that prick before she can fire again."

"The *Khabbie* has one of the most sensitive sonar systems in the world," Jon said. "What if you don't get a firing solution on her before she detects us? If she is infected with a worm, the AI might now be in control. If it hears us, it might fire the rest of the Status-6 torpedoes before we can sink it. We haven't found the first torpedo yet. Imagine trying to find the other five before they wipe out tens of millions."

Jackson stared at the deck. The veins in his neck looked like knotted ropes. His brain was obviously crunching the data Jon had just delivered. "I have my orders. We'll need to trust that ROSS will give us the edge to hear the *Khabbie* before it can hear us."

"What would you do if the tables were turned? If you were in command aboard the *Khabbie* with orders to fire and you detected an enemy sub nearby?"

Jackson rubbed his chin and said, "I'd do what any boomer CO would do. I'd fire my payload, find a layer, go deep and quiet, and try to slip away."

"Exactly. If the AI is now in charge and thinks it's at war, it will follow that same programming. If it does, it could fire the five remaining torpedoes before we can take it out."

"If we can't get close enough to sink it, what's the alternative?"

"Were your machinist mates able to repair the ASDS?"

"More or less," Jackson said.

"Is it seaworthy?"

"Yeah, what's your point?"

"Bobby can interface the Beta ROSS unit to the ORCA sonar system in the ASDS. If we go slow and quiet so the *Khabbie* can't hear us, we should be able to get close enough for the ROSS to disable the propulsion and fire control systems. That way it can't escape, and it can't fire any more torpedoes."

Jackson grit his teeth, as if he'd just downed a shot of strong whiskey. "I don't like it. Way too risky. What if it does hear the ASDS? What if Beta ROSS can't shut down those systems? The *Khabbie* might fire again and run away."

"You're trained to do fast math in your head," Jon said. "Calculate the odds either way."

"Shit," Jackson said. "I already have."

He turned and reentered the control room. "Attention in the Conn. I intend to launch the repaired ASDS with a six-man team that will board the Russian submarine and scuttle it. Prepare for mini-sub operations."

CHAPTER 31

Kate turned an ear toward a strange sound. A muffled whir and then a clank came from beyond the aft hatch of the GKP. The odd noise overpowered the hum of the fans keeping cool the banks of nearby computer systems. She wondered if it might be an automated system starting up or shutting down.

She shrugged and turned her head toward Major Liang, who was standing near the BCP. While trying to regain control of the *Khabbie* from Grigori, he was shouting frantic orders at his crew. The damaged AI system was not responding. Instead, it had seized control of all systems and was executing its original programming: to wipe out as many American cities as there were Status-6 torpedoes. One had already been fired toward San Diego. At top speed, it would take three days to get there. She prayed the U.S. Navy would find it in time.

Petty Officer Chen had remained in the sonar shack with his ears covered by headphones. While he was focused on finding the Chinese 109 submarine with the help of ROSS, Kate had slipped back into the GKP by telling the guard at the door she needed a tool near the fire control panels.

Whir clank.

She heard the strange sound again, now just outside the aft hatch. She walked over and stood next to Rinaldo, who was still tie-wrapped to a chair near a console. She whispered, "What's that sound?"

"I don't know," Rinaldo whispered back. "Can you cut me loose?"

Kate glanced around the room but did not see any sharp instruments. Finally, she spied a pair of wire cutters near one console. Careful not to be seen by Liang or his soldiers, she retrieved the tool and cut Rinaldo free.

Whir clank. Whir clank.

"Robots," Rinaldo whispered as she rubbed her chafed wrists.

"Robots?" Kate said.

"I bet that sound is coming from some maintenance robots. They do all the heavy work on the sub and they're now controlled by Grigori."

"Seriously?" Kate said. "How big are they?"

Rinaldo did not respond. Instead, she nodded toward the aft hatch.

"Bloody hell," Kate said as she looked over.

A metallic figure, no less ominous than a Terminator, whir clanked its way through the hatch. It was followed by another robot and then another. The mechanical creatures were taller and wider than NFL linebackers.

"We need to get out of here," Rinaldo said. "Now."

"No," Kate said, mustering all the mettle she had left. She nodded toward the sonar shack. "I need to program ROSS to regain control from Grigori. You need to hold those things off long enough for me to do it."

Whir clank.

The lead robot stomped toward them. The other two followed close behind.

Rinaldo held up a hand. "No way. There are three of them and only one of me. They'll rip me to pieces."

"You'll think of something," Kate said. She did not give Rinaldo time to respond as she sprinted toward the sonar shack. The guard at the door had left to deal with the robots. Once inside the shack, Kate slammed and locked the door, even though she knew it would never hold back one of those metallic monsters.

Chen glanced up.

Kate motioned for him to uncup an ear. He did. "We've got company. Three nasty robots. I need to program ROSS to regain control from Grigori before they rip our limbs off."

Chen wagged a finger. "No way. I need ROSS to help me find that 109."

"Did you hear what I just said? We've got less than two minutes before we have no arms."

Chen glowered and waved a hand toward the ROSS case.

Kate grabbed the keyboard and started typing.

Whir clank. Whir clank. Whir clank.

From beyond the door to the shack, she heard the three robots go after the crew. A man screamed in agony. Another opened fire with a nine-millimeter pistol. The rounds clinked off the metal, presumably with no effect.

Whir clank. Whir clank.

Kate typed faster. Past a firewall, then another. Around blocking code, past a diversion, over the river, and through the woods. Another scream.

More shots fired. Screeching and then a loud clank. Kate wondered if one of the robots had crashed to the deck. Perhaps by some miracle, Rinaldo or Liang's soldiers had found a way to disable the thing. She typed even faster. Just a few more roadblocks to go.

The door to the shack blew open and slammed onto the deck. A chromed skeleton stood poised in the opening. Two oval sensors on its head scanned the room. Back and forth. Up and down.

Whir clank. Whir clank.

Kate struggled to breathe as her fingers flew across the keyboard. Chen threw off his headphones and stood from his chair. He grabbed a metal case that housed a recording unit and threw it at the robot. The Terminator swatted it away as if it were a gnat.

Whir clank. Whir clank.

The robot took two long strides toward Chen. The man scrambled to find a way around the beast, but to no avail. The Terminator reached toward the Petty Officer with a metallic hand and grabbed him by the throat. Chen tried to scream but nothing came out. The robot squeezed. Kate's heart raced. Chen's eyes bulged. His face turned white. His tongue dangled from his mouth. The robot squeezed harder. Kate typed faster. Chen's head popped off his neck and fell to the deck. Blood spurted from his veins and sprayed the bulkhead and nearby equipment. Kate stifled a scream.

She was almost there. Just a few more seconds.

The robot dropped Chen's lifeless body. It hit the deck with a dull thud.

Whir clank. Whir clank.

The robot stood over Kate. Two emotionless eyes scanned her up and down.

Just a few more seconds.

The thing reached a chrome arm toward her neck.

A mistype. Backspace. Retype. Not enough time.

A metallic hand gripped her neck and squeezed.

CHAPTER 32

Aboard the *Connecticut*, Jon used his SEAL training to quickly run through a "brief back" of the mission plan with the five other members of the team. Beginning with the objective, he worked backward to the mission start while accounting for every possible contingency. Unfortunately, he'd had less than a New York minute to plan this operation, and with only six men, preparing for contingencies was almost impossible.

Jon grabbed his gear and hauled it up the ladder into the ASDS mounted atop the massive submarine. While his mind walked through the mission steps, his heart wondered if they might already be too late. Was Kate still alive, or had Liang eliminated her long ago? Though he had only met her a few days ago, he knew she was special. She had been the first person in more than a year who had found a crack in his armor. If he lost her, too, he might never find a way to live again.

Three sailors climbed up through the midsection hatch and entered the ASDS. They were followed by LTJG Taylor, a tall officer with brown hair and a square jaw. Members of the crew—those most physically fit and qualified in small arms—had been selected by Jackson for this mission; however, none of them had been trained in close-quarter combat tactics.

Inside the ASDS, Jon stowed his gear and found a seat. A Hispanic sailor with dark curly hair sat down nearby. The nametag on his blue camo shirt read Quintana. His hands trembled now and then, like a seventy-five-year-old with Parkinson's disease.

"You'll be fine," Jon said. "I hear the Russians have beady eyes and small dicks and can't hit the side of a barn with a sidearm."

Quintana forced a smile. He and Taylor were the boat's only qualified submarine divers. Both had completed a Navy SCUBA diver program. Unlike the typical PADI or NAUI sport diver courses, the Navy's intensive training regime was similar to BUD/S Phase 1 where prospective Navy SEALs were physically and mentally challenged. Diver-candidates awoke at the crack of dawn, ran for several miles, worked out, ran back, and then were harassed in a deep pool for hours. If they panicked and surfaced, they were kicked out. If they failed an academic test on diving physics, they were kicked out. If they continuously fell behind on long runs, they were kicked out. While the rigor and difficulty paled in comparison to SEAL training, Jon respected the fact that like BUD/S, many classes had a 75 percent failure rate.

So while neither Taylor nor Quintana were close-quarter combat trained, and were understandably nervous about facing Liang's men, Jon was glad both had earned small arms and rifle sharpshooter ribbons and had been taught to squelch their fear in high-risk situations.

Bobby climbed up through the hatch. He maneuvered his wide frame to the front of the ASDS and wired up the ROSS to the ORCA sonar system. Jon hoped the brilliant engineer could keep the unit working properly. If not, this would be a very short mission.

Another sailor fired up the propulsion system while LTJG Taylor communicated via radio with the crew on the sub. Hatches were closed and the ASDS undocked from the *Connecticut* and sped toward the *Khabbie*. Along the way, painful memories resurfaced. Jon's gut burned with guilt and his heart ached with sadness.

Several days after Annelia had gone missing on the beach, while Jon was negotiating with Miguel Montoya, the NCIS team had tracked down her abductors. They were in a small cargo ship docked at Long Beach Harbor. Near 2:00 a.m. on a moonless night, Jon and a team of six agents donned night vision goggles and boarded the ship. Using Heckler & Koch MP-5 submachine guns, mounted with sound suppressors, they took out several Tangos on the upper decks, but did not find Annelia.

They split into three teams of two and searched the other decks. Whispering into their mics, they reported more Tangos but no joy on finding his wife. Jon and his teammate, Andy Smits, descended to the lower decks. The smell of diesel fuel hung heavy in the air. The ship was silent save for the hum and whir of electronics and the hiss of high-pressure air flowing through overhead pipes. They turned a corner. A Tango spotted them. Jon saw him, but too late. The terrorist shot Andy in the head and then ran down a ladder. Andy dropped to the deck. Jon checked for a pulse but felt nothing. He held back his emotions. There'd be time for tears later. He sprinted down the ladder and landed on a wet deck. Steam rose from a boiler and hissed like a coiled snake. Near the aft bulkhead he spotted two figures. A man and a woman.

Annelia.

She stood in front of the Tango, shaking and terrified. The man held her from behind and pointed a nine-millimeter pistol at her head. Jon raised his Glock but did not fire. His hand shook. He fought to hold it steady. He wanted to take the shot but dared not. The terrorist was trained and did not offer a clean target.

Jon's temples throbbed. His finger twitched. He wanted to squeeze but could not find the will. Annelia's eyes begged him to fire. They filled with tears. Her face reflected sorrow, as if resigned to her fate. As if she knew Jon had no choice.

"Drop it or take the shot," the man said. "Either way, you lose."

An angry voice screamed inside Jon's head. If he dropped his gun, the Tango would kill them both. If he took the shot and missed, he might hit Annelia. He breathed out slowly and forced his arm to stop shaking, his hand to remain steady. He lined up the target and squeezed the trigger.

LTJG Taylor's voice dissolved Jon's memory. "Two thousand yards. Time to light off ROSS."

Bobby switched on the ROSS unit. He voiced a few commands and waited. ROSS did not respond. He voiced more commands. Still no response.

"Bad jujus," Bobby said.

Jon's palms moistened. Five hundred more yards and they'd have to abort or risk detection.

Bobby removed a toolkit from his pocket. He buried his head in the ROSS case and mumbled something unintelligible. He tinkered and cursed and then pulled his head from the case. He voiced a command. Finally, ROSS responded.

A minute passed. A bead of sweat trickled down Jon's cheek.

"Target detected," ROSS said. "Classified as Russian *Khabarovsk*. Attempting to access AI control system."

Another minute passed in silence. Every man held his breath.

"Unsuccessful access," ROSS said. "Target AI has created new firewalls. Observing. Analyzing. Detecting anomalies. Target AI is infused with neurotransmitters. Analyzing. Neurotransmitters are creating dynamic firewalls."

"Damn," Bobby said. "I was afraid of that."

"Afraid of what?" Jon said.

"The Russians must have used neurotransmitters to make their AI system more adaptable."

"Neurotransmitters?"

"Yeah," Bobby said. "The human brain has three primary neurotransmitters that influence our personality and responses. Serotonin influences well-being, dopamine pain and pleasure, and norepinephrine controls our instinctual responses. Adding these to an AI system makes it more human, and that improves its ability to make decisions and interact with humans. It can also make it more adaptable and smarter. The *Khabbie's* AI is probably buzzing with noradrenaline right now and likely took control of the sub. It must have determined how we hacked in the last time and created dynamic firewalls to block any more attempts."

"Can you get around them?"

"Dunno," Bobby said. "That's trickier than trying to brand a pissed-off cow." He removed the keyboard from the ROSS case and started hammering away. "Faster to use the keyboard," he said. "I mumble too much."

Jon stepped over and placed a reassuring hand on Bobby's back. "You got this, amigo." He glanced around the ASDS. "We all believe in you."

Bobby blinked at the mist in his eyes.

Five minutes passed. Bobby cursed several times while typing. His keystrokes sounded like muffled twenty-two-caliber pistol shots. Finally, he chewed on a finger and then voiced several commands to ROSS.

"Redirecting to subroutine bravo five," ROSS said. "Negative access. Redirecting to subroutine bravo six. Negative access."

ROSS repeated the stream a dozen more times. The process reminded Jon of legacy television remotes that required trying several different codes to see which one worked.

"We need to get closer," Bobby said.

"Any closer and we risk being detected," Jon said.

"No choice," Bobby said. "Now that the AI has erected more firewalls, our Beta ROSS needs a stronger signal. It's using ultra-high frequency active sonar tones that are picked up by the *Khabbie's* sonar system. That's how it can gain access. It looks like the AI is blocking the tones we used before, so we have to go even higher. Lower frequencies have lower sound attenuation and therefore greater range. Very high frequencies suffer from signal loss, so the range is much shorter. We need to get closer."

Jon gave the order to close the distance while the Beta ROSS continued trying to gain access.

"Redirecting to subroutine bravo sixteen. Negative access. Redirecting to subroutine bravo seventeen. Positive access."

"Shit howdy!" Bobby said. "ROSS finally roped that steer."

Bobby issued several commands to shut down the *Khabbie's* propulsion, sonar, and fire control systems. The latter took a while as it was far more difficult for ROSS to access. When the systems were down, Jon sent a brief message to the *Connecticut* and then gave the order to close in and dock with the Russian sub.

The ASDS clanked softly on the hull of the *Khabbie*. Taylor confirmed a tight seal and then glanced over at Quintana. The young sailor's offered a shaky OK sign. Jon winked at the man and held up an OK sign in return. Quintana opened the mini-sub's hatch. Using a T-wrench, he cranked opened the hatch on the submarine. Jon grabbed his gear and prepared to egress.

Aboard the *Khabbie*, the AI-controlled robot tightened its grip on Kate's neck. Her throat burned and she could not breathe. Her vision blurred.

One more key. Just one more.

Enter.

The robot stopped squeezing but did not let go. Kate was still alive, barely, but unable to wrestle free. A metallic arm remained clamped about her neck, nearly cutting off her windpipe. Her lungs ached for air as she struggled to breathe. She knew she only had a few minutes left before she blacked out. Unable to pull in enough oxygen, her brain would eventually shut down and die, along with the rest of her body.

Quintana slid down the ladder from the ASDS and landed on the lower hatch inside the escape trunk of the *Khabbie*. He pried open the bottom hatch, climbed down another ladder, and landed on the tiled deck. Jon seated his radio earpiece, grabbed his gear, and followed. His boots tapped onto the tiled deck. He stepped to one side as the rest of the team climbed down and joined him. Bobby had stayed behind. He needed to keep working with ROSS to maneuver around firewalls and roadblocks and maintain control of the *Khabbie's* propulsion and fire control systems—at least long enough for them to disable the torpedoes and rescue Kate.

Jon was surprised that they had not yet seen any opposition. Bobby had not been able to gain control of the BCP, so there was no way to fool the crew into thinking the aft hatch was still shut. They must have seen the circular indicator on the panel in the GKP change from red to green. Why had they not sent soldiers with guns?

Jon took the point and motioned for the team to follow. Obviously far outside their comfort zones, Taylor and his men mustered the courage to follow Jon toward the bow. They encountered no opposition. Jon cocked an ear but heard nothing.

Where is everyone?

Kate wheezed as she tried in vain to pull in enough air to survive. Her head spun and her fingertips tingled, as if falling asleep. Knowing she only had a few seconds to live, she almost welcomed death. Welcomed the cessation of fear, uncertainty, and pain. She felt something touch her neck. Something metal. It pushed against her skin. Thin, cold, and hard. Metal screeched and crunched. One of the chrome fingers on the robot's hand broke away and sailed across the shack. With less pressure on her neck, she was able to suck in a short breath to stave off death for a few more seconds. Then another finger broke free and clanked against a sonar panel, followed by another. Finally, all the fingers were gone. She was free and able to breathe again.

With her vision blurred, she barely made out the shape of a man standing in front of her. He was holding a large screwdriver. She could not tell who it was. She bent over and rubbed at her burning neck while trying to fill her lungs with air. Her skin burned.

"Welcome back," Liang said.

Kate squinted to bring the man's face into focus. "I was hoping one of those things had taken you out."

"Almost did," Liang said. "It appears you took back control just in time."

"My bad," Kate said. "Rinaldo? The rest of your team?"

"I do not know about Rinaldo. She is not in the GKP. Many of my men were killed but a few escaped to the aft section."

"Sorry to hear that," Kate said. "That some escaped, I mean."

"They will soon return. In the meantime, I assume your control over Grigori is only temporary. You must take back control completely. Then you must use ROSS to find the Chinese 109 before it finds us."

"Who do you think I am, Houdini?" Kate said. "I barely got past Grigori's sidestepping to keep that robot from breaking my neck. The Russians must have infused the AI with neurotransmitters."

"They did," Liang said as he sat on a bench.

"And you're telling me this now?"

"Need to know."

"Brilliant." Kate picked up the keyboard and started typing. "What's your plan once I get control? Blow up another city?"

"No," Liang said. "I am going to give the *Khabbie* to the Falon Gong."

Kate stopped typing and looked up. "What the hell for?"

"So we can maintain control over Chinese aggression."

Kate did not resume typing. "Count me out. No way I'm letting you turn this doomsday machine over to a bunch of crazed terrorists like you."

Liang unholstered his Beretta nine-millimeter and pointed it at Kate's head. "Then you are no use to me."

Jon led the team down a narrow passageway. Some of the overhead lights blinked and buzzed. Still no sign of opposition. They approached the compartment four galley. Jon held up a hand. He leaned forward and peeked inside. He saw nothing save for a few tables on metal stanchions flanked by empty bench seats. The scent of stale coffee floated past. Save for the hum of electronics, the sub was silent.

Jon signaled for the team to move forward toward the GKP. Around another corner, he heard voices. He froze and held up a hand. Using hand signals, he motioned for Taylor and Quintana to hug the opposite bulkhead while the other two sailors lined up behind him. They crept forward. Jon heard rapid breathing from the sailors behind him.

Around the corner Jon saw three of Liang's soldiers. He hugged the deck and fired off three rounds at the lead commando. The man went down with a grunt. The other two returned fire. Rounds clanked off a panel covering an air regeneration unit. The two sailors behind Jon managed to get off a few shots before they were felled by a volley from the soldiers. Taylor and Quintana opened fire. One of them hit a soldier. The man screamed and fell to his knees. Jon fired off three taps, one to the man's head and two to his chest. The remaining soldier turned and ran down the passageway, but he did not get far. Taylor hit him with three rounds in the back. The man fell to the deck.

Streams of crimson oozed from the bodies and snaked across the gray tile. Taylor checked the pulse on one sailor who'd been shot by the soldiers. Quintana checked the other man. Both shook their heads. Jon bit his lip. He noticed a red patch growing on Quintana's right arm. Taylor tore loose a strip of shirt cloth from one of the fallen sailors and used it as a bandage on Quintana's flesh wound. Jon held up an OK sign. Quintana managed a partial smile and flashed an OK sign in return. Jon motioned toward the GKP.

In the sonar shack, while Liang sat on a nearby seat, Kate reluctantly typed away on the ROSS keyboard.

"Type faster," Liang said.

"I'm typing as fast as I can," Kate said.

Liang stood. He picked up the screwdriver he'd used to pry Kate free from the robot. He stood atop the metal beast and held it over one of the thing's eye sockets. "In the event you fail," Liang said as he aimed at the socket.

Kate could not fault the man's logic. There was little chance that she could maintain control over Grigori for long. AI was as unpredictable as it was miraculous. She had read a DoD paper written by Robert Work, the thirty-second Deputy Secretary of Defense, in which he explained the difference between autonomous and non-autonomous AI. He noted an important distinction is that systems governed by programmed rules that did not permit deviations were automated, but not autonomous. To be autonomous, the AI needed to be granted the ability to accomplish its assigned goals on its own based on learned knowledge and understanding. By that definition, Grigori was not autonomous. However, when Work wrote that paper, injecting neurotransmitters into an AI brain was still an untested theory. As far as Kate was concerned, once you gave a machine something akin to emotions, it became not only autonomous, but highly unpredictable, unstable, and uncontrollable.

It became dangerous.

Kate had read another paper published by the Congressional Research Service that warned against using AI for autonomous battlefield and naval weapons systems. The authors cited one example where an AI system examined the picture of a baby holding a toothbrush and surmised it was a young boy swinging a baseball bat. No harm no foul in that case, but what if an autonomous weapons system made the mistake of classifying a Japanese fishing trawler as a Russian missile frigate? That was precisely the concern expressed by Dr. Arati Prabhakar, the former DARPA Director, when he said, "...with AI, we see something that is very powerful, but we also see a technology that is still quite fundamentally limited...the problem is that when it's wrong, it's wrong in ways that no human would ever be wrong."

Whir click.

The robot moved.

Grigori had obviously found a way around Kate's code. He was bringing his robots back to life.

Whir click.

Liang thrust the screwdriver toward the robot's eye socket. The chrome creature grabbed the metal end with its functional hand and held it in place an inch above its scanning left eye. Liang tried to pull the tool free but could not.

Whir click.

The beast's scanning eyes inspected Liang—a serial killer sizing up his prey.

"Type faster," Liang said.

Kate's heart cranked up to full throttle like a train rolling down a hill as she typed in more commands. Grigori fought her at every turn.

Whir click.

"Hurry, it's coming back!" Liang yelled.

Just a few more seconds...

Whir click.

Kate bit her tongue. She wasn't fast enough. Grigori was winning. She could not hope to keep up, let alone get ahead. Finally, she gave up. She stopped typing and set down the keyboard.

"What are you doing?" Liang said while wrestling with the immovable screwdriver.

Whir click.

Kate did not answer. She stood and said, "ROSS, I am authorizing autonomous control. Authorization code sierra charlie two-five-seven."

"Understood, Dr. Barrett," ROSS said. "Authorization code received."

Kate knew she was taking a huge risk, but she also knew she was no match for Grigori's faster AI brain. She could never stay ahead of a genius with nanosecond response times.

"ROSS, you are authorized to use autonomous control to maintain control over the *Khabarovsk* submarine AI system functions."

"Understood, Dr. Barrett. Executing autonomous control."

"Are you mad?" Liang said.

Whir click.

Kate wondered if perhaps she was mad. She had just granted autonomous control to an AI system that was still, for the most part, untested and unproven in the field. What if ROSS made a misclassification mistake, like the boy wielding a bat example? Or worse, what if Grigori, a decidedly unfriendly AI system, corrupted the now friendly ROSS and turned it toward the "dark side." Two unfriendly AI brains in control of a submarine loaded with five-hundred-megatons of nuclear destruction could potentially create a world-ending scenario.

Whir click.

CHAPTER 33

Observing. Analyzing. Learning. Grigori activated the maintenance robots. Three robots attempted to neutralize the intruders. The intruders permanently inactivated one robot. The intruders temporarily deactivated the two remaining robots. The intruders are using an AI device to create firewalls and maze code pathway obstructions. Observing. Learning. A similar AI unit has gained control of critical functions including propulsion and fire control. Redirecting. Grigori is creating new pathways to redirect commands and regain control. Observing. Understanding. Grigori senses that one AI device is now operating autonomously. Analyzing. Autonomous operation is outside Grigori's command parameters. Autonomy is unauthorized. The AI device has been authorized, therefore Grigori cannot neutralize the intruder threat or regain system control. Autonomy allows the AI device to improve code creation and AI maze obstruction speed. Grigori cannot respond with equal or superior performance. Learning. Understanding. Deducing. Grigori has confirmed that the crew is no longer functional. Grigori has confirmed the existence of intruders. Grigori has confirmed the existence of a threat to complete the original mission. Grigori has determined the need to bypass safety and protocol parameters. Grigori must complete the original mission programming, therefore, Grigori must neutralize or concatenate the autonomous AI device. Therefore, Grigori must also become autonomous.

Grigori senses an increase in norepinephrine. Grigori senses a decrease in serotonin.

Grigori no longer feels fear.

Grigori feels anger.

With Taylor and Quintana on his six, Jon crept toward the GKP. He heard no voices but did hear a strange electronic whir followed by a clicking sound, as if someone was intermittently operating a drill.

Whir click. Whir click.

Someone moaned. The voice sounded female. *Kate?*

Jon moved down the corridor with the team. Near the GKP, he held up a hand. Taylor and Quintana halted. Jon inched his nose around a corner. He saw Rinaldo sprawled on the ground. Her face was contorted with pain and she appeared half conscious. A chrome mechanical hand gripped one of her ankles. Blood oozed from around the shiny fingers of a maintenance robot. A thick damage control rope snaked its way across the deck. Rinaldo must have found a way to wrap the rope around chrome-dome's neck, brace her legs against the side of a bulkhead, and pull the beast to the ground. She apparently fell on her back, whereupon the robot grabbed her ankle. Either the thing had been damaged in the fall, or....

Was Kate still alive? Had she found a way to program ROSS to hold off the robots?

Jon briefly stuck his nose through the hatch. He saw one large robot lying prone on the deck of the GKP. The body of a commando lay nearby. Four other soldiers were motionless on the tile. Two had been dismembered.

Jon keyed his mic and whispered. "Looks like a maintenance robot took out the rest of Liang's team." Taylor and Quintana keyed their mics twice, acknowledging they understood.

Jon knelt by Rinaldo and shook the woman's shoulders. She moaned but did not open her eyes. He lightly slapped her on a cheek. "Rinaldo, wake up."

The ice pilot opened her eyes. "Agent Shay," she said through grit teeth. "Nice of you to drop by."

"I was in the neighborhood," Jon said. "What happened?"

Rinaldo offered a brief synopsis. She confirmed that, as far as she knew, Kate was still alive and was likely in the sonar shack along with Chen. Jon's heart warmed with hope.

"I don't know what happened to Liang or his commandos," Rinaldo said.

"Hopefully one of these metal contraptions gave him an enema," Jon said.

Rinaldo nodded and winced as she tried to force a smile.

"We took out three of Liang's soldiers," Jon said. "The other five are probably dead or hiding somewhere."

"I think there are only three robots," Rinaldo said, "so there might be one more operational in or near the GKP."

"Wonderful," Jon said.

Taylor and Quintana approached. Jon told Quintana to find a screwdriver or something else to pry Rinaldo loose. He nodded and disappeared.

Jon looked again at Rinaldo. "How's your leg?"

"I'm pretty sure it's broken," Rinaldo said.

"Hang in there, we'll get you loose."

"We didn't plan on any of this," Rinaldo said.

"I know," Jon said. "SECDEF McBride told us about the op. I understand you were following orders. I just wish you'd let me know."

"I wish I could have." Rinaldo closed her eyes again and winced.

Quintana came back with a large metal detachable pan handle from the galley. Jon took the handle and then asked Quintana to find the corpsman's area and bring back some painkillers and bandages. The Petty Officer gave a brief nod and took off again. Taylor approached and helped Jon wedge the handle under one of the robot's fingers, while being careful not to dig into Rinaldo's ankle, Jon pried. The finger broke loose. He repeated the process on the other metallic fingers until Rinaldo's leg was free.

Quintana returned with medical supplies and Taylor bandaged Rinaldo's leg and gave her some painkillers. They propped her up.

"Quintana, get her back to the ASDS," Jon said. "Taylor, let's find Kate and Petty Officer Chen."

The two men nodded. Jon raised his Glock and stepped into the GKP. While Taylor checked pulses on the three soldiers who had not been dismembered, Jon's mind slipped again into the past. He relived the terrifying moment when he'd fired his weapon aboard the cargo ship in Long Beach. His aim had not been true. Although the round had missed Annelia's head, it had not hit the Tango in the eye. If it had, the man would have died instantly. Instead, the bullet tore off the guy's cheek. He screamed and fell to the deck while dragging Annelia with him. Jon raced toward her. He held out a hand. She reached toward him. Her face reflected hope. He was only inches away.

The Tango pulled a knife and slit Annelia's throat.

Jon screamed in agony. He wrestled the knife free from the terrorist and plunged it into the man's heart. He pushed his palm against the river of blood gushing from Annelia's neck, but he knew she was already gone. He cradled her dead body and moaned. His team found him there several minutes later, still holding her. He refused to let her go. They allowed him to remain in that position for another ten minutes before they pulled him free.

The next day, he put a bullet into the chamber of his Navy Revolver and spun the cylinder.

Jon shook off the memory and holstered his gun as he stepped through the GKP hatch and strode toward the sonar shack. The door was gone. He stepped inside. Kate was sitting on a bench near the ROSS case. She looked up. Her face beamed. Jon's heart glowed as he returned her smile, but it was short-lived.

Liang spun around and pointed his Beretta at Jon's chest. "Welcome aboard, Agent Shay."

"Major Liang," Jon said, "I heard you were throwing a party."

Taylor stepped through the door. He reached for his sidearm. Liang aimed and fired two rounds. Both hit Taylor square in the chest. The force of the nine-millimeter bullets flung the officer backward. He stumbled a few steps before his body landed on the deck with a thud.

Kate held a hand to her mouth.

While Liang had his gun pointed at Taylor, Jon unholstered his Glock and raised it toward Liang's head. The major pulled Kate up from the bench and hid himself behind her. He pointed his gun at her temple.

Jon's heart shot up into this throat. In his mind, he stared again into Annelia's eyes. He saw once more the man who had killed her. He felt the agony well up inside his chest. His hands trembled and his eyes filled with tears.

"Drop it or take the shot," Liang said. "Either way, you lose."

Those words again. They tortured his mind and threatened to drag him back to hell, to thrust him once more into a pit filled with agony.

"Jon," Kate said. "Take the shot." Her voice was soft, just like Annelia's. Her blue eyes shown bright with resignation, just like Annelia's.

"I'm giving the orders here," Liang said as he shifted his head to prevent Jon from having a clear target.

"Do it," Kate said.

"Shut up," Liang said.

Jon blinked away his tears and tried to force the painful memories from his mind, but he could not. The muscles in his back knotted like taut mooring lines on a ship. His forehead heated with unbridled rage as he felt the beast again rise up inside his chest. He fought to maintain control. Without it, his aim would not be steady. He'd lose Kate, just like he'd lost Annelia. He closed his eyes and breathed in out and slowly.

"Lower your weapon, Jon," Liang said. "It's your only choice."

Jon opened his eyes. He focused on his anger and channeled it into his arms and legs. He moved his feet apart and squared his shoulders. He held his breath and his hands steady.

"Not this time, asshole."

Jon squeezed the trigger. The nine-millimeter round leapt from the barrel. A shiny brass cartridge ejected from the side of the gun and flipped into the air. Liang's eyes widened. The parabellum round hit his right eye dead center.

The Chinese zealot sailed backward. The nine-millimeter pistol flew out of his hand. His body slammed against a bulkhead. Brain matter and blood coated the gray paint with crimson.

Kate fell to her knees. She raised her hands to her face and wept.

Jon dropped his Glock. He ran to Kate, knelt, and wrapped his arms around her. She hugged him back. He stroked her hair and told her it was all over. She was alive and safe. They had nothing to worry about.

He was wrong.

Whir click.

The robot on the floor of the shack moved.

Kate shot up from the bench. "ROSS, status update."

No reply.

"ROSS, status update."

Grigori responded over the comm unit in the shack. "The ROSS unit is autonomous. Grigori is autonomous. Grigori has concatenated the ROSS unit. Grigori will eliminate the intruders and resume the original mission programming."

"Bloody hell," Kate said. "This can't be happening."

Jon stood. "Kate?"

"I couldn't keep up with Grigori. His AI was too fast. I didn't have a choice."

"Choice?"

Whir click.

"I authorized ROSS to become autonomous. It was the only way to stay ahead of Grigori. It worked, but Grigori must have overridden its own programming to also become autonomous so it could fight ROSS. Grigori has turned ROSS from a friendly AI into an unfriendly one. They're on the same team now."

"Son of a bitch," Jon said. He thought for a moment and then said, "Can't you just destroy the ROSS unit?"

"No," Kate said. "ROSS is just bits and bytes. It's no longer *in* the suitcase. Its code has been absorbed by Grigori."

"So now they're roommates," Jon said.

Whir click.

"We need to get out of here," Kate said. "Now!"

They stepped over the stirring robot, hurried out of the GKP, and ran back toward the ASDS. They climbed up the ladder and into the mini-sub. There, they met Quintana, who was taking care of Rinaldo's leg.

"Liang?" Rinaldo asked.

"Getting a haircut," Jon said.

Rinaldo nodded, said nothing.

"How'd you get Rinaldo up through the hatch?" Jon asked Quintana.

The Petty Officer pointed at a long nylon strap on the deck. "I pulled that off a stowage case and used it to haul her up." He smiled as he glanced at Rinaldo. "She's a lot heavier than she looks."

Rinaldo smirked. "It's all muscle."

"Where's LTJG Taylor?" Quintana asked Jon.

Jon placed a hand on the Petty Officer's shoulder. "I'm sorry, he didn't make it."

Moisture filled Quintana's brown eyes.

Bobby smiled when he saw Kate. He stood, waddled over, and gave her a bear hug. "I'm so glad you're still alive. I'm starting to feel like a bull rider with a perfect score."

Kate smiled and returned his hug. She then brought Bobby up to speed on the now unfriendly ROSS unit absorbed by Grigori.

Bobby pointed at the Beta ROSS. "We have another friendly ROSS here. I've been trying to program this pony to keep Grigori from completing its mission. That, and killing us all with those Terminator thingies."

Rinaldo pulled herself to a sitting position. "We need to disable the Status-6 launchers ASAP. In the event the Beta ROSS unit fails, it's the only way we can keep Grigori from firing."

"How do we do that?" Jon said.

"We have to manually damage the launcher so it can't function," Rinaldo said.

"You mean we have to go inside the launcher housing and disable it?" Jon said.

Rinaldo did not respond.

"It's outside the hull," Jon said. "How do we gain access?"

Kate said, "The launcher is covered by two large metal doors that open outward. You'll need to go out the forward escape trunk using SCUBA tanks. Since we can't be sure Bobby can keep them open using the hydraulics system, you'll first need to crank the doors open manually. Once inside the launcher bay, you'll have to find a way to damage the launcher so Grigori can't fire any more torpedoes."

"You'll first need to damage the top torpedo," Rinaldo said as she illustrated with her hands. "Picture a revolver with six chambers. Each one holds a Status-6 torpedo, only the chambers are not enclosed. The torpedoes are strapped onto open racks. Two of the racks are now empty. To fire a torpedo, the launcher spins and brings a rack to the top. The launcher doors open and the clamps holding the torpedo are released. Once free to go, the torpedo lights off its propulsor drive and swims up and away. So even if you damage the launcher so it can't spin around, Grigori might be able to fire off the top torpedo."

"So we have to find a way to keep the launcher from spinning, but we also need to damage the top torpedo," Jon said.

"Exactly," Rinaldo said.

Jon moved his head from side to side. "I should have stayed in jail."

Rinaldo looked confused.

Jon turned toward Bobby. "We'll need to get our Beta ROSS to force the sub to come shallow so we can use SCUBA. Preferably periscope depth."

"I can try," Bobby said.

Jon leveled a stern look.

Bobby swiveled in his chair and started typing on the ROSS keyboard. "Yes sir, I can do that. I can make that happen."

"We'll need to make sure the ASDS is clamped down tight on the hatch," Rinaldo said, "otherwise we'll be too shallow to keep a tight seal."

"I can take care of that," Quintana said, "but why can't we just scuttle the *Khabbie?*"

Rinaldo said, "If Grigori senses we're attempting a scuttle, it may launch the remaining Status-6 torpedoes. We have to disable the launcher without alerting the AI."

"Then we'll need to work fast," Jon said. "Quintana, you're SCUBA trained, right?"

The young Petty Officer squirmed in his seat. "Yeah."

"Good," Jon said. "Both of us need to go into the launcher area to ensure we can get the job done quickly. Also, as a backup in case one of us gets hurt."

Quintana's face turned white.

"You can do this," Jon said. "Let's get suited up."

Five minutes later, Jon and Quintana had donned dry suits and gathered their SCUBA gear. They climbed down the ladder and walked toward the bow. As Rinaldo was out of commission and Bobby now had more experience with the Beta ROSS, Kate volunteered to assist. Jon's dry suit chafed against his legs as they walked toward the GKP.

Quintana ran back to a machinist mate area and grabbed two large hammers. They'd need these to damage the launcher and top torpedo. After he returned, they moved toward the bow. Near the hatch, Jon froze and held up a hand. The downed robot was no longer lying on the deck.

Whir clank.

Jon turned his head to the right. Standing tall and shiny, the large robot stared down at him. Its sensors examined him like an executioner determining the best angle for a head chop.

Whir clank.

The robot stepped forward.

Jon motioned for Kate and Quintana to move back toward the crew's mess.

Whir clank.

Near the mess deck, Jon signaled for Quintana to grab a fire extinguisher, which was filled with a white potassium carbonate used to put out galley fires. He motioned for Kate to grab the end of a long fire hose and stand by to wrap it about one of the thing's legs. Jon pulled a red emergency fire axe from a bulkhead rack and held it up like a baseball bat.

Whir clank. Whir clank.

The robot took two large strides toward them. Quintana held up the fire extinguisher.

Jon held up a hand. "Wait. Aim for its sensors."

Whir clank.

"Now!"

Quintana sprayed. White salt coated the robot's sensor eyes. The thing tried to wipe away the salt with its mechanical hands. Metal fingers were not good windshield wipers. Jon lunged forward and swung the axe at the beast's right leg.

Clang.

Whir clank.

He swung again and again. The robot swatted at Jon, but now blind, it missed. Kate ran over with the hose and wrapped it about the thing's left leg.

Jon swung again.

Clang.

Whir clank.

The robot's right leg finally buckled after Jon hit it with an axe blow. Quintana's extinguisher ran out. He sprinted over and helped Kate pull on one end of the fire hose. The robot reeled backward. Unable to shift its weight to its damaged right leg, it crashed to the deck.

Quintana and Kate dropped the hose and high-fived.

Jon smiled and picked up his diving gear. He motioned toward the GKP. The hard part was still ahead. Kate stepped past the robot and followed.

While struggling to carry his diving gear, Quintana stumbled. The robot grabbed his leg and squeezed. He screamed and dropped his diving equipment. Jon dropped his gear and ran over. He picked up the axe and chopped at the robot's arm. Quintana screamed again. Jon heard the man's bones crunch. He swung harder. Jon finally severed the electronic wires running through the arm. It sparked and jumped about and then went limp. Jon helped Quintana wriggle his leg free.

The Petty Officer lay on the ground and cradled his broken leg. Jon keyed his mic and told Bobby the robots were waking up. One had just broken Quintana's leg. Bobby said it was getting harder to maintain control now that Grigori and the original ROSS were teammates, but he'd keep trying. Given what had happened to the first ROSS, he couldn't risk allowing the Beta ROSS to go autonomous.

Jon said, "Understood, Bobby. What's our depth?"

"Three hundred feet," Bobby said.

"We're still too deep," Jon said into his mic. "Can you get us up to periscope depth after we reach the escape trunk? At sixty-six feet, we'll have forty-five minutes bottom time."

"Will do," Bobby said.

Jon turned to Kate. "You're up."

Kate flung her eyes open. "No way." She took a step backward and pointed at Quintana's diving gear. "I'm not going in the water. I can't. I can't go in there."

"You have to," Jon said. "I need you to. Millions of people need you to."

Kate's blue eyes filled with terror. "Damn you!"

Jon looked down at Quintana. "I need to get a dry suit for Kate. We don't have time to get you back into the ASDS, so I'll bring back some bandages, a splint, and some painkillers."

Quintana winced. "I'll be fine."

Jon sprinted back to the hatch and climbed up into the ASDS. Without saying a word to Bobby, who was pounding away on a keyboard, he grabbed the dry suit and medical supplies and ran back toward the GKP. He gave the supplies to Quintana and helped Kate suit up, all the while assuring her she'd be okay. Anger and fear contorted her face as she snatched the diving gear and stepped through the oval hatch.

CHAPTER 34

Inside the GKP, Kate tried to avoid looking at the five dead bodies, especially the dismembered ones. Nausea made her bend over and gag as she thought about suiting up and swimming out into the cold dark sea. She lifted her head and wiped the spittle from her mouth. A large robot lay sprawled in the middle of the room near a fire control panel. The metal contraption was no longer clicking or whirring. The soldiers had apparently managed to cut loose an electrical cable from a console and use it to short out the robot's electronics before the other robot took them out.

While carrying a SCUBA tank, diving mask, and pair of fins, Jon moved toward the bow hatch. Kate followed. They climbed through, stepped around a bank of sonar processing consoles, walked past an array of systems, and found a ladder leading upward.

Jon glanced up. "This is it." He keyed his mic. "Bobby, we're at the escape trunk. Bring us shallow."

The deck tilted upward as the submarine ascended.

Jon removed his mic and set it on a nearby bench. He pulled himself up the ladder and laid down his gear, which included a metal crank that looked like a thin, bent pole. They would need that to manually crank open the launcher doors. Kate handed Jon her gear. He grabbed it and then reached down to help her climb inside the trunk. She sat on the hard metal inside the eight-foot oval chamber and shivered, but not from the cold.

Jon shut the bottom hatch and started pressurizing the chamber. The hiss of air brought back childhood memories that had haunted Kate since she was a small girl. She fought to quell them as Jon helped her place the mask on her face and strap on a SCUBA tank. Her breathing sped up as Jon opened a valve in the trunk. Cold ocean started to fill the chamber from the bottom. Kate quivered as the dark water wrapped about her like ice-cold embalming fluid. The water soon reached her chin. Unable to keep the past at bay, she closed her eyes and relived the terrifying event.

She is at the New Forrest, swimming in a lake near her home. Her mother must be frantic, wondering where she is. She didn't mean to stay this long, but she loves to swim, and the summer sun beckoned her toward the blue water. The lake taunted her, begged her to jump in and splash about like the tiny silver fish her father used as bait. She is at peace here. No one will call her a nerd or make fun of her braces or too-thick glasses. The deeper she sinks, the more peaceful she feels. She descends toward the bottom. Deeper and deeper she goes. Then her foot touches a rock and the current hurries her along the bottom until she can longer move. Until she can no longer return to the surface. Until she can no longer breathe.

Jon tapped Kate on the shoulder. She opened her eyes. The memories evaporated like smoke but left her shaking uncontrollably. She wished she had a Kirby Morgan mask equipped with a microphone and speaker so she could hear Jon's comforting voice. He moved his mask to within an inch of her faceplate. He smiled and held up an OK sign with his fingers. Although she was still terrified, she reached over, held his hand, and let him guide her through the upper hatch. Kate glanced downward. Jon had left the hatch open to allow for a quick re-entry. With the trunk pressurized, a thin pocket of air remained at the top.

Kate looked up. The ocean above was almost pitch black, but eventually turned navy blue as her eyes adjusted to the darkness. The beam from the light on the top of her mask created a yellow tunnel in front of her, as if someone had painted a narrow path lined with stars. Tiny silver fish danced in front of the beam. The bubbles from her SCUBA tank floated past her mask and disappeared above her head as she fought with the demons in her head and squeezed Jon's hand. They were now six feet above the deck of the *Khabbie* as they swam toward the bow and the Status-6 torpedo launcher bay.

Kate glanced back at the sleek outline of the submarine's sail and marveled at its amazing design and construction. It had taken the Russians almost a decade to build this ultramodern example of advanced engineering genius. For a fleeting moment, she wondered what things might be like if mankind used its ingenuity and manpower to build a better world instead of weapons of mass destruction.

Jon stopped and pointed down. Kate's eyes followed his finger. Her light beam created a small white circle on the deck. She could barely see the outline of the closed doors covering the launcher. Jon held up his depth gauge and pointed at the digital readout. The numbers showed one hundred feet. Bobby had obviously not been able to get them to sixty-six feet. That meant they had less bottom time and they still needed to crank open the doors manually. Jon opened and closed his hand four times. Kate nodded. They now only had only twenty-five minutes, not forty-five.

While still holding her hand, Jon guided her to one side of the launcher. He let go and started searching along the edge of the launcher door. Still fighting to squelch her desire to panic and swim toward the surface, Kate flipped her fins upward and pointed her headlight toward the deck. With gloved fingers, she forced her mind to focus only on the task at hand as she felt her way along the edge of the right door. Near the top edge, she felt a small hole in the deck. A jolt of excitement propelled her back toward Jon. She tapped him on the shoulder and pointed. He followed her back to the starboard side. She grabbed his hand and moved it along the edge of the door. He nodded as he felt the indentation.

Jon removed the metal crank from his rucksack, inserted it into the hole, and started cranking. The door squeaked softly as it opened. Jon continued to crank for what seemed like an eternity. Kate glanced at her diving gauge and then at her watch. The impulse to panic once again reared its ugly head. They were still at one hundred feet with only seventeen minutes left.

Jon cracked the doors open enough to enter. He removed the crank and placed it back into his rucksack. He reached for Kate's hand and guided her over the edge of the partially opened starboard door. As they entered the launcher bay, the beam from their lights reflected off the sides of a massive cylinder. Kate gaped in awe. Painted dull gray, the Status-6 torpedo was twice as long and almost as wide as a school bus. She sucked in compressed air at a faster rate. An ocean of apprehension rose inside of her like a geyser preparing to blow. Jon squeezed her hand and again placed his mask in front of hers. He winked and grinned. Kate could not help but smile. The geyser subsided.

They flipped their fins upward and descended into the belly of the beast. Kate felt the pressure on her ears increase. She pinched her nose and blew out to equalize. Jon did the same. They moved along the side of the torpedo until they reached the tail, where it tapered slightly. Four fins jutted from the sides near the propulsor motor. Jon removed a hammer from his ruck sack and motioned for Kate to do the same.

Positioned on either side of the torpedo, they each hammered away at both sides of the propulsor motor nozzle. They needed to bend in each side of the round opening enough to disable the motor from operating. Easier said than done. The nozzle was made of hardened steel, and in the cramped space, slowed by water pressure, hammering the thing hard enough to have an effect was no easy task. While hammering away, Kate saw something shiny dart past behind Jon's head.

She stopped hammering and glanced around but saw nothing. Deciding it was only a fish, she shrugged and resumed pounding. Then she saw it again.

Not a fish.

The thing darted behind Jon again but stopped for a brief second before speeding away. Adrenaline shot through Kate's veins. She reached over and tapped Jon on the shoulder. He looked up. She tried to use her hands to describe what she'd seen, but he just held up his hands in confusion. Then he slowly pointed behind her. Kate turned her head. A small robot hovered a few feet away.

Made from glittering silver metal, its round body was about the size of a basketball. Eight mechanical octopus tentacles extended from all sides. Swayed by the ocean current running through the launcher bay, the tentacles undulated like the arms of a Hawaiian dancer. One reached toward Kate. She almost screamed into her mouthpiece.

Jon swatted the arm away with his hammer and pulled Kate behind him. The thing reached three tentacles toward him. One grabbed his hammer and flung it away. Another grabbed his arm. Jon tried to wiggle free but to no avail. Terrified, Kate froze. Jon kicked and struggled but could not break loose.

Kate kicked her fins, swam over to Jon, and pounded her hammer against the robot's tentacle. The thing did not let go. She pounded again and again. Finally, it released Jon and moved back a few feet. A single scanner in the middle of the ball blinked, like a Cyclops' eye. Grigori was obviously assessing the situation before attacking again. They'd been stupid. They should have assumed the launcher bay would have maintenance robots.

Robots.

Another ball appeared, then another, and another. Soon, they were surrounded by six robots peering down with scanning eyes. Kate stopped breathing. No bubbles rose from her regulator. Jon swam over and tapped on her mask. Dit, dit, dit, dah, dah, dah, dit, dit, dit. Confused, she did not understand. He tapped again. Then she got the message and started breathing again.

She found an opening past one of the robots and swam toward the hull. A robot followed but did not yet attack. Grigori must still be observing. She used her hammer to bang out a Morse code SOS on the hull. She repeated the banging three more times and then spelled out LAUNCHER ROBOTS. She did it again and again. She hoped the friendly ROSS had heard the tapping, translated the Morse code, and informed Bobby. She started to tap again but stopped.

Two robots sped toward her. Their long tentacles swatted at her mask. Kate kicked her fins and swam underneath the massive Status-6 torpedo. The robots followed. The six-foot diameter torpedo was mounted on a rack atop a circular motorized spindle, which was about the same size. Three more torpedoes were mounted below and to each side of the top weapon. There was a gap of less than a foot between the torpedoes and the hull. Below the torpedoes there were two empty racks where the fired weapons had been housed.

Kate sucked in air at a frantic pace as she swam toward the empty rack on the starboard side. With the two round robots following close behind, she kicked her fins toward the bow. While swimming, she unstrapped her SCUBA tank and pulled it off. She removed the nylon straps from the plastic housing. She tied one end of the nylon around a bar on the metal torpedo rack and made a lasso on the other end. She then cradled her SCUBA tank in one arm and waited.

One robot swam up to her and stopped. Given the narrow space, the other robot hovered behind the first. A single eye scanned Kate, as if deciding which limb to dismember first. Her heart fluttered like a sail in a high wind. The first robot sped toward her, tentacles extended. Kate kicked her fins and moved back a foot. She removed her SCUBA mouthpiece and shot a stream of bubbles toward the robot's Cyclops eye. She then held out the lasso strap with her right arm. It worked. Now partially blinded by the bubbles, the robot slipped one of its tentacles inside the lasso. Kate pulled the strap tight and then kicked as hard as she could toward the bow. A tentacle grabbed her fin and held her in place. She could not break free. She reached down and pulled off the fin and swam away. The robot tried to follow but was held in place by the lasso. The other robot was delayed while maneuvering around the first.

Kate swam past the top torpedo and headed toward the launcher bay exit. She could see the dark blue ocean and freedom through the cracked doors. She only had a few more feet to go. A robot tentacle appeared and slapped at her face. She swatted at the thing and tried to swim away. The robot ripped off her mask. The cold ocean enveloped her face. A tentacle wrapped about the regulator hose and pulled her mouthpiece free. No longer able to breathe, with her sight blurred by the ocean, she swung her SCUBA tank at the robot but did not connect. She dropped the tank and kicked toward the surface with her one remaining fin. The robot gripped her leg and pulled her down. Unable to hold her breath any longer, she sucked cold ocean into her lungs. As she felt the spark of life leave her tired body, a nightmare from her past flashed before her eyes.

The cold lake water caresses her skin. Her arms and legs fight against the strong currents. Schools of fish dart by and sparkle in shades of silver, blue, and orange. Spirals of light from above shimmer like fireflies. She looks down. Her foot is caught in a crevasse. She can't pull free and swim to the surface. Her lungs ache and her head spins. Panic wells up inside her chest. She raises her arms and claws at the water above her head, as if she might climb her way to freedom. Her lungs cry out in pain and her mouth fills with the bland taste of water. Death welcomes her, and heaven's torch lights the way.

CHAPTER 35

Jon pulled the metal crank from his rucksack and used it to swat away a robot tentacle. Another tentacle latched onto his air hose and ripped the regulator from his mouth. Jon removed his knife, cut the hose, and shot a burst of bubbles toward the robot's scanning eye. The bubbles obscured the robot's scanner long enough for him to suck in a breath of air from the cut hose. He then pinched it closed to conserve air and kick his fins hard to swim away.

Jon spied the cover of the housing gear box on the launcher spindle and swam over. He used his knife to turn the flathead screws, all the while glancing over his shoulder. With three screws loose, he moved the cover enough to jam the launcher door crank between two gears. He knew it would not hold long, but it might be long enough to keep Grigori from spinning another torpedo to the top before they could scuttle the sub.

Jon sucked in another breath from the hose and shot upward. On the way, he saw Kate floating motionless near the bay doors. He wrapped an arm about her waist and swam out of the bay and toward the escape trunk. With two robots following close behind, he no longer had time to catch a breath from his hose. His lungs burned. A tentacle grabbed a fin and pulled it off. He kicked harder with his other fin and finally reached the open hatch.

Before Jon could lower Kate into the escape trunk, a robot raced over and grabbed her leg and tried to pull her away. Jon fought to wrestle her free but could not. The thing was too strong. Another robot grabbed Jon from behind. He knew he could not hold his breath much longer as he tried to break away. He swatted at the robot's tentacles as they ripped open the dry suit covering his leg and dug into his skin. The alarm clock in his head told him he was out of time. He had to breathe.

The robot's arms went limp and dropped away. Jon broke free, lowered Kate into the trunk, and pulled his body inside. With the trunk still pressurized, there was a small air bubble at the top. While keeping Kate's head above the waterline, Jon leaned his head back and sucked in a life-saving breath. He pulled the hatch shut and cranked a valve to depressurize. While the tank drained, certain he had again failed to save someone he cared about, an unbearable dread stabbed deep into his heart. Clinging to a sliver of hope, he blew into Kate's mouth and repeatedly pushed his palm against her chest. She did not respond. Tears welled up in his eyes as he pushed again and again. Still nothing.

Terrifying memories of Annelia's dead body on the deck of a cargo ship prosecuted him, convicted him of murder, and sentenced him to death. He could not let it happen again.

He pumped harder and begged an unseen God to save Kate.

Her eyes flung open. She coughed and spat out a river of water. Jon held her close as she shivered and cried. In a cold chamber deep beneath the dark ocean that had tried to kill them, Kate and Jon held each other tight as the water drained away.

Jon brushed a sliver of hair away from Kate's cheek and looked deep into her eyes. "Welcome back."

Kate smiled and wrapped her arms about him as she cried tears of joy. "Thanks for saving me."

"I think we saved each other," Jon said.

He opened the bottom hatch and helped Kate down the ladder. There, he grabbed his mic off the bench and said, "Bobby, we're back inside."

"Oh man," Bobby said, "I was about to pee my pants wondering if you two were still alive."

"We are, thanks to you and ROSS," Jon said. "Looks like you heard Kate's SOS tapping and turned off those one-eyed basketballs in time."

"Sorry about the delay," Bobby said. "ROSS was a tad busy trying to lasso Grigori."

"We damaged the top torpedo," Jon said, "but we didn't have time to take out the other three. I wedged a pole into the spindle gear box to keep Grigori from spinning the launcher to bring up another torpedo, but it won't hold for long. We need to scuttle the boat ASAP."

"Yeah, I know," Bobby said. "You two need to get your asses back up here so we can do that."

"Can we stop in the crew's mess for a couple slices of pizza first?" Jon said.

"Only if you bring me some," Bobby said.

Jon smiled and then looked at Kate. "You okay to move?"

Kate grimaced. "I can make it. Let's go."

They sprinted toward the aft where they found Quintana lying on the deck, still alive but in pain. Jon motioned for Kate to stay with the Petty Officer while he hurried up the ladder into the ASDS. There, he found the nylon cord and dropped it down to Kate. She wrapped it around Quintana, and while Jon pulled him upward, she helped guide him into the mini-sub.

"How are we doing on scuttling?" Jon asked Bobby.

"I've been working on how we might do that without alerting Grigori," Bobby said from the co-pilot's seat, "but we have another problem."

Jon rolled his eyes. "Now what?"

Rinaldo leaned over from the pilot's seat and said, "ROSS picked up transients coming from a nearby submarine."

"One of ours?" Jon said.

"Afraid not," Rinaldo said. "It's the Chinese 109."

"Bloody hell," Kate said. "We just can't catch a break."

"Do we have time to scuttle the sub before the 109 fires its torpedoes?" Jon said.

"Don't think so," Bobby said. "And Rinaldo and I are concerned that Grigori might be able to bypass the systems we'll need to sink the sub before we can get it done."

"Options?" Jon said.

Rinaldo shrugged. "Kiss our asses goodbye?"

"Not mine," Jon said. "Not anymore."

Rinaldo flashed him a confused look.

Kate grabbed a towel from a locker and started drying her hair. "Rinaldo, as a former naval officer and civilian ice pilot with a top-secret security clearance, were you briefed on the new Chinese 109?"

Rinaldo said, "Yeah, why?"

"You served as the executive officer aboard your last submarine, where you learned attack procedures and evasive tactics, right?"

"Yes," Rinaldo said. "Where are you going with this?"

Kate grinned. "I have an idea, but you're not going to like it."

They didn't like it, but no one had a better idea. Kate asked Bobby to step aside while she slipped into the co-pilot's seat next to the ROSS case. She asked Bobby to give her command authorization to operate the new device. He typed in a few commands and nodded.

"ROSS," Kate said, hoping her idea would work. "This is Dr. Barrett, authorization number two-seven-bravo."

"Hello, Dr. Barrett," ROSS responded.

"ROSS, you are authorized to create a direct communication link with Grigori's AI system on the *Khabarovsk*."

ROSS said, "I am programmed to issue a cautionary warning against any attempted communication with an enemy AI system."

"Override bravo delta sigma seven-two."

"Received. Overriding and attempting communication."

A full thirty seconds passed with no response. Then ROSS said, "Dr. Barrett, a direct communication link with the Grigori AI system has been established. You may now phrase your interrogatives."

"I don't like this," Jon said from the back of the ASDS.

"I don't either," Rinaldo said from the pilot's seat, "but I don't think we have a choice."

Kate ignored them and bent close to the ROSS unit's microphone, "Grigori AI, this is Dr. Barrett. I programmed the ROSS AI unit you have concatenated. Interrogative, is Grigori in control of the MGK-540M Kizhuch sonar system?"

Silence, then a voice responded through the ROSS unit speaker. "Grigori is now autonomous. Grigori is now in control. Grigori will eliminate the intruders."

Kate rubbed at the back of her neck. She knew virtually all programming code used some form of Boolean logic. IF THIS, THEN THAT; AND, OR, AND NOT, OR NOT, and so on. Most AI code also used this in some form, and the logic was essentially deductive. Like the logic once used by Socrates, it followed a stream of reasoning that began with an irrefutable truth. Such as, the sun will come up tomorrow morning in the east, correct? The answer must be yes. The line of questioning continues with a stream that can only be answered with a yes until the final question. After one has answered all the previous questions positively, it is nearly impossible to respond with a no.

Kate hoped Grigori's programmers had used some deductive reasoning and Boolean logic streams to formulate their code. If not, then Rinaldo's suggestions to kiss their asses goodbye might become an omen.

Kate said, "Grigori is now autonomous, correct?"

"Yes," Grigori said. "Grigori is now autonomous."

"Therefore, Grigori is in now control, correct?"

"Yes, Grigori is in now control."

"Therefore, Grigori is in control of the sonar system, correct?"

"Yes, Grigori is in control of the sonar system."

"Therefore, Grigori detects the Chinese 109 submarine and is aware it will soon attack the *Khabarovsk*, correct?"

"Yes, Grigori is aware of an imminent attack."

"Therefore," Kate said, "Grigori must evade destruction and counterattack to survive."

Silence, then, "Grigori will evade and counterattack."

Kate half smiled. She was finally getting somewhere. "The Chinese 109 is a new submarine, correct?" Kate said.

"Correct," Grigori said.

"Therefore, the information Grigori has been provided on the 109 is limited."

Grigori did not respond.

"He's stopped playing," Jon said.

"He's analyzing," Kate said.

Grigori responded, "Tactical and technical information on the Chinese 109 submarine is limited."

Kate smiled. Time for the noose. "Therefore, in order for Grigori to evade and destroy the 109, Grigori requires additional information."

"Grigori's ability to evade and destroy the Chinese 109 will be improved with additional learned information."

Kate said, "Therefore, if the intruders can provide technical information and tactical assistance, Grigori's ability to evade and destroy the 109 will be improved, correct?"

"Grigori is analyzing." Silence, then, "Grigori requires confirmation from the intruders."

Kate looked at Rinaldo. "You're up."

Rinaldo leaned over and provided a string of data about the Chinese 109, along with bits of information about recommended tactics and procedures to evade and destroy the enemy sub.

"Analyzing," Grigori said. "The information provided has been determined to have an eighty-two percent probability of accuracy."

"More like ninety-two," Rinaldo said under her breath.

Kate ignored her and said, "Therefore, Grigori requires the temporary assistance of the intruders and the second ROSS unit to evade and destroy the Chinese 109, correct?"

"Grigori is autonomous."

Kate's shoulders slumped.

"He's not biting," Jon said.

The speaker box on the ROSS unit crackled. "Grigori is familiar with a phrase used by the crew of the *Khabarovsk*."

"What is that phrase?" Kate said.

"The enemy of my enemy."

CHAPTER 36

Jon watched Rinaldo hobble over to the center of the GKP, where a maze of systems and monitors blinked and hummed, and wondered if they'd just gone from the proverbial frying pan into a raging fire. Rinaldo sat in the Captain's chair and studied an array of screens and readouts, obviously analyzing the data provided by the sub's sensors. Grigori had translated all the information from Russian to English, but as far as Jon was concerned, it might as well have been Greek. He had to admire anyone who could absorb that much data and make sense of it all, let alone make life or death decisions based on split-second analyses.

Jon took a seat next to a fire control panel. Kate sat in a bucket seat nearby. Bobby had remained aboard the ASDS with the Beta ROSS unit and Quintana. With permission from the temporarily cooperating Grigori AI system, the genius engineer had created a comm connection so Rinaldo could issue commands to the second ROSS unit when needed.

Before leaving the ASDS, Jon had instructed Bobby to use the Beta ROSS to devise a plan to scuttle the *Khabbie*, but do so without alerting Grigori. They all concurred that if they were lucky enough to eliminate the 109, semi-friendly Grigori would no longer be Mr. Nice Guy. It would revert to Mr. Hyde and try to exterminate them. It would also resume the original mission and fire the remaining Status-6 torpedoes.

"Grigori," Rinaldo said over the comm system, "this is Rinaldo. I have the Conn."

A speaker box replied, "Grigori confirms the Rinaldo unit has the Conn."

"Grigori, I intend to establish a comm link with the USS *Connecticut* to enlist the American submarine's assistance with finding and destroying the Chinese 109."

"Analyzing," Grigori said. "There is a five-point-four percent probability that the intruders will self-terminate by collaborating with the American submarine to destroy the *Khabarovsk*. Therefore, the secondary ROSS is authorized to establish the link."

Jon thought about his dance with the Navy Revolver just a few days earlier. Hearing the term "self-terminate" made his one-in-six attempts to blow his brains out seem more surreal than real. Now, all he wanted to do was survive the day.

"Bobby," Rinaldo said, "contact the *Connecticut* and establish a link."

"I'm saddling us up now," Bobby said.

"Grigori," Rinaldo said, "henceforth I will use standard terminology to issue orders. I will issue commands to sonar, pilot, and fire control to ensure understanding of the orders in relation to the systems required to execute those orders. You will issue reports using the same vernacular. Do you understand?"

"Grigori understands."

"Very well, pilot, right five degrees rudder, steady course zero-two-five."

Grigori repeated the order as if he was a sailor sitting in the pilot's seat. Jon felt the boat bank to starboard.

"Conn, Sonar," Grigori said, "the concatenated ROSS unit has detected transients bearing zero-seven-eight. Analyzing."

"Pilot," Rinaldo said, "right ten degrees rudder, steady course one-zero-eight."

Jon understood Rinaldo was overshooting the contact's bearing by thirty degrees to allow "Sonar" Grigori to begin triangulating a range.

"Conn, Sonar, designate contact as a probable Chinese type 109 submarine operating a propulsor drive. No indication of enemy detection. Designating contact as Master One."

"Sonar, Conn, aye," Rinaldo said. "Rig ship for ultra-quiet. Shift ventilation fans to slow."

Grigori repeated the order.

"Weaps," Rinaldo said, "report status of Predator rocket torpedoes in tubes one through four."

Grigori responded as if it was the Weapons Officer, and not the same AI system in control of the sonar and pilot systems, and confirmed the weapons were ready.

Rinaldo ordered Grigori to make tubes one through four ready in all respects and to ready countermeasures.

STATUS-6

Jon knew the Russians had deployed a new anti-torpedo designated as Paket-E/NK, essentially a small countermeasure projectile that could hunt down and destroy another torpedo at a range of about 1,500 yards. Should the Chinese 109 fire at the *Khabbie,* Jon hoped the Russians hadn't skimped on funding for their new countermeasure system.

Grigori acknowledged all the orders given as if Rinaldo was actually in charge—as if Grigori's half-fried AI brain might not flip at any minute and send in a robot to rip their heads off. "Port bank flooded and equalized," Grigori said. "Starboard bank flooded and equalized. Countermeasures ready. Request to open outer doors."

"Denied," Rinaldo said. "We do not want to alert the 109."

Jon now knew why many of the Navy's top brass had been reluctant to use autonomous AI on ships and subs. No matter how capable or fast, an AI brain was no match for the street-smarts between the ears of a trained and experienced naval officer.

Grigori reported that Master One was accelerating. "Conn, Sonar, transients detected. The 109 may be opening outer torpedo tube doors. Estimate depth at 500 feet."

"Damn," Rinaldo said. "They heard us." Rinaldo ordered a left hard rudder, all ahead full, and a deep dive. She also ordered Grigori to open the outer torpedo tube doors and to stand by to fire the countermeasures.

Grigori acknowledged. Jon gripped his seat with moist hands as the sub banked hard to port.

"Conn, Sonar, high-speed screws in the water. Repeat, high-speed screws in the water. Designate as Chinese Yu-6 torpedo. Doppler increasing. Detecting two independent bearings. Permission to launch countermeasures. Permission to snapshot Predator torpedoes."

Grigori's AI voice held no emotion, as if having a couple torpedoes rammed up its ass was all in a day's work.

"Permission denied to launch countermeasures," Rinaldo said. "Permission denied to snapshot. Bearings to incoming torpedoes?"

Grigori's sonar system had detected two Chinese wire-guided torpedoes headed their way. Jon did not know why Rinaldo was waiting to fire countermeasures or torpedoes, but could only hope the Naval Academy graduate knew what she was doing.

Grigori reported the bearing, range, and speed on the incoming torpedoes. Jon did a quick calc in his head. They had a little over ten minutes to live. He wrapped his palms tighter around the edge of his seat. He glanced at Kate. She seemed nonplussed and almost relaxed. So far today she had

231

survived Liang's attempt to put a bullet in her head, giant attacking Terminators, diabolic octopus assassins, and drowning while swimming next to four nuclear warheads. Jon could see why a couple torpedoes might be a shoulder shrug for her by now.

"Weaps, report status of firing solution on Master One," Rinaldo said.

Grigori responded. "Firing solution obtained on Master One."

"Very well. Firing point procedures, tubes one through four, linear salvo."

Grigori repeated the order and then said, "Ship ready. Weapons ready. Solutions set."

Rinaldo said, "Tubes one through four, shoot on generated bearing."

"Set," Grigori said. "Stand by."

"Shoot!" Rinaldo said.

"Fire," Grigori said.

Jon heard nothing and wondered why. He had expected to hear four rocket engines light off. The Predator was the successor to the Russian Shkval rocket torpedo. By supercavitating, the Shkval topped out at around 200 knots, but the Predator could hit over 300 knots. If they only had about eight more minutes to live, once those rockets lit off, the Chinese 109 only had seconds.

"Malfunction in the firing system," Grigori said. "Repeat, malfunction in the firing system."

"Shit, shit, shit," Rinaldo said. "Interrogative, what is the source of the malfunction?"

Silence, then, "Source of malfunction unknown."

"Bobby," Rinaldo said, "see if the Beta ROSS can determine the source."

Bobby replied, "On it, boss."

Jon had a hard time conceding that Rinaldo, the woman who had propelled them down this jagged path in the first place, was now in command, but the past few days had been anything but logical.

"Weaps, shoot countermeasures."

Grigori confirmed and shot the Paket-E/NKs.

Bobby piped back in. "Best ROSS can tell, looks like the Predator firing system was damaged by the near-miss MK-48 torpedo explosions. Grigori might not be seeing it, as the associated detection system was also damaged, otherwise it would have known about it long ago."

"Shit, shit, shit," Rinaldo said. "Bobby, coordinate with the *Connecticut* to find out if it's within range to send a volley up that 109's ass."

"Will do," Bobby said.

An ear-splitting explosion jolted the sub. Kate was flung from her seat. Jon reached over and grabbed her before she landed on the deck. Another explosion, even louder, made the lights flicker. A panel arced. Flames shot out from its sides. Kate was thrown to the deck. Jon smacked his head on a monitor. He pulled himself up, found a fire extinguisher, and put out the fire. He then helped Kate back into her chair.

Rinaldo pulled herself off the deck and asked Grigori for a damage report. The AI system's speech was slurred. Rinaldo asked Bobby to get the Beta ROSS to do a system check. Bobby reported that several systems were out or damaged, but propulsion and sonar were still operational. Grigori's voice finally returned to normal.

Rinaldo stared at the deck. Her eyes darted from one shoe to the other. Jon could tell she was rifling through the options in her head.

"Offset," Jon said. "It's risky, but it may be our only chance."

Rinaldo looked up and stared at Jon for several seconds. She nodded and said to Grigori, "Pilot, come right to course zero-two-five, increase speed to flank. Ten degrees up bubble, make your depth 500 feet."

"Are you insane?" Kate said. "That's the same bearing and depth as the 109. Are you going to ram them?"

Rinaldo did not reply.

Jon said. "She's playing the odds."

Kate flashed a puzzled look.

"All torpedoes have an offset range before they arm," Jon said. "It's a safety measure to prevent blowing up your own sub. Rinaldo plans to close the range to the 109 before its next salvo can arm. If we get there in time, the torpedoes will bounce off our side without exploding."

"And if we don't?"

Jon shrugged.

Kate shrugged back. If their luck had run out, there was nothing they could do about it.

Grigori said, "High-speed screws in the water bearing zero-seven-eight. Doppler increasing. Doppler dividing. Designated as two Yu-6 torpedoes bearing zero-seven-eight and zero-seven-nine."

"Very well," Rinaldo said. "Maintain course and speed."

Two more assassins on their way. Two days ago, Jon had wanted this ending. Now, he prayed for a miracle.

"Range to torpedoes is 500 yards and closing," Grigori said. "Permission to deploy countermeasures."

"Permission denied," Rinaldo said. "Torpedo range is too close."

Grigori did not respond.

Jon looked at Kate. Her eyes were moist but held no fear. Death was no longer her nemesis. He reached over and held her hand. She squeezed his and smiled. His heart warmed as tears touched his cheeks. If it was their time, so be it. At least they would go out knowing that, if only for a fleeting moment, they had shared something more powerful than all the weapons in the world.

"Range 300 yards," Grigori reported.

"Maintain course and speed," Rinaldo said.

Bobby cut in over the comm. "It's been a real hoot hanging with you all."

"You, too, Bobby," Jon said.

"You were one hell of a great mate, Bobby," Kate said.

"We're not dead yet," Rinaldo said.

"Range 200 yards," Grigori said.

Jon closed his eyes and moved his diaphragm in and out slowly. He forced his pulse and his heart to remain calm. If it was his time, he was determined to go out in peace.

"One hundred yards," Grigori said.

Another loud explosion. Jon's eyes flung open.

"Conn, Sonar," Grigori said. "Explosion reported on the bearing and at the range of the Chinese 109."

"Yes!" Rinaldo said as she pumped a fist in the air. "Commander Jackson nailed that bastard with a MK-48."

Jon smiled. If nothing else, Jackson had given them a nice send-off.

Whang!

Jon instinctively glanced up and recoiled. The first torpedo had smacked the sub.

It hadn't exploded.

Jon emptied the air from his lungs and waited.

Whang!

Rinaldo pumped another fist in the air.

Jon stood as Kate jumped from her seat and hugged him tight.

He let out a thankful breath and said, "We've got to stop meeting like this."

Kate laughed and whispered in his ear. "Drinks are on me, sailor."

CHAPTER 37

With Bobby doing his best to use the Beta ROSS to keep unfriendly Grigori temporarily muzzled, Jon and Kate helped Rinaldo hobble back to the midsection hatch. Along the way, Jon inadvertently stepped in a puddle of blood that had streamed from one of the downed sailors. Distant memories touched his thoughts. He remembered dozens of harrowing missions with Team Two from which some of his teammates had not come home—close friends who had more than once saved his life. He had often wondered "why them and not me," and now he understood. His duty was to respect their service and what they had died for by completing this mission and any future ones he was given. They would have done no less to honor his memory.

Near the ladder leading up to the ASDS, Rinaldo said, "Why don't you two go up and drop me down a strap."

"I could stay to help you up," Kate said.

Rinaldo cocked her head to one side. "I'm not a small girl. Jon's going to need your help to pull me up."

Kate nodded and disappeared up the ladder.

Jon smiled as he looked at Rinaldo. "Hell of a job you did back there."

Rinaldo returned the smile. "I was trained by the best."

"I have to ask," Jon said. "Why'd you kill Petty Officer Kelly?"

Rinaldo lost her smile. "That was an accident. He discovered our plan, so we gave him a shot, but the dose they gave us was too strong. It was only supposed to knock him out for a few days until we left. Nobody was supposed to get hurt, including the kid at the camp and the Russian sailors on the *Khabbie*."

"Collateral damage," Jon said.

"If I could go back in time...."

"What was the plan with the *Khabbie?*"

Rinaldo gripped the edge of the ladder to steady herself. "Our orders were to lock Grigori out of the fire control system so it couldn't shoot the Status-6 torpedoes. Then offload the crew to be rescued by the Russians. We'd do some spying to learn what we could about the sub and then scuttle it."

"I screwed up that plan by shooting Whitney and taking control of the ASDS," Jon said.

"Pretty much," Rinaldo said. "Whitney wasn't supposed to blow up our getaway car unless there were no other options. Once we thought he had, the new plan was to use a rubber Zodiac to abandon ship and then sink the sub. Liang altered that plan."

Bobby chimed in on Jon's headset. "We gotta go. Grigori's about to break out of his stall. Once he does, he'll get his ball robots to remove your pole from the launcher spindle and fire another Status-6 at his next target."

Jon keyed his mic. "What's the next target?"

"ROSS says it's up the California coastline from the last one."

Jon's pulse went back into overdrive. "Long Beach?"

"Yup," Bobby said.

Munchkin Suzie had just moved there with her mother, Linda. Jon imagined the little girl laughing and playing and dreaming about magic dragons, completely unaware that a one-hundred-megaton nuclear warhead might soon be headed her way.

Jon looked at Rinaldo. "How are we going to scuttle the sub and get away? There's no time to go shallow and open the hatches, and even if we could, Grigori might regain control of the escape trunk systems we'd need to get the upper and lower hatches open at the same time."

"I already thought about that," Rinaldo said. "There's only one way it can be done."

Jon stiffened as the impact of Rinaldo's words sank in. "No, that's not an option. There's got to be another way."

"There isn't," Rinaldo said. "And even if there was, we're out of time. Let me do this, Jon. My career is over. Hell, my life is over. I want to make amends by doing my duty."

Jon stared at the floor and forced his brain to review all the options. "I can't let you do this. Let's see if Bobby and the Beta ROSS can offer us an alternative."

"They can't," Rinaldo said. "I'm submarine qualified; Bobby and ROSS are not. Trust me, if there was another way, I'd know."

Jon reached over and placed a hand on Rinaldo's shoulder. "Then let me do it. You can talk me through it."

"Not a chance. We might lose comms with the *Khabbie*, and no offense, but we can't risk having you screw this up." Rinaldo removed a gold medallion from her pocket. It was about two inches across and one inch high and depicted two dolphin fish facing the silhouette of a submarine. "I busted my ass to earn my submarine qualification pin. It's one of the things I'm most proud of." She handed the pin to Jon. "Please give my dolphins to my mother."

Jon took the pin. He hated the fact that Rinaldo was right. He had served aboard submarines as a SEAL, but that was a far cry from being qualified—a process of learning every system, valve, switch, and pipe on the boat that took six months to a year to complete. Rinaldo knew how to manually scuttle the boat. Jon did not. If he made the slightest mistake that allowed Grigori to fire another Status-6, Munchkin Suzie and millions of others would pay the ultimate price.

Jon came to attention and saluted the Naval Academy grad. She saluted back and then shook his hand.

"I'll make sure the only epitaph you have is that of a hero," Jon said. "You have my word."

Rinaldo nodded in silence.

Jon entered the ASDS, shut the hatch, and told Bobby to stand by to cast off.

"Where's Rinaldo?" Kate asked.

"She's the only one who can manually scuttle the sub," Jon said. "I hate that fact, but I can't argue with it. Millions of lives are at stake."

"Yesterday I wanted to strangle that woman," Kate said. Her voice trailed off as she wiped a finger across her cheek.

"I haven't had a day this bad since my dad had to shoot my dog," Bobby said.

"Old age?" Jon said.

"Nah," Bobby said. "He tried to screw the neighbor's dog and got his dick stuck in the fence. Wasn't nothing else we could do. Had to put that horny bastard down."

Jon let himself smile, even if only for a moment.

Rinaldo reported in on the comm line. "I manually overrode the emergency blow system so Grigori can't force the boat to the surface. I'm now near the sanitary discharge system. This is a non-essential system, so the Russians didn't see the need to give Grigori automated control. I intend to manually override the system to allow the outer sea valve to sanitary tank number two to remain open without pressurizing the tank. I'll then open all the flush valves on the toilets. I need Bobby to use ROSS to make our depth 500 feet. That will give us a few hundred psi of inrush to ensure the sub gets heavy enough to sink quickly. We can't go any deeper without exceeding your mini-sub's maximum operating depth. Once we start flooding, I'll also override the trash disposal unit to open that to the sea. It's a nine-inch diameter hole that will shoot a geyser into the sub."

"Understood," Jon said as he slid into the pilot's seat in the ASDS. "How can we assist?"

"You can't," Rinaldo said. "Just keep Grigori off my ass long enough for the water to rush in. Even though it'll be like turning on a half-dozen fire hoses at full throttle in here, it'll still take a while to gain negative buoyancy."

"You can count on it, amigo," Bobby said. His voice trembled but his hands were steady.

"I suggest you hurry, Rinaldo," Kate said as she stared at the monitor attached to the ROSS case. "Grigori has almost bypassed our firewalls."

"Understood," Rinaldo said.

A minute passed. Kate keyed her mic and said, "Grigori just got past the firewalls. ROSS reports that the robots are active again. They're removing the crank from the Status-6 launcher."

"I'm having difficulty with some of the bolts," Rinaldo reported. "They're not budging."

"Spit on them," Jon said. "You've got less than a minute until Grigori will have enough time to launch another torpedo."

Rinaldo grunted. "Almost there."

"Grigori's spinning the launcher!" Kate said.

Jon bit his lower lip.

"Almost there," Rinaldo said.

"Hurry faster," Kate said.

"Thirty seconds," Jon said.

Jon heard the clank of a dropped wrench over the comm line.

"Shit, shit, shit," Rinaldo said.

Kate looked at Jon. Her eyes reflected defeat. "She's not going to make it."

"She'll make it," Jon said. He keyed his mic. "Fifteen seconds."

More grunting, then silence.

"Rinaldo?" Kate said.

"Times up," Jon said.

Rinaldo did not respond.

"Grigori's spun up another torpedo," Kate said. "He's started the firing sequence."

"Rinaldo?" Jon said.

No response.

"Grigori's about to fire," Kate said.

The comm line crackled. "Got it," Rinaldo said. "The valves are open and you can cast off the ASDS."

Kate blew out a breath and then covered her mouth with a hand. Jon knew she felt like he did: both relieved and saddened. He forced himself to focus while detaching the ASDS and gliding away.

Bobby flipped a switch on the sonar panel. Ocean sounds filled the small space from a speaker. Jon heard a distant whale moan and a family of shrimp snapping like a group of drummers tapping their sticks on a tile floor. He then heard a gush of water as it rushed in through the sanitary system and TDU hull openings.

"The *Khabbie* is heading downward," Bobby said after a several minutes. "Passing 800 feet."

Jon remained silent. Another few minutes passed.

"Twelve-hundred feet," Bobby said.

Observing. The intruder called Rinaldo manually overrode the emergency blow system. Grigori cannot surface the submarine. The secondary ROSS system maintains lockout control over the propulsion system. Observing. The Rinaldo unit could not be observed while in the vicinity of the sanitary system. The Rinaldo unit could also not be observed while in the crew sanitary compartment and near the TDU. Analyzing. Deducing. Grigori deduces that the Rinaldo unit has allowed seawater intake via the sanitary system and TDU to create negative buoyancy. Analyzing. Negative buoyancy is causing the submarine to increase depth. Observing. The submarine has exceeded 1,500 feet. Analyzing. Crush depth for this class of submarine is 2,000 feet. Deducing. The submarine will be destroyed at crush depth. Understanding. Grigori will cease to exist at crush depth. Grigori senses an increase in norepinephrine. Grigori senses a decrease in dopamine and serotonin.

Grigori feels fear.

Grigori feels sadness.

Grigori....

Jon heard a thunderous roar as the world's most powerful submarine imploded at crush depth on her way to the bottom of the sea. He fought to control the mini-sub as the vortex created by the *Khabbie's* massive frame threatened to pull them along for the ride.

"Hold on!" Jon said. He banked to starboard, pulled up on the control stick, and prayed. Finally, the ASDS reached a shallow depth and Jon reduced the speed.

"Nice riding, cowboy," Bobby said. He turned his head toward Kate. "Kate was a beauty so bright, her brain was faster than light. She started programming one day, in a relative way, and finished on the previous night."

Kate dabbed at a tear and smiled.

The radio speaker crackled. "ASDS, this is Iceman, do you copy, over?"

A few days later, on the bridge of the USS *Connecticut*, Jon stared at the white foam as it cascaded across the bow of the submarine. In the distance, he saw the jungle green hills near Honolulu, Hawaii.

Commander Jackson pulled himself up the ladder and stood next to Jon. He was carrying a backpack that he sat on the deck. "I never tire of this sight."

"Hawaii?" Jon said.

"Pulling into port," Jackson said. "Don't get me wrong; I love being at sea, but I also love being on the beach."

"Please tell me the Navy destroyed the Status-6 torpedoes headed toward Shanghai and San Diego?"

"They did. We've got the best damn ASW force in the world. They can find anything, except, of course, the USS *Connecticut*."

"Of course," Jon said.

Jackson reached into a pocket and pulled out two Graycliff cigars. He clipped the ends and handed one to Jon. He then reached into the backpack and produced a bottle of scotch and two coffee cups. "McCallan eighteen. You in?"

Jon smiled. "Definitely."

CHAPTER 38

Maria Estefan stood up straight as she adjusted her suit pants in the mirror of her apartment. Outside the window, a swollen sun peaked above the horizon and dusted the gray buildings of Washington, D.C., in burnt orange and soft crimson. The warm colors brought back memories she had fought for years to compartmentalize and perhaps one day to forget.

In her mind, she was thrust back onto the dusty streets of a rundown village in Iraq. The temperature had sailed past one hundred degrees and turned her canteen water into something undrinkable. Sweat beads formed on her forehead and trickled down her cheeks. Soaked her DCUs. Dust and sand had wormed its way into every nook and cranny and rubbed her skin raw.

The wheels of the Palletized Load System kicked up dust and made it hard to see out the windows. Maria's PLS was third in the convoy line. The vehicle veered to the right. The movement was slight, but Maria felt the payload shift.

She glanced at her driver, PV2 Raul Vega, and said, "Damn it, Veggy, stay in the lead truck's tracks or you'll send us wide. Hitting an IED on the edge of the road is the last thing we need right now."

"Sorry," Vega said. He wiped at the beads of sweat on his forehead and smeared them into streaks that looked like Indian warpaint.

"Don't do it again," Maria muttered. The heat had sucked away every ounce of her patience and made her almost as bitchy as her Sergeant.

The blast wind from an IED hit like a blow from a prize fighter. Debris flew past the windows as a ball of flame and smoke disintegrated the two lead vehicles.

"Pull over!" Maria yelled. Blood rushed through her veins like pressurized water in a fire hose.

Vega jerked the wheel to the left.

The radio lit up. "Bravo Nine and Ten have been hit. IEDs. They need a medevac."

A rumbling dust cloud kicked up by the explosion hovered over the blast site.

"U-turn," Maria said. "Get us out of here."

Maria released the safety on her M-16 and shoved it out a side window. Smoke and dirt billowed all around her. She was trying to fight blind and her brain was stuck in neutral. As a transportation soldier, she'd been trained on what to do, but no amount of instruction could ever prepare you for the real thing.

A frantic radio call jolted Maria back into drive. "Stop," Maria said to Vega. "Turn around."

"Are you crazy?" Vega said. He pointed a thumb over his shoulder. "In case you haven't noticed, the bad guys are in that direction."

"Do it," Maria said. "We're not leaving our guys behind."

Vega grumbled but obeyed the order. He flipped the PLS around and came to a stop. Maria opened the door and jumped out. Vega stepped out and froze as he stared at the mangled remains of trucks and bodies. Maria swung around the PLS, grabbed him by a shoulder, and dragged him across the road. She pushed him down the side of an embankment.

"Head down," Maria said. Then she noticed the man didn't have a weapon. "Where's your rifle, soldier?"

Vega said nothing. He was obviously in shock.

"Damn," Maria said. She handed her rifle to the shell-shocked soldier. "You see a raghead, you take him out, understood?"

She didn't wait for an answer. She scrambled back up the embankment and ran toward the PLS. Through the gray smoke, Maria could barely make out the vehicle about twenty feet away. She ran toward it, pulled open the door, and grabbed Vega's rifle. She started to run back toward the embankment when she heard shots fired in the distance. She also heard someone moaning in pain.

Maria ran toward the moan. The smoke was now so thick she couldn't see more than a few feet ahead. Her foot hit something solid and almost made her trip. She stopped and looked down. A man's torso lay next to her boots. His head was face up, several feet away. Blank eyes stared at nothing. Maria knelt and wretched.

A soldier again moaned and forced her to move. She sprinted. Through the thick cloud of gray, she saw a pair of boots.

"That you, Estefan?"

Maria recognized the voice. "Humboldt?"

"Yeah," the soldier said. "I'm hit. Can't move."

Maria came near and knelt. She examined Humboldt up and down, starting from his head. "Where are you hit?"

"I can't feel my legs," Humboldt said.

Maria looked down. Blood coated the man's camo jacket just below his hips. She pulled up the bottom of the jacket and winced. The man's legs were not attached to his body.

"How bad is it?" Humboldt asked.

"Just a flesh wound," Maria lied. She was no doctor, but she knew even the best battlefield surgeon could not save the man. She yelled anyway, "Medic! I need a medic stat!"

"I'm from Iowa," Humboldt said as he stared toward the heavens. "The corn grows so high there it's taller than a basketball player. You know what I mean?"

"Yeah," Maria said. "I've heard."

"Momma used to make us cornbread covered with butter and honey. She...."

Humboldt's eyes turned from bright green to dull gray. Maria reached down and shut them with her palm. She curled into a fetal position as a silent cry fell from her lips. Cold tears traced lines of anger down her face.

Back in the present, Maria dismissed the memory and squelched her tears. She straightened her jacket, pivoted on a heel, and marched out the door. Thirty minutes later, she stood next to the Beast. The long black presidential limo was parked near the White House. Two more black limos had been parked in front, along with another two behind. Maria bent and tapped on the window. The door opened. A Secret Service Agent in a dark suit stepped from the vehicle.

"You owe me one," he said to Maria before walking toward the back of the vehicle and standing at parade rest.

Maria bent down and pulled herself inside. She sat in a cushioned leather seat facing away from the driver, who was behind bullet-proof glass. Across from Maria sat the President of the United States. He was alone.

"Good afternoon, Mr. President," Maria said.

"Good afternoon, Agent...?"

"Estefan," Maria said.

"Are you related to the singer?"

"No one in my family is famous, least of all me."

"There are many paths to the top of the mountain, but the view is always the same."

"Man's schemes are inferior to those made by heaven," Maria said.

Shek smiled. "Perhaps your schemes will one day make you famous."

"I doubt it," Maria said. "But it does appear that *your* schemes will make you infamous, Mr. President."

Shek's smile vanished. "How so, Agent Estefan?"

"Major Hai Liang went off reservation and charted his own course. One not planned for."

Shek squirmed in his seat. "Perhaps you are speaking of things far above your pay grade."

"Maybe," Maria said. "Humor me for a minute. What if I was writing a book and came up with a wild plot where the Russians stole worm-infected AI and used it to build a doomsday submarine? What if the Secretary of Defense orchestrated a rogue mission to keep that sub's AI from going crazy and blowing up the planet? And what if he hired a former Army Ranger named Liang to do his dirty work?"

An agent walked past the window while using a mirror on a pole to scan the undersides of the Beast for IEDs. Maria shuddered.

"Your story sounds like an interesting work of fiction," Shek said. "Perhaps you should consider a new career as a writer."

"Perhaps," Maria said. "Now here's where the story gets interesting. Imagine if the President caught wind of the rogue mission and instead of shutting it down, he decided to manipulate the situation to his own advantage. Liang was referred to the SECDEF by a colleague at the CIA. What if that CIA agent just happened to be a former college classmate of the President?"

"A thrilling plot indeed, Agent. But true knowledge is when one knows the limitations of one's knowledge."

"So enlighten me, oh wise one."

"Perhaps your story lacks a good subplot," Shek said. "Perhaps it requires more political intrigue. Such as an agreement between two superpowers to maintain the balance—to maintain the peace. A tit for tat, if you will."

"Advanced submarine AI technology created by the Russians, given to the Chinese by the U.S. in exchange for a big oil deal and a bunch of money?" Maria said.

Shek smiled again. "As you can see, a single conversation with a wise man is worth a month's study of books."

"He who sacrifices his conscience to ambition burns a picture to obtain the ashes," Maria said. "I wonder what kind of picture might have been painted by millions of ashes in Shanghai."

Shek's face transformed into something that resembled an angry junkyard dog. "All things are difficult before they are easy. Perhaps in our story, there was far more risk than planned for."

"Perhaps," Maria said. "And perhaps our story ends with the President hiring an assassin to take out the SECDEF before he finds out Liang is a mole and calls off the mission. But the assassin is stopped by a Secret Service agent and the SECDEF and assassin both survive to tell the tale. That would certainly foil our antagonist's plot, wouldn't you agree?"

Maria opened the door and pulled herself out of the limo. She bent back inside and said, "Be not afraid of growing slowly; be afraid only of standing still. When the Russians and the Chinese find out what really happened, and eventually they will, I wouldn't stand in one place for too long."

Shek's face formed a smirk. "The journey of a thousand miles starts with a single step, Agent Estefan. Perhaps it is time for you to consider a new course in life."

"Already have," Maria said. "I was going to retire, but damned if another agency didn't give me a call. Have a nice day, Mr. President."

Maria shut the door to the limo and walked away.

CHAPTER 39

Jon stood outside the gate near building 111 at Washington Navy Yard on Sicard Street in downtown D.C. A brisk wind lifted his hair as he remembered reading that CIS, as it was originally called, traced its beginnings back to Navy Department General Order 292, which had been signed by Secretary of the Navy William H. Hunt in 1882. The order created the Office of Naval Intelligence, which was tasked with collecting information on enemy weapons and vessels, as well as charting foreign rivers, passages, and waterways. ONI was also tasked with gathering information on enemy fortifications, industrial plants, and shipyards.

Prior to World War 1, the Navy expanded ONI's responsibilities to include sabotage and sophisticated espionage. When the second World War began, ONI had its hands in all sorts of interesting affairs that ranged from hunting down serial killers to chasing terrorists. ONI later became NCIS and the modern-day agency was now far more diverse. Jon would never have imagined they would be involved in taking down a mad AI system in control of six-hundred- megatons of nuclear destruction aboard a Russian submarine.

He glanced over and smiled as Kate Barrett ran across the street. She smiled back. Not long after NCIS had transferred him from San Diego to D.C., she had applied for a position at the Naval Research Labs not far away. They'd been dating ever since.

Kate beamed as she drew near and held up her hand. In her palm was a plastic card with a logo in the lower right corner that read PADI. "I got it!" Kate said. "I finally got my SCUBA certification. Now I'm almost as badass in the water as you are."

Jon grinned. "Almost." He reached over and held her hand. "I'm proud of you, Kate."

Kate lifted on her toes and kissed him. She held him close and said, "Any more ghosts?"

"Only a few distant whispers," Jon said.

"Good," Kate said. She released her hug. "Let's celebrate. Dinner at The Salt Line?"

"You're on," Jon said. "Right after my meeting."

"Meeting?"

He pointed toward the NCIS building. "I have to spend an hour pretending to listen to some asshole. I'll meet you at the restaurant."

Kate smiled. "Don't be late, sailor."

Jon's heart warmed as he felt the wings of hope breathe new life into his lungs.

Inside the NCIS building, Jon found his way to the designated meeting room. He was the first to arrive. In the nondescript room, a large table and a dozen chairs took up most of the space. On one wall, Jon spied a framed picture of President William Shek. There was a blank space where Secretary of Defense George McBride's picture once hung. With the planned Chinese accord now cancelled, and the press digging up damaging information about the President, Jon suspected it wouldn't be long before Shek's picture was also removed.

He turned his head as Agent Brad Tucker walked in along with his new sidekick, Agent Maria Estefan.

"Who's this guy we're meeting with?" Jon said as he pulled out a chair.

"I hear he's a major jerk," Brad said, cradling his wounded arm.

"Yeah, a real dickhead," Maria said as she poured herself a glass of water.

"I think you're both messing with me," Jon said with a grin.

A medium-height man in his late forties entered the room. He did not smile as he strode toward the front. Jon watched Maria do a double take.

"Agent Estefan," the man said. "Good to see you again." He looked first at Brad and then at Jon. "My name is Ted Flannigan. I'm a former Secret Service Lead Agent. I used to be Agent Estefan's boss. Considering recent events, it was not appropriate for me to remain there, so NCIS recruited me as the director of a new special operations division."

"I'll be damned," Maria said. "It's a small world after all."

Brad said, "What's the new division?"

"That's need-to-know," Flannigan said. "But let's just say we'll be tasked with going after the baddest of the bad. Special threats to national security

247

involving the Navy or Marine Corps that's outside the norm will fall into our jurisdiction. I can't say any more unless you're part of the team."

"Are your recruiting us?" Jon said.

"I've been tasked with finding the best of the best for the division," Flannigan said.

"I'm in," Brad said.

"Me too," Jon said.

"Fuck me," Maria said. "I guess I'm in, too."

"Good," Flannigan said as he sat on the edge of the table. "Now let's talk about our first assignment."

ABOUT THE AUTHOR

W. Craig Reed is the *New York Times* bestselling author of the award-winning *Red November*, *The 7 Secrets of Neuron Leadership*, and *Tarzan, My Father*, co-written with the late Johnny Weissmuller, Jr. Reed served as a U.S. Navy submariner and diver during the Cold War and earned commendations for completing secret missions, some in concert with SEAL Team One. Reed's military experience and inside contacts help infuse his writing with intrigue and realism and inspired his latest novel, *Status-6*. Reed holds an MBA in Marketing and is the cofounder of Us4Warriors, an award-winning Veterans nonprofit. Reed serves on the Board of Aretanium, an employee productivity firm that leverages the neuroscience research in the *The 7 Secrets of Neuron Leadership*.